Also by Kathryn Kramer

Rattlesnake Farming

A Handbook for Visitors from Outer Space

SWEET WATER

SWEET WATER

KATHRYN KRAMER

ALFRED A. KNOPF
New York   1998

This Is a Borzoi Book
Published by Alfred A. Knopf, Inc.

Copyright © 1998 by Kathryn Kramer
All rights reserved under International and Pan-American
Copyright Conventions. Published in the United States by
Alfred A. Knopf, Inc., New York, and simultaneously in
Canada by Random House of Canada Limited, Toronto.
Distributed by Random House, Inc., New York.

www.randomhouse.com

Library of Congress Cataloging-in-Publication Data
Kramer, Kathryn.
Sweet water / by Kathryn Kramer. — 1st ed.
p.   cm.
ISBN 0-375-40083-4
I. Title.
PS3561.R2515S94   1998
813´.54—dc21   97-49474   CIP

Manufactured in the United States of America
First Edition

The handwriting overlying the jacket photograph
is from a letter by Henry James to G. T. Lapsley.
Reproduced by permission of the Houghton Library,
Harvard University, bMS Am 1094.4 (44).

Acknowledgments

My heartfelt thanks to those people
and institutions whose various forms of
assistance greatly expedited the writing of
this book: the John Simon Guggenheim
Memorial Foundation, the Ingram Merrill
Foundation, the Ludwig Vogelstein
Foundation, and the Threshold Institute;
Ann Close, Melanie Jackson, Lindle
Lawton-Sutton, Richard Powers, Virginia
Barlow; and especially Mary Kramer and
Arthur Feinsod, for their many heroic
efforts on my behalf.

PART ONE

Sometimes rain can be heard before it is felt. A sound like wind would rise from the valley dividing Thrush Hollow's property from the main road and sweep across the unused pasture towards the house, visible as water falling from the sky only when it reached the straggling barbed wire that marked the near boundary of the field. If you stood in the open doorway, breathing in the rich air that precedes rain's arrival, you could listen to the curtain of sound growing louder and louder as it approached the house—climbed the valley, crossed the pasture, struck the Hollow's road, and then advanced through the sugarbush and up the lawn. To Greta it felt as if the house and she were the rain's destination and she wanted to prolong the anticipation forever, to remain suspended in that interval before the inevitable happened; yet even before she could articulate the wish the water would be upon her, for an infinitesimal instant pecking at the gutterless edge of the steep silver roof but then, as if having found only what could be expected, splattering loudly on the tin, proclaiming its indifference to the building's obstruction of its path.

The old house had once been a hotel, a summer resort; when the breeze swelled from the south in the previous century, young men in white flannels and boaters and young women in soft gowns and vast hats, tapping croquet balls across the lawn, had waited until the last possible moment before racing to the safety of the veranda, gleeful at having an excuse to huddle together, laughing, their clothes splotched by the first, foretelling drops; fire had destroyed one wing of the hotel early in the 1960s, an agent of nature invited in by the bankrupt owner, who put the torch not only to his own insured property but also, if belatedly and unwittingly, to a century and a way of life that would never come again.

"Water cures," Thrush Hollow's 1890 brochure advertised, but what water did it mean? The small accordion booklet belonged to Nora Sleeper, a woman who had already been living for fifty years, her entire life, in the village of West Stilling, a mile and a half from the old hotel, at the time Greta and Ned Dene first happened upon it; the brochure was Mrs. Sleeper's sole souvenir of the two summers in the late 1930s when as a girl she worked in the hotel kitchen, but she didn't know the answer to this question. "They had baths," she commented. "Queerest-looking contraptions. They were all sold at auction, of course."

Of course. As if it should be evident to everyone that the present had no use for such gimcrackery.

Even then it had been hard for Greta to believe that the water of the "cures" meant the local brook no wider than the backstairs Nora had been deputized to climb with meals for the guests who took breakfast in their rooms—though there were few guests then, those final years of the hotel's operation, and those "scarce knowing how to enjoy themselves," Nora recalled with irritation, as if the Depression and the war that followed were inadequate reasons for people to mope. Seeming to fear that her present guests might think her annoyance directed at them, she announced, "There's a photograph," and brought out her ultimate reference, the *History of Stilling;* in the photograph Thrush Hollow still wore not only its east wing but its two-story wraparound porches; a gazebo stood sentinel on the lawn; down over the bank in the direction of the abandoned copper mines on Trout Hill the swaybacked roof of the since caved-in carriage house was visible. (Ned and Henry had taken down the decrepit structure and made a bonfire of the unsalvageable lumber one summer after the horses had already been shipped back home.)

Next Nora had turned the page to a photograph of a striking young woman in nineteenth-century coiffure, and this was the first time that either Greta or Ned had heard Lucinda Dearborn's name: the daughter of a Captain Rufus Dearborn (captained at Appomattox), who had nurtured Thrush Hollow to the height of its prosperity. When he died suddenly in 1870 his daughter, in her early twenties then, had kept the hotel open; she ran it until her death in the second decade of the next century, after which it was handed off like a baton in a relay race among a series of owners until the Second World War forced them and their guests to acknowledge what the First had failed to: that time of long, leisurely holidays and the kind of guiltless ease they represented, when entire families might spend the summer at a resort hotel looking for no greater excitement than a summer rainstorm, was really over.

Though Greta had then known nothing about Lucinda, something about the young woman's expression had focused her attention and she hadn't raised her head from the photograph to look at the corner of the graveyard across the road in which Nora Sleeper was pointing out the Dearborn family monument. "She died by drowning," Nora was saying, sounding complacent. "When she was in her sixties she took a train to the seashore and she drowned." "Why does she look so sad?" Greta had asked, and Nora exclaimed "Who?" in such astonishment that Greta laughed. Ned remarked that Nora must have thought Greta commented not upon Lucinda but upon a figure who'd "cast off cerements" and was to be seen strolling about among the headstones. "This young woman, I meant," Greta said, annoyed with Ned for talking in his professorial manner in front of Nora, "this Lucinda Dearborn." "She never married," Nora replied. "But, surely," Greta said, "even if that could account for it, she must have been too young when this was taken to know for a fact that she wouldn't. Did she drown herself?" Nora shrugged, as if the question were impertinent. "I'm afraid I couldn't say."

Whoever had originally built on the knoll on the north side of the valley after which the old hotel was named—Captain Dearborn had expanded an existing structure—must have known how riveting was its prospect; something seemed to inhere in the site's dual nature as surveyor of the valley and shelterer against its slope that gave the building a feeling of inevitability, as if it completed an inclination that already existed in the terrain. Hudson Sleeper, Nora's husband and a waterwitch, maintained that lines of force lay hidden in the earth—he said he could tell by looking at a place where they came together—and when Ned and Greta were considering buying the old hotel, he mentioned that the Hollow contained some "powerful intersections." However one chose to explain it, something invisible combined with the topography to give the place a greater density than others, to make of it something more than itself—though Greta knew that to conceive of place in this way might make it impossible to recognize what was there to begin with. Maybe the salubrious effects boasted by the nineteenth-century brochure referred to subterranean waters—although Lucinda Dearborn's diary, preserved in the metal box located in the cellar by Hudson's dowsing rod earlier this summer, with Lucinda's complaints of interminable baths "too warm, lukewarm, gelid, and hot," suggested something more mundane, something to occupy the great-aunts while the grandnieces and -nephews disported themselves upon the croquet lawn.

Lucinda Dearborn could have been one of those gleeful fugitives from rain; she, like the others, might have gone on to enjoy whatever further interludes life held in store—enjoy them for themselves—had it not been for the fateful visit of a young man who was to become one of the country's renowned writers; the encounter, in the summer of 1865, would pluck Lucinda right out of her life, and, in a way Greta knew only too well, never really drop her back into it.

All summer now there had been a relentless drought. The previous winter's snowfall had been low, too, and by mid-June gardens were half dead and springs were already running dry—the reason Ned, swallowing his lowlander misgivings, had agreed to ask Hudson Sleeper to dowse for a new well. Water to water runs, Hudson claimed of the sap in his dowsing rod, to explain why the forked apple branch dragged him towards the ground when it sensed water beneath, and to him this explanation also served for what drew the rod to metal, to any lost or hidden thing; it was the water in everything, he said. You could find anything, if you let yourself be drawn.

When the forked wand had first curved towards the ground, Greta couldn't believe that some trickery was not involved, but then Hudson had invited her to take the stick and she couldn't stop remembering the sensation of its trembling in her hands and then the sharp tug as it buckled towards the ground. The sensation had reminded her of nothing so much as Henry's birth, by cesarean section: the pulling out of something within her that was a part of her and yet not a part. At the time she had been pressing her lips tightly between her teeth and Ned, stationed by her head, had thought that she was in pain and shouted at the doctor that the anesthesia hadn't taken, but that wasn't it; she'd been trying to prevent herself from crying out for Crain, who should have been with her: it was his child; it was he the doctor was separating her from, after all those months of carrying him securely inside her; but Crain refused to claim his child and the child needed a father.

As the divining rod strained at her hands the force was such that Greta could scarcely hold on to the branch, whose narrower ends she gripped, but she hadn't wanted to relinquish it when Hudson, chuckling, had taken it back and continued pacing slowly across the field, following the vein, which led directly to the house.

"You say the spring's dry? Because you've got no shortage of water," he said as he went down cellar, Ned and Greta following, Ned laughing in a way not scoffing now but incredulous, as he ducked so that he wouldn't, as he always claimed he was in danger of doing, "crack his skull open on the floor joists." Then Hudson told them that Thrush Hollow's main foundation had been laid in a rectangle at whose center point two water veins intersected, the first eight feet below the surface, flowing from the northwest at six miles an hour; the other three feet below the first, travelling nearly due east, at two miles an hour. While Greta and Ned were still trying to guess whether or not Hudson was serious (water there might be, but how could he gauge its speed and depth?), he asked for a shovel, and Ned, thinking that he meant to set out to dig a well in the cellar, protested, but Hudson said it was something else—not water, exactly—close to the surface.

After only a few minutes' digging he unearthed a metal box whose padlock was so rusted that he was able to release it with one thud of the spade, and then Greta and Ned had stared at each other (what sort of disbelief had they been exchanging? Greta wondered now). Hudson, having lifted the lid and glanced at the contents, had handed the box to Ned. "More your line than mine, looks like," he said, meaning (they assumed) that the packets of yellowed letters and the swollen-looking copybooks the box contained were a biographer and history professor's domain, not a logger and sometime water-witch's. (Legally, as Ned found it necessary to point out later, the box would have belonged to them in any case.) As Hudson headed back up the stairs to trace the first vein across the lawn to the spot beside the carriage-house foundation where they ultimately dug the new spring, he remarked, "Curious." Why, Greta berated herself now, had she registered this as an all-purpose country comment and not asked Hudson what he meant? He was so taciturn, but he had that glint in his eye that was part native amusement at the folly of "low country" folk, yet also seemed to promise that he could find whatever you were looking for if only you could tell him what it was. If you could ask the right question. But what would be the right question? Was there magic in the earth? And what was magic? Who could use it?

It was late July now, and the suggestion of breeze had brought Greta to stand, as she so often did, in the doorway of the ramshackle summer house—the warped screen door, which had long since lost its spring, drooping wide open against the clapboards. She stood waiting, it seemed to her, like a parishioner in line for communion for water to advance across the pasture, to bring her relief, however momentary, from the desolation that living had become since Crain's death, already three and a half months ago now; why did the prospect of water falling from the sky call forth this unfounded hope? Her pulse quickened in the same way that the butternuts at the corners of the lawn and the sugarbush along the road to the village had begun to quiver, as if her blood, however inadequately perceived by her, responded with the same consternation and excitement in its invisible branchings.

The rain always came from the south when it approached in this annunciatory way; south, beyond the valley, lay civilization, if by that one implied a population greater than the forty or fifty in the village of West Stilling, the eight to nine hundred in Stilling township (numbers yearly augmented by the northern migration of the "summah people"—a phrase enunciated with a never explicit disdain by those who lived in Stilling year round); though one could exercise one's identity as a consumer, as Ned put it, in Dalby, Silkburg, or Rye, fifteen miles east, west, and south of Stilling, the towns grew larger the farther one travelled, as if up here the law of diminishing perspective had been reversed. While the population had grown elsewhere, here it had dwindled; the 1850 map hanging in the dining room recorded habitation not only all along the now grassy road between Thrush Hollow and West Stilling but in back of the Hollow all the way up to the Trout Hill copper mines and beyond, but now the Hollow's nearest neighbor was over a mile away. Greta and Ned had cheerily advertised Thrush Hollow to visitors as the last outpost of the civilized world, but they had meant this as a warning that people had better know how to entertain themselves if they came. Greta had never felt it to be her world at whose edge Thrush Hollow stood.

Sometimes since Hudson Sleeper's discovery, surreptitiously, even though she was alone when she did this, Greta had broken off a forked branch and, closing her palms around the two narrow ends, paced slowly back and forth as Hudson had; she had tried to think only of water flowing beneath the ground—you had to keep in mind a picture of what you were looking for, Hudson said, and then let yourself be drawn—but the stick never moved. Greta knew she hadn't imagined the pull when Hudson handed her his divining wand, but it must have been Hudson the water wanted to summon; it didn't want her.

"Why won't you answer me!" she had exclaimed recently up in the field where she and Henry picked blackberries, then, shocked, looked around. Though who had she imagined might possibly be there? Berry-picking had always been one of her and Henry's favorite shared pastimes, and in a few weeks the blackberries would be ripe and Henry would be home from camp, but how could they enjoy anything anymore, with Crain dead, Henry's father dead, and who was Henry, without his father? Then she had been sobbing, the stick jettisoned into a thicket of the wild cherry and poplar that threatened to engulf the field if they weren't cut back soon; sobbing because the stick wouldn't move for her, because she hadn't even known she had it in her to weep anymore until she heard herself, alone in a field, arguing with the *ground;* sobbing to realize that she could think with such coldness of her own child.

Ned maintained that Thrush Hollow's last owner could not have been aware of the material he held, encrypted, in his possession, since *he* (the arsonist) would not have balked at converting the discolored, brittle pages into crisp, green rectangles with pictures of presidents on them—and "rather more presidents than letters, more Grants than Washingtons," Ned said sententiously, "given a find of this magnitude," the letter writer's identity apparent to him after he'd read a mere three lines. "Good God, only one person ever wrote the English language like this," he said grimly, turning to the signature and staring at it as though he were going to be sick. Simply the one letter in which the writer addressed Lucinda Dearborn as his "one untarnished darling" could have earned Thrush Hollow's previous owner enough to make it unnecessary for him to set his property on fire!

This Greta doubted. No one's private correspondence was that valuable, not even evidence that O. (to whom Ned, absurdly, insisted on referring by his initial) had felt the great passion of which no one had believed him capable. What difference could it make to anyone to know? The evidence was hardly conclusive; if anything, passionate outpourings on paper only showed that the writer had spent his passion through his pen. Of course, as Ned pointed out, Greta was hardly in sympathy with the man or his work, finding it too long-winded and analytical for her taste, which ran to mysteries (she having for her own mother "Priscilla Thwaite," a doyenne of the genre), naturalists' accounts, and stories of exploration; but she did know O.'s reputation. Her mother had been a die-hard fan and had pressed her favorite titles on Greta, though Greta had merely browsed through them until recently. In other circumstances, maybe, she wouldn't have doubted Ned's assessment, but his awestruck attitude combined with his insistence on total secrecy (whom did he think she would tell?) had made her dubious. Ever since the "find," Ned had closeted himself a good part of each day in his study, rereading O.'s biography and skimming his oeuvre, trying to ascertain how much and where his fifty-year almost entirely epistolary relationship with Lucinda, about whom no biographer had known, might have influenced his novels and stories—though at the moment Ned was in Dalby, buying a newspaper and getting the chain saw sharpened.

Originally, Greta had looked with distaste upon the prospect of publishing something so private; she felt protective of Lucinda; Lucinda had hidden the letters for a reason, but lately she'd found herself fearing just the opposite: that Ned now meant to suppress the papers. At first he'd claimed that he simply wished—opportunistically, he acknowledged, but how often in life was one granted such an opportunity?—to take advantage of the serendipity before opening the cache to other scholars, but then recently he'd remarked, in a flip way that filled Greta with mistrust, "You know, Greta, I sometimes think that you were right. What difference does it make if our friend was in love with a girl in the last century? Who are we to disturb the peace?"

Maybe she was allowing her imagination to run away with her in a manner befitting some of the writer's own more neurasthenic heroines, and yet she was convinced that Ned's change of mind—his change of mind and his whole strangely possessive attitude about the letters and diaries—was a response to the change in her since Crain's death, even though Ned hadn't challenged her explanation that her near-breakdown tension and insomnia resulted from "too much stress" at work, too many people wanting the impossible from her—to transform either them or their horses into world-class material without any effort on their parts. Which was true enough, but nothing out of the ordinary.

Ned couldn't know, having never suspected Crain's existence, that Crain was dead (she had been alone at Thrush Hollow the first, numb month), but he sensed something, how could he not?, some crack in the carapace—and Greta could not now comprehend how she'd been able to keep her life with Crain secret all these years. Whether or not he knew it, Ned meant to hold Lucinda Dearborn hostage, to trap her in silence until Greta broke hers.

Finally, at last, the rain began, swelling towards the house with the purifying eloquence of a choir, and Greta, still standing in the doorway, began to breathe, lightly at first, cautiously, but then more deeply, until finally she permitted the exhalation she'd been withholding to wash through her, as if the water Hudson had reminded her she was largely composed of sought the water all around. She waited until she was sure that the rain was no wayward summer shower but was settling in for a long sermon before she hoisted the crooked screen back into the tilted door frame and climbed the narrow backstairs to shut the south-facing windows on the second floor. At night, however, no matter how wild and insistent the storm, she never wanted to close the window beside the bed; she liked to lie on her side facing the weather, the blankets tucked around her ears, the rain wetting her face, while from the far side of the bed Ned complained that if she'd wanted to be splashed while she slept she should have slept in a boat.

Back downstairs, Greta sat beside the cold wood stove in the kitchen in the rickety overstuffed rocking chair that, though since reupholstered, had stood in the identical spot since the first time she and Ned had entered the room, trespassers sixteen years ago; she picked up a book, one by Lucinda's correspondent—they practically infested the house, borrowed by Ned from a college library an hour's drive away—though she knew she had no intention of looking at the novel because she was still listening, not only with her ears but with her blood, to the rain pounding on the flower beds, drumming on the faraway roof, trying as if with every pore to inhale the rich air and the exalted smell of the wet earth. She held the book self-protectively against her chest, like the schoolgirl she had been when she first met both Crain and Ned, as she absorbed the sound of the rain in a state of receptivity she knew was less like listening than prayer, even though no prayer could bring Crain back to life or alter the fact that her more than twenty-year marriage was founded on a lie.

Greta could not remember even once, in all that time, when she'd woken in the night and been unable to get back to sleep that Ned hadn't said, "What is it, Greta? Can't you sleep, darling?" in his gentle, really fatherly way—and where had he acquired this, when they'd known each other since they were teenagers? By what trick or secret marriage agreement? She had often been amused by Ned's insistence that she hadn't woken him, he'd already been awake, but in her present mood the habit seemed to stand for too much else. Why couldn't Ned admit that it was her wakefulness that aroused him even before she herself knew that she was awake; aroused him so instantaneously and completely that he seemed, even to himself, to have been awake all along?

The habit went back, she was sure; as with so much else from which the habits of their marriage had grown, this never fully articulated argument found its source in the time they'd met, under then Bishop McAndrew's auspices—when she had been *Margaret,* that poor afflicted girl Ned had been led by McAndrew to believe in need of his succor. It was Margaret Ned had fallen in love with, even though nine years later he'd agreed to marry Greta; yet always, Greta suspected, Ned had been hoping that she would become again that lost girl for him, so that he could finally save her.

In the midst of her grief and shock it astonished Greta, even as it left her uncertainly, fearfully grateful, that Ned hadn't confronted her, insisted on more information—why was she so on edge? Why had she suddenly decided to come to Stilling six weeks early? How could it simply be work? She had been a riding professional for many years without showing this kind of strain—why now? And she had brought only the one horse with her instead of the three or four she usually did; how could she suddenly afford to have no horses in training? How was she planning to pay Henry's tuition in the fall? And why, after refusing to consider it in the past, had she, this year, not only allowed Henry to go to camp but in fact urged him to?

Though Ned was no master of directness, intentional subterfuge had never been his style either, and it frightened Greta that he seemed to be making a point of not questioning her at the same time that she was afraid he was going to, for if he asked her in a certain way, kindly, without accusation, what was wrong, in the voice he used when she was having trouble sleeping, she knew she would tell him.

Henry isn't your son! All these years I've lied to you! I remained his father's lover. But now his father is dead, and I can't keep the secret anymore. I haven't the strength. I don't know who Henry *is.* I don't even know if I love him!

Greta could never sit still once her fear drove her into this corner; she sprang up now and hurried to the sink to wash the dishes waiting from lunch but then, instead of filling the dishpan, stood staring out the window at the rain: beating down hard now, bending the half-closed daylilies in the back yard, sending rivulets down the slope into the vegetable garden. The great elm, one of the few of its size left anywhere in the region, whose long branches reached down and swept the grass, back and forth, back and forth, with increasing urgency when rain approached, now stood mutely, bowed to receive the water.

She saw, then, why Ned might say nothing: not out of strategy, not even strategy unknown to himself, but because he thought *he* was undergoing the upheaval, his tendency the opposite of most people's. He took on others' feelings, instead of supposing his feelings to be theirs. Thus he would try to make sense of everything privately, not liking, as he put it, to hear the exegesis before he'd read the text. That was his way, and they were alike in this—keeping their own counsel, as if they were weak natures afraid of being influenced. The stupidity of this struck Greta, the arrested development of it: parentless, grown-up, from what or whose contradiction were they protecting themselves?

But there was no one to talk *to*. No one she, anyway, could talk to besides Ned. Rachel was not down the road as she usually was but in England and anyway angry to discover that Greta had never confided fully in her; only Rachel, besides Crain, had known that Henry was Crain's son. Flippantly, Greta tried to imagine speaking of her circumstance to anyone in the village: to Reuben Bliss, the farmer from whom they bought milk, or to Nora Sleeper, sitting in her spanking clean kitchen gazing across the road at the plots reserved for herself and Hudson. How would she respond if Greta asked her advice about whether or not to tell her husband that their fourteen-year-old son, whom he loved more than anyone or anything on earth, was not his own? Greta imagined Nora gasping and staring across at the graveyard for advice.

Greta had sometimes comforted herself by picturing how, with Ned (assuming she could not be with Crain), she might someday lie among the Chubbs, the Osgoods, the Burroughses, the Dearborns (they ought to reserve a space, Nora urged her and Ned; the sites were nearly all spoken for)—the cozy Anglo-Saxon names conjuring images of lives lived in sweet self-contained hamlets, even though Greta knew that this could only be a vision from outside, spun from wishes and half-knowledge, a romance she carried on with her nominally native land. (She'd grown up overseas, she'd insisted; inheriting a passport didn't make her a citizen.) To envision her name and Ned's on matching slate tombstones among these country dead had permitted her, however artificially, to imagine their marriage as other than it had been, as someone, reading their names and dates years hence, might imagine it.

In Thrush Hollow's kitchen, Greta blinked to contain tears—no chance anymore of that. No lifelong confidence and trust. She had no one to blame but herself; no right to self-pity, or to anyone else's either, and she forced herself back, with a reflexive sensation of culpability as if she'd been inattentive to someone in conversation, to the sound of rain on the tin roof, as if *it*—this repetitive reminder of a world not infected by human deceit and uncertainty—were what she'd been detained to, where she had to start over, to learn the instinct for wholeness somehow gone wrong in her nature. She listened to it—the same sound, new each time yet the same as before—as if to a patient teacher trying to instill a foreign language solely by repetition, hoping that understanding would arise not through translation but out of familiarity, the way children learn to speak.

That afternoon in Dalby, Ned Dene bought a newspaper, a large metropolitan daily, and left his chain saw off at Arnie's Small Engine Repair to be sharpened. Then he visited the Dalby Public Library, open only on Monday, Wednesday, and Friday mornings and Saturday afternoons, where he asked to be directed to past issues of the *Dalby Gazette*. It had recently been microfilmed, thanks to a deceased patron's bequest, and the machine, bought cheaply from a better-funded library updating its equipment, squeaked and whirred. Ned was looking carefully through the late winter and early spring of 1915. News of the war did not take away space from agricultural advice and the usual local reportage, he noticed. Finally, on April 23rd, he found the article he'd been searching for: a description of Lucinda Dearborn's death. She had been observed walking into the sea near Portsmouth, New Hampshire, fully clothed, wearing her hat, and carrying her "portmanteau"—looking as if she were "setting forth to swim the Atlantic, baggage and all," in the words of an eyewitness who couldn't swim and whose shouting to her to turn back Lucinda either had not heard or had ignored. The witness, a Mr. Willis Orn of Kittery, Maine, had run for help; boats were launched, but too late. The article didn't mention, but Ned knew, how icy the water still would have been at that time of year; hypothermia wouldn't have been long setting in. Lucinda must have known this too; in her diaries she wrote with expertise of the various effects of water—hot and cold, running and still—on the body. Though she could swim (she wrote of swimming in the pond down the hill from Thrush Hollow to support some of her more infirm patients—the "pond" now a marsh overgrown with cattails), she couldn't have held out long given the water's temperature and the weight of her clothes.

Newspapers were still relatively genteel in 1915, and the article was circumspect in its suggestion that Lucinda had lost her mind—"might not have been in the fullest possession of her faculties"—but Ned didn't believe this. At least she wasn't out of her mind in any way that would have made her unaware of the consequences of her action. The reporter didn't know that Lucinda had walked into the sea less than a month after learning of O.'s death at his winter home outside of Florence. The poor woman, Ned thought, had had to come upon the news in her local newspaper (the same which now reported her death) several weeks after the fact: "NOTED AUTHOR DEAD IN ITALY—KNOWN FOR PORTRAITS OF AMERICANS ABROAD." Ned had found the little clipping, yellow, brittle, pressed between pages of Lucinda's diary, on one of which she had written the short sentence: "I cannot continue." If only O. could have entrusted someone with the task of notifying Lucinda of his death, maybe the shock would have been mitigated; it was the least he could have done, Ned thought acerbically, after Lucinda had devoted her entire life to him—but O.'s silence on the matter had evidently been complete. Not long before his death he had burned the bulk of letters written to him, among which must have been Lucinda's.

In the obituary article the *Gazette* noted that Miss Dearborn, proprietress of the Stilling resort hotel Thrush Hollow, had left no immediate heirs, and it was not known what would become of the property. Ned considered looking for follow-up articles, but the progress of the hotel's decline was self-evident; further facts weren't going to help him decide what to do about the papers so fortuitously come into his possession. That they *had* still seemed so incredible to him—he, Ned Dene, the repository of this century-old international secret, as it seemed to him—that he had toyed with the notion that the papers had been planted; but why would anyone have bothered? And who would have had the skill? To forge the nearly two hundred letters in O.'s inimitable style, the many more hundreds of pages of Lucinda's diaries, aged them somehow, buried them at Thrush Hollow, and then bribed Hudson Sleeper to "discover" them? What could have been the motive? H. Edward Dene was no renowned O. scholar whom a rival might wish to discredit.

Ned copied over the article about Lucinda by hand, since the Dalby Public Library didn't possess a copy machine; he had had to drive an hour to the university town where he borrowed books and did research to photocopy, laboriously, the letters and diaries, which he had done immediately after their discovery, afraid they would deteriorate on exposure to air. He felt irresponsible not to have deposited the originals in a climate-controlled environment; he depended in his own research on the careful preservation of just such documents as these, and he knew he needed to make a decision soon. But when he couldn't even decide whether or not to mention the article he'd just read to his wife, who had so aptly guessed the nature of Lucinda's death years ago, before they knew anything about her, how was he going to decide how and when to publish his discovery? Did he call up the *New York Times* and tell them he had some front page news? It *was* front page news, in his opinion, but it would never make today's front page. The man who more than any other had foreseen the alienation of the sexes in modern-day America had carried on a nearly lifelong, if nearly unrealized love affair: the ramifications were stunning, if ambiguous. Should Ned invite famous O. scholars to Thrush Hollow and announce the find in a manner befitting one of O.'s own dramatic scenarios? They would apprehend the letters' importance but Ned didn't want them to take charge of interpreting it until he'd made up his own mind.

This was all stalling, though, on one level; he didn't need anyone to tell him that. If he spent all his time unravelling O. and Lucinda's story, then he could avoid thinking about whatever was transpiring between him and Greta—or not transpiring—though by some subterranean method it appeared that he couldn't think about the one without thinking about the other. "Did O. bear a moral responsibility for Lucinda Dearborn's suicide?" translated into "Was he himself responsible for Greta's unhappiness?"

If he hadn't pressed her to elaborate on her trouble, it wasn't because he didn't speculate as to its source; it was because he feared the discussion that lay in wait. He wasn't an idiot—a coward, but not an idiot. Standing a month earlier in the dank cellar, his head uncomfortably craned forward because the ceiling was too low for him to stand upright, his eyes glazing as he leafed through page after page covered by O.'s spidery nineteenth-century Arabic-looking handwriting, he had felt as if years and years of his life were funneling into that one moment, time and history sucked back into his present experience like a genie recalled to a bottle. The cellar echoed: the fieldstone foundation had become quarried, the floor stone instead of dirt, and the dangling electric lightbulb flickering candlelight. He wasn't in Thrush Hollow's cellar anymore; he was back in that moment in St. Stephen's crypt just before Bishop McAndrew had announced his presence and disrupted Ned's reverie; he had been on the *verge*—Ned remembered the feeling so clearly—of toppling into the past; he had been experiencing that vertigo as he ran his fingers over the dead bishops' names and dates, about to be translated into that unseen density, and then Bishop McAndrew had interrupted him with a witty remark, something about divine silence, and labelled the boy Ned's still unformed experience.

Now here was a second chance, which he hadn't expected to be afforded in his lifetime, to pursue his own, unmediated experience of the past, and this time he'd be damned if he'd let anyone interfere. Once scholars descended upon the find, his private encounter with a place where what he had come to know as intransigent reality was still in the process of becoming, would be all over, and along with it his last hope of resolving his own life's salient question. What would his life have been like, in other words, had he not, at his impressionable age, become mixed up with Margaret Sayre and her "miracle"?

It was why he had written, wasn't it? Ostensibly to learn how his subjects' lives made manifest the larger forces at work in their era, but really to use those lives as a doorway into another time—thence to sneak back, catching it unawares, into his own? He and Greta had never talked about St. Stephen's, after that first abortive attempt when they'd met up again in their twenties, so he had to ask all his questions by proxy. If Greta had, in fact, been "chosen," why had *he* been chosen along with her?

He could see that his naiveté lay in having supposed that time would stand still, like a painter's model, while he walked all around it, examining each perspective at his leisure. It hadn't occurred to him, in his dimwittedness, that something could happen, now, that could affect what had happened then. People woke up, after twenty years, and discovered that they didn't know the person they were married to; this was a cliché, and Ned was revolted to think that it might apply to him. He had always known there were places in each other to which he and Greta did not travel; he knew that very well, but had they not made their peace with that fact? Now it seemed that Greta wanted to renegotiate the terms and he—well, he wasn't sure he did. That his marriage might appear unsatisfying when viewed from an outsider's point of view, he could grant—the extraordinary past they never discussed, the relationship's relative sexlessness, except for brief periods mostly after, it seemed, Greta returned from one of her trips—but, for one, he was not an outsider, and, for another, the relationship was also affectionate, a source of stability, and had produced a child to whom they were both devoted and whom they both adored.

But something was threatening all that, and Ned knew quite well that, regardless of his wishes, things couldn't go on as they were. If nothing else, they had to spare themselves the embarrassment of Henry's coming home from camp and demanding what was going on—"Rain on your parade, guys? What's the story?" Ned could hear him.

This summer, the house felt so empty. Henry had brought his friends. Henry had brought friends, period. He had forged most of their Stilling acquaintanceships, other than the Tollivers, and they were in England. Greta had asked Ned to put off visitors this summer; she wasn't "up to" entertaining, she'd said.

Thrush Hollow, the old hotel, had always been such a refuge, provided such a conducive atmosphere for Ned's biographical forays—looking, with its peeling white clapboards and silver roof, like its black-and-white photograph in the town history, as if it, alone among the trees and fields and sky, had not been colored in. As if it partook, in its three dimensions, of the two-dimensionality of dreams or reading, which was so much more comfortable to contemplate. He had been able to count, here, on the quotidian's not refuting the imagined, but now it seemed to Ned that there had been something rotten at the heart of this vision—literally there had been, buried in the old hotel's cellar—as if his enjoyment of his nineteenth-century summers, as he'd gloatingly thought of them, had *depended* on O.'s neglect of Lucinda, his own pleasant state of suspension actually made possible by O.'s refusal to, so to speak, take the plunge.

"They came *up* here," Ned had used to say, holding forth at dinner, "all together, on a train. Mother, father, children, grandparents, maiden aunts, bachelor uncles—can you imagine? To spend the whole summer..."

Driven out to the Hollow in a buggy from Dalby, having arrived there by train—the guests' first sight of Thrush Hollow's Resort Spa and Hotel for Ladies and Gentlemen would have been inevitably startling: as they rounded the bend in the maple-arbored road the driver would remark, "There she is," as if the hotel were a ship, and yet the guests would see nothing until they glanced up to their right where the driver was indicating with his buggy whip, and there the secretive place would be, up on a knoll, having been watching them: doubly secretive, since it had loomed there all along in plain sight.

"This place, this *place* . . . " Ned would say, inarticulate, weighed down by his vision, as he made a sweep with his arm to include not only the sweetly wallpapered and wainscoted dining room but the view down the valley outside, hill overlapping hill like the soft flakes of a milkweed pod, in the dusk of the redolent summer evening a distant light or two faintly glimmering. "What century *is* it?" he would ask, and guests would nod, and he would think that it wasn't gone, that time, with, as he believed, people's shared understanding of life—such a strange compression in these gatherings, as if they *were* aboard a ship, or besieged in a mountain fortress, all the significant events of the past along with them, packed in a travelling bag for easy carrying.

"Let's have coffee on the porch," he or Greta would say, and they would all glide out back and disperse themselves among the creaky wicker rockers and deep canvas deck chairs—and here the hills and woods were close, the spaces between the trees filling in now with dark— and he or Greta would carry out a tray of cups and saucers, and the other would bring the coffeepot. He had felt so happily married then.

Ned had read with self-conscious pleasure, in one of O.'s first letters to Lucinda, the remark that, visiting the Hollow, he had "verily proved the sense—as the French would have it—of being at civilization's final fastness. One knows with such intensity, seated about your hospitably disposed tables in that so charming dining room, in the midst of absolutely, I do believe, nowhere—not, assuredly, the untamed wildness of our fabled West, but wildness reencroaching because abandoned by ancestors who could construe no further adventure to be prosecuted in it—of holding artful and invigorating converse on a ship about to go down. One feels, in truth, that one may literally fend off the gush of water with one's talk!"

A dark irony, given O.'s letter, in Lucinda's having drowned; Ned hoped she hadn't remembered it. It sickened him to imagine the desolation she must have felt in the moments before she breathed in the water, her lungs no longer amphibious, as they'd been before her advent into the unaqueous world, the water a foreign substance now, which her lungs could take in but not expel. That life-giving element, with which she herself had healed others, had turned on her like a person she had always believed in, asserting its deadly, impersonal volition.

But maybe it hadn't been like that; maybe the anguish that had driven her to the act had stayed with her to the end and cleansed her of every other feeling; maybe she had felt relieved to be, finally, taking matters into her own hands, to be going to join the man she'd waited all her life for—but Ned didn't believe this. She must have felt sick with horror when she read O.'s obituary and realized how little, in the end, she had meant to him, and the end mattered, what could be written in that summarizing news article. It mattered, at least, to the survivors. Lucinda had clung to the belief that her role as muse, her being the figure to whose shadow O. had given substance in his tales, equalled a personal commitment—how many women, after all, were called upon to represent an entire nation? she'd breathily written—but when she read the stark news of O.'s death, with no mention of herself in connection with him, her faith must have tasted bitter indeed.

Ned saw very well, even if he would prefer not to, how one might spend a lifetime believing oneself to mean something to another that one did not. He saw this, yet at the moment the perception threatened to descend into his own experience, he fled from it. *Not again,* he said to himself, *not again,* but then did not pursue what he meant by that.

He had never believed, he meditated instead, in ghosts; if they did exist, however, they would have to be the residue of lives like Lucinda's: so unrealized. One had only this one life—how could one not have what one wanted? Wasn't it promised? He didn't know by what or whom, but this belief was so inveterate he'd never really questioned it and this now flabbergasted him. How long could one fool oneself? Like Lucinda, until the moment she'd read of O.'s death in the *Dalby Gazette?*

Well, if she were going to come back, now would be the time, he thought with some giddiness; they'd disturbed her reliquary. He liked to imagine she'd be his ally, comprehending the strange stasis in which it was beginning to seem to him he'd spent his interior life. He trusted she wouldn't blame him for the dilapidated condition of the old hotel, with its wing lost to fire, most of its furniture auctioned off, its fields half swallowed by woods. He and Greta had done little to the house beyond assuring its structural soundness, and most rooms remained in the faded, semi-furnished, shabby condition in which they'd found them when they climbed in through an easily pried-open shutter sixteen years ago. What had they been thinking? That they'd restore the hotel to its original splendor? It had been a grand house—in the main section lofty ceilings, ornate woodwork—how had they imagined they'd ever have the money to bring it back? Not to mention bringing back the life that had once animated the place?

The truth was, they'd lived in it like caretakers, anticipating the true owners' return, whereupon they could subside into their appropriate role, as houseguests. Recalling his feeling, on those vivid summer evenings when the talk had seemed so brilliant and the common understanding so complete, that they were perpetuating a vanished way of life, Ned now heard the unanchored quality in the talk, and struck, like someone digging for metal hearing the telltale ring, the anxiety underlying the elegiac mood. He heard, like an instrument off-key, the bravado underlying his assertions, as if his celebrating what he'd considered a delightful escape from the larger, rotten society in which he lived were a pretense and instead he and his kind were stranded out among these green hills, Thrush Hollow an earthbound ark, wrecked out here in this secluded valley, and all they'd been able to carry on board was their longing for what they had once cared about, out there beyond the darkening tree-line.

Ned groaned. He had fallen into a trance at the microfilm machine. He rewound the reel, put it back in its box, and returned it to Mrs. Whitcher, the librarian, who asked him if he'd found what he wanted. He didn't know her; Henry had read through the children's collection a couple of years ago and the former librarian had since retired.

"I think so," he told her, and went to sit in the round reading room at the polished octagonal oak table, where he spread out the newspaper he'd bought earlier so that it wouldn't look as if he were malingering, though he barely glanced at it.

Get on with it, he exhorted himself—wherever "on" led, whatever "it" was—except that for him forward, in any direction, usually turned out to be backward. He professed history and wrote biography—occupations, so called; they had occupied him in the sense of a conquering force before he even knew what else life might offer; he had cleaved to them as a way of holding everything still. They had taken possession, a word he disliked for its supernatural connotation, but it was an accurate description of what happened to him. Not even Greta had a true idea of what he went through each time he stepped in front of a class; she didn't know how he paced back and forth in his office, swallowed cup after cup of coffee and then had to hurry to the men's room when his bowels rebelled, deciding he had to give up teaching—he simply couldn't endure this crippling anxiety one more day; he would climb out the window and shimmy down the drainpipe (this image of escape never seeming to feature the simpler expedient of descending the stairs) . . . Rarely a teaching day passed in which he didn't entertain this fantasy. And yet he always found himself, on the hour, entering his classroom, greeting his students inaudibly, fiddling at his lectern with notes whose subject he had already forgotten, notes he couldn't have read if he'd wanted to since anxiety made it impossible for him to focus—eventually looking up and saying vaguely, "Are we all here? Yes? What was our subject last time, Miss _____ or Mr. _____?" and when the student ventured an apologetic synopsis, he would come out from behind the lectern and chime in like an eager fifth-grader, "That's right, and today we're going to discuss . . ." and then would wait, not infrequently as ignorant as the class of how he would conclude his sentence. He would hear what he'd said and think, Really? You really believe that? or That's interesting, as this individual who had usurped his voice and body went on to expound a thesis about a particular period in history, to render in their "full pathos" the lives of historical figures. Through a haze he would occasionally notice a student or two looking rapt, and would wonder how this imposter had managed to put one over on everybody.

With each of his three published biographies their subjects had taken him over in a similar manner: something about the way the person was mentioned in whatever he was reading, a minor detail, would awaken him from the spell cast by his absorption, and he wouldn't be able to rest until he'd located the source of his curiosity. Yet in each case he had thought, What a nuisance. Why me? *I* don't know anything about this time and place. How incredibly irritating to have to engage in several years' research and write an entire book that he—*on his own* (though what did he mean by that?)—would have had no interest in writing. When Hudson Sleeper had handed him the rusty strongbox in Thrush Hollow's cellar last month, and Ned had recognized the letter writer's style even before he saw his signature, his exclamation of what Greta had properly interpreted as dismay had sprung not solely from his immediate comprehension of either the remunerative or scholarly implications of the find, but from his distress at the telltale lighting up of the material. *This* was to be his next assignment? This great master, about whom inordinate amounts had already been written; to whose critical canon he, Ned Dene, could hardly have anything worthwhile to add? He was a historian, he protested, not a literary critic; he'd been attracted heretofore by minor, marginal subjects, liking to discover reflected in their relatively insignificant lives the sweeping forces of their times; he'd never aspired to wrestle with a figure who himself might be considered such a force, or at least the symbolic apogee of one. He had felt outraged at the amount of work being demanded of him and yet even as he'd read through O.'s letters and Lucinda's diaries that first evening, he already knew that no amount of whining would get him off this hook. How he wished—then and now—that Greta's shrewd eye had not been upon him; it would have been enough to grapple with the material on its own terms without his decisions being scrutinized by her for their personal import.

And here he was sliding into dishonesty again, pretending there could have been a way to avoid the reckoning they'd put off for over twenty years now. That it should have been provoked or accompanied by the O.-Lucinda revelation was no more extraordinary than the way in which he had become a part of Greta's life in the first place. (Which was how he thought of it, he noted: he'd become a part of her life, not she of his.)

Ned, in the circular reading room of the Dalby library—a brick turret attached to a Victorian house, the Victorians pretending to be medieval—said to himself, Go back to the beginning, just go back, an oracular phrase with which he sought to inspire his students.

How unoriginal, Ned thought, at my time of life. Don't we all go back like lemmings. Though how many to a dimly lit cathedral crypt, a bishop's game in which he and Greta had both been pawns? And what did he mean, thinking that? Was he *proud* to be distinguished in this way? A bit player, but still in arguably the most potent drama so-called Western civilization had yet come up with?

Ned glanced up and noticed that it was raining. The sky had grown dark since he'd last looked out the window. Forgetting it was summer, he'd simply thought that night was falling. Mrs. Whitcher seemed to be bustling about suddenly, as if the books might get wet and she needed to protect them. On Main Street, people were running and ducking into stores. A woman ran out of Aubuchon's Hardware, opened the door of her car, rolled up the window, and ran back inside. A man coming out of the post office thrust envelopes inside his shirt. Everyone had been complaining incessantly about the drought, but now that it was finally raining all they thought of was how not to get wet. Ned thought it was funny. If there hadn't been a drought, he noted, they would never have discovered O.'s letters, and he wondered, without achieving any result, whether any significance could be derived from this fact.

T he next morning dawned gray, not raining anymore, but with impassive, featureless clouds slung low in the sky, thick, slow drops oozing from the motionless leaves like blood, and Greta woke up, groggy, at seven-thirty, shrouded in a bad dream. She turned from the staleness of the bed to look out the window, but this morning the sight afforded no relief; the unbroken green undulations of the wooded hills seemed menacing, as if their swallowing of pasture and habitation had been intentional and swift, instead of involuntary compliance with a near-century of human neglect. Ordinarily the view—lawn sloping to sugarbush, the few open fields preserved in the clefts of the overlapping hills, a silver roof or two glinting in the early sun—reassured her, amalgamated as it was with her memory of the more dwelling-punctuated English landscapes against whose backdrop her mother's mysteries had mostly taken place, those bucolic scenes promising a mystery-novel solution to the most complex human problems. That her mother, as Priscilla Thwaite, had known and even exploited this had not diminished the sight's efficacy for Greta.

On most days Greta was up and out at the paddock by six, preferring to ride King's Ransom, the eight-year-old of whom she was sole owner since Crain's death, in the cool clear air of early morning. She would be back at the house and finished breakfast by the time Ned woke at eight or eight-thirty. In previous summers she had kept him and Henry company while they ate and then returned to the ring to ride another two or three horses before lunch; in the afternoon she worked in the garden, went swimming or hiking with Henry and Ned, or, if it rained, read while the two of them played chess. This year not only had she no other horses in training, there was no Henry to keep company or chauffeur; no Rachel down the road to visit; no Crain to write letters to—though she had never written him much in the summer since he couldn't respond; in Stilling she had nowhere to receive mail privately. Sometimes she would find a moment to telephone him from town, if she'd gone in alone (a rare occurrence), but then often he wouldn't be in his office, and for all of August he was off with his family on vacation.

Now she slipped out of bed, taking care not to wake Ned, who lay on his back with an arm flung over his eyes; he had come to bed after she was asleep—staying up late with O. and Lucinda, Greta thought irritably, as if he had excluded her from a visit with friends.

She dressed in the bedroom across the hall where she kept her clothes. The upstairs was scarcely furnished, but they lived in the luxury of unoccupied space: eight large bedrooms in the central section of the house and five smaller ones in the ell. In its heyday, with its wing still standing, Thrush Hollow had been able to accommodate between thirty and forty guests.

In the kitchen, Greta made coffee, then wandered down the back hall in the ell to the "bathing room," pipes removed, which Ned had furnished as his study. Steaming cup in hand, she stood, still trying to shake the dream, gazing at Ned's paper-strewn desk. He was always berating himself for his disorderliness, but he couldn't work in a neat room—the mental effort required to ignore the mess seemed to free him to concentrate on other matters. So why pretend to be a neat person who was simply too busy to tidy up? This self-deception, which had previously amused her, struck Greta now as symptomatic. She considered looking through the papers, though what she thought she might find she didn't know. She'd already skimmed Lucinda's diaries and as many of O.'s letters as she could stand. His effort to articulate his thought to the greatest degree of magnification which Ned so admired exasperated her. "What's his *point?*" she'd exclaim. "Why doesn't he just get to the point?" "The point has ramifications," Ned would say good-naturedly. These were habitual roles—Greta the athlete, impatient with indirection and subtlety; Ned the scholar, advocate of the complex and obscure—and she had been at ease in hers as long as Crain was waiting in the wings to welcome her when she came offstage.

Her impulse to snoop upset her; she'd never felt it before, and it was a cruel joke that she should be feeling suspicious of Ned when she was the one hiding something. Yet she had felt terribly uneasy ever since he had come home yesterday afternoon from Dalby; she had the distinct impression that he was up to something, though what anyone could be up to in Dalby, she couldn't imagine. There was some new resolve in him, some private almost cheerfulness—but what could possibly be its source? He couldn't have found written evidence of her deceit; she'd kept her promise to Crain to destroy his letters, though she regretted it now. In any case, Ned couldn't have discovered that Henry wasn't his and put on an upbeat air. The only evidence she had that she'd even known Crain was a photograph of the two of them taken at the boarding school in France where they'd met and a recent one of them with Ransom, taken when they'd bought him, neither picture even a close-up; an old school friend, an investor, Greta could have told Ned if he'd asked. She had many clients and business partners he'd never met; he wouldn't have given it a second thought. She had destroyed Crain's letters to keep her word to him (he had seemed to fear—what? Not discovery, exactly; they risked that every time they met), but she would have given anything now only to look at pages of his handwriting, let alone reread phrases of which there now existed no proof he'd ever uttered them.

Greta had always counted on there coming a day, when Henry was older and living away from home, when he would meet his real father. He might hate his mother for her long deception; he might never forgive her, but he would be grown up then; he would have lived a happy, secure childhood and in time he might come to understand that to give him that was partly why his mother had lied. He would see that he still had Ned, and now he would have Crain too . . . There would come a day—she had been waiting sixteen years for it—when she wouldn't have to lie anymore, when the life she said she lived and the life she did live would be the same. She had never considered the possibility that Crain could leave her stranded between the two.

For one thing, there remained only her word that he was Henry's father. Greta found it incredible that she could have had such little forethought as to destroy all the letters in which he wrote of his hopes for his son's future, his fear that his son might never wish to know him. How could she have believed Crain—that everything would turn out all right in the end?

"You worry too much, Greta—" (pronouncing her name as he always had, somehow in three collapsed syllables) "—so typically American of you, wanting to know how everything will turn out before it happens . . ."

He knew how to annoy and so manipulate her; she was certainly *not* typically American; she'd scarcely lived in this country until she was in college, and, besides, what were the last fifteen years but an exercise in resisting the conclusions that could be drawn about her life? The only person now alive other than herself who knew who Henry's real father was was Rachel, and the only "evidence" a letter Greta had written to Henry shortly after his birth in which she told him the truth. Rachel kept it in a bank vault with her family valuables and had promised to give it to Henry when he was twenty-one if Greta should not be around to tell him.

Ned's desk stood under a window that looked down the front lawn; Greta had been staring, unseeing, at the view Crain had never seen until this fact occurred to her and she turned her head with a sharp intake of breath and found herself looking, instead, at a portrait of herself. Ned had commissioned Rachel to paint it two years ago from a photograph Henry had taken a year or two before that: Greta sitting on Thrush Hollow's back-porch steps in her riding clothes, the crop resting across her knees, as she gazed into the distance in the direction of the abandoned Trout Hill mines. Her hair was longer than she wore it now—parted on the side and falling below the shoulder; it looked marcelled, the way women had waved their hair in the 1920s.

The painting startled Greta in the same way it had when she'd first looked up one evening at dinner to see her own face gazing down at her from above the dining-room mantel. Ned and Henry had laughed at her exclamation—"What am I doing up there?" In some ways the portrait didn't even look much like her and yet Rachel, who preferred painting landscapes to people, had captured something idiosyncratic about Greta's pose and expression. Greta knew she'd been missing Crain at the moment Henry had happened along with the Instamatic she and Ned had given him for his tenth birthday. She had just come back from the American Horse Show finals, where Crain had spent five days with her—their "cover" his ownership of the horse she was riding.

Greta had disliked being reminded of this every night at dinner, but she hadn't wished to offend Ned; he'd been so proud of himself for having thought up the scheme. An inspiration had come to her finally: last summer she'd traded Rachel riding lessons for her twelve-year-old daughter Olivia for a painting of Lucinda Dearborn, using the photograph in the town history as model. She'd given it to Ned as a late birthday present, suggesting that it was really Lucinda's place to look down from the mantel, and he hadn't objected.

Greta was struck this morning—she hadn't looked at the portrait since they'd found Lucinda's letters—by the similarity between her expression and Lucinda's: a kind of defiant wistfulness, a sadness that dared anyone to attempt to palliate it. No substitutes accepted for what was missing, thank you. It must have been Rachel's signature—Greta didn't think she often looked like that. She thought she generally conveyed competence and good will, if not warmth particularly. Yet this was the snapshot Ned had chosen to represent her. This was the image of her—sixteen-year-old Margaret Sayre standing up to the Catholic Church, refusing to let anyone explain her inexplicable experience—that Ned had kept in his heart for three decades.

Greta envied that person now. The integrity of her solitude—if she could have even that back, she wouldn't ask for anything else. She'd felt that pure loneliness only in the days immediately following the phone call from Crain's secretary—Mrs. Dene was among Mr. Crain's "important business contacts," so first there was the disorientation of hearing him called, as he actually was, *Mr.* Crain—it rarely happened that she heard him called by his "real" name. The secretary apologized for not knowing how well anyone on her list had known Mr. Crain—her apology preceding the actual news although Greta's body had understood on its own and, standing in the tack room, she'd slumped down upon a trunk; no one was there, thank God no one was there at the moment, although later she'd wished there had been, a witness. She'd believed for a moment that the secretary meant to insinuate that she *did* know who Greta was, later knowing she'd hoped that, despite everything he'd said, Crain had left news of her with the world.

He had been with her as soon as she heard the word "crashed," right beside her; she could hear him, feel him, see him, smell him—she only could not touch him, and she could survive like that; it was how she had had to survive for years, after all, except that this time his presence had been so all-consuming that she'd had to leave at once, go up to stay with Rachel, lest Ned see him too.

Then afterwards she had pleaded with him, she had screamed out his name, but by then he would not stay. She remembered that pleas had never been effective, so she had tried logical argument. He would appear to be persuaded, but by the next day seemed to have no recollection of what they had discussed. Since then his plain loss, which she had found she could stand—didn't she have to?—had fractured into contradictory recollections of their time together and questions about the way she had lived for so long, the way he had been willing to let her live, and this she couldn't bear. Absence, pure, was fluid; she could move in its medium, but these sharp, granular thoughts, each of which wanted to insist that *it* was the truth—piece by piece they were turning her to stone.

This was last night's nightmare, which she still couldn't shake: not the first, but to date the most sinister, dream she'd had about Julia, Crain's wife, since seeing her for the first time at Crain's funeral, standing between her children, Teresa and Felipe (Philip to everyone except his family), first in their pew as the bier bearing its draped coffin, suddenly modernly movable, was wheeled down the aisle and outside by rigid men in black suits, and then near the door of the church, while the mourners filed past one by one and shook Julia's hand. They congratulated her, so it seemed to Greta, upon being Crain's widow. Julia was the one he had chosen to stand there, dressed in black, to receive the mumbled apologies of people for being inadequate in the face of such a loss; he had not chosen Greta. It was not complicated; how had she ever believed it was? He had loved her as he'd never loved anyone; he had said so and she knew it was true, but what did that mean when she did not stand there, as Julia did, to listen to people say how shocked they were, how sorry? Who had told *her* that? Only Rachel, and Rachel's sympathy had been tempered because at the same time she'd learned that Crain had died she had also learned that Greta had continued to see him, that they were still lovers when Greta had told her that she only wrote letters, in order to keep Crain up to date on Henry's welfare.

Greta had believed Crain—it was what she herself believed—that things were what they were, it didn't matter what names people gave them; but he had been wrong; it *did* matter. Death fixed the names in place, once and for all.

In the receiving line, Teresa and Felipe's attention never strayed from their mother except when they glanced with undisguised hostility at the people none of them knew who introduced themselves as "a business associate" of Crain's, an "acquaintance of your husband's." "Mrs. Dene," said Felipe to his mother, since he was first in line. "Another business connection of Papá's." The "Papá" might have struck Greta as an affectation, but in this instance reminded her of their distinctness from everyone else. Though both Teresa and Felipe had been born in the U.S., to Greta they and their mother possessed the aura of recent refugees, carrying memories of an experience that no one who hadn't shared it could understand.

You have a younger brother you've never met, Greta had imagined saying to Teresa and Felipe. To Julia, Your husband is the father of my son. Because he did not want you or your children to suffer, I have had to lie all these years. Their shock would have at least confirmed the reality of her relationship to Crain.

"You didn't have to be bound by his rules," Rachel had said. "You could have told Ned. Ned is *your* husband." "And deprived Henry of the father he knows when his real father wouldn't take his place?" "You don't know what Ned would have done. You denied him freedom of choice. At least you didn't have to keep seeing Crain." "I did," Greta had said. "I did have to."

How else could she have found the strength to keep lying—their relationship, from the time they met up to the last time she saw him, having an incontrovertibility that nothing else in her life, with the exception of her feeling for Henry, had ever had?

Greta had gone to the funeral imagining that she would be able to tell—if she could but once, after all these years, look into Julia's eyes—how much Crain had loved his wife; there would be some discordance, in which Greta might read the fact of her own existence. But instead all she had seen was how much Julia had loved him. Her depth of grief, her unquestioning devotion . . . how could Crain have looked at anyone else? That was the mystery—and in that one thought Greta had felt herself cease to exist.

"How could you leave me like this?" she said aloud. Her voice was quiet, her tone reasonable. Then she heard the way she sounded and, sickened, left the study. She set her coffee cup in the kitchen sink and, in her knee-high rubber boots, tramped down the wet lawn to the barn to feed Ransom. She was late and he stood alert, waiting, in his stall. She wouldn't ride this morning, and, recognizing her mood even before she spoke to him, he didn't whinny but instead pushed his forehead against her shoulder.

"Old goat," she said as she stroked his neck. "Old billy goat."

He watched as she measured grain into his feed bucket and hung it from a hook in his stall. She broke several flakes of hay off a bale and tossed them in, refilled his water buckets, shoveled out the manure, then leaned against the gate post to watch him eat. She was fond of saying that one couldn't afford to be sentimental in her profession; she earned her bread and butter training other people's horses and giving riding lessons, but the "real" money she made—the kind that permitted her and Ned to afford Thrush Hollow, to send Henry to private school, and to travel during Ned's sabbaticals—she acquired in buying horses for next to nothing and selling them for a large profit after training them up to the Grand Prix level; she had an eye for potential other people either couldn't see or couldn't tap.

But Ransom Greta refused to sell. Already this summer she'd turned down two offers in the six figures; she'd instructed her barn at home not to give out her Stilling telephone number, but there was always someone who hadn't heard, or who decided that if the call involved money, the order could be countermanded. Even if she'd wanted to sell the horse she wouldn't have done so now; she'd have waited until he'd won a gold medal or two at the next Olympics, as she had no doubt he could do, though to date no U.S. rider had ever won an individual gold; the country hadn't the tradition in this anachronistic sport that others did—but she had no intention of asking it of him. She had ridden him before judges for the last time. Let other people parade their private relationships in front of strangers. Maybe they didn't know what a private relationship was, if they were so eager to have other people pronounce upon its worth for them. "Why do you care what they think?" Crain had said, shrugging in the Gallic way he'd acquired in school. "It's a game—you have only to play it. Every livelihood possesses that element. Think of showing what you can do as doing other people a favor."

Maybe he could do that; maybe she could have too, when he was alive. He'd been half-owner, so could pretend he had a stake in promoting Ransom's reputation. But he wasn't here, not here to object, not here to remind her of the private life they'd shared—though it wasn't private, but *secret,* since privacy was a quality particular to the inside of something whose outside was known. Now she wasn't going to traduce Ransom's trust by allowing his performance to be measured according to a scale of values that assessed his relationship with her based on what could be seen in public, that cared nothing for the bond itself but only the measurable manifestations of the bond.

"I'll have to come back later," Greta said to the horse, who had finished the oats and was looking at her, though she was merely verbalizing out of politeness what he already knew. If she had been going to ride, she'd have been wearing her breeches and boots, and by now would have carried his saddle and bridle out of the tack room and hung them on a sawhorse while she brushed him.

"I'm no good this morning," she said. She couldn't concentrate and he would know it the moment she hoisted herself into the saddle. He would be courteous, and do what she asked—Ransom had never not done what she'd asked, ever since as an unruly five-year-old he had let her ride him around the ring and at her request performed several maneuvers that other trainers who had ridden him had asserted he would never achieve in his entire career—but she would feel his disappointment. Sometimes she could work herself out of a low mood by forcing herself to concentrate, thinking only of the pressure of her knees on his flanks, the feel of the reins across her palms, until she was no longer herself but a creature she and Ransom had become together, and her thought a liquid thing, following their motion rather than directing it, but today was not one of those days. She was going to have to think about the dream to be rid of it—Julia standing, flanked by her children, just as she had been at Crain's funeral: dressed in the same widow's black and clasping her nineteen-year-old son's hand with her left hand while extending her right to the mourners who waited in line to offer their condolences. But in the dream she had held both children's hands and instead of being in the church in New York, they had been in Mexico, in the square of a small town in the central highlands where Greta had stayed with Ned and Henry for a few days on a sightseeing trip during Ned's last sabbatical; they had been renting a house for six months in Cuernavaca so Ned could do research in Mexico City.

The square, named El Jardín de la Libertad, was closed to automobile traffic and accessible only by narrow walkways called *andadores;* those leading in the direction of the town's main plaza were lined by women squatting on the paving stones, tiny collections of pots or hair combs displayed hopefully on scarves spread out on the ground, their babies tied in their shawls or fidgeting nearby, often dirty and sick-looking. Guiltily Greta had tried to leave the square in another direction so she wouldn't have to walk past them.

The square itself, in contrast to the noisy and exhaust-choked central plaza, was serene, surrounded by well-kept nineteenth-century buildings painted rich yellows and ochres, prosperous but not ostentatious. A colonnade ran along one side of the square, and beneath it were set out the white cloth-covered tables of a small restaurant where she and Ned and Henry several times ate meals—the waiter soon greeting them as if he'd known them all his life. Opposite, a large archway opened into the courtyard of the hotel where they were staying.

Over the course of their visit, the three of them had often sat in the square, but one particular evening, re-created in her dream, stood out in Greta's memory. It was not dark, but it was evening, and the gas had already been lit in the old-fashioned gas lamps that stood at intervals throughout the square; the white-painted tree trunks (Henry called them the trees' socks) and the white wrought-iron benches gleamed in the dusk.

It had been lightning for some time, off to the east, though there'd been no thunder. Greta had been watching the other people in the square; those who, like her, rested on benches in the cooling evening, also saw the lightning, but those heading home along the square's diagonal paths—vendors with baskets on their backs, workers in suits coming from the government building catty-corner to the restaurant, or couples, holding hands, beginning an evening out—didn't notice the lightning unless they happened to be walking towards it.

Greta, with Ned and Henry, had been sitting on a bench that faced the fountain in the center of the square; there was a statue in the middle of the fountain commemorating the man responsible for first bringing drinkable water to the city: at each corner of his pedestal a sleek-looking stone dog, crouched as if about to pounce, spurted water into the basin in a continuous stream. What part the dogs had played, if any, in bringing water to the city, or why the sculptor had otherwise deemed their presence appropriate, was not explained in the plaque embedded in the fountain's rim. (Henry had entertained them with various theories.)

There was something odd and compelling about the fountain, and children, who loved fountains anyway, seemed to feel at once that this one required a response from them. One tiny girl, holding the hand of an older brother, was walking around and around on the fountain's flat rim, humming. Another little girl, older, had picked up branches left behind by pruning gardeners earlier in the day and was dancing with them, slapping them against the ground, twirling them in the air, executing a ritual hop every few steps. Several other children, strolling decorously with their parents, broke away when they caught sight of the fountain and catapulted themselves towards it.

As the lightning continued to flash, dark clouds had slid in, and when the first roll of thunder came, everyone glanced up expectantly as if the curtain were finally being lifted for a performance. Some rose from their benches, collected belongings, and hurried on their way—as if suddenly realizing that they had tickets to a different show—but the rest, like Greta and Henry and Ned, didn't stir. As the thunder began to boom and the lightning to flash more urgently, the people crossing the square walked faster; when the first occasional raindrops fell, experimenting, umbrellas appeared from nowhere, yet it wasn't until the rain began to fall in earnest that everyone else jumped up, laughing and running; Greta and Ned and Henry ran for their hotel holding hands, as if they might otherwise have found themselves separated.

Although originally Greta had looked forward to spending Ned's sabbatical in Mexico because Mexico was where Crain had grown up (though his family was not Mexican but English—originally Danish) and she'd wanted Henry to experience his father's culture, or one of them, while he was young enough to absorb it uncritically, it had turned out to be the time, more than any other, when she'd come closest to forgetting that Henry wasn't Ned's son. She hadn't been writing to Crain; he'd been angry with her for going to "his" country when he could never go back; too many "painful circumstances" to forget, which, untypically, he wouldn't specify. At least, it had seemed untypical then. He was usually so forthright, so expressive and unguarded—even his mannerisms suggested it: that way he had acquired, because of a hearing loss early in life, of leaning towards you, though he had worn a hearing aid since his twenties; his habit of sculpting everything with his hands as he spoke, as if to make sure you could see what he was talking about—a mannerism of the cultures he'd lived in but more exaggerated with him, as if he were speaking his own sign language, maybe another practice acquired before his hearing trouble had been properly diagnosed. He was generally so candid that his occasional balking at telling her something (sometimes as perverse as where he'd purchased a pair of shoes) had seemed like the petulant proprietorship of a small child, inexplicable and amusing. That, she saw now, had been a stupid misjudgment. *She* was one such secret, which he'd no doubt protected in the same endearing way.

She had known that Crain had had a falling-out with his younger brother; he'd spoken of Federico often and then at one point no longer did. Two years ago Federico had died; Greta learned this only because she'd called on a pre-arranged day and been told by the secretary that Mr. Crain was away at his brother's funeral.

"Are you afraid I'm going to contact Federico's family and expose you?" she'd asked, before the sabbatical trip. "Is that what it is?"

"Of course I'm afraid of no such thing. I do not wish to be reminded of things I prefer to forget. If you go there, kindly do not write to me."

Whether or not their not corresponding was the reason, she'd felt that she and Ned and Henry were an entity in a way they'd never been before, closer to the real family they would have been had circumstances been otherwise. It was the only enduring time in her marriage that making love to Ned had been something in itself, not an offshoot of her feeling for Crain, as it usually was. When she'd awakened this morning, she especially resented Julia's appearing in that location, as if now she, and the family Crain had left behind—his official, public family—meant to insinuate themselves into the only identity Greta had left to cling to.

In the dream, she'd been sitting on the bench as before but had begun to sense a presence behind her; it seemed to take a very long time to become aware of it, or she had been reluctant to acknowledge what she sensed. Finally, turning, she was incredulous at seeing Julia and her children standing right there, like a sacred trinity. *"Perdóneme,"* she exclaimed in the dream, meaning, What are you doing, standing so close to us? *"Querrían sentarse?"* Do you want to sit down?

But Julia had not answered. Clearly she had heard the question, because she looked right into Greta's eyes as she spoke; the children also stared silently.

"Ned . . ." Greta had tapped him on the shoulder.

"What, darling?"

She had indicated behind them, but though Ned, and then Henry, had turned, and Julia and her children still stood there, Ned and Henry did not see them. Then Julia smiled—a hideous, purely evil smile—and pursed her lips and whistled.

Henry jumped. "What was that?"

"Look!" Ned exclaimed.

Greta turned back. Before them, at the fountain, the stone dogs had come to life. They leapt down, still spewing water, knocking over the little girl on the rim, and bounded towards Greta.

"More water," Julia said. "More and more water. Good dogs."

The gentle spurts now gushed forth like geysers, sparing Greta but hitting Ned and Henry with the force of water cannons, knocking them from the bench and sweeping them across the square. At first they clung together, gasping and choking as they tumbled in the torrent, but then they were forced apart and Greta, trying to run after them, had to decide which one to abandon. In waking life she would, unthinking, have gone after Henry, but in the dream she was paralyzed by her indecision, and Julia said, "Children come first," in a bitter, mocking tone. "Most mothers would give up their lives for their children."

Henry was floundering, going under, resurfacing, screaming for help. Yet every time Greta tried to move towards him Julia's children took her hands and pulled her back. Their hands were cold and hard, their grip merciless, and when Greta looked down, unable to free herself, she saw that their hands were made of the same stone as the dogs, and when she looked back up at their faces, they too were made of stone, immobile now. She looked for Henry again, saw him go under, but then she could no longer move; she also had been turned to stone and stood now as Julia had, holding the hands of Julia's children while Julia, disguised as Greta, said, "Don't worry, they will be safe with me. I will know how to love them."

She had whistled again, inserting two fingers beneath her tongue, curling it back, and blowing, the way Greta whistled for her horses when they were out in the field, and the dogs had sprung back onto the fountain, the water had vanished, and Ned and Henry had reappeared from the walkways into which they'd been washed. They waved gaily at each other and laughed, as if they'd been competing to see who could reach the square first from different directions, then waved to Greta—the false Greta—and the three of them came to sit on the bench where Greta, as herself, had been sitting just moments ago.

Greta had woken then, sweating, one of her hands trapped beneath her, numb—which she realized had been translated into the grip of the children; nor had she any difficulty in understanding, in a general way, the message of being usurped by Julia, even if she didn't try to work out the dream's more subtle symbolism. There was the desire for water perverted, traceable to the longing she invariably felt during rainstorms, and had felt that evening in the square, for the thunder to grow louder and louder, the rain to come down harder and harder until all separation— from others, from life—was obliterated.

"Did she *know* about me?" Greta said aloud, leaning against Ransom's stall, and the horse, unsettled by her tone, lifted his head from the hay and looked at her.

"Should I have told Ned? Right at the beginning?"

And what then? Gone away to have Henry by herself, with no father at all? Maybe if she'd done that, Crain would have left Julia to be with them.

The stupid thing was, Ned was so completely happy to be a father. Watching Ned with Henry was when she had really begun, for the first time, to love him.

Greta was shivering, and she let herself into the stall so that she could lean against the horse, to feel the warmth of another creature—one who would not demand to know what was wrong.

Crain was dead, but his death was not simply an ending, as at first she had believed it would be, and now there was no relief even in sleep. She had become obsessed by the fact that she had not seen his body; there had been no funeral-home visiting hours; he had crashed his plane, she did not even know exactly where. She did not know where he had been buried—or even if he had been; Julia was Catholic and so was the service, but Crain had observed no religion and perhaps his request had been for cremation. If he had made any such request. Maybe Julia was still in possession of his ashes. Could Greta think of an excuse to call on her, bringing along a container of wood ashes in her handbag to replace the ones she would steal—were there shards of bone? Whom could she ask? Both of her parents had been buried. Then she would possess all that anyone could anymore of Crain; she would be able to say to Henry someday, "Your father's ashes are buried here. His family doesn't know. This is where I want to be buried." Although Henry might be so angry at her for depriving him of his real father that he would refuse.

"What am I going to do?" she repeated. "What should I do?"

Things could not go on as they were, but what could change them? She couldn't continue to live in this silence, but if she told Ned not only would she devastate him and Henry, it would also be the end of her, the person Crain had loved. Only he had known her, but he was dead. If she did speak, she would dissolve into the hurt in Ned's eyes, the disbelief in Henry's. Yet if she did not, she would also disappear, her life drained of its nourishment by the secret inside her, whose hunger to be made known could no longer be kept in check by Crain's sharing it.

It was that afternoon and Ned sat hunched over his desk at Thrush Hollow, copies of O.'s letters spread out before him; on the left-hand side of a yellow legal pad he was listing the dates of what he judged to be significant letters along with a brief synopsis of their subjects. He underlined those which referred to topics in previous letters of Lucinda's. On the right-hand side he had listed chronologically the dates of composition and publication of those of O.'s short stories and novels whose plots seemed to pertain in some way to his relationship with Lucinda. In block letters, on the left-hand side, he had also noted the dates of O.'s five visits to Lucinda: 1865, 1870, 1874, 1881, 1905. Five visits over the course of forty years. When O. and Lucinda met, he was twenty-two and she nineteen. The last time they saw each other, he was sixty-two and she fifty-nine.

When Ned looked at the five dates and contemplated the intervals of time they marked, a sense of bleakness crept over him. The last interval was longer than his entire marriage to Greta, and when he considered all the days, all the hours of being together that that span represented, he couldn't comprehend how Lucinda could have kept her feeling for O. alive. How could it have been for *him,* the actual person? Ned's compassion for Lucinda was mixed, however, not with condescension but with a sense of his own inferiority; he could sympathize with the conviction that no one could measure up to a particular person, but he didn't think he would have been capable of such single-minded devotion, of maintaining his integrity at the expense of companionship. (Though what would he have done, if he and Greta had not met up again? Clearly she had been the figure against whom he'd measured all the other young women of his acquaintance, his encounters with whom it still mortified him to recall.)

Ned wished he could figure out the extent of O.'s understanding of his effect on Lucinda. Had O., who found so heinous the ways in which people made use of others, himself used someone? Had his frequently told story of one intimate's flourishing at the expense of another been not simply something he'd witnessed and feared but something in which he'd participated?

It seemed clear that O. had understood the effect Lucinda had had on *him*. "The longing to cast myself down in your verdant valley, to close my eyes in the dappled sunlight beneath one of the spreading maples, comes upon me at many odd moments. Yet I dare not heed it; the world calls. Your lush and yet as it were upright Hollow is not the world."

O.'s unconsciously sexual language had been provoked by something that had occurred between him and Lucinda on his first visit to Thrush Hollow, something O. referred to in subsequent letters as the "episode," a term Lucinda adopted in her diary. "I cannot bring myself to record the particulars of the episode whose very instant I shall recall all of my life," she wrote. "To do so would be to contort it by the telling, just as certain sacred mysteries must remain unspoken, but—oh, until the moment I breathe my last, I shall remember the water on my skin, the heat of his eyes on me . . ."

From this, and other cryptic entries, Ned guessed that the episode, so called, had involved O.'s chancing (or arriving as planned), through a grove of trees, upon Lucinda doing something in the brook for which she was in a state of complete or partial undress—though to say even this much required reading with microscopic zeal between the lines.

Lucinda wrote that "all was pale; when my beloved left, he drained the world of color." "My desolation will know no end. I have found the love I have always sought, but it is not to be." But had she written as much to O.? In the latter part of the nineteenth century it was unlikely that a young woman would have taken a man to task for not proposing to her, especially if he had not made love to her, in either the archaic or the modern sense of the term, which, strictly, it seemed, O. hadn't.

For a period after each of O.'s visits to Thrush Hollow, he reacted in his letters to the emotionally straitened circumstances in which he found Lucinda; at these times he glimpsed the long empty years she had spent worshipping at his altar and was horrified. "I would shudder to suppose were it not too overwhelmingly vain to think it," he wrote to her after his second visit, "that you might have entertained a notion of my nature as distant from the truth as it might be compelling. . . ."

This seemed to be as close as O. had ever come to admitting in print that he might bear some responsibility for Lucinda's privation. Usually his correspondence after each visit was full of exhortations to her to "get about more," to visit "our great metropolises and imbibe their raucous, maddening, invigorating life." But after a time the cheerleading tone disappeared, and he returned to the intimate, vivacious, and intermittently adoring one that characterized the bulk of the letters.

What happened, each time, to reestablish the epistolary intimacy? Ned wondered. It could only be that Lucinda had reassured her correspondent. She was far too sensitive not to have felt his shock when he visited her—"Did he expect to find me still nineteen?" she wrote. "He is ever too much the gentleman to have manifested his dismay, yet nonetheless I perceived it"—but his distress had only increased her loneliness, as if he were suggesting that she was to blame for it. "Must I then smile, and welcome my pain as a reminder of the love I am blessed with? Is to complain of my loss an ingratitude for what I *am* given? Surely I have known an understanding that others do not even dimly imagine. . . ."

She must have convinced O. that she didn't suffer as he dreaded, that he was not responsible for her isolation. To have expressed to him the despair evident in her diary entries might have provoked him to stop writing her altogether, and "without his letters," she had written, "would remain only great emptiness." She had freed him from any sense of obligation, but he had been complicit in her self-denial.

In 1865, when O. first visited Thrush Hollow, he was not yet as disenchanted with his native land as he was afterwards to become. He had felt disenchantment, but had not yet, as might be said, nationalized it. He chafed at American society and longed to go abroad, where he sensed that life might be lived more expansively, but he had not yet experienced enough of the contrast between continents to form the lasting judgments of both that would inform his life's work. Had something in him sensed that Lucinda could prove an impediment to his neat analysis?

It was "devilishly hot" in Boston in August of 1865, and a holiday in New Hampshire with a brother and a couple of friends had already been planned. Then his brother (call him S., Ned decided), a Civil War veteran, had urged O. to accompany him on a visit to his former captain, "describing him to me [O. wrote to Lucinda in his first letter] as a courtly and educated man who, for reasons unclear, had elected to remove himself from the onrushing flow of his country's life when he could have been anything, as S. avowed, done anything. He left 'on principle,' S. told me, and though I confess to being disgruntled by my brother's inability to furnish the all-important details that would substantiate the thesis, my curiosity was nonetheless aroused—my writer's curiosity, dare I say. This self-exiled gentleman, this 'captain,' I thought, might prove a fit subject—for a small tale, perhaps; ten thousand words or so. I might offer it, I encouraged myself, to one of the better magazines. A gentleman who, for obscure reasons, chooses to live out of the way and to make his living as the proprietor of a resort hotel in Vermont's faraway hills; a widower, the father of a delightful daughter (so S. styled you, seeming quite infatuated with you by hearsay. There was no one up there estimably 'good enough' for you, as your fond papa had told him—one evening, so I presume, when the Confederate guns fell silent)—yes, I said to myself, I could quite see how something might be got up."

In this letter, Ned believed, O. was both testing Lucinda to ascertain her willingness to be considered "material" and confessing to her his difficulty in transforming her into it. He would need her collusion, in other words. After he met her, it had been quite evident that the captain's daughter could not so easily be "got up" as anything, and the truth was that he would spend a lifetime trying to contain her, to define her, to kill her off, in fact, every way he could think of, whether by having her catch her death of influenza as a result of being so naive as not to recognize the social strata in European society or, more subtly, by putting her in the way of the intrigues of a money-hungry fellow countryman and his mistress whose wiles the Lucinda-character was too idealistic and trusting to recognize.

The echoes in O.'s letters to Lucinda of themes elaborated in his published work (or vice versa) were not hard to find. What was trickier was to trace the mutations whereby Lucinda, in her full aliveness, had been transformed into a symbolic entity. Upon meeting her, O. had praised Lucinda's "unstudied grace, her natural sophistication, her serene liveliness," and there were other such oxymoronic combinations: the civilized alchemized with the natural, the European with the American, the contemplation of life with its striving. And yet in his published work, O. had

maintained these qualities in opposition, as if to write about them introduced a chemical agent that artificially separated what ordinarily would
not be. Had finding this marvelous mixture in Lucinda, Ned wondered,
interfered with O.'s belief that it nowhere existed? Not only didn't, but
couldn't?

"Your bloom would not survive transplanting," he had written. "I
doubt you could practice your magic in other waters."

What Lucinda had replied to this would never be known, but it was
evident from her diary that such statements, of which this was not the
last, had troubled her. Was he correct in his judgment?—after all, he
knew the world, not she—or did he say this because it was convenient to
believe? Otherwise he might have had to consider taking his "nymph of
the north woods" across the ocean with him.

And what if he had? His features might have aged more softly; he
might have looked more at ease; maybe he'd have been happier, but
would he have written his great books? How many successful writers'
careers were founded on the kind of apostasy O. had practiced? To Ned
the critical question was whether O. had practiced it inadvertently or to
be true to the time he lived in; to maintain his integrity had he had to
abstain from a fulfillment society at large could not know? Or was his private paralysis cast like a giant shadow across everything he looked at? If
the latter, though, one wouldn't have heard the ring of truth one did in
O.'s social analysis.

Furthermore, the stories in which O. tried to bring about a happy
finale to his dance of opposites were never convincing. In an early story,
for example (written when, abroad, O. learned of Lucinda's father's sudden death), a proud, independent-minded young American girl, tellingly
named "Miss Brooke," travelling with her widowed father in Italy, met a
fellow countryman, equally revealingly named "Mr. Hargrove." The latter, intoxicated by architectural and pictorial loveliness, and a life of the
senses such as he had never imagined possible, could conceive of
responding to this voluptuous experience only by developing a corresponding intoxication for Miss Brooke. She, however, saw his infatuation
for the "in essence poetic" emotion that it was, and sent him packing.
This seemed realistic to Ned and perhaps the message would have
proven salutary to Lucinda; why couldn't O. have left it at that? Instead,
O. had Hargrove, not long after, come upon Miss Brooke kneeling in
St. Peter's (the majority of their encounters, for reasons ominously

inscrutable to Ned, took place beneath the dusky domes of Italy's basilicas or before the masterpieces of her painters—depictions of the Crucifixion, the Last Supper, the Adoration of the Magi), dressed in black, orphaned, and in her loneliness and weakness she now accepted Hargrove's factitious sentiment as real love. O.—it was a somewhat mechanical, early story—had evidently intended the marriage contracted at the end to seem happy, but he hadn't pulled it off. Mr. Hargrove was so blatantly callow that Miss Brooke's change of heart could be attributed only to her present helplessness.

Ned could not be positive that Lucinda had read this story. She had read all of O.'s work that she could get hold of, having sent a standing order to a bookseller in Boston for "whatever of Mr. O.'s should appear in print" (she had retained a copy of the letter in her diary), but the order was for books, and though she subscribed to the *Atlantic Monthly* and, later on, to *Collier's,* in both of which magazines she knew that O. published, she knew that she wouldn't find everything. He was generally evasive to her about when and where his work saw print, remarking that he'd "penned a macabre tale or two" or was "still enmeshed in the coils of a very *constricting* opus."

If she had seen the story, Lucinda certainly would have been able to read O.'s ambivalence about her integrity and independent spirit in the thinly disguised portrait of "Miss Brooke." O. might admire these qualities in theory, but, he seemed to say, they did not permit for the leaning on of someone's shoulder that (from his side) was necessary if the physical aspect of passion (and the marriage which propriety dictated would follow) were to be admitted to the relationship. The suggestion seemed to be that, if Lucinda had only been more yielding, O. would not have had to take himself off. The artificial quality of the ending prevented one from believing O. could have seriously meant this—he'd been trying it out and learned from his inability to make it believable, Ned guessed— but Ned still wished he could know how Lucinda would have judged it.

In a short entry whose brevity tantalized Ned, Lucinda wrote, "Z. S. came late afternoon yesterday to offer condolences for Father. I read O.'s Italy story again. He wants to get himself 'off the hook.' " This was the only entry anywhere near the time of the Miss Brooke story's publication that could conceivably have referred to it, but why so cryptically when usually Lucinda reacted at length to O.'s published work, who "Z. S." was and what his visit had to do, if anything, with Lucinda's rereading of

O.'s story were not clear. Neither Z. S. nor O.'s "Italy" story was ever mentioned again (O. set many stories in Italy); nevertheless, Ned felt sure, that terse entry marked a milestone in Lucinda's feelings about O., even if Ned could not corroborate this inference by anything she specifically said. After that point, he had the feeling, Lucinda was writing in her diary almost as if she were in fact the character O. kept fashioning out of her. Again, Ned could locate his impression in nothing Lucinda explicitly stated—perhaps she was unaware of the change herself. Yet it seemed to him that she acquiesced more in O.'s portrayal of her. Her language subtly began to echo his. It was at this time that she first wrote, "I am all that he has left behind. I am his boyhood and his youth, and to think of me at liberty in these woods and pastures he so loves, but is constrained from dwelling in, provides his spirit with a tranquility he can attain in no other way." Though O. had never spoken directly to the expectations Lucinda had obviously formed (unspecific as they may have been) as a result of whatever had taken place during his first visit, he had also written to her in such a way that he had not discouraged her either. To be fair, Ned thought, one might judge that the intimacy O. had shared with Lucinda was so out of his ordinary experience that once he had left Thrush Hollow he couldn't even credit it. His memory, in self-preservation, had diminished it, and Lucinda, herself exiled back into propriety, hadn't dared object to the picture he'd painted.

Yet her acquiescence in O.'s neglect had not prevented him from stepping up his murderous campaign over the years, as if even her acquiescence in her own destruction bound him, or as if the reality of her being kept flooding back to him no matter how hard he worked to contain it, until finally there came the most explicit story of all: the famous tale of the governess, besotted by an employer she saw only once, whose thwarted desire took on dimension as villainous, sordid ghosts who destroyed the children in her charge. This one might read, Ned thought, not only in the usual way—suppressed sexual impulses wreaking havoc—but more specifically as censure of Lucinda for devoting her affections to someone who would never provide her with children, thus denying life to the children, and all that they symbolized of a healthy future, she might have had with another.

Increasingly in O.'s work, such denied impulses, recognized too late for what they were, figured as the unspoken horror at the heart of the mystery, the "it" with its unstated reference inevitably directing readers' attention to the place unreferenced pronouns always directed it—which had of course inevitably incited O.'s biographers repeatedly to ask whether the extent of the writer's own sexual experience could be determined via internal evidence in his literary work, since it could not be ascertained from any hitherto extant biographical material. This was only one reason that Hudson Sleeper's dowsing discovery of letters O. had written over a fifty-year period to a woman no biographer—and, it seemed probable, no friend—had ever known O. knew, with their suggestive references to an undefined "episode," would, as Ned had known upon his first cursory glance at the correspondence, only intensify the pursuit of these questions. The letters to Lucinda (it already sounded like a title) could not confirm a sexual experience, if by that one meant a sexual act, yet it had been adumbrated, and seemed to explain something that had always been missing in O.'s biography. And now Ned held the missing piece of the puzzle, yet the missing piece of the puzzle did not solve the puzzle.

Ned considered the two principal dimensions of O.'s work: the personal and psychological, the national and international. On the personal level, O.'s great subject (and to him the greatest evil) was the ways in which people used each other; in the classic plot there turned out to be a stark reality underlying all the convoluted self-examination and elaborate self-deception in which the characters, not knowing, afraid of knowing, the plain facts, had engaged—usually some aspect of the crude sexual or economic heart of things exerting its existence. O. seemed unable to construe an intimacy in which advantage was not taken by one partner of the other. The psychological turned international when you noted that the willfully naive dupes were usually Americans. On the other hand, their innocence had much to recommend it when set against the disillusion and hence the corruption of the Europeans. You couldn't, another way of saying it was, look forward and back at the same time.

The nineteenth century was in its death throes—O. recognized this—and the way of life he'd known and cherished was vanishing. What he valued—human gentleness, generosity, integrity, a code of behavior sometimes so refined that his sensibility alone could register its transgressions, the time for thinking and contemplation, the art of conversation, not to mention architectural and scenic loveliness—would be belittled and replaced by what newfangledness claimed of more vigorous worth: money-making, exploration, invention, industrial expansion. Forging ahead. The life *he* had wished to live—devoted to seeing and expressing what he saw—would seem rarefied to succeeding generations; nor could one pose intricate moral questions when people had ceased to care about their answers.

Yet, Ned thought, O.'s concerns were not antique. He had seen how a terrible fissure had opened and would widen in human nature, until the private life of the individual would be completely detached from the larger society. But even in privacy there would be no union. In the early part of the century, O., coming back to his homeland for the last time, had already seen how the distance between men and women had grown so great that they might never again be able to bridge it. It was the single most noticeable thing about the native atmosphere, he had written. This was almost a hundred years ago. What, one had to ask, had changed?

On this final return trip, O. had paid Lucinda his last visit. It was forty years since they had first met. Since that time, he had developed into a successful and respected writer, an international figure, but what had she done? She had continued to run Thrush Hollow, to effect water "cures" of an ambiguous nature—faith-healing, essentially—and to write letters to O., on average once every couple of months. That added up to well over two hundred letters during the time between O.'s first and last visits, and there would be nearly another hundred before he died.

All of these, burned. The final cruelty—to leave no record of Lucinda's devotion. What had O. been afraid of? Had he anticipated the contemporary biographer's habit of denigrating his subject (Ned liked to think of himself as not among the majority), as if to find that the flower of a life's work was rooted in its author's life devalued it? Why else the current craze for biographical detail, the more scurrilous the better, not confined to the lives of writers but drawing people in droves to TV "talk" shows, to discuss and hear discussed the most intimate details of people's lives before total strangers? Turning privacy inside out in a last hysterical attempt to bridge the gap between public and private, as if by delving deep enough in the trough you would find an incident so shocking as to reinstate you in the life of your time.

Knowing all this, what did he do? Ned wondered. Respect O.'s wishes and suppress the material that would convince people they were right to say, "Oh, he just needed a good roll in the hay, that was his problem"? Or did Ned—he cringed at the thought of the investment of time this would represent—try to write a revised biography, or a kind of joint biography of O. and Lucinda, in which he would try to show (assuming that this was what he believed) how O.'s choice could have been a sacrifice to make a point, every bit as heroic as immolating oneself to protest a hostile occupation of one's country or—dare he say it?—letting oneself be nailed to a cross because one couldn't stand everyone else's suffering?

Ned had been brought up to mistrust self-sacrifice, in particular the organization that had made a religion of it, but that did not mean it hadn't exercised an attraction for him in certain deep, inscrutable ways. He couldn't tell, now, if he was bringing that attraction to bear where it didn't apply or whether he was actually onto something.

Not long after his final visit to Lucinda, O. had written a story which told of a man returned, like himself, to his native land after many years abroad. The only other character was a Miss Swallow, who had known the protagonist, Mr. Livingstone, in his youth, and who, it was clear, had nursed an unrequited affection for him. Mr. Livingstone, dismayed but also fascinated by the changes that had taken place in his homeland during the interval of his absence, was haunted by the anxiety to know what he might have become had he remained at home instead of, as it now seemed to him, escaping abroad. He might have "had power," he said, when Miss Swallow questioned him about his regret.

In an at first seemingly quixotic effort to know this other, unlived life, Mr. Livingstone spent the wee hours, night after night, roaming his empty family mansion, which builders were after him to sell so that they might tear it down and construct a bigger, more lucrative apartment building in its place. The house represented Mr. Livingstone's mind, and, as he wandered up and down stairs, through its manifold doors (the number of which modern architecture, the point was made, would do away with, having no recognition of their usefulness to the psyche), into its nether regions, his state of nervous tension nightly increasing, the figure he would have been had he not gone abroad gradually began to take on dimension. Finally, one night, it seemed to have attained an independent life. A door Mr. Livingstone knew without doubt that he had left open—he had established it almost as a matter of principle to leave all the doors open—was, upon his retracing his steps, inexplicably shut. Except not inexplicably, as Mr. Livingstone, his terrified heart pounding in his chest, was forced to realize. His other self, the Mr. Livingstone he could have become, was loose in the house.

Mr. Livingstone, after enduring some moments of horror before the closed door, chose not to open it: a magnanimous gesture, this failure presented itself to him; he would leave the poor beleaguered fellow alone—and it, him. He would cease to torture himself with the what-might-have-been.

Leaving the room, he went to another and opened a window onto the street, deserted just before dawn, and leaned out in the hope of making contact with present-day, everyday humanity. While leaning out into the fresh air, he realized that, were he to return to the door and find it open, he would be completely undone. The shock to his psyche would send him rushing straight back for the open window, this time to fling himself out of it, to dash himself to bits upon the hard ground of the indivisible present, since the alternative—to go on existing in the world of the real-ized conditional—would have been an unending horror.

He did not risk a return; he descended, flight after flight, to the lower stories, feeling lighter of heart with each landing he left behind. Halfway down the final flight, gazing with happiness at the black and white marble squares of the foyer, he was struck by how light it seemed to be in the hallway—a fortuity he for a moment attributed to his own mental relief—until he noticed that someone had opened the door to the vestibule. Between it and the outer door, he realized, someone stood. Someone stood waiting for him. And who, of course, but his "other self"? Roused now from his sleeping potentiality by Mr. Livingstone's nocturnal pacing, this other self would not allow the being who had stolen *his* life from *him* to go away unscathed.

The creature appeared. Gruesome, venal, revolting—no words were too strong to express Mr. Livingstone's horror at the sight of this entity he might have become. His other self was hideous, grasping—peculiarly, he had lost two fingers on one hand, a detail that Ned thought must have seemed woefully obscure to readers who didn't possess, as Ned did, the information that, during his last visit to Lucinda, O., in assisting her to move a heavy parlor stove from one room to another, had slipped and let his side fall, pinning two of his fingers beneath it and bruising them badly. ("A visit to my brother's physician has reassured me that they are not bro-ken," he wrote to Lucinda the next day, "though their variegated vermil-lion and russet rival the most magnificent of sunsets.")

In the story, Mr. Livingstone fell to the marble floor in a faint, awaken-ing hours later with his head cradled in the lap of the perspicacious Miss Swallow, who had guessed what he was up to and had lain in wait for the daily charwoman to let her in. As, shuddering, he tried to express to Miss Swallow the horror he had experienced, she bent over and kissed him—not he her, Ned noted—and informed him that now he was hers. Instead of, as one might have anticipated given his earlier diffidence, recoiling from her act of possession, Mr. Livingstone begged her please, oh, please to keep him.

And what was this supposed to mean? Ned wondered, hearing the question enunciated in the aggrieved voice Henry used when he thought his father or mother too adultly cryptic. What's *that* supposed to mean?

How had O. intended what struck Ned as another gratuitous, implausible resolution, like that in the early, Miss Brooke story? He hadn't sent the story to Lucinda, so it couldn't be read as an invitation to her to follow in Miss Swallow's footsteps, unless he'd expected she would read the story in print. But in either case the message would have come too late; O. was already back abroad, never to return, so the story could only have taunted Lucinda with her missed opportunity. Years ago, she had not been submissive enough. Now, she had not been bold.

Or had the message, conversely, been, This is what I would have become, if I'd stayed to be your lover? The power I would successfully have wielded would have corrupted me—corrupted my very flesh. (Miss Swallow had taken Mr. Livingstone in her arms only after he'd been successfully vanquished by his alter ego—he was lying on the floor, a shell of himself.) Is that what you would have wanted me to become? Yes, you've suffered by my absence, but think how we'd both have suffered if I'd stayed. Our country, ironically, given its birth in the minds of exalted thinkers, is no place for thinking men to take power. The kind of power available here can only destroy them. If this means they must pay with a private as well as a public exile, then so be it. We are the real patriots, those of us who deny ourselves our homeland, not those who stay and eat of her flesh. Our loss of country and of those human beings we might have loved had we remained at home is a small price to pay for living in the truth of our clear sight.

This is what Ned imagined that O. might have said.

W hile Ned was at his desk subjecting O. to scrutiny, Greta was in the attic of the old hotel rummaging through a trunk of papers, looking for the address book she'd used when she was in boarding school in France. She had long ago lost touch with everyone she had used to correspond with, but if she could contact one or two of them—particularly her roommate during two of the three years she'd gone to the Collège, Marie-Agnès, or Crain's closest friend, Dominic—she would write to them that Crain was dead; they would reply, and then perhaps she might tell them about Henry and her secret life with Crain. It seemed to her, trying to reinstate herself in the past as she was, that if anyone could understand, without condemning, how this had come about, it would be someone who had actually known them together, seen them during the three years they'd spent as much of every day and every evening together as they could, given their separate class schedules and the school's restrictions, which on weekdays separated the sexes except during classroom hours and lunch.

Settled into these well-worn thoughts, Greta found it as strange as she always had that if her mother hadn't been dying she would never have met Crain. Even at the time she had felt there to be some unclear causal relationship between her mother's withering away and the vehement passion she felt, as if her mother had sent her away so that she would find Crain, knowning Crain would be the only person Greta would ever be able to stand asking her how she was—but her mother couldn't have known that her father would send Greta to school at St. Stephen's the fall after her mother died, despite Greta's pleading to be allowed to return to Le Cleuzet.

"It's time I came home for a while," he said. "Time we all came home."

"It's not home to me," Greta told him. How could it be, when she'd never spent any time here? Summer visits to a grandmother in Maryland, another in Michigan—that didn't make the States *home,* just because she carried its passport.

"But Sally lives in Marby," her father had argued, "and if I'm suddenly called abroad, I want you near family. It's not a time to be off on your own, Greta."

Neither was last year, she didn't say—I was off on my own then. It had been pointless to protest—to remind him that she'd be less on her own in a familiar place with her boyfriend and close friends than in a new, religious school in a country she hardly knew, near to a sister ten years older to whom she was not particularly close. This was her father's blind spot, both his conviction that, despite years of expatriation, his children were true Americans at heart, and his cherished belief that Greta, the child of his second marriage, and Sally, the child of his first, were devoted comrades and would stand by each other in their mutual motherlessness. If anything, Sally found it hard to sympathize with Greta's grief because she, Sally, envied Greta's at least having known her mother long enough to grieve for her.

Before the previous year, whenever their father had been posted to a location judged "too unstable" for families of diplomatic personnel to take up residence in, Greta and Sally, with Greta's mother, Anna Sayre, had remained in Europe, primarily in England and France (the countries which came to furnish the chief settings for "Priscilla Thwaite's" mysteries). The two girls had always attended local schools. Since Greta was nine, Sally had been back in the States, first to go to college and then, after her marriage, to live in Marby, and Greta and her mother had become closer than ever. They were playmates and confidantes—even, at times, collaborators—and Greta had not been able to understand her mother's insistence that, for the first time, she go away to school.

"I'll be travelling, Greta, doing research for the new book. A lot of genealogical material—you know how that can take me all over."

"But I've always gone with you," Greta pointed out. "I help you take notes. Why can't I this time?"

"Greta, please don't press me. You simply can't."

Baffled and hurt, Greta obeyed. Something was wrong, and she didn't understand why her mother didn't trust her enough to tell her what it was. Later, even when she realized that her mother had already been diagnosed with lung cancer (how could she have had lung cancer? She had never smoked) and hadn't wanted Greta to have to suffer through the treatments with her, the feeling of not having been adequate remained.

When she met her mother in Paris for the Christmas holiday, her mother was weak, and her hair had thinned, but despite Greta's demand to be told the truth—no matter how bad it was she could take it—Anna Sayre had insisted that she'd had a recurrence of her last "foreign service disease" but was recovering. Until sometime in May, she wrote Greta regular, cheerful letters, discussing her difficulties in making Throckmorton, her chief detective, behave as she wished him to. Did Greta have any suggestions? Greta had always found this way of speaking about something her mother was inventing disingenuous and was particularly infuriated by this levity now.

When Greta saw her mother in the States in June, where she had gone for a last desperate attempt at treatment, she was bedridden and even Greta, who had never seen anyone near death before, knew at once that her mother was dying.

"Why didn't you tell me?" she said, weeping. "I would have taken care of you. Why didn't you let me? I'll never forgive you!"

"Oh, Greta," her mother whispered, stroking Greta's hair, her ordinarily melodic voice raspy and barely audible. "I know you would have. It was wrong of me, I know, but I couldn't bear for you to watch me go through this. It was selfish of me, but try to understand. Every day I would have had to think of you in the world without me, of not being there if you needed me. It helped me to think of you living your life and being happy. To know that you'd met a nice young man—you did help me, dearest."

A month after her mother's death, Greta was a student at St. Stephen's, trying to keep her mother's memory intact in a place her mother had never been, rereading Priscilla Thwaite mysteries under her covers by flashlight—*Destiny in Derbyshire* or *A Killer Comes to Kent* . . . Alliteration sells, her mother had often repeated; British place names sell, and she and Greta had entertained themselves by inventing the most ridiculous they could think of: *Lethal Laryngitis in London, Hiccups Wreak Havoc in Herefordshire* . . .

Sometimes Greta could hear her mother's soft voice for a moment, and she would be transported into the past, maybe arguing with her mother about a scene Greta had been helping her to write, since her mother was squeamish about describing murder scenes and Greta didn't mind. "Youth can afford to be cold-blooded," her mother had said.

"Write," Greta would direct her, " 'Then he felt rather than saw . . .'"— she well apprenticed in Priscilla Thwaite's language, in which there was an abundance of "feeling rather than seeing," "sensing rather than hearing," "apprehending just beneath the threshold of consciousness" . . . "Write, 'Murdock felt rather than saw the long white fingers reaching around the doorway to retrieve the knife he only then realized had been lying on the bookcase. "Who the bloody hell is *that?*" he shouted, but those were the last words he ever spoke. The next morning when Camilla, the maid—' " "Since when does Murdock have a maid, Greta?" "Well," Greta said, "someone has to find him. Who else would just walk into his flat at eight in the morning? He isn't married, he doesn't go to an office, so no one would find him. If no one finds him, then you'll have to describe how his body is decomposing by the time someone smells him and breaks down the door. I don't mind doing that, but I don't know if you want it in your book or not."

Many of "Priscilla Thwaite's" spectacular deaths had been Greta's inventions, and, paging through her mother's books as she had at St. Stephen's to help her recall her mother's living presence—or even now, in Thrush Hollow's crowded attic (besides their own discarded possessions, she and Ned had stored here the Dearborns' water-cure paraphernalia that had not sold at auction), sorting through the trunk that contained not only letters and school papers but some of her mother's manuscripts—Greta enjoyed coming across the sections she had contributed, such as the penniless earl suffocated by cats: the earl, Lord Wildbury, identified with animals, whom he considered barred from their rightful place in the natural order; he'd been investigating a lab that experimented on stolen house pets, and had hidden himself in a compartment of an evil animal-theft gang's collection truck, not realizing that it could be opened from the top as well as from the side. He certainly had not expected a crateful of howling, hissing, clawing, screeching cats of all sizes and colors to be dumped all together on top of his head. Either he fainted from shock or the weight knocked him "senseless," so that he was unable to make an air space for himself and so was suffocated. Greta had felt some compunction about casting cats as murderers, even though it wasn't their fault—"inadvertent murderers," her mother had reassured her, laughing. "Inadvertent cats. Man suffocated by inadvertent cats."

When the truck arrived at the lab, the gang had fitted a big catching cage—"What on earth is a 'catching cage,' Greta?"—up to the lower door of the compartment, but instead of, as customarily happened, its issuing forth furious felines ("Alliteration lightens the atmosphere," her mother said. "It tells people not to take the murders too seriously"), a dead earl's head lolled out, and in the ensuing confusion "all the cats escaped and ran off into the night, vowing revenge—" "I can't put 'vowing revenge,' " her mother complained. "That would turn it into a story about the cats."

At St. Stephen's, the January after her mother died, after Greta had received Crain's letter announcing that he and Julia had become "formally" engaged, she had attempted to comfort herself by thinking of the sores on her hands in terms that would have amused her mother. *Mysterious Marks Manifested in Marby; Heathen Has Holy Hands . . .* Her mother would have liked setting a mystery in a cathedral, Greta knew, though she would have relocated it overseas and attached it to a ruined abbey, overgrown with vines, where a demented monk would be hiding out, brewing the evil potion that he would selectively apply to things that his victims would handle. ("Demented" was a word Anna Sayre had been fond of, as had been "potion" and the phrase "overgrown with vines.") In a mystery, however, Greta's would have been only the first case of the Mysterious Marks: the perpetrator inevitably repeated his evil deeds, since repetition was the foundation of the deduction process.

Her mother, Greta had understood even at the time, would have enjoyed casting a bishop in the role of evildoer. Anna Sayre had had a penchant for making villains out of figures who were members of age-old hierarchies, such as the Church or the nobility or the military; the criminals either became disillusioned and went sour or fulfilled their roles too zealously and went crazy. Writing about these figures, Anna Sayre had explained to Greta, let her feel as if she'd penetrated these forbidden enclaves. She wasn't content with the guided tour, she'd told her daughter; she wanted to sneak off into those sections of the castle visitors weren't supposed to see. She wanted to see the Pope eating breakfast, not delivering benedictions from a balcony. Maybe there'd been some envy of Greta's father's "top-secret" status—his carrying out "sensitive" diplomatic missions while Anna had to stay in "safe" countries with their daughters.

At St. Stephen's, Greta had attempted to think of Bishop McAndrew as a character in a Priscilla Thwaite mystery, pretending boredom with his priestly life but really looking for a miracle, pretending skepticism so that Greta would fight to convince him. The most devious villains wore a false front. "If you meet someone whose words don't seem to connect all the way down to something deep inside him, Greta," her mother had said, "don't trust that person." It was possible that Bishop McAndrew hadn't been deceitful on purpose, yet even so the route from what he said to its source twisted and turned so tortuously that you'd have lost your way before you got there.

Ned would be surprised to hear this, but she didn't *hate* McAndrew, for all that she'd resented and still resented the way he'd tried to use her experience to learn what he himself was feeling.

"Tell me about life at your school last year." "Do you miss your friends there?" "Sister Mary Catherine tells me you often receive letters from France."

What had been his point, exactly? That she'd caught the stigmata (as Greta still thought of it) because her boyfriend had become engaged to another girl? (She hadn't told McAndrew about Crain, but in his worming way he had guessed something.) What had one thing to do with the other? She had entertained fantasies of summoning Q. L. Throckmorton, her mother's favorite detective, to St. Stephen's; he would have made short work of the busybody bishop and his nosy nuns.

"Mistlefits, Chatterlane, and Windeminion, Solvers of the Insoluble, good morning," Miss Conan-Drum, secretary of the firm for which Q. L. Throckmorton worked, habitually answered the phone. "Throck?" Greta had imagined her saying. "Why, I do believe he is in, Miss Sayre! Quite the coincidence. You've caught him in between Cairo and St. Petersburg. He'll be so happy to hear from you. Any way we can repay our debt to your dear mother. She put us on the map, as you Americans say. . . ."

Q. L. Throckmorton was a combination, Anna Sayre had explained, of Tom Jones (for sheer lustiness and love of life) and Lawrence of Arabia (for ascetic devotion to a cause), though his two governing impulses frequently battled one another and landed him in sticky predicaments. Descended in ways both legitimate and illegitimate from the Hapsburgs, the House of Tudor (which people mistakenly thought had died out), and the Bourbons, among others, Throckmorton, as a result, knew certain key phrases that could extricate him from many a tight spot or admit him past many a locked door. He was impoverished, hampered, despite owning various estates around Europe, by a lack of ready cash, though this never seemed to prevent his going anywhere or doing anything he wanted. Most of the crimes he solved were committed in England and France, but a few took place in countries where Greta's father had happened to be stationed at the time Greta's mother was devising her plots.

Anna Sayre preferred not to set her stories in warm climates, however; something was lost when wind could not whistle across moors or icicles dangle threateningly from eaves. The sorts of mysteries "Priscilla Thwaite" authored depended on types of architecture not readily found in Cyprus or Borneo: the *brooding, overgrown manor;* the half-ruined uninhabited *great house* in whose windows lights were nevertheless *still sometimes seen at night;* towers and wings, hidden passages, secret stairways, doors *no one had ever noticed before.* The house needed to be at least two centuries old and possess enough rooms so that someone, even someone who already lived there, could get lost in it, could absentmindedly open the fourth instead of the fifth door from the left and stumble upon something he or she hadn't been supposed to see which would *change everything.* "Can you imagine a detective solving the kinds of mysteries I write in a place where he'd drive along roads studded with fast-food restaurants?" Greta's mother had scornfully asked. "If my detective investigated an issue of paternity in such surroundings, it would be because the poor mother wanted to collect child-support checks, not because her offspring was disinherited from a castle on the moors." "What's the difference?" Greta had asked. "They're both money." "No, they're not," her mother had retorted. "One's money; the other is a place in history, authenticity, a life full of meaning—there's all the difference in the world."

The murders Throckmorton worked to solve were all motivated by family rancor. The disinherited returned to wreak their deadly revenge on those who had usurped their places; the usurpers committed foul deeds to protect their names and property from the dispossessed. Q. L. Throckmorton was especially adept at solving these crimes because he, although not a criminal himself, knew from his own experience how someone robbed of his rightful position in society or afraid of this happening would think. Though the details of Throckmorton's own usurped rights were only hinted at in the many alliteratively titled mysteries in which he starred, it was implied that if he chose to employ his wits in the interest of unravelling his own lost heritage instead of devoting himself to the service of others, he would have prospects whose splendor and continent-wide influence could scarcely be imagined; it was also hinted that, if he were to take this step, his life wouldn't be worth a "plugged nickel—to use an Americanism," wrote Greta's mother, born and raised in Ohio.

Greta was remembering now the warm October afternoon when she and Crain had first sat drinking heavily sugared coffee and eating brioches and mille-feuilles near the open door of the only pâtisserie in the tiny village outside of which their school was located. Crain had sat with his back to the door; Greta had been able to gaze out over his shoulder at the shops on the other side of the town square: the boulangerie and the charcuterie with their striped awnings; the quincaillerie and the papeterie where she bought the flimsy blue paper she wrote to her mother on; she'd watched in a pleasant haze as short, rounded women in dark cardigans and headscarves had entered and exited, carrying string bags filled with paper-wrapped parcels and loaves of bread, greeting each other in the vivid, energetic voices French people used when they ran into each other completely expectedly.

Crain had been talking, but Greta hadn't been listening to him. It was a bad habit she had; she knew it, but she couldn't help it; so much else seemed to demand her attention besides what a person said. She'd already discovered the way Crain's eyebrows moved when he talked; she liked his voice, which had a kind of huskiness that broke at moments into a high tenor, like a younger boy's voice changing, though Crain was already halfway to seventeen. (She'd thought since that the unevenness might have been connected to his deafness.) Greta had heard "Denmark," "ancestral estates," "before William the Conqueror," and, by inserting judicious questions, had caught up with the family history Crain had decided it was now the moment to tell her. A step further into intimacy, she'd realized, although what he was telling her she found hard to take seriously. It sounded like one of her mother's novels. He had a destiny, was what he was confiding. There was land to win back from "swindlers." His branch of the family, its name since Anglicized (Crain was the surname, which Crain had used ever since going away to school; he detested his first name, Lars—this Greta had already known), had fought with its Danish branch and had settled in the North of England, but then this branch too had feuded. "We have a history of bad blood," Crain announced, leaning across the table.

"You what?" Greta exclaimed, laughing aloud.

"What is it?" he asked, hurt. "Did I misuse the word?"

Though his English was fluent, Spanish had been his first language (his mother was Mexican—"but pure Castilian," he said) and was the language he spoke at home; Greta, attempting to explain that he'd used a rather melodramatic and old-fashioned phrase, had only made matters worse.

Sitting up straight, Crain asked if Greta found his family story so amusing.

"Not amusing. Just—well, isn't it kind of out of date?"

"You are sadly misinformed, Greta."

"I guess," she said.

She had kept waiting for this suddenly destiny-conscious *heir* to revert to the down-to-earth, bright, easy-going, witty person she'd so quickly become attached to. He had to be teasing her in some way—this talk of winning back an inheritance, reclaiming the family title . . . She'd always considered her mother's characters exaggerated, even though she believed that somewhere, sometime, people had felt violently enough about lands and titles to do anything to keep them, but not in this day and age. Not here, not now. Not Crain.

Was this some kind of test? To see how much he could get her to believe?

But she'd known even as the idea occurred to her that Crain wasn't calculating in that way—it was why she trusted him. He seemed incapable of using people; despite his culture and sophistication, he was innocent and open-hearted in an almost childlike way.

Was this new business rooted in the fact that he was foreign? The way the French, for example, with their detesting *absolument* and their finding things completely *insupportable,* took themselves more seriously than other nationalities? But Crain wasn't French, even though he'd been in school there for a year already; he wasn't any more or less foreign than she was. Neither of them belonged anywhere, they'd agreed on that already; they weren't native to the countries they'd been raised in, but neither did they feel at home in their "own" countries. Someday they would find an island and start a new homeland, they'd promised each other, specifically for people raised as expatriates. So why was Crain now insisting he really did have roots, that there *was* somewhere he belonged?

Greta wished she could remember how the conversation had concluded, but instead all she could remember was that, walking back up the hill to school, Crain had taken her hand. First he'd kept bumping into her; she'd said *Pardon* several times until she realized that it wasn't an accident. Was he being playful? She'd been about to say, What do you think you're doing? Trying to push me off the road? when he had knocked against her again, but this time, as if to keep himself from falling, he'd grabbed for her hand. It wasn't until he didn't release it that she'd realized he *meant* to hold it.

In November, by which time they had already begun their first fumbling attempts to become lovers, when Crain began to tell Greta about his being "promised" to the daughter of a distant cousin and business partner of his father's, who owned the next hacienda over, Greta again had to struggle to believe that he wasn't joking. By then she knew he loved her and yet he meant to marry and have children with "this Julia" (as Greta thought of her) in order to tie up the claim to the family estates in England—maybe, in fact, Crain added, to those in Denmark as well. Even when he began to supply increasingly specific details of the family history—an illegitimate son, a great-grandfather of his father's, denied by *his* father, as a result of which the estate which should have gone to him had passed out of the direct line into a branch to which Julia would, with a "little luck," be sole heir—Greta couldn't believe he was serious.

"But you love me!" she said. "How could you marry *her?*"

"Oh, love . . ." Crain said, like a world-weary habitué of life's more arcane emotional regions. "Oh, love . . ."

"What is that supposed to mean?"

"There are other things in life besides love."

"Like cars and toothpaste," Greta said. "So what? Does she love you?"

"I believe she may, yes."

Greta had tried other approaches, searching for a way through this impasse, which seemed scarcely real and was inaccessible to thinking, like a logical puzzle; if she could figure out the correct method of argument, she could wake Crain up from the spell he was under.

"How do you *know* that you'll get back the family estates even if you do marry Julia? Can you *prove* you're descended from the Crains back then? Your ancestor was illegitimate."

It wasn't easy, Greta had learned at a young age, to prove consanguinity when people were dead. No paper trail could ever satisfactorily demonstrate that anyone was anyone's son or daughter, though people tended to accept written evidence—at least if written by a parent—since people rarely if ever had anything to gain by pretending that a child who wasn't theirs was. The reverse, of course, was not the case.

"It's known," Crain said airily. "It's common knowledge in the family."

"That would never hold up in court," Greta scoffed.

"We will win back in the end," Crain said. "You'll see."

There was a lie in all of it somewhere, but where? Something didn't ring true, but what? Had she been too naive—had she remained too naive for thirty years—to see how he was using *her?*

Yet he loved her. If that had not been true, then nothing in life could ever be true. It was not a feeling open to interpretation. It existed, as plainly as they themselves did. It wasn't a feeling that was going to change—it wasn't like that. It wasn't, in fact, anything like what Greta, in her younger childhood, had imagined that falling in love would be like. She had thought that it would be very drastic, two people desperately stretching out hands to each other across stormy waters as their separate boats drifted off in opposite directions—then deciding to jump into the roiling seas to struggle to shore together. This image was a distinct one, perhaps from a movie she'd seen. She hadn't expected loving someone to be like finding a member of her own family, a stranger she'd immediately recognized, so that it would make no difference what Crain did or didn't do. She would never be able to say, That's it. I want nothing further to do with you. She could *say* it, but it would change nothing since she would always be related to him.

Later, even after he had married Julia, Greta had continued to notice resemblances between him and characters in her mother's books, increasingly between him and Throckmorton himself, as if his teenage readings of Priscilla Thwaite had exercised a formative influence: like Throckmorton's, there was Crain's incognito coming and going in the "highest circles," though Crain, who'd become an economist, was hired to assist in the restructuring of broken national economies ("voodooing them back to life," he called it, now interlarding his stilted upper-class idiom with slices of American vernacular), while Throckmorton had worked to solve crimes revolving around the attempts by the would-be-titled to claim their rights or those of the titled to prevent them; there was Crain's choosing, like Throckmorton, to invest in horses, a hobby developed as a way of spending time with Greta; there were other things.

That first year, though, after a few more conversations, there had been an end to it—she had given Crain a couple of her mother's mysteries and he'd come to her and somewhat sheepishly said, "I more or less take your point." After that she'd had only to call him "Throckmorton" when he began to get "all noble-bloodish" for him to say, "It's just an *idea,* Greta—I never said I meant to *do* it. A person can entertain an *idea,* you know." She had had the tact not to point out that, until he'd met her and she'd teased him out of it, he'd considered it the only fate that lay in store.

It had been the end of it, that is, until a year later, when he wrote to her in Marby to tell her that he and Julia had become engaged. Yet even so something in Greta refused to believe he meant it—even now that he'd been married to Julia all these years, had two children, and died without admitting that it was all a bizarre kind of pretense. Anyone looking at it from outside would have to say that she had deluded herself, but that made no difference; she knew what she knew.

Q. L. Throckmorton had had a "lady friend," residing in a "secluded manse," named Phoebe Wilmot; Mrs. Wilmot's husband had vanished in the North African desert during the Second World War, but because his body had never been found he had been declared officially dead only by virtue of the time elapsed since he'd last been seen alive. Though Phoebe Wilmot was "indubitably" in love with Throckmorton and he with her, she refused to marry him on the off chance that her husband, whom she insisted she also still loved in spite of not having seen him for fifteen years, should turn up again. She nevertheless consented to meet Q. L. at various vacation spots, though she wouldn't entertain him at Riddley Dale, her "manse," since that would constitute too flagrant an infidelity. Q. L., who loved her "to distraction," was "utterly besotted by her," thought the "moon rose and set in her eyes," mostly accepted the state of affairs, was confident in her love for him, and, in his less sentimental moments, realized that their arrangement conferred advantages that a conventional marriage would not have: it never, for instance, interfered with his freedom to pick up and travel in pursuit of whatever clues he required to unravel whatever mystery he happened to be entangled in. From time to time, however, Q. L. would fall into the "depths of despond" about his lady love's refusal to "regularize their relationship," and this would give way to an inordinate suspicion that she wouldn't because in fact she couldn't: Wilmot was alive and well and living quite happily as master of the manse, a fact of which everyone was in possession except for poor, benighted Throckmorton. When these suspicions overcame him, Q. L. would disguise himself and lurk about the village of Whimsy-on-Wold outside of which Riddley Dale was located; he'd trenchantly query shopkeepers and the various individuals—gardener, housekeeper, chauffeur, et cetera—who worked at Riddley Dale, and eventually it would get back to Mrs. Wilmot, who would stalk angrily into Whimsy in her "sensible walking shoes" and rip off her lover's fake moustache in front of the, by now, amused villagers, and shout at him not to be "such an inordinate goose." She'd escort him back home for tea and offer to let him search the premises, an offer which, though he wanted nothing more than to accept, his small remaining sense of honor would not permit. Mrs. Wilmot never let Throckmorton spend the night there—"It wouldn't be seemly," she maintained—but, after scolding him "roundly," would comfort and reassure him, so that he would leave quite confident in her affections, determined not to let his doubts get the better of him again. They always did, though, at least once every mystery.

Sometimes, over the years, embarrassed to admit to herself what she was doing, Greta had temporarily assuaged her missing Crain by reading about Throckmorton: Throckmorton's periodic doubts of Phoebe's affections and his need for reassurance had particularly comforted Greta, not solely because these traits found a parallel in Crain's character, but because she could imagine that they derived, as they did with Throckmorton, from the frustrated desire to marry the woman he loved—something he was prevented from doing by "circumstances." But really, *she* was Throckmorton, loving someone who could never free himself from another; maybe her own father had never stopped mourning Sally's mother, who'd been killed in one of the last bombings of London when Sally was five, and Anna Sayre had bestowed *her* frustration with this unshakable fidelity on her character and, in the inevitable way of families, on her own daughter. Had Greta somehow "known," even before she became involved with him, that Crain was bound to another? Did she love him *because* he had taken this excluding vow?

Such thinking repelled her, this reasoning that attempted to attribute to every circumstance some prior, secret volition, as if the fact of something's being willed, however painful the outcome, was preferable to something's having simply happened. And she was attempting just what her mother had advised her never to do—"Never let anyone else explain your life to you, Greta," her mother had said, and Greta had abided by this advice; while Crain was alive, she'd had the strength to. She knew people's stories only touched at points, then sprang away from each other; similarities were only that, similarities, and should not be mistaken for the Rosetta Stone that would thenceforth translate into familiar terms all that had hitherto been obscure. Yet now she grasped at similarities, these sharp false islands in the mind, anything to keep from drowning in the loss that was even greater than her loss of Crain—though here her mind went blank: What could be greater than that?

Her loss was not what she thought it was—or there was another loss besides Crain's—but what? She felt the same incredulity at his death as she had felt when he wrote to her at St. Stephen's of his engagement to Julia, or, later, of their marriage. At the first news, she had broken out in stigmata, the way some people broke out in hives—though *why* this should be she had never understood and no longer particularly cared to. At the second, she had married Ned, counteracting an incredible act with an incredible one of her own, cancelling Crain's out. If he could marry someone he didn't love, then so could she—let him see where that brought them.

Ned had been fourteen, Henry's age, when he took the job at St. Stephen's that had led to his meeting Greta. He lived then in the small coastal town of Marby, the only town of its size in the country to "boast a cathedral"—at least, he recalled, so claimed the guidebooks sold in the gift shop down the street from St. Stephen's; the shop was run by the St. Stephen's Women's Auxiliary, and its proceeds helped to maintain the cathedral and its adjacent buildings, including those of St. Stephen's School. This comprised two schools: a boarding school for girls and a day school for boys.

To Ned, growing up three blocks farther down Cathedral Street in a brick row house, St. Stephen's had simply presided: its spire signalled sailors and its bulk prevented the town from slipping down its hill into the harbor, as if only something as massive as the cathedral could counteract the natural slide of everything towards the water. As a boy, Ned had been confused by his parents' scornful words: that "monument to man's credulity," they called St. Stephen's; that "splendid reminder of centuries of torture and oppression." Fervent skeptics, they'd wanted their only child to understand that there was something about "believers" that could not be apologized for; the clergy were "white-collared simpletons"; nuns, "sanctimonious wimples." The route away from doubt, they made clear, led straight to damnation.

Nevertheless, though conscientiously carpooled to a private and satisfactorily unreligious day school ten miles outside of Marby, Ned had secretly admired the gray blazers and blue neckties of the boys who attended St. Stephen's; the girls in their identical gray and blue plaid jumpers, white blouses, and navy-blue kneesocks seemed surreptitiously plain to him, like royalty in disguise. He'd had no classmates in the neighborhood and since he was small had depended for after-school companionship on a boy named Anselm Atterbury who attended St. Stephen's. If Ned's parents exempted Anselm from their general disapprobation of anyone and anything connected with the cathedral, it must have been because they regarded Anselm as someone brought up in a primitive culture who couldn't be expected to know any better. When Anselm broke his leg in a skiing accident one Christmas vacation, it seemed natural to both him and Ned that he should ask Ned to substitute for him at his afternoon job at the cathedral (though they didn't mention the arrangement to Ned's parents); Anselm told Ned that, if he asked a schoolmate, it might be difficult to reclaim the job once his cast came off.

"Each year, Marby," asserted the guidebook, "known for its steep streets of old brick and shingled houses as well as for its unique cathedral, plays host to thousands of visitors who flock to St. Stephen's to admire its Gothic arches and flying buttresses, the only ones of their kind to be found in North America. . . ." Many of these tourists also spent a quarter to light a votive candle at the altar before St. Stephen's statue, but if any of them noticed that, when many candles were lit, few were short, they most likely didn't deduce the reason: it was Anselm's, and then Ned's, task to remove the longest-burnt whenever the stands became overcrowded. "Discretion is the better part of valor" was an ambiguous statement which, at the time, seemed to Ned to apply here. Dressed like Anselm in an acolyte's robe, he could glide along the aisle bearing a candle in each hand, a one-boy holy procession, without arousing suspicion, but he had to be careful that no one was looking when he slipped down the stairs to the crypt, where the candles were left to sputter out. There was a trick to opening the iron gate so that it didn't squeak—Anselm had taught him how to do it with one swift hook of the elbow.

Anselm had inspected the candles both at lunchtime and before he went home; however, since it was January and cold—thus fewer visitors—he had told Ned that once a day after school would be enough. Anselm had informed the bishop "in charge of the cathedral" (as Ned had thought him), who had personally hired Anselm, that he'd asked a friend to replace him until he could walk without crutches; Bishop McAndrew sometimes prayed alone in a back pew in the late afternoon, Anselm told Ned, and he didn't want the bishop surprised by the sight of a stranger performing Anselm's job. Anselm laughed at Ned's nervousness; Ned was picturing a black-gowned priest thundering down at him from his holy height, accusing him of being an imposter. "He's just a bishop," Anselm said, Ned felt irreverently. "He's not the Pope or anything. He's pretty friendly. You'll see."

Despite Anselm's assurances, Ned was certain that, he having been raised a scoffer at all things religious, the bishop could only be displeased by such a heathen carrying his sacred tapers. Ned held in reserve a plan to confess, if caught and catechized, to a longing harbored since early childhood to be among those who climbed Cathedral Hill every Sunday to Mass, so casual in their privilege. The bishop, he felt, would be merciful if Ned confided his secret disapproval of Anselm's cavalier attitudes towards religious practices (practices which he, Ned, knew nothing about).

Thirty years later, Ned could still recall the atmosphere of St. Stephen's on those cold, motionless winter afternoons: the gray, arched nave with its dark, respectful pews and unpadded kneeling benches; the subdued light awaiting the moment when the lingering sun would shoot a ray through a particular, faraway stained-glass window and make the colors ricochet across the pews. At such moments it would seem to him that silence swelled up from the paving stones like a cry, rising until it pressed up against the vaulted arches, as if there weren't enough room in even all that vast space to contain the longing in it. The cathedral itself replied in a way Ned could not contradict to his parents' mockeries and Anselm's easy indifference. Yet always, as Ned stood gazing, transfixed, at the mutely blazing window, just as he felt himself on the brink of responding, of moving from wistfulness to whatever unimaginable state lay beyond it, it would come to him with a lurch of nausea that the refined glass, which he'd been admiring as a glorious abstraction, had been artfully arranged to portray something particular—specifically, to celebrate a death. Ned didn't know who St. Stephen was, how he had come to be a saint, or that there were numerous St. Stephens, of whom this one was prototype (Bishop McAndrew was eventually to regale him with details of the various Stephens' martyrdoms), yet he was repelled sufficiently that, as he wandered along the aisles and threaded his way through the pews, he took care not to step into the rainbowed beams lest they infect him with belief.

The afternoon on which he first met the bishop, Ned had taken the last candle he could without overdepleting the altar stand down to the crypt and was dawdling, scaring himself by imagining the lids of the sepulchers slowly opening. He never switched on the electric lights, and the sputtering candles splayed huge misshapen shadows that seemed to stagger among the tombs—the dead bishops, Ned liked to pretend, aroused by the presence of an unbeliever. He had been tracing an inscription with a finger, holding a candle close to it, translating the Roman date, when a voice broke out of the gloom. "Awareness of divine silence is what separates man from the animals," it said.

Ned jumped, dropping the candle, which he watched with amazement roll several feet along the paving stones before extinguishing itself.

"Who's there?" he asked weakly, turning in the direction of the voice, his fright augmenting to horror when a figure materialized from the outer wall of the crypt; paralyzed, Ned watched as his doom approached, wondering how he could have been so arrogant as to imagine that this cathedral's god would bother with conversion when destruction of the infidel would be so much more entertaining; but when the figure drew closer, Ned could see at once that it was no vengeful messenger. It was a man of his parents' age or a little older, somewhat stout, dressed in shabby corduroys, a plaid flannel shirt, and a corduroy jacket that didn't match his pants. His sandy brown hair was rumpled and his cheeks were rosy, as if he had just awakened from a nap. Except for his air of being so at ease, Ned would have pegged him for a tourist who'd decided he'd have a look at where the bishops were buried—that and entertain himself by scaring an acolyte into the bargain. Emboldened by this notion, Ned demanded, "What are you doing down here? Who do you think you are?"

"You pose deep questions," the man replied.

"How did you get in? You couldn't—" But then Ned stopped, having meant to say that no one could have opened the gate at the top of the stairs who hadn't practiced it; had this individual then been in the *habit* of sneaking around the cathedral? All those moments Ned had luxuriated in stained-glass solitude, a stranger had been spying on him?

Instead of answering Ned's question, the man hopped up on a marble tomb and lay on his back, steepling his hands above his chest. "How do I look?" he asked. "Today above, tomorrow below. Now that's security."

"Ha ha," Ned said. "Don't you know you're not supposed to come down here?"

"I had always supposed that I was," the man said, then leapt off the tomb and extended his hand. "I'm Bishop McAndrew. You must be the new snuffer."

"The new what?" Then, "You expect me to believe you're the bishop?"

"I take it I don't precisely fit the picture you've formed of me."

"I haven't formed any picture of you," Ned lied. "I never give you a second thought."

Ned had never spoken rudely to a stranger in his life, and though he still couldn't believe that this youthful, irreverent man, resembling an overgrown middle-aged cherub, with his curly hair and full, well-defined lips, could be a bishop, holy head of an entire region, his irritation sounded extreme, even to him. He felt as if the bishop had been playing a game with him—playing a game without his having known it was one until suddenly it was over and the bishop had won.

"What's your name?" the man asked. "If Anselm mentioned it, I've forgotten."

"Anselm?" Ned repeated. Then, "Henry Edward Dene," he said, having never thus introduced himself to anyone. "Actually, most people call me Ned."

"Ned. A pleasure."

The bishop held out his hand again; this time Ned took it.

"I didn't know you could wear regular clothes," he muttered.

"Sacrilegious, you deem it? I hadn't intended to startle you, but I found the sight of Youth Confronting the Ages too compelling to resist."

Ned ignored this—another invitation to a game he didn't recognize— and asked, "How did you get in?"

"There's a back door that leads to the priory. I'm surprised you haven't discovered it."

The bishop led the way to an alcove like the ones upstairs that held what Ned thought of as the "assistant" saints; in the candlelight the outline of the recessed door hadn't been visible. The bishop opened it; steps led up to a bare, frozen garden surrounded by pillared arcades.

"The cloister," he said. "Would you like to be shown around?"

That day Bishop McAndrew (who Ned couldn't convince himself much longer the "spy" wasn't, though he still half hoped that the real bishop would rush out and confront this fraudulent one) escorted Ned through the private quarters of the brothers. They were Dominicans, and Bishop McAndrew explained to Ned what that meant, but besides the fact that Jesuits were scholars, Franciscans lived frugally, Dominicans wore black robes, and Benedictines manufactured a sickly-sweet liqueur Ned's parents kept and which Ned and Anselm had secretly tasted, Ned didn't absorb much. For someone who didn't know the difference between a Catholic and a Protestant, these were too great subtleties. He was more impressed by how modern everything looked. His only experience of monasteries (one of which he still thought this was) came from films, but here, instead of wooden planks on trestles, he saw Formica-topped tables and metal folding chairs, the kind he and his fellow students slouched upon in assembly hall. A common room was furnished with an ugly tangerine-colored couch and several reclining plastic-leather armchairs, stuck in various positions, as if everyone had leapt up suddenly to escape dentists. Books lay about, swollen paperbacks—thrillers and westerns—and boxes of games were stacked on an up-ended metal milk crate: Scrabble, Checkers, Parchesi, Monopoly; Ned was amazed that the brothers were permitted to play games with money, even play money, in them—what had happened to relinquishing your worldly goods? It had begun to strike Ned, without his precisely so articulating it, that his parents had been frozen in their rebellion in the Middle Ages and were railing alongside Luther against the lavish fees levied by Rome for admission into heaven; they'd instilled in their son a purity of resistance that bound him more passionately to principle than was the very entity they so violently opposed. As he followed the bishop through the cloister, and saw the bedrooms—simply furnished, but hardly cells—where the brothers slept, Ned daydreamed, once he got to know the bishop, of inviting his parents over one day and giving them the tour: "You see— they're just like other people. You had it all wrong." Or the bishop might come over to his house, insisting he wanted to meet the parents of "such a fine young man." Mr. and Mrs. Dene, astonished by the bishop's youthful urbanity, would invite him to dinner. "We'll have to revise our estimate of your institution in light of you," they'd say.

In the meantime McAndrew, delighted by Ned's naiveté about religious life, was instructing him in the differences between priests and abbots, monks and friars, clerics and lay brothers. Ned could tell that his inability to grasp these distinctions put the bishop in great good humor; maybe, Ned thought, the bishop liked the idea of having someone to convert.

"But you, Ned," McAndrew remarked suddenly, "I can see that you're a votary of a different order. You don't require a badge to certify you— you're an automatic member of your brotherhood."

"What brotherhood?" Ned asked.

Later he grew accustomed to McAndrew's oracular remarks and gave up expecting, if not wishing, the oracle to elucidate them, but now he felt stupid and this irritated him.

"You probably expect people to do what they say—to live up to their promises, isn't that right?"

"What promises?" Ned asked. "What are you talking about?"

But McAndrew didn't answer; instead he led the way upstairs to his study. This was to be the first of many afternoons that Ned was to visit him in this cozy room, which looked out not only onto the cloister with its skeletal rosebushes but, from the other side, all the way down Cathedral Hill to the harbor; it gave Ned a strange sensation to look down, never before having seen the harbor from this height and distance, and to know that the boats were bobbing on the water even though he couldn't see their motion. To him there was something sinister in this, and he thought of the fact that, when he walked along the piers with Anselm, the bishop could have been observing them; he felt the same sense of having his privacy invaded that he'd felt in the crypt, along with the contradictory sense that he had no right to consider private what he did in a place that didn't belong to him.

Like everything else about the brothers' living quarters, the study surprised Ned by its inausterity. Long Christmas-red curtains hung over windowseats to the floor, which was covered by a richly detailed Persian carpet Bishop McAndrew once remarked was as "thick and soft as Calvary." Ned would lounge upon it many a cold afternoon in front of the fireplace with the bishop's huge old boxer, Venerable Bede (that day being walked by one of the brothers, who in general seemed not to be about, though Ned had been introduced to a couple as McAndrew gave him the tour); together they'd stare into the flames as the sun fled the cloister, looking up from time to time to acknowledge the bishop's opaque remarks. On the other side of the study hulked a huge dark desk with a large sheet of green blotting paper spread across it—something that impressed Ned since he had always coveted blotting paper, but hadn't realized that it was something one could simply go out and buy. He had thought that it was antique. That January day, as on subsequent ones, there was a fire burning and the bishop took one of the red leather buttoned armchairs that sat on either side of the fireplace and motioned Ned to take the other.

"It's not easy for a man in my position to find an unprejudiced listener," he said, smiling at Ned. "Anselm's a fine fellow but you can understand that he's possessed of certain preconceptions."

Ned nodded, feeling disloyal, and wondered if McAndrew had said something earlier that he'd missed.

"Things come up," Bishop McAndrew went on. "A man needs someone he can trust. Someone who won't tell him what it's thought he wants to hear."

"What do you want to hear?" Ned asked, his insolence feeling like a blow on Anselm's behalf.

But McAndrew simply laughed, went to his desk and pressed a buzzer, then spoke into an intercom and ordered tea and sandwiches for two. When a brother appeared with a tray holding not only sandwiches and tea but gingerbread and cookies—and, on leaving, gave Ned what Ned interpreted as a suspicious look—Ned asked the bishop if he always ate this much now, a question he recalled years afterwards because of McAndrew's response.

"Why? You think I'd be too full of communion wafers?"

Ned, having no idea what these were, said nothing, but the bishop pursued the question.

"Tell me, my friend, don't you know that Catholics eat the body and drink the blood of their Savior?"

"I doubt it," Ned answered, not because he necessarily found such cannibalism unbelievable, but because he was beginning to have the uncomfortable feeling that this game, whose rules had not been explained to him and which he had been tricked into playing, might have consequences.

"Ah, Ned, you're a breath of fresh air," McAndrew exclaimed. "Just what the doctor ordered."

"What's the matter with you?" Ned asked.

When the bishop didn't answer, Ned thought, almost with relief, that he'd finally offended him. He knew there had to be a protocol he wasn't following, but the bishop had given him no clues and the most Ned really knew about bishops at that time was that in chess they were slightly less valuable than knights until the board thinned out. Yet in spite of his discomfort he felt flattered by the bishop's interest, by what he secretly believed to be the first ever accurate assessment of his virtues, and his sense of privilege only increased over the next few days, when each afternoon he found a note left for him in the crypt, inviting him to tea. Thereafter it was simply understood that he would come.

All these years later, Greta could still faintly make out the denser, whiter skin in the center of her palms and remember how, when she first noticed the strange tightness there and saw the round, hard, reddish marks, she had thought that she must have caught poison ivy. The spots itched in the same persistent but obscure way that poison ivy did in the beginning—yet it was January, and even though Marby winters weren't severe Greta wouldn't have thought the plants could still be alive, or, if alive, virulent; moreover, she hadn't been in the woods; she hadn't even gone into Sally's back yard—and she hadn't been to Sally's since the previous weekend. Yet maybe Sally had brought it into the house with her, maybe even a couple of months ago, and the oil had remained—on a doorknob, for instance, a doorknob that Sally and her husband rarely touched. An out-of-the-way closet, a stairway to the attic? Unfortunately, Sally's house had no attic. Could someone have brought it into the school? Greta's roommate? Yet her roommate didn't leave on weekends. None of the other girls did. Greta was allowed her absences as a special privilege, since her mother had died in August and the powers-that-be (as her mother would have described them) had determined that it would comfort Greta in her grief to pay frequent visits to her sister.

Greta had instructed her mind to please stop leaping among subjects in this distracting way, and, furthermore, to desist from such demented imaginings as thinking that Sally's house had an attic, when it didn't, or that oil from poison ivy could remain on a doorknob for weeks or months, when even the least informed, most unscientific person in the world would know that it couldn't. It was the kind of thinking that had helped her mother write novels, but it wasn't useful in real life, and Greta implored her mind to just get on with it. Her mother had once told her that when someone close to you died, you could find yourself expressing aspects of that person's personality—craving food they'd liked, using their mannerisms, inventing puns if they had; maybe that explained what was going on. Her mother's plot-inventing talent had usurped her brain.

When the marks did not disappear but instead became harder and redder—the bright fiery red of flesh frozen with cold—and instead of itching began to throb, Greta knew that they were not poison ivy, yet still had no idea what they could be. A school nurse held hours every morning from ten to twelve, but seeing her meant requesting permission to leave class, and Greta did not want anyone to know about the marks: she was embarrassed about them, for the plain reason that she had one on each hand. They were identical, and in the identical location, so that Greta was sure that she had caught one from the other (she often clasped her hands and propped her chin on them), and she did not want to be seen as unhygienic, as having childishly scratched something she should have known to leave alone. Because the marks were on her hands, not feet, or even arms, she must have acquired them by doing something, touching something, and, obviously, if these marks were the result, it was something she should not have touched.

Nevertheless, despite her vague shame, Greta was becoming fascinated by the spots on her palms. Whenever she was alone, or felt sure no one observed her, she would turn her hands over to see if there had been any noticeable change. In the beginning the spots had been the size of a dime; as they protruded and hardened, they attained the size of a quarter, and finally the round hard knolls had reached the size of a half-dollar. How much larger would they grow? Greta had wondered, half fascinated, half horrified. Would they eventually take over her entire hand, then spread up her wrist and down her fingers? Was it leprosy, was it some exotic disease that her father had contracted in one of the countries whose "unstable political situations" he investigated, and passed on to her without catching himself? How long would she be able to hide the marks? Though they hadn't yet appeared on any other part of her body, they had to be contagious, since she had caught one from the other. She tried now not to touch herself anywhere without the intervention of a tissue or a washcloth, but it was easy to forget; she would brush hair back from her face, or rest her forehead on her palm to think during a test, and then feel seized by terror and wipe her forehead with her sleeve. Yet, despite these lapses, no other marks appeared. She had looked in the school library for a medical encyclopedia that might suggest a diagnosis; and on an afternoon when the boarders were allowed to do errands in town she had visited the Marby Public Library, but the only book she could find listed diseases alphabetically, not by symptom; after reading into "C," and having dismissed arthritis, beriberi, and catalepsy, she gave this up.

Three decades later, thinking back on that time, Greta wondered how differently her life would have turned out if the marks had not been discovered. She would never have met Ned, or, even if she had, he wouldn't have been McAndrew's undercover agent. Then their relationship might not have developed as it had—making it possible for him to want to marry her when he must have realized that she didn't love him. (Though she did love him—not as she loved Crain, but she loved him.)

It was probably inevitable that the marks be discovered, anyway, given how obsessed she had become with them—preoccupied to the point that they interfered with her concentration; her happiest moment came in the evening, in study hall, when Sister Mary Catherine or Sister Evangelina would ring the small silver bell and the girls would close their books and recite evening prayers. The murmuring sound was soothing, incantatory; it distracted her from the nearly incessant itching that now taxed her self-control to the utmost. She often wished that the prayers would last for hours, for once she was in bed there was nothing else to think about but her hands, and even though scratching did not relieve the itching she could not prevent herself from indulging in it. Then, once she'd scratched, she was afraid that she'd touch herself somewhere else so she'd get up and tiptoe down the hallway to the bathroom to wash her hands, fearful that Sister Mary Catherine, who slept at one end of the hallway, or Sister Evangelina, who slept at the other, would hear her.

Greta knew that Sister Mary Catherine thought she was making fun of the evening and other rituals because she was assiduous in partaking of them, when in fact she was merely doing what she had always done when she had to adjust to a new environment. Because she had travelled and resettled so much, she had learned that the more quickly she adopted the customs of a new place, the more comfortable she would be, and that it was better to be sincere in her efforts, even if the customs seemed absurd. If nothing else, as her parents said, it would help her to understand what the people around her were feeling. At St. Stephen's, she had miscalculated through no fault of her own, discovering too late that only a few "weird" girls took religion with any true seriousness. To all the others, the duties—genuflecting when one crossed before the altar, repeating the responses in Mass, offering prayer before meals—did not differ from anything else they'd had to do all their lives because someone had told them to, like brushing their teeth or writing thank-you notes. Even most of the nuns and the friars seemed not to enact their duties with undue solemnity, perhaps taking their cue from Bishop McAndrew, who was nothing if not unsanctimonious. Afterwards Greta understood that her eager compliance with conventions she had not been brought up to could only seem to Sister Mary Catherine to be effrontery, but by the time she had begun to realize this, it had been too late to change her tactics, to overlay her zeal with indifference. What had been an opportunity to disappear into the group became a torture of visibility—of being observed by a predator when she had nowhere to hide.

Then the marks changed character again. Hard, round, and solid for weeks, they now became softer, seeming to contain liquid, like a blister, and then one morning, after a night during which Greta had been awakened several times by the throbbing in her hands, she was shocked to see that the welts had opened. There was a semi-clear liquid on her palms. The marks had become miniature volcanoes; in the night whatever substance was in them had collected and risen with enough force to push through the membrane of skin. Despite her fright, Greta was still intensely interested—what force was at work that could break through her skin from the *inside?* She was also relieved, for it seemed now that a natural process was taking place, a poison of some kind working itself out of her body; she felt hopeful as she had not before that, though it might take time, the spots would heal themselves. In addition, she was delighted to find that they no longer itched, and in her excitement at these new developments it was difficult not to summon her roommate to come and see.

Unfortunately, this stage also posed new problems. Did the suppuration mean that her hands were infected? Had she not washed often enough? Could she have blood poisoning? She knew that her tetanus immunization was up to date, but maybe she needed to be on antibiotics. She decided that, on the weekend, she would go to a drugstore and show *one* of her hands to the druggist and ask him what kind of first-aid cream she should use for it. Furthermore, on the off chance that she should have some recognizable, deadly disease, she preferred for it to be an unknown person who broke the news to her. She could then decide in privacy what to do about it—whether to tell Sally and her father, or simply to go off somewhere by herself to die. It would depend, she supposed, on how long she had left before the end. *Moribund in Marby,* she thought, and wished that the person best able to appreciate the quip were alive.

At first, during the morning, the oozing was minimal, and the chief problem Greta encountered was how to hold her pen in class, since to cross her thumb to meet the other fingers now exerted a painful pressure on the sores and intensified the oozing. She discovered that she could hold the pen with her three middle fingers well enough to scribble notes; when she had to write answers more legibly on a test, she had to grit her teeth and hold the pen in the usual way. By late afternoon, however (it was on a Tuesday morning that Greta had first discovered that the sores had opened), the clear yellowish liquid had turned viscous and then begun to show traces of blood. Now Greta had to worry that she would get bloodstains on her papers or on her clothes, and this was when she decided on what was, she realized too late, a foolish scheme (though what else could she have done?): she would wear gloves to class. If anyone asked her why, she would say that she was cold. This was not entirely unreasonable, for the classrooms were often chilly; she would also wear a scarf to reinforce this impression.

In retrospect, it was obvious to Greta that if her perspective had not been so attenuated she would have realized that the nuns, like most teachers, would assume that any aberration from the norm was intended as an affront to their authority—certainly the rest of the class would regard it in this way. Yet she had thought that she would have to wear gloves for a few days only; on the weekend, which she had already arranged to spend with Sally, she would buy antiseptic cream and gauze bandage, and upon returning to school would tell everyone she had fallen and scraped her palms; even if she were sent to the nurse, Greta felt confident that the nurse might be fooled by then too, since the sores would probably have continued to progress—continued, that is, to open—so that the marks would more legitimately resemble the usual sidewalk injuries. But there were three long days to get through before the weekend, and she didn't make it.

She nearly did, but on Thursday evening, after study hall, Sister Mary Catherine, irritated by who knows what gesture during evening prayers that she interpreted as insolent, ordered Greta to take off her gloves. Greta's protest—overheard by everyone, thrilling to the contest to come—that she wore them because she was cold, could be met only with laughter, because study hall took place in the dining room of the girls' residence, and the dining room was so warm that Greta had unthinkingly taken off her sweater and rolled up the sleeves of her white oxford-cloth shirt. This Sister Mary Catherine now pointed out.

Still Greta would not give up. "Please don't ask me to," she entreated, as everyone, many yet sitting with their hands clasped for prayer, watched. "Please," she repeated. She clung to a weak hope that her earnestness might awaken a dormant sympathy in Sister Mary Catherine's heart—Sister Mary Catherine might recall a moment when, as a child, she too had wanted something for a reason she could not make clear—but Greta had forgotten that Sister Mary Catherine had challenged her before spectators and would not be able to back down now even if she wanted to.

"I have asked you to take off your gloves, Margaret," Sister Mary Catherine said. "Why do you not obey me? Are you hiding something?"

"Please don't ask me, Sister," Greta said again. "I'm not trying to be rude. Just please don't ask me."

Sister Mary Catherine frowned, yet there must have been something in Greta's appeal that convinced her that Greta was not being solely impudent. She said, "Study hall dismissed," and when no one moved she repeated sharply, "Study hall dismissed! Are you all stricken deaf? You will remain here, Margaret."

When the room had emptied, Greta's roommate and friends casting perplexed, sympathetic looks her way as they filed out, Sister Mary Catherine came to stand on the other side of the table.

"I don't know why you resist my authority in this fashion, Margaret. I understand that you are not happy about being at St. Stephen's, but we have all done our best to make you feel at home and it is difficult to understand why you shun our kindness so."

"I don't, Sister," Greta said. She knew it was hopeless now, but the longer she stalled, the better chance she had of thinking up a convincing explanation for having hidden the sores. Yet her mind refused to work at the problem.

"Then why do you flout my authority? Why do you mock our sacraments? Do you think I don't notice the condescending expression on your face during Mass, your offensive display of compliance at prayers? You may not be a believer yourself, but there are others around you who are and your behavior is thoughtless and disrespectful."

"But I don't disrespect people for believing!" Greta exclaimed. "I don't have a condescending expression during Mass!"

"You can't see your own face," Sister Mary Catherine replied, rather childishly.

"I know what I'm thinking and usually people's faces show what they're thinking."

"Margaret, I will sit here all night if necessary. Obedience, do you understand? Obedience is not only a virtue, it is an indispensable part of our lives here together. I obey my superiors, and in turn you must obey me."

By now Greta realized that she could continue to hold out and enrage Sister Mary Catherine to the point at which the nun cornered her and tried to pull the gloves off herself, or she could spare them both a humiliating ordeal.

"All right," she said, "I'll take them off. But you'll wish you hadn't asked me."

She meant by this only that Sister Mary Catherine would be made squeamish by what she saw; it had never occurred to Greta how the marks might be interpreted by a nun, almost certainly would be interpreted. The only information that at the time would have revolted her more than the news that pure and devout believers in Christ might acquire replicas of his wounds as a divine mark of approval would have been the possibility that young girls seeking attention of a certain sort might inflict such wounds upon themselves.

As Greta pulled the gloves off, they stuck, which provoked the sores to bleed more actively. She had attempted various methods to prevent the gloves—a pair of thin, unlined deerskin that had belonged to her mother—from sticking to the sores: she had padded the palms with tissues, but then these had stuck as well. She therefore simply wore the gloves and, when she was ready to remove them, wet the discolored palms with warm water, which usually allowed her to remove the gloves without reopening the wounds.

She had taken off the gloves now without turning over her hands, which she kept palm down on the table, feeling the blood spread onto the cool Formica surface. This last futile resistance merely exacerbated the melodrama of what happened next. Sister Mary Catherine picked up the gloves and examined them; she observed the stains in the palms. She said, "Turn over your hands."

"What do you mean, turn them over?"

"Turn them face up, Margaret."

"All right," Greta said, "but don't say I didn't warn you."

"Warn me?" Sister Mary Catherine repeated, and then stared as Greta turned her palms face up on the table and revealed what now looked like oozing punctures. Sister Mary Catherine reached out a hand as if to steady herself, but there was nothing for it to come in contact with and she took a stumbling step. She stared at Greta's hands, then at her face, without speaking, but suddenly seemed to recollect herself and pulled free a chair and sat down.

"What did you make them with, Margaret?" she asked, in the quiet, matter-of-fact manner that reputedly sometimes provokes criminals, who have been adamantly insisting upon their innocence in the face of violent accusations, to break down and confess. But in this case the method had no effect, since Greta had nothing to hide.

"Make them with!" she exclaimed. "You mean you think I did this on *purpose?*" In her wildest imaginings, the chance of someone's thinking this had never occurred to her.

"Then how did you come by them?" Sister Mary Catherine reasonably asked.

"I don't know," Greta muttered, upset now, feeling guilty and falsely accused at once, though she still had no clue as to what Sister Mary Catherine thought the marks were, or, that is to say, were intended by Greta to resemble.

"How can you not know?" Sister Mary Catherine asked. "You don't expect me to believe that they simply appeared, do you? To *you!*"

What did Sister Mary Catherine mean by that? Greta wondered.

"They started about three weeks ago," she said. "I thought I had poison ivy at first, but then I realized that that was impossible because it's January. I don't know what they are or how I got them. I don't have them anywhere else," she added.

"Don't have them—well, I wouldn't imagine you do." Sister Mary Catherine looked disturbed by this information. Then she said, "Why did you hide them, if you didn't make them yourself?"

"I just thought they would go away," Greta said. "I was afraid . . . I was afraid they might be contagious and I would be put in quarantine or sent away from the school. I realize that it was irresponsible of me not to say anything, but that's partly why I wore gloves," she added, inspired. "To keep anyone else from catching what I have."

"It's never been my impression that you would find leaving us such a hardship," Sister Mary Catherine said.

Greta thought it wiser not to answer this.

"May I ask you," Sister Mary Catherine now said, trying, Greta could tell from her tone, a new approach, "what on earth makes you think you should be chosen?"

"Chosen? What do you mean? Chosen for what?"

"Don't play games with me, Margaret. It's unseemly as well as a waste of time. Perhaps you'd prefer to tell the truth to the bishop."

"The bishop! What does he have to do with it?"

"Margaret, if you insist upon perpetuating your ruse—"

"What ruse? I'm not lying to you, Sister Mary Catherine. I don't see why you want me to see the bishop."

But Sister Mary Catherine had already gone to the cubicle off the dining room where the boarders received telephone calls from their families (and where Greta had, until she'd written to him to stop calling her, sometimes talked to Crain) and dialed the bishop's study. She'd then attempted to drag Greta, pulling her by the wrist and walking faster and faster, out of the residence hall and across the frozen cloister yard to the side of the square where the brothers and the bishop lived. She knocked peremptorily and barged in with a kind of triumph as if, Greta thought, the bishop had put Greta up to it and Sister Mary Catherine had found him out. It was only after Bishop McAndrew had asked Sister Mary Catherine, by this time nearly hysterical in her unrequited urgency, to leave him alone for a while with "this renegade," and had spelled things out for Greta that she had begun to understand what Sister Mary Catherine (and perhaps McAndrew as well, although Greta could tell that he wasn't as quick to make assumptions) believed the marks to be— though whether self-imposed, hysterically acquired, or divinely bestowed was the question they now wished to have answered.

On a Monday afternoon about three weeks after his first encounter with McAndrew, Ned entered the bishop's study to find a girl of his own age, or slightly older, sitting up very straight on the edge of the red leather armchair he usually occupied opposite McAndrew, drinking a cup of tea. Both of her hands were bandaged, though her thumbs and fingers were free, and she had no difficulty holding the cup. It looked strange; she had no bandages anywhere else, and Ned wondered if she'd had some kind of an operation. Venerable Bede, Bishop McAndrew's boxer, lay on the hearthrug with his head resting on the girl's foot. Obviously this wasn't the first time she'd been there.

"Welcome, Ned," McAndrew said, standing. "This is Margaret Sayre, one of our students here. Margaret, this is the young friend I've spoken to you about. Henry Edward Dene, although he permits his familiars to address him as Ned."

"Hello," Greta said, unsmiling.

"Hi."

Ned didn't enjoy being introduced as McAndrew's "young friend," as if Margaret were the same age as the bishop and he years younger. He thought about offering to shake hands with her but decided it would be awkward if she couldn't. He felt embarrassed to ask about her hands, but he'd look like an idiot if he pretended not to notice.

"What happened?" he blurted out finally, after he'd been seated, at McAndrew's insistence, in McAndrew's armchair, and served tea and a blueberry muffin. McAndrew brought over his oak desk chair and placed it between Ned and Greta.

"I fell off my horse," Greta said.

"How?" Ned asked.

"How?" she repeated.

"I mean, were you jumping a fence or did he buck you off or what?"

"I just did."

Taken aback, Ned glanced at McAndrew and was even more surprised by the expression on McAndrew's face: he looked almost smug—amused and pleased—as if Ned were behaving just as McAndrew had expected him to.

"I think I may safely say that Margaret is not one who likes expanding upon her experience," McAndrew said. He was watching her as he spoke. "Am I right?"

"Suit yourself," she said.

She wouldn't look at McAndrew, and Ned wondered what was going on. Something was strange, even stranger than things usually were around the bishop, as if he were both planning to punish Margaret (the way she sat so stiffly, not touching the plate of food in her lap) and asking her forgiveness for something.

At the same time, Ned felt mortified to have thought himself singled out, the only person McAndrew could talk to freely. He had even kept his visits to McAndrew secret from Anselm, thinking that Anselm's feelings might be hurt if he knew. Ned had felt sneaky about this at first, but soon had begun to perceive Anselm as dimwitted for not figuring out what was going on.

The girl—Margaret—wore the gray and blue plaid jumper, long-sleeved white shirt, and navy-blue kneesocks of the St. Stephen's girls' uniform, and Ned learned (this before McAndrew gave the first of his implausible reasons for leaving them alone together) that this was Greta's first year at St. Stephen's; her older married sister lived in Marby; Greta was an experienced rider; and she had lived in various foreign countries because her father "did something" for the government. That was how Greta put it—"He does something for the government"—which Ned thought very sophisticated. After McAndrew left, with a spurious excuse about having to "ascertain the level of spirituality" in the cloister that day, she told Ned that she was going to St. Stephen's only because her mother had died that past August of cancer and her father "in his brilliance" had thought she'd be better off in the United States near her sister.

"I'm not religious," Greta said.

"Neither am I," Ned said.

She seemed to brighten at this. "Why are you here then?"

After Ned had given the history of his employment and his visits to McAndrew, she said, "No one except Bishop McAndrew and the nuns calls me Margaret. Everyone else calls me Greta. I guess they think Margaret's a more religious-sounding name." Then she added, "He thinks you'll get the truth out of me. That's why he's leaving us alone together."

"The truth about what?"

"My hands. He thinks I'll tell you something I haven't told him."

"You mean about how you fell off your horse?"

"I didn't fall off my horse. You didn't realize I was making that up?"

"Why? Was I supposed to? Do you even have a horse?"

"Yes, although she's not here. Everything else I told you is true. I'm sorry I said that, but I wasn't going to tell you anything in front of the bishop. He was just waiting to see what I'd say. 'I've a young friend I'd like you to meet,' " she mimicked. "But you don't seem like you'll report back to him."

"Report back to him?"

"What else? He can't get anywhere with me himself, so he's trying to think up some other tactic."

"What do you mean, get anywhere with you?" For a moment Ned thought she meant in a romantic sense.

Greta sighed. For the first time she set down her cup and sat back in her chair. "I may as well tell you. I don't have anything to be ashamed of, even though they try to make me feel as if I do."

"Ashamed about what?"

"What happened to my hands. They think . . . How much do you know about all this stuff?" She gestured around the bishop's study. Venerable Bede, on the rug, looked up with his plaintive boxer look. "Religion, I mean. What they believe."

"Mainly things Bishop McAndrew has told me. My parents aren't religious. They kind of scoff at it."

"Same here. Maybe not scoff, but they never took it seriously. Not churches, anyway. They would much rather attend some African tribal ceremony. I guess I knew Jesus Christ was crucified—how could you miss it?—but it didn't occupy my every waking hour."

Ned smiled.

"Now they're trying to tell me that these sores . . . I don't know where they came from. They just started by themselves a few weeks ago. They're trying to tell me that they're the same things Jesus had on *his* hands after being crucified. Supposedly they're marks people get who are especially holy because they identify with him. They're called stigmata."

"What are?"

"The marks. It's like a sign, like you're stigmatized. Do you know what that means?"

"Like a scapegoat, right?"

Greta looked pleased. "They think that that's what I have on my hands. Either that or I made them on purpose to get attention. What would I do? Take an ice pick and stab myself perfectly symmetrically? Can you imagine anything more sick? The last thing I want is their attention! The third possibility is that I didn't make them on purpose but somehow imagined them into existing out of hysteria."

"That sounds pretty insane," Ned said. "How could you imagine sores on your hands?"

"I guess there are girls who do that. Maybe boys, but mostly girls for some reason. But they're always very religious and they want to be saints. Why would anyone think I'd want that? I go along with their prayers and crossing themselves to be polite, and now Sister Mary Catherine is telling me I'm *jealous.* I wish I belonged to their church and this is my way of getting attention. They don't believe I never heard of such a thing as stigmata before they mentioned them. You'd think that if you were going to imagine something happening to you, you'd have to have heard of it first, wouldn't you?"

"What does Bishop McAndrew think?" Ned asked.

"That's a good question. I don't think he knows what he thinks. He doesn't believe in miracles but he can tell I'm not lying. He's looking for a clue. I know he's hoping you'll be a good sleuth and find something out for him."

"So he's just been buttering me up all this time so I'd do his dirty work for him," Ned said bitterly. "I always thought he had some ulterior motive."

"What do you mean?" Greta asked. "How long has he been inviting you up here? He only found out about my hands last week."

"Oh," Ned said. "I guess I take it back. How long have you had the sores, though?"

Greta shrugged. "About three weeks. It's hard to remember."

"That's kind of weird, though. He still started inviting me up here around the time you got the marks on your hands."

"So?"

"It just doesn't seem like a coincidence," Ned said. "Maybe he put some poison in your gloves or something."

"I don't think so, Ned."

Greta looked depressed then, and Ned was sorry for playing Sherlock Holmes when she felt so bad.

"Do they hurt?" he asked.

"Not so much since they opened up. It stings when the nurse changes the bandages."

"How long will it take them to get better?"

"That's just it," Greta said miserably. "Sometimes they never get better. Some people go on bleeding for years."

"For years!" Ned exclaimed. "Wouldn't you die from loss of blood?"

"It just bleeds a little. Your body can replace blood if you don't lose it too quickly."

"But if you don't think they're really—what are they called?"

"Stigmata. Don't make me say it again. I don't *know* what they are. I just wish I could get out of here. But where can I go? So far, I've convinced Bishop McAndrew not to say anything to my sister—talk about hysterical. She'd summon my father and get him paged in the middle of a revolution."

Ned laughed. Greta brightened.

"I can just see it. 'Could you please hold your fire, gentlemen? We have a problem Stateside that requires Mr. Sayre's attention.' I wish they'd just leave me alone, but they won't. It drives them crazy not to know what the marks are. Sister Mary Catherine practically had to be hospitalized, she got so worked up. The thing is, it's *their* religion. If they believe in these things in the first place, why are they so amazed when they happen? Are they jealous, because it didn't happen to them?"

"Do you believe they're really marks from God?" Ned asked. "It seems like that's what you're saying."

"All I'm saying is that it's bizarre for them to be so skeptical when they're the ones who believe. The way I feel, even if they are from God, whom I don't believe in in the first place, I wouldn't accept it. I don't approve of this way of getting someone's attention. You wouldn't believe the kind of cross-examining they've put me through—cross-examining . . ." Greta made a face. "Now I know where that expression comes from. First they had a doctor look at them—that was okay. At least I could officially have bandages then."

"What did he say?"

"He said he was baffled. Quote unquote. He said that in his experience the only thing the sores resembled was a poisonous bite—a spider or maybe a mosquito bite that had become infected. But the 'duplicate nature of the lesions makes that implausible,' he said. Since I don't have any overall symptoms—like a fever or uneven heartbeat—and no marks anywhere else, there's no immediate danger. He didn't say from what. He's especially baffled that they're not starting to close up. It's been almost a week since they opened—they were just these hard bumps before—and they're not showing any signs of healing."

"If yours don't stop bleeding, will you believe they're . . . what the bishop says they are?"

"No!" Greta almost shouted. "I'll never believe it! The more someone tries to convince me the less I'll believe them. For all they know, all these times people have had these so-called marks of God they might have been something else which nobody can identify and people just *said* were marks of God. I'm not saying Christ wasn't crucified and if people want to think he was the son of God and rose from the dead that's their business, but personally I wasn't there and I don't listen to rumors. I'll tell you something else. Bishop McAndrew let this slip and I could tell he wished he hadn't. Jesus Christ probably wasn't even crucified through his hands. If you nail someone up by their hands, the weight of their body will tear them right off the nails."

"That's disgusting."

Greta held up one bandaged hand and pointed. "Feel in the middle of your hand and then up towards your fingers and you'll see what I mean. There isn't any bone for the nail to catch on. But if you nail through the wrist . . ." She pinched her wrist between thumb and forefinger. "You can see how it would catch. When McAndrew told me that, obviously I asked him why people don't get stigmata on their wrists. He said—you know how he talks—'A penetrating observation, my friend.' He said it was because painters and sculptors had always portrayed Jesus with wounds through his hands, not wrists. I said, 'Well, that explains the hysterical cases'—the ones people imagine into existence—'but what about the supposedly genuine ones?' He said he was afraid I was going to ask that."

"And what did he say?"

"He said that the Church has never really given a satisfactory answer on this subject. According to him, popes and cardinals are always arguing about it. I'm not sure I believe him, the kinds of things he says people in the Church argue about."

"I know. Like how many angels can fit on the head of a pin. Has he told you that one?"

"No." Greta laughed. "But I'd like to hear it, wouldn't you? Assuming he didn't make it up. All these men in their robes sitting around arguing about something like that. I'd like to know what they could think of to say.

"Anyway, I was going to tell you that, after the regular doctor, they made me talk to a psychiatrist. That was annoying. He asked endless personal questions—I won't even tell you some of them, they were too humiliating. Most were about my mother. Obviously he believed that I was having some kind of hysterical reaction to my mother's death. The nuns told him they'd never heard me cry—what do they want? For me to sob in public? It isn't any of their business what I feel about my mother. Of *course* I miss her. We were very close." Greta looked away, then bent to scratch Bede's head. When she sat up, she said, "The thing is, if I had a hysterical reaction to my mother's death, you'd think I'd have symptoms that had something to do with her, wouldn't you? Like imagining I was one of her detectives, for example."

"Her detectives?"

"She was a mystery writer."

"That sounds pretty interesting," Ned said.

"It was. I'll lend you some of her books sometime." Then Greta said, "It's like I've caught their ideas. Like I've got the flu in my *mind*. Before they found out, I thought the marks were weird. They were revolting and bizarre—especially that they were on both hands in the exact same place—but, this may sound strange, I was actually kind of interested in them. I didn't know something like that could happen to your body. But after people found out, I felt so creepy. Even if you don't believe what they say, you can't help wondering. I just feel as if—if I don't get out of here soon I really could go crazy. There are all these slippery places in my brain. It's hard to explain what I mean."

Ned, absorbing all this, nodded sympathetically and leaned over to pat Venerable Bede's head. Bede groaned and stretched, and Greta laughed. Ned glanced up.

"You could stay at my house," he offered. He'd suggested it without thinking of what he would say to his parents, but realized that they would probably be thrilled to harbor a refugee from the Catholic Church.

"Oh, thanks, Ned," Greta said, "but they'd never let me. I'd either have to go to my sister's or run away."

"Would you do that?"

"I might, if things don't let up."

"You could hide out in our attic. I've made it kind of nice and I could fix it up more for you. My parents never go up there, and they're both out all day so you'd only have to be really careful at night."

"Thanks," Greta said again. "That's very kind of you, but I think Bishop McAndrew would figure it out. It would just be embarrassing. If I have to run away, I'd better do it right."

Ned nodded, and they sat in silence for a while, both staring into the fire. Ned was considering putting another log on when there was a knock at the door. He and Greta exchanged a look of alarm. What would someone say who found them sitting alone together in McAndrew's study? But then the door opened and McAndrew himself stuck his head in.

"Coast clear?" he asked.

They shared another look, this one conveying their mutual disgust with his insinuating tone.

"I wish I could say you resembled cats who'd swallowed canaries," he said as he shut the door, "but you both look too annoyed with me for that. Might I offer either of you more tea?"

They shook their heads and then remembered to say, "No, thank you."

All the rest of the week and for the first four days of the next, Greta was already in McAndrew's study when Ned arrived, and each time McAndrew excused himself after a few moments' chat. After the first afternoon, Greta and Ned didn't discuss her hands again. Ned was eager to hear about the places she'd lived and about her mother's books, and each day they spent a pleasant hour or so in conversation. Ned liked Greta; he thought she was witty and interesting, and she didn't fall into any of the categories in which he had heretofore placed girls: "flirt," "brain," "sap," "whiner," "cheerleader." None of his friends were girls, a fact he'd never considered strange until he found himself so comfortable talking to Greta.

As the second week went on, however, McAndrew seemed increasingly distracted and preoccupied, not friendly and mischievous as he'd been in the beginning, but when Ned asked Greta if she knew what was going on she said McAndrew was "avoiding her" but she'd prefer not to waste her time worrying about it.

On the second Friday afternoon, Ned barged into the bishop's study expecting to find Greta and McAndrew in their usual places, but instead found two unfamiliar men in clerical collars seated in the red leather armchairs and McAndrew standing between them with his back to the fire, one arm resting on the mantel. The boxer wasn't there.

"Hullo, Ned," McAndrew said. "What brings you here this wintry afternoon?"

"This . . . What brings me?" Ned repeated. He could feel his face flush.

"A young friend of mine," McAndrew said to the two men, who were staring—Ned felt disapprovingly—at Ned. "Ned, allow me to present Archbishop Clarendon and Monsignor Brunelli."

"How do you do," Ned said. Was he supposed to kiss their rings? McAndrew had told him people did that to the Pope.

The men nodded at him without smiling. When McAndrew said nothing else, Ned said, "Sorry to bother you," emphasizing "bother" as much as he dared. He was angry, but he was also frightened. He was afraid that something had happened to Greta, but McAndrew clearly expected him to leave. Now he would have to spend a miserable weekend wondering if she was all right. Maybe longer—he wasn't going to the bishop's study again, that was for sure.

On Monday afternoon, however, when Ned carried the first batch of tapers down to the crypt, he found a note propped up on one of the sepulchers. "Your presence respectfully requested above," it said.

Ned considered ignoring it, but no other means of hearing about Greta occurred to him. This time he knocked. "Come in," McAndrew called; today no one was there but the bishop and Bede, who, seeing Ned, vibrated his stub of a tail.

"Sorry about Friday," McAndrew said at once. "Those two give me the ecclesiastical willies. I'm not myself when they're around."

"It's okay." Ned's resentment immediately dissipated. "Where's Greta?"

"At her sister's. I thought it best if she got away from this hornet's nest for a time."

"Hornet's nest?"

"It seems a miracle's been had in the parish, Ned."

"What do you mean, a miracle?"

"Our Lord has made His presence known. Here in Marby, U.S.A., of all places. The archbishop came to investigate. It seems I haven't reported to the authorities with enough alacrity."

"Enough what?" Ned pretended not to know that McAndrew was talking about Greta. "What were you supposed to report?"

"The signs of the Lord's grace—if that's what they are. The archbishop refused to disclose the identity of his informer, but I'm guessing that one of the sisters felt that I was remiss in my responsibilities. Call it insubordination, but the damage is done. I pointed out to the archbishop that you can't sanctify someone who doesn't want to be sanctified. I can't subpoena the girl to appear before a church tribunal. Even if I could, I wouldn't."

"Do you think they really are—whatever you call them?" Ned asked. He remembered the word, but out of loyalty to Greta didn't say it.

"*I* don't call them anything," McAndrew said. "Not until I have more evidence, and neither should you."

"But you're the bishop," Ned said.

"Indeed. So I keep being told. I'm inclined to believe they are whatever Margaret says they are."

"Greta doesn't know."

"No, but she may learn."

"She said you cross-examined her," Ned accused him.

"I had to, didn't I? As you pointed out, I'm the bishop. That's my job. I don't apologize for that. I had to see what stuff she was made of, and I could do that only by playing my official role. I must say, I came away impressed. I'm glad she has you, though, Ned. What serendipity that you came along—good luck for both her and me, I should say. I hope you don't find your responsibilities too heavy."

"What responsibilities? What do you mean?"

McAndrew gave a rueful smile but didn't answer, and suddenly to Ned's mind, in the midst of his conflicting feelings—his concern for Greta, his simultaneously being envious of McAndrew's high opinion of her—there came the memory of a fairy tale he'd read once, about a princess who'd had to weave shirts out of nettles in order to undo a witch's spell that had transformed her brothers into swans. The witch had given the princess a deadline. If she didn't complete the shirts in time, her brothers would remain swans forever. So she wept and sewed and sewed and wept, and though her fingers stung and bled it never occurred to her to give up. Yet despite the fact that she worked as fast as she possibly could, time gained on her, and it seemed unlikely that she would finish. At the very last moment, however, when all hope seemed lost, her brothers flew to her and she tossed the shirts over their heads and they were changed back into princes, except that the oldest brother still had one wing instead of an arm, because she hadn't had time to finish that sleeve. He ruled like that when he became king.

And that was what Ned had always thought love was—the knitting of nettleshirts—something painful you had to do to save another person; and it had always seemed so sad and yet so beautiful to him, to think of the king's forever after having had a wing instead of an arm to remind him of what he would have been without his sister's devotion.

It was a token of the strangeness of the day, of the whole accumulation of his days in the cathedral and his visits to McAndrew that Ned found himself telling this story to the bishop, who listened to him with a kind expression in which, for once, Ned could discern no hint of irony. Ned had expected some clever rejoinder from McAndrew, but, when he'd finished, McAndrew merely gave him a small, painful smile and said, "It's a seductive story, but what makes you think people want to be saved, Ned?"

The next afternoon, Tuesday, when Ned knocked, no one answered, and afraid of what he might find—who knew what group of white-collared interrogators—after listening a moment in the hall, he went away. On Wednesday, the bishop answered, but he was sitting at his desk writing and looked up only to say, "Ned, you'll have to excuse me today—I've had a blow. Come back tomorrow, will you?"

Ned had to swallow his questions—how was Greta? How long would she stay away? Could he have her phone number?—and since he was too restless to go home he walked down to the harbor, always soothing to him, with its clutter of canvassed-over sailboats and motorboats bobbing at their moorings, then walked along Currier Street, which curved around the north side of the harbor and out towards the peninsula called Ravens' Point. Greta's sister Sally, whose last name Ned didn't know or he'd have looked her up in the phone book (he had already tried

"Sayre"), lived there, and he might run into Greta, who had told him she liked to walk in the area of abandoned boatyards and decrepit boarded-up summer houses, out beyond the narrow streets of small row houses where her sister lived. Ned rarely walked out this way, although it wasn't far from Cathedral Street; something about the place had always made him uneasy: an entire section of town deserted—not a few people deciding to move but a whole neighborhood at once, as if they'd been under attack.

At the entrance to the peninsula a metal historical plaque, with raised letters like braille, proclaimed ambiguously that Ravens' Point had "once been a popular summer resort" but had "been abandoned some time between the two World Wars." The Marby Historical Society, which erected such notices, did not explain what had happened, whether people had had any warning or had had to leave in a hurry. History had closed in on them, Ned saw that; he had never before thought of history as something to be prevented but wondered now whether, if you watched closely, you could see the forces gathering at the edges of your life before they set upon you and left you without a home. Something like history, he felt, was closing in on Greta; the bishop was trying to ward it off but might be too interested in seeing what it was, exactly, that was bearing down, to take effective measures. As the image of McAndrew preoccupied at his desk came back to Ned, it was with a sense of wanting to warn Greta that he strode up and down the gray silent cobblestone streets hoping that he would find her.

The next afternoon, Thursday, Ned knocked with trepidation; McAndrew was in, sitting this time by the fireplace, but there was no fire, and he hardly glanced at Ned when Ned came in. There was no tea tray either, and McAndrew didn't offer to ring for one. Ned sat down opposite, and, as usual, when he was uncomfortable in the bishop's presence, leaned over to pet the boxer, who, as if he too had experienced a disillusionment, seemed to lift his square head off his paws only with great effort to give Ned a disappointed look. Finally, Ned couldn't stand it anymore and asked McAndrew if something had happened to Greta. He was afraid of what he might hear, but it would be better to know the truth.

"Happened to her?" McAndrew said, glancing up. "Yes, I suppose you could put it that way."

His eyes were bloodshot, and his normally ruddy face looked splotchy.

If it hadn't seemed such an impossible idea to Ned, he would have said that the bishop had been crying.

"Where is she?" Ned asked nervously.

"How would I know?" McAndrew said. "In Rome, chatting with the Pope? Maybe she'll drop us a card. 'Having a rip-roaring time in the Vatican—wish you were here.' "

He looked over his shoulder at the window, as if in the direction of Greta's sister's house, then back at Ned.

"Evidently the archbishop came at her request. I spent all day yesterday composing what I thought was a very restrained but eloquent letter protesting the archbishop's taking matters into his own hands without consulting me first—I pointed out that I'd been respecting the girl's right to privacy, among other things. Before I had a chance to send it, he summoned *me* to appear before *him*. He'd been going into the matter 'more thoroughly' and had come to the conclusion that I'd 'refused to take the girl seriously'; I'd mocked her 'sincere beliefs' . . . He didn't mention when he was here last Friday that she'd somehow smuggled a note into my weekly packet to him because he didn't want to 'prejudice the case'—of course he had to know that it was from me she'd acquired enough information to communicate with him in the first place."

"Greta wrote to him?" Ned repeated. "I can't believe that. Don't you think that maybe that nun, Sister . . ."

"Forged the letter?" McAndrew half smiled. "I was right to put my faith in you, Ned. I have to admit that the reprehensible notion occurred to me as well. But the archbishop saw Margaret earlier this week too. I can hardly believe she wouldn't deny the letter had it not been hers."

"Saw her where?" Ned asked.

"I presume at Headquarters. It's an hour by bus."

"I just can't believe that," Ned said. "All she wanted was to be left alone."

"All she said she wanted," McAndrew said. "You're a staunch supporter, Ned. Everyone should have such a friend. But I'm afraid that in this case your allegiance may have been too precipitately given. I can hardly fault you, though—I was taken in myself. I thought she was the pinnacle of integrity. I'm afraid, though, that our friend Margaret is quite a confused young woman. That's the kindest thing I can say right now, I'm afraid. She's a very lost and confused young soul."

"I just can't believe that," Ned said again. Greta, lost and confused?

The person who seemed lost and confused to him was McAndrew, although he didn't dare say so. And why had Greta said nothing about writing to the archbishop, if she had? Didn't she trust Ned? Had she thought he would tell McAndrew?

"Perhaps there's another explanation for her turnabout," McAndrew said, "but I can't find it. Maybe you can."

Ned left McAndrew's study feeling ill. He could tell that McAndrew had not been lying to him, yet at the same time he didn't see how what McAndrew had said could be true. As he descended the stairs and walked slowly across the cloister garden, scrutinizing the minute details of the carved banister post, the herringbone pattern of the brick paths, as if they might reveal something he had failed to notice earlier that could make sense of the paradox, he tried to encompass all the events that had occurred in such a short time. He'd met a bishop; he'd made friends with a girl who was at the center of a church scandal; he'd learned that his parents had been right about religious people using "abstract controversies" to explain what they were personally all worked up about. He'd never known what they meant, but now he was getting an idea.

He retraced his steps, as usual, back through the unrisen dead, as McAndrew referred to the entombed bishops, but today he didn't linger in the crypt in proud proprietorship but took the circular stone steps two at a time and ran back down the right aisle of the cathedral. The sun had set sometime earlier and, though it was not completely dark, the cathedral interior was deep in shadow. Ned, who had been running, a hand knocking against the corners of the pews as he passed, abruptly pulled it back and shoved it into his pocket, he having suddenly imagined someone crouching in a pew waiting for his hand to come in contact with him so that he—or she—could grab it. Anyone could be there, eyes better adjusted to the dim light than Ned's, and now he felt convinced that someone was watching him and he walked as fast as he could without running towards the vestibule—running would provoke pursuit, he knew, as if what he feared stalked him were a mountain lion instead of an ill-defined yet still human menace. Ned had never felt nervous in the darkened cathedral before and now this seemed incredible to him, as if he'd been playing with cobras under the impression that they were garter snakes. When he finally stood outside and could gaze down Cathedral Street towards the harbor, the descending gas lights like sentries guarding an innocence he knew he was losing even though he'd scarcely known he had it, and didn't know what its loss might mean, he thought he might cry from relief. What had been going on these past weeks? What had been happening to him?

He felt far away from all that was trusted and familiar, as if he'd been drugged and abducted to a strange place and forced to act like the person his kidnappers had mistaken him for if he wanted to preserve any chance of getting away alive. As if in affirmation of his relief, it was beginning to snow, an infrequent event in Marby—a few flakes drifting lazily, like an afterthought, down into the light of the streetlamps—and Ned stood looking up, trying to see where in the night sky the snow first became visible, wishing he could keep standing and standing there until everything that had happened since he had first started working at St. Stephen's just disappeared. With a vague purpose of effecting this by beginning again at the source, he started down the hill but, instead of stopping at his house, continued several doors farther down to Anselm's. He rang the bell and when Anselm, thumping to the door in a new, abbreviated cast, appeared, Ned said, "Hi! I wondered if you felt like playing chess."

Anselm stared, then said, "Why? The bishop stiff you?"

As his face reddened, Ned's impulse was to turn and run home but he said weakly, "Who told you?" Then he felt more embarrassed when he realized how his choice of words made it sound as if he had something to hide.

Well, didn't he? Why else had he kept his visits to McAndrew secret from Anselm?

"I followed you," Anselm said.

He was standing in his open doorway and didn't move or invite Ned in, as if Ned were an encyclopedia salesman Anselm was trying to get rid of.

"You *followed* me?"

"When a person who's your friend basically stops speaking to you, you kind of wonder what the story is," Anselm said.

"I didn't stop speaking to you," Ned objected.

"Maybe not technically. It's not like you'd hang up on me, but lately you're just so *busy.* I knew it didn't take you two hours to do the candles. But then when I'd ask you to do something you'd have to do extra chores around the house. You'd have to work on your science project. Since when do you give a crap about science projects? We used to hang out most afternoons, or are you too madly in love with the bishop to remember?"

"What?" Ned said.

"Hey, if that's what turns you on," Anselm said.

"If what is?"

Then Ned understood what Anselm was suggesting. When Anselm moved to shut the door, Ned panicked.

"Anselm, wait!" He pushed the door open and stepped into the house. "I can't believe you think that!"

Anselm shrugged. "All the brothers are queer. It's common knowledge. The bishop isn't any different."

"I don't believe you."

"Why else would they live like that? They can't get married. It's normal to get married. I mean, eventually."

"Well, maybe," Ned said, feeling a little relieved when he realized how much Anselm was exaggerating, "but all I did was talk to Bishop McAndrew. Mostly *he* talked. To tell you the truth, I didn't understand half of what he said. Lately there's this thing that happened." He hesitated—he would be using Greta to bargain for Anselm's friendship—but then said, "This girl, Greta—Margaret Sayre—maybe you know her . . ."

"The whole school's heard about it," Anselm said, bored. "She stabbed herself with a steak knife so people would think she had the wounds of Christ. You've got to be sick in the head to do something like that."

"That's a lie!" Ned exclaimed. "She wouldn't do that!"

"Oh, are you in love with her too?"

"No!" Ned shouted. "Why do you keep saying that? I just—"

"Look," Anselm said, pulling the door closer to himself so that there was just barely room for him to stand between it and the door jamb. "Do me a favor and get out of my life, will you?"

Ned, stupefied, opened his mouth to protest, but before he could say anything, Anselm had shut the door in his face. Ned stood on the wide top step staring at the brass knocker in the shape of a fist hanging upside down as if ready to deliver a punch to an intruder. Then he turned and descended the steps. As he reached the sidewalk, the door opened again and Anselm stuck his head out.

"By the way, I get my cast off next Wednesday. I'm taking my job back after that."

That night Ned couldn't sleep, and he went up to the attic of his house and sat for a long time in a broken armchair he'd moved some months ago to the one window so that he could see to read. He looked out at the snow-dusted roofs descending Cathedral Street to the harbor, and at the lights of the harbor glowing down below, but instead of the familiar sights reassuring him, they made him feel as if he were leaving home, as if this were the last night of his life in Marby, and, like the houses on Ravens' Point, his would soon be deserted and boarded up and someone might stand outside and wonder what had happened to the people who used to live there. Only yesterday he had been imagining that you might learn to see coming whatever events were gathering to force you from your home, but here he'd been right in the middle of them and he hadn't noticed. He'd worried that events were collecting to crush Greta, but the truth was that they'd been collecting to crush *him.* He had realized by this time that Anselm's accusations and disdain had arisen out of jealousy, and Ned felt bad for not having guessed how important his friendship was to Anselm. Anselm had spoken frequently about his many friends at school, and Ned had simply assumed that Anselm wouldn't be spending time with him if he could have spent it with them. He'd thought that, as with his own school friends, Anselm's lived in other parts of town, and that his friendship with Ned was based mainly on proximity. Now Ned saw that he'd been mistaken; he even suspected that Anselm had asked him to sub for him at the cathedral not because he was worried about reclaiming his job later but because Ned was the only person he could ask. The story about the bishop's having chosen Anselm "personally" might or might not have been true. The job didn't pay much and maybe no one else had wanted it. Maybe McAndrew had tried to talk to Anselm as he had to Ned, but, as his remarks had suggested, had found Anselm inadequate company.

Sighting along the line of roofs, Ned counted down to Anselm's and remembered their plans—never materialized—to set up a railroad track travelling over the rooftops between their two houses along which they could send messages at any hour of the day or night. Ned had liked the idea of surreptitious communication *right over people's heads,* but they'd never built the track and now his friendship with Anselm was over, something it had never occurred to him could happen since he'd never even realized it was important.

Ned thought again about Anselm's insinuations about his relationship with the bishop. Was the bishop in fact "queer" and his interest in Ned derived from sexual appetite instead of, as he'd stated, the need for an "unprejudiced listener"? Ned thought back over his afternoons in McAndrew's study, looking for hints that he might have missed, for comments McAndrew might have made about other things that might have revealed such a predisposition, for any indications at all that Anselm's suggestion might be justified. The thought horrified Ned, though less because the particular suggestion revolted him (it didn't specify anything to him) than because other people might understand a significance to events of which he was unaware. It sickened him to think that something could have been *obvious* to others about which he was in the dark. He couldn't deny that a murkiness had always hung over McAndrew's motives and remarks, and since Ned could offer no other clarification of them he could not easily detach Anselm's label. Though Ned entertained a vague picture of himself explaining to Anselm that he'd just liked *talking* to Greta and the bishop—they were just *interesting,* could Anselm possibly understand that?—he knew that he didn't have the resources to stand up for these friendships, so out of his ordinary experience; he even knew that, if once he went downstairs to sleep and woke up in his usual world, the one antedating his initiation into McAndrew's, he might not want to.

On Friday, Ned stayed away from the cathedral, but, by Monday, restlessness got the better of him. As he carried his first candles down to the crypt, he saw a note propped up on a sepulcher but resisted reading it; he told himself he had just come to do the candles and go home. He had his obligation to Anselm to fulfill, after all. Many times during the loneliest weekend he'd ever spent in his life, Ned had resisted the urge to call Anselm and "explain"—because what was there to explain? He'd even considered telling his parents some abbreviated version of his experience at the cathedral in order to hear their predictable reactions. "Behind enemy lines, eh?" But by now he doubted even *their* doubts; that was what had come of listening to McAndrew. Why had his parents always insisted that the best thing was to be skeptical about everything, and to mistrust anyone who said they believed?

At the same time, Ned felt mortified to have let himself think that there could have been a friendship between someone like him (whatever he meant by that) and a bishop, or between him and a girl like Greta, with all her experience—to let himself imagine, on occasion, how they would go on being friends: maybe someday ("eventually," as Anselm had put it) even fall in love; the bishop, their great friend, could marry them; if they had a son, they might name him after the bishop (whose first name was James) and young James would grow up thinking nothing of running through the cathedral to visit his godfather; cathedral stones, stained glass—it would all be as homey as nursery school to him.

On his second trip down to the crypt, Ned couldn't stand the suspense any longer and read the note. It was from Greta, not McAndrew. She wrote:

> *Dear Ned,*
> *You told me that the bishop left messages for you down here, so I hope you get this. I'm not coming back to St. Stephen's. I wrote to my father and I'm going back to the school in France I went to last year. I'm leaving in a few days, and I'd really like to see you before I go. If you can meet me today when you finish with the candles, I'll be down at the harbor near the fish-market, loitering.*
>
> > *Sincerely,*
> > *Greta Sayre*

Ned hurried back upstairs and, without even looking around the cathedral, picked up the entire tray of votive candles and carried it across the transept and back down the nave, deciding, halfway to the stairs, to hoist it up to shoulder height as waiters did with food. It was surprisingly easy to carry that way. He walked faster than he ever had, though when he lowered the tray to maneuver it through the iron gate, he saw that some of the candles had been blown out. He felt bad. It was the church and its bishop or some entity not even so explicit that he'd wished to affront, not the people trying to bless their dead relatives and friends and he mentally apologized to them. The phrase, "Innocent people could get hurt," came into his mind, and when he had placed the tray on the tomb in the crypt, he relit the extinguished candles. Had the souls of the departed been endangered because the candles had not burned to the end without interruption, the way there was supposedly an opening for the devil to capture you when you sneezed if someone didn't say "Bless you" in time?

Then Ned shook his head to wake himself from these thoughts. He understood what Greta meant when she'd said that she thought you could "catch ideas like flu." They beckoned like Halloween witches crooking bony fingers: Come this way, my child . . . You could refuse to go, but you didn't dare turn your back on them. You had to stay suspended in a state of watchfulness.

On the way to the harbor it occurred to Ned that Greta might have left the note on Friday; it could have been there all weekend, and who knew who might have seen it; she might have already left for France— but as panic began to overwhelm him, he saw her. She sat on one of the pilings, swinging her legs, looking in fact as if she were trying hard to loiter, like someone obeying a stage direction: "Girl, sitting on dock, loitering." What did "loiter" mean, exactly? Ned wondered. When did waiting for someone change to loitering, something with a purpose to something without one, something quite normal which no one would think twice about to something you could get arrested for?

"Hi," Greta said, sliding off the post. She was wearing blue jeans and a heavy sweater and a hat with matching mittens, the first time Ned had seen her dressed in anything other than the St. Stephen's uniform. She looked just like anyone else.

"Have you been here long?" he asked.

"Centuries. Not really."

They took a walk, covering the same territory Ned had the previous Wednesday when he'd gone looking for her, though he didn't mention this to Greta. He was waiting for her to fill him in so he could tell her how worried he'd been about her and how confused by what McAndrew had told him, but instead of talking about the cathedral Greta discussed her travel plans: she was going to meet her father in Paris next week and then he would drive her to school. Ned could tell she was very happy about going back, and he was jealous. He had seen Greta as friendless and himself as able to come to the rescue, but now he could see that she had many friends, if none in Marby; he was awed by Greta's command of another language—she had used several French phrases when speaking of her school, which she called "le Collège," the accent on the second syllable—and he saw that there were whole worlds already in her experience to which he had no access and in which he could play no part. His own one-town, one-country Marby upbringing seemed dull and empty in comparison.

"I'll probably never see you again," he said.

Greta stopped walking for a moment, startled.

"Don't feel that way, Ned. We can write letters. Besides, my sister lives here, and I'll probably visit her sometime."

"You wouldn't be afraid of running into the bishop?" Ned asked. It was an underhanded way of getting to the subject, but Greta didn't seem to notice.

"Why should I be scared of him? He gives me the creeps, but that doesn't mean I'm scared of him."

Something about the way she was talking now—miffed, but also indifferent—made Ned uneasy.

"Tell me, Ned," she said. "I've never really asked you. Do you *like* him?"

Ned, recalling Anselm's remarks, stammered, "Sort of. I don't know. I guess."

Greta laughed. "How definite can you get. To tell you the truth, he gives me nightmares."

"Nightmares!"

"Actually I did have a nightmare about him." She looked around—they had come to a stop at one of the dead ends on the harbor side of the peninsula—a vacant lot strewn with some broken-apart barrels, an anchor, rusted chains, and a wrecked dinghy. Greta sat down on a tall hoop of coiled rope beside an empty boathouse and Ned prevented himself from warning her that it might dirty her jeans.

"I was riding a bike," she said, "on a highway, a thruway with huge trucks and everyone driving a million miles an hour. It was nerve-racking, but I was doing okay. Then we come to tollbooths, and I'm afraid that if I try to go through, I'll get arrested. But trucks are honking at me and I have no choice. Then I see that the tollbooth operator I'm headed for is McAndrew. So I try to change lanes, which makes everyone furious; the truck drivers are all shouting things like 'Girlie' and 'Bimbo' at me but finally I manage, but then I see that the next tollbooth operator is McAndrew too. I look down the row of tollbooths and they're *all* McAndrew. It was such a sickening feeling. I know it may not sound like a nightmare—he didn't do anything; he didn't even say anything—but you know how things get a particular feeling in dreams. I wish I could describe it. I can still feel it. It was just so sickening."

"Do you think it's about how he acted about your hands?" Ned asked cautiously.

"How should I know?" Greta retorted. "I'm not Sigmund Freud."

Ned, amazed, said nothing.

"I'm just trying to forget everything as fast as possible, that's all. I didn't think it would take any great genius to understand that."

"But McAndrew said you wrote to the archbishop yourself," Ned blurted. "At first he thought that that nun had, but he said you went to see him too. Did you?"

"What are you, the police?"

"No, I just—"

"It's a free country. Why shouldn't I?"

"Well, I—"

"That's what you're implying, isn't it? That it was a wrong thing to do?"

"I didn't mean that. I just—"

"Look, Ned," Greta said.

"I'm not . . . ," he started to say.

She was talking to him as if he were on "their" side, and he wanted to tell her that he wasn't, but he was no longer certain what either side stood for and besides, she probably wouldn't believe him. He wanted to say, Why didn't you tell me? But she obviously didn't need his friendship the way he'd thought she did.

"I didn't like the way McAndrew was treating me," she said. "I felt as if he were studying me under a microscope, using me for his own private research. At first I trusted him because he wasn't as stupid as the nuns, but then I could see that underneath all his sympathy he was always *observing* me. It's as if he wanted me to crack up so that he could take notes. Like those people who cut animals open while they're alive . . ."

"Vivisection," Ned said.

"Vivisectionists. That's what he reminded me of. When he introduced us, it was like he was adding another chemical to a beaker to see what the reaction would be. Don't you remember that look he has? That gleam in his eye?"

"Yes, but I don't think he . . ." Ned was going to say, "means any harm," but Greta interrupted him, and Ned wondered why he found himself defending the bishop. Maybe he wouldn't have if he hadn't seen him so upset the other day.

"It's not like he really cares what happens to you. He cares what what happens to you *means*. Oh, I can't explain it. It's not even just that. I can understand why what happened to me would be interesting to a bishop. But I can't stand the way he's waiting to see what happens to me so that he can decide what to do about himself. He ought to decide on his *own.*"

"What do you mean, decide what to do about himself?"

Greta looked surprised. "About the Church. Didn't you know? I thought he talked to you about it too."

"What about the Church?"

"Whether he should leave it. All his doubts about his profession."

"I guess kind of. He talked about his doubts, but—"

"Well, that's what it was about. Don't look so shocked. It's nothing new. Priests are leaving the Church in droves. I know from some research my mother did for one of her books. Bishop McAndrew acts as if he's the only person on earth who's ever had religious doubts."

"He does?"

"He's just a coward, when you come right down to it. He can't make up his mind to go through with anything."

"But I thought you wanted them to leave you alone," Ned said, bewildered. "That's what you said. So why did you write to the archbishop? I don't understand. If you don't think the marks are religious, what's the point of having him in on it?"

"Oh, I already wrote him back and told him to forget it," Greta said casually. "I realized I just didn't have any more energy. It's just that I was so mad. And then Sister Mary Catherine kept telling me I *owed* it to people to find out if I really bore the wounds of Christ. I could see her point." Greta shrugged again. "But I don't know, do I owe something to people? What do you think?"

Ned had no idea what to say.

"I mean, if their god is trying to get a message to them through me, Greta Sayre, it would be rude not to pass it on, don't you think?"

"Are you serious?"

"I'm not *joking* about this, Ned," Greta said angrily. "What kind of person do you think I am?"

"I don't—"

"It's irrelevant now. The wounds are closing up." Greta pulled off her mittens and held out her palms. She wore no bandages, and in the center of each palm was a dark scab.

"They should be all better before I leave. I hope so, anyway. My father gets sick at the sight of blood. Besides . . ." She laughed. "I never specifically told him what was going on. I just wrote him that the school was trying to convert me and begged him to let me go back to the Collège. He'll ask for details, but if I tell him they were trying to convince me to look at the world the way they do, which is after all more or less true, that will be enough. He hates any organization trying to make individuals think a certain way."

"What about your sister? Did you tell her?"

"I told her I burned my hands holding a hot pan handle. I said I had started carrying it from the stove to the sink before I noticed how hot it was—that really happened to a girl at school last year. Some of us took a cooking class from a lady in town and Sophie said she was more afraid of what Madame LeGrand would say if she dropped the pan full of hot oil than of burning her hand. I told my father that an atmosphere of fear and distrust reigned over everything. I doubted the bishop or the sisters would contradict my story, if my sister asked them. They wouldn't exactly want it to get around that students attending St. Stephen's might catch the stigmata."

"That's what you think, that it was because you were here?"

"I didn't have them before I came and they're going away now that I've left."

"I guess," Ned said.

"What's that supposed to mean, you guess?"

"I don't know."

"All I need is for you to start doubting my word."

"I'm not doubting your word. I just . . ."

"Just what?"

When Ned didn't answer—he didn't know how to express all the thoughts he was having simultaneously—Greta stood up and walked away. She stopped at the edge of the wharf, looking down into the water. Ned gazed at her back, hypnotized by his inability to think clearly. Nothing Greta had said had been untrue; she hadn't denied sending the letter that was causing McAndrew so much trouble, but she dismissed its importance. Did she have any idea how much it had upset him? Should Ned tell her? First she had been resentful because people were making too much of what had happened to her, but then she'd raised a stink because they weren't. Yet as soon as the archbishop took her seriously she changed her mind. Ned had never once considered the possibility that Greta might have made the marks on purpose, but now Anselm's matter-of-factness combined with Greta's strange new attitude made him wonder. How could everything that had mattered so much to her a week ago seem so insignificant now? Was it because she was leaving?

There were some dead grasses, or weeds, bent over in clumps throughout the vacant lot—grown up between cracks in the cement— and Greta now leaned over and pulled out a handful of them, still without looking at or speaking to Ned. It suddenly occurred to him that she might be having a nervous breakdown. He had always thought that people just started screaming wildly and throwing things and flailing around, but maybe that wasn't how it always happened. Maybe that was the movie version, like his picture of religious life as taking place in ancient abbeys where the only sound was Gregorian chant.

He should do something; he should say something to Greta to bring her back to reality—maybe he should go over and put his arm around her shoulders. He was taller than she even though she was a year older. But what if she was fine and thought he was making a big thing out of nothing? Or, worse, thought he was making a pass at her?

Ned couldn't move—he wanted to help her, but he couldn't unless he knew for sure that she needed to be helped, unless, for example, she started to climb over the railing to throw herself into the water, though even then, he thought, full of self-disgust, would he do anything in time? Wouldn't he wait to make sure she really meant it before he committed himself? Would she have to *drown* before he could believe she really needed him?

He kept hearing McAndrew's sad voice. "What makes you think people want to be saved, Ned?"

"They *marry* Jesus, did you know that?" Greta asked.

Ned jumped. "What? Who does?"

"The nuns, when they take their final vows. That's what they're doing—they're marrying Jesus. They wear white wedding gowns and veils. They actually walk down the aisle. Their fathers give them away."

Greta held the weeds out in front of her like a wedding bouquet and began to take slow bridal steps across the vacant lot.

"Why are you mentioning that now?" Ned asked. Wild possibilities occurred to him—she had decided to become a nun; she wanted to marry *him* . . .

But she said, "I can't stop thinking about it, ever since Bishop McAndrew told me. I know he was watching for my reaction, so I didn't let him see I had any, but the truth is I haven't been able to get it out of my mind. I asked Sister Mary Catherine about it the time she said I owed it to people, et cetera—what it felt like to get married to Jesus Christ—and I didn't think she would answer me, but she said, 'Overwhelmed with love.' She *meant* it, too. I can't imagine saying that about a *person,* I mean to someone else, let alone . . ." Greta looked at Ned and laughed. "At least with a person you're not marrying the same guy everyone else is. Jesus Christ with his harem."

Ned felt shocked, and then wondered why he felt shocked. It was the kind of thing he'd heard at home all his life—why was it different when she said it?

"How could they marry someone they can't even *see?*" Greta asked, throwing down the weeds. "They're marrying an idea, not a person— how can they feel 'overwhelmed with love'?"

"I don't know," Ned said.

"It makes me feel inferior," Greta astonished Ned by saying. "As if there's something wrong with me that I can't feel that. So in love with an idea, I mean. But then sometimes I think I could, if I would just take one little step. It would be like falling off a cliff, except you'd have to do it believing you'd be all right and then you would. I think that's why I wrote the archbishop—besides being angry. Kind of like taking one step off the cliff. Luckily I came to my senses before I really went over, though I wish I knew what they would have done next. Taken me to Rome to see the Pope? Would I have become a saint?"

Ned remembered McAndrew saying, "Do you know what that child would have to go through, if those worthies you saw here Friday were to report her case to Rome? Do you know the kind of scrutiny, the battery of tests—things none of *us* is ever asked . . ."

"Saint Greta," Ned said, bowing.

"Saint Margaret, *please,*" Greta said, steepling her hands. "Saint Margaret of Marby. It sounds like one of my mother's mysteries. *Margaret Murdered in Marby.* What do you think? Maybe we should write it. We could set it at St. Stephen's."

"Who would be the victim?" Ned asked.

"Well, that's obvious, isn't it? The bishop. *Death Comes to the Bishop.* I think there's a book with that title already, though."

"It's *Archbishop.* My parents have it."

"It would have to be all 'b's, anyway. *Bishop Buried in B-something*— that's not really right, though."

"Who would be the killer?"

"Hmm . . ."

"Sister Mary Catherine?"

"Too obvious. You need someone no one would suspect. Nuns are always going off their rockers and stabbing someone with sharpened crucifixes."

"Since when?"

"It's common knowledge. No," Greta said, "I have a better idea."

"Who? Venerable Bede?"

"That's a good one. He could lick the bishop to death. Except I don't think he'd have a motive."

"Who, then?"

Greta smiled. "Guess," she said. "Someone no one would suspect but who has—have—a perfect motive."

"I give up," Ned said. "I hate guessing."

"Us!" Greta shouted.

He was a coward from way back, Ned could see that. Even the self-knowing, gently ironic tone of that remark was only another evasion. He sat at his desk at Thrush Hollow, feeling as useless and discouraged as he ever had in his life, messily piling the photocopied sheets of O.'s letters without regard for chronology and looking with distaste at his own fastidious lists, wondering when his sense of impotence would give way to anger. It was such an old anger that he scarcely recognized it, maybe that was why. He was being lied to. Someone . . . Was he going to lie to himself too? Who could it be but Greta? She didn't trust him enough—he was too inexperienced, too unsophisticated, too *young*. Such self-loathing. It was as deep and nauseating as if he'd just left McAndrew's study that day of his unforgettable final visit, his legs still tingling after the hour he'd spent cramped beneath McAndrew's desk, listening to McAndrew vilify Greta to the archbishop. If he was still being deceived, Ned thought, there must be something about him that invited deception, some morbid naiveté, an inability to look at the world as it was. The mystery was how he'd avoided confronting this for the past two decades. Was it because, for reasons of her own, Greta had permitted him not to and now was changing the rules?

If that walk with her on Ravens' Point had been the final event, he might have come away from the whole experience at St. Stephen's thinking, Pretty bizarre—or whatever catch-all term he'd have used in those days. He might have been left with an impression of Greta as a nice girl who'd been having a rough time and had behaved a little inconsistently as a result. They had exchanged addresses and he had been eagerly anticipating receiving letters from abroad. He remembered feeling that, though he might be stuck living in the same unexciting country, where nothing ever happened, at least he'd have a friend somewhere interesting.

He had met Greta by the docks on a Monday afternoon. This he clearly remembered. Only two more days of his duties had remained; Anselm would be back on the job on Thursday.

On Tuesday nothing happened. It was a dull, gray, cold day and there had been few tourists. Ned didn't need to take candles to the crypt, but he picked up a pair for old times' sake—and on the off chance that Greta might have left another note. She wasn't leaving until the end of the week. When they'd said goodbye the day before, her departure had felt imminent, but now it seemed distant and he wondered why they'd made no arrangement to see each other a second time. There was no note, but on Wednesday—same weather, even heavier and grayer, only nine or ten candles lit since the previous afternoon (Don't die in the winter, Ned had wanted to warn people. No one will pray for you unless the weather is nice)—when Ned carried a pair down (he having decided, in order to prolong his last day, to transfer all of the candles, two at a time), he found a note on one of the tombs. His heart beat fast as he reached for it, but it wasn't from Greta. "Tea, four-thirty sharp. *Please,*" it said. "J.M." James McAndrew. Previously McAndrew had always signed his notes, "His Excellence." (Not "Excellency," he'd had to point out.)

Now what? Ned said to himself. If he hadn't come down to the crypt, he would have been able to say honestly that he'd never seen the note. He hadn't expected to hear from McAndrew again. Their last meeting had had a final feeling, and Ned didn't want to become more confused. Maybe Greta had been angry and upset, but she wasn't a "lost soul," as McAndrew had said. All Ned wanted was to go on with his life, look forward to corresponding with Greta, borrow some of her mother's— "Priscilla Thwaite's"—mysteries from the library (even though he thought of mysteries as books his mother read in bed), figure out how much to tell his parents about Greta if he didn't intercept the first letter from France.

Then Ned saw a quick way back into his peace of mind. He would return the candles to the tray upstairs and pretend he'd never seen the note. If the bishop came later to check, he'd find it still there and realize that Ned hadn't been down. It was a kind of lie, but it was better than having McAndrew pry into his meeting with Greta. Ned felt certain that somehow McAndrew would guess that he'd seen her. McAndrew could always write him a letter if he really had something to say to him, and then Ned could . . . Well, he could tell McAndrew that his parents had found out and wouldn't allow him to visit any longer. He would be polite; he'd thank McAndrew for his friendship—could you thank a bishop for his friendship? Already McAndrew, the specific person, was fading back into the original image Ned had held of "the bishop," that unknown figurehead, and Ned was thinking maybe he and Greta really could write a mystery; they could take turns writing chapters and send them to each other. He was debating methods of murder—poisoning, shooting, stabbing? Poison seemed by far the best, the quietest and easiest for younger murderers to pull off, though where would they get the poison? Did rat poison have a taste in food?—and he had replaced the note on the chest of the effigy, propped against the crossed wrists as McAndrew had left it, and was turning towards the stairs when the bishop's voice called, "A prior engagement?" Ned jumped exactly as he had on the first occasion of McAndrew's accosting him. He turned to see him materializing, just as he had then, from the shadow of the recessed doorway.

"Were you watching me this whole time?" Ned demanded angrily—what he'd wished to ask the first time but hadn't dared.

"I'm in the dark, Ned," McAndrew said. "Completely in the dark."

"What do you mean?"

"Put those down, will you please, and follow me? I have one last favor to ask of you."

"What favor?" Ned was clutching the candles, whose heat he could feel on his chin.

"No effort is required on your part. It's merely to witness; I want a witness . . ."

The bishop looked dazed, like someone who'd just woken up and didn't remember where he was. He was dressed in his usual corduroys but today had on his black shirt and the white collar that, because of its stiffness, made Ned think of those kept on dogs after they'd had operations on their ears, to keep them from scratching. McAndrew called it his "choker."

"Are you going somewhere?" Ned asked.

"Not today, no. Nowhere except back to my study. Please, Ned, indulge me?"

As Ned reluctantly set down the candles in their reusable tin holders, McAndrew asked, "Will you light one for me when I'm dead?"

"Why? Are you planning to die soon?"

"Rhetorical question, Ned. Doesn't require an answer. You should learn that. Save you a lot of trouble."

The bishop looked nervously around as he hurried across the cloister, and Ned, recalling his hope, that first day, that the real bishop would appear and stop McAndrew, asked, "Who do you think's after you? The *Shadow?*"

"This is not a time for levity, Ned," McAndrew said.

"Excuse *me,*" Ned muttered.

When they reached the study, Venerable Bede fishtailed over to them, but McAndrew, who usually greeted him elaborately, brushed him aside, exclaiming, "Confound it! It stays light so late now!"

"So what?"

"It will seem peculiar if the drapes are drawn this early."

"Why do you have to draw the drapes?"

"For you to hide behind, of course."

"What?"

"From the tribunal, Ned. The inquisitors. They'll be here any minute."

"What inquisitors?" Ned noticed then that McAndrew's desk chair had already been pulled out to face the fireplace.

"I've got it!" McAndrew shouted suddenly, like Henry Higgins in *My Fair Lady,* Ned thought, yelling at Pickering when Eliza Doolittle finally learned to pronounce her "h"s. "Under the desk! Why didn't I think of that before? Quick, scrunch up. Don't make a peep."

Ned protested, but McAndrew took hold of his wrist and pulled him towards the desk. Its back faced the door, and no one could see under it without lying right down on the rug.

"Trust me, Ned. It's for the best."

Ned wondered what he would have done if, at that moment, someone hadn't knocked; the sound confirmed him in complicity with McAndrew as they both froze; then Ned dove under the desk. McAndrew waited a moment for him to arrange himself before he walked to the door and opened it. His legs disappeared, was how Ned perceived it, and then he heard various people saying hello and imagined them all kissing each other's rings, bumping their heads like the Three Stooges.

"May I offer you tea? Sherry?" the bishop asked.

"I think not," replied a voice.

"Please sit down, your Excellency. Monsignor," McAndrew said, and Ned knew then who the pair were.

He heard creaks as they sat, then the slow squelching of the leather chairs readjusting around them. There was silence, and then the archbishop's voice began to speak.

"To be frank, Jim, we don't know what to make of it. The first letter, then the second, withdrawing her claim—I feel I owe you an apology. You evidently read the situation better than I. When I spoke with you last week, I was irritated by your flippant attitude, but now can understand it better, if not justify it. The girl said in her letter that she's left the school?"

"It's simple, don't you think? She got cold feet."

"Do you mean you think she *was* faking?" the archbishop asked, sounding surprised. "Last week you assured us that that was impossible."

"I do think it's impossible," McAndrew said. "What I mean is that she wrote you in the beginning to get even with me."

Ned, under the desk, gave a mental sigh of relief. This was what Greta had said, and he was glad that McAndrew's version and hers were going to agree.

"For what, Jim?" the archbishop asked. "You have me confused. You mean, wrote the letter to get even, since you didn't take her claim seriously?"

"She made no claim to me. To me all she *claimed* was that she wished to be left alone."

The archbishop sighed. It sounded a lot like one of Bede's sighs, and Ned imagined Bede sitting up in a chair, wearing a white, stiff collar and a black shirt. If he laughed under the desk, what would the archbishop think then?

"For what did she wish to get even? You might make an effort to be less obscure. If you don't believe she was faking, then do you believe that she truly received the holy marks or do you believe her to be one of those fans of martyrdom one sometimes finds among our Catholic girlhood?"

"She's not 'among our Catholic girlhood,' your Excellency. I wonder how I forgot to mention that. She has no formal religious background whatsoever, so far as I can ascertain. She came to St. Stephen's only because her father, who works abroad and is recently widowed, wished her to be near her older sister, who lives in Marby. We're the only boarding school for girls within thirty miles. We don't require our students to come from a Catholic background, though as a matter of course most of them do. She didn't even know what the stigmata were until I explained them to her."

"She didn't . . . You mean that she took the idea from you," the archbishop said.

"I don't mean that," McAndrew said.

"You don't mean . . ."

"I explained them to her in order to clarify Sister Mary Catherine's—shall we say, exuberance?—at discovering them on her hands."

Ned, cramped under the desk, one of his feet already asleep, had begun to feel uneasy again. He could tell, even if the archbishop couldn't, that McAndrew was leading up to something, building a kind of trap; it was quite apparent, listening to the hints in McAndrew's voice, and Ned wondered what he might have learned about the bishop before now if he'd been able to listen to him without seeing him.

"Then you *do* stand by your allegations of last week!" the archbishop exclaimed. "I had convinced myself I must have misunderstood you. I had thought you were saying that you *did* believe the marks to be genuine, but intended to say nothing to anyone about it, despite your clearly defined responsibilities. When I received the girl's second letter, I was perplexed, and thought that perhaps you had frightened her off. When we first began to speak a little while ago, I thought that you had not believed they were genuine. Would you be so kind as to tell me precisely what it is you do believe?"

"Oh, what I believe . . ."

Ned could imagine McAndrew rolling his eyes as he said this.

"I believe the marks to be genuine, as you put it, if by that you mean that they are neither self-inflicted nor the physical manifestation of some metaphysical mania. They came, somehow, from outside her. Beyond that I am not prepared to go."

There was a silence and Ned heard someone get up, he could not tell who, and he stopped breathing, but evidently whoever it was—he guessed McAndrew—had not moved far, probably gone to stand in front of the fire.

"Father McAndrew," the archbishop said, "there's a question of doctrine here into which I am not, for the moment, prepared to enter. I would simply like you to explain, as clearly as you are capable, what you mean by 'getting even.' What have you done to the girl—what does she think you have done—to justify such a measure on her part?"

"I scorned her," McAndrew said.

"I beg your pardon?"

Ned could tell that the archbishop was furious now and thought that McAndrew was being vague on purpose, though Ned, with his new, discerning ears, could tell that McAndrew wasn't being vague, but clever.

"Forgive me," McAndrew said. "A perhaps too archaic term. My inveterate delicacy. Spurned—would that synonym do? Refused? I dislike our contemporary idiom: rejected. So clinical-sounding. It seems to divest the act of all intention—"

"Enough!" the archbishop exclaimed. "Enough!"

"It sounds," the monsignor said, "as if Father McAndrew is saying that the girl made advances to him."

"Advances, yes, I like that," McAndrew said. "Like an army. The avant-garde. She would like that," he added.

"And did you reciprocate?"

"Ah, reciprocate . . . Another one of those eviscerated words."

"Did you respond in any way, Father McAndrew?"

"I'm only human," McAndrew said, "as the saying goes. Even bishops have their weaknesses, I'm sure you know."

They can move only on the diagonal, Ned thought automatically.

"I suppose I invited it—I allow too much familiarity. She and the boy—the one who appeared the other day—they both possessed a similar attraction—intelligent youngsters who haven't been indoctrinated early. Fiercely schooled in skepticism, in fact. I introduced them. I suppose I thought I'd divert her attention to someone of her own age, but it was clear from the first how young she thought him. Of course, with her amount of experience . . ."

"To what do you refer?"

"Oh, she's lived abroad much of her life, been given her independence. My impression is that I'm not the first."

Ned's feet were both sending throbbing pains up his legs by now, but he noticed them only as a physical manifestation of his emotions. The bishop was saying that Greta had been in love with him, but it wasn't true! It couldn't be true, yet it made sense of Greta's two letters to the archbishop—if you didn't know Greta. But did he? It had been only a little more than three weeks since he'd first seen her, sitting in the armchair with her bandaged hands. She probably had thought him too young, and it made him feel sick to think how she'd have reacted if he really had put his arm around her. He made a note to himself for the future never to make the mistake of liking anyone he wasn't completely positive already liked him.

"I suppose there must be an additional thrill in seducing a celibate away from his vows—not only a celibate but one advanced in the hierarchy. Perhaps you've encountered something of the sort yourself, your Excellency?"

"That's enough," the archbishop said. "We've heard enough. If what you say is true, the girl is to be pitied. I still don't know what happened, but I am convinced you've betrayed a trust."

"Would that I had had it to betray," the bishop said.

But Ned didn't want to hear anymore, and he laid his face down against his knees and held his elbows over his ears. His cheeks were wet—he hadn't realized he'd been crying.

Why had the bishop wanted him to listen? It could only have been to hurt him—to bring him to his senses in this harsh way because he'd been too stupid to get the hints that McAndrew, and maybe Greta too, had been dropping. McAndrew must have figured that Ned wouldn't believe him if he'd talked to him privately. But that would mean he'd set this all up for Ned's benefit, besides which he was jeopardizing his career. Was *that* what he'd wanted Ned to witness? But why?

It wasn't until Ned felt the vibrations of footsteps and then the door shutting that he released the pressure on his ears: complete silence in the room; McAndrew must have gone out with the other two. When, after a moment, he still heard nothing, he finally let his sobs come, stifling neither their sloppy noise nor his misery. He knew he should get out before McAndrew came back; McAndrew had probably left on purpose to give him an opportunity to get away, but he couldn't move. He hated McAndrew but he sickened himself . . . To have thought he was *worthy* . . . To have made a fool of himself . . . Thinking McAndrew valued his companionship, that Greta relied on his friendship . . .

Finally crawling out from under the desk, Ned lurched to his feet, stumbling on tingling legs. And McAndrew was there—had been there ever since the two visitors had left: leaning against the door with his back the way one braced against an intruder, and he was heaving deep, silent breaths, as if to ride out a spasm of pain. He didn't look at Ned but acknowledged his emergence by reaching back and turning the doorknob. Then he stepped forward, pulling the door along with him, so that when the door was wide open he was standing behind it, out of sight. The doorway yawned into the upstairs hallway, with its sickening indifference to all that had happened, and Ned didn't know what else to do except step through it.

Sitting, three decades later, in his own very differently furnished study in the ramshackle former hotel in Stilling, Ned could still instantly summon up the feeling of that moment, that one step over the threshold into the vacant hall that had seemed silent like something *keeping* silent: resentful, taunting, refusing to care what had happened in the room since it, the hallway, wasn't part of the room. But what else could he have done? Followed the bishop around to the other side of the door and asked him why *he* was so upset?

Though Ned now understood that McAndrew had intentionally disgraced himself—by clever implication, wanting, it seemed, to be relieved of his position without having his real reasons (assuming he had known what these were) to be subjected to the scrutiny of his superiors—Ned had never satisfactorily figured out why McAndrew had wanted him present. Had knowing that Ned was under the desk, listening, helped McAndrew to play the role he'd assigned himself? An audience he was familiar with, whose reaction he could gauge? Yet he must have known how what he said would hurt Ned, and he certainly could have disgraced himself in some other way than by impugning Greta; and what had been the purpose of that gratuitous bit about Ned's being "too young"? After all, Greta was leaving. It still seemed to Ned that the whole plan, in some inexplicable, inchoate way, had been formed the very first moment that McAndrew had laid eyes on him fingering the epitaphs in the cathedral crypt. Even if he hadn't known why himself, McAndrew had recognized in Ned an avenue of escape.

Over the years Ned had considered, but rejected, the possibility that McAndrew had been telling the truth. McAndrew's story had made a kind of sense of things that hadn't before made sense, and yet Ned's imagination simply couldn't encompass Greta's being interested in McAndrew in such a way that "spurning" would have been possible.

He hadn't seen the bishop again. He had returned to the cloister one afternoon the following week, not knowing what he would say yet needing to revisit the room to believe that McAndrew had really said what he had; to find an explanation for McAndrew's behavior that he could live with. Ned had felt as if the numbness he had suffered physically while cramped under the desk was spreading into every aspect of his life, and that the bishop alone could break the spell, but as Ned stood in the hallway gathering his courage to knock, one of the brothers had appeared—he must have seen Ned go in the door downstairs—and said, "His Excellency isn't here."

"He isn't?" Ned asked. "Where is he? What about Bede? Would he like a walk? I used to walk him sometimes," he lied.

"Who are you?" the brother asked. "You're not one of our boys."

"I used to do the candles in the cathedral for Anselm Alterbury when he broke his leg."

"Anselm—I see. Well, the bishop isn't here, and the dog is with his master. Neither will be coming back."

The issue wasn't, Ned said to himself as if to an interlocutor, that he couldn't live without fully comprehending McAndrew's motives. Obviously he could—he'd lived for thirty years without comprehending them. Nor had he, in fact, given much thought to McAndrew over the years. Only at odd moments, when he'd felt what he might have labelled the "open door feeling," the feeling that he was being forced by outside circumstance or someone else's will to take a step for which he was unprepared and from which there could be no turning back—only at these times did he recall that first experience of being pushed into what he didn't want to think about. Usually it turned out that he wasn't being forced, or he found a way to get a foothold and hedge. One of those moments faced him this summer, he knew, and his impulse, this time, to return to its prototype, was probably just another kind of hedging—just as it was, in his private cosmology, to make O.'s being conscious (or not) of his effect on Lucinda Dearborn stand for McAndrew's so being of him. This time, Ned swore, he would refuse to step through the door and instead tell McAndrew to shut it and explain himself. Tell me what's going on, he would say, and in terms I can understand. Why did you sow in me these suspicions of my future wife, why? Just to see what they might grow into? Well, come see what you nurtured. After all these years, your seeds of mistrust have finally germinated. Time has fallen in on itself, and it's your fault. Come now and stretch it back out again.

Though this was not the language in which Ned actually wrote to McAndrew, swivelling in the oak desk chair much like the one in McAndrew's study except that McAndrew's had been stationary, rolling a piece of the yellow foolscap he used for first drafts into his ancient Smith Corona as if it were the most ordinary undertaking: to write to someone he'd neither seen nor spoken to in over a quarter of a century. The strangeness of it was that it felt ordinary (though Ned suspected that he'd pay later for this drunken disregard of scruples), and Ned's letter was chatty, friendly. He didn't explain what had prompted it. Let McAndrew worry that one, Ned thought. McAndrew might or might not be surprised to hear, Ned wrote, that he'd been married for over twenty years to Greta Sayre and that they had a son, now fourteen ("my age when you knew me," Ned noted), named Henry. As they had for many years now, they were spending the summer in Stilling, in northern Vermont, in a house that had once been a hotel. Its ghosts, Ned wrote, had "lately been agitating" for him to "bring them to the attention of the larger world." Let McAndrew ponder that one, too. If he were alive, that is. Presuming he received the letter, which Ned addressed to "Former Bishop James McAndrew, c/o St. Stephen's Cathedral, Cathedral Street, Marby . . ." with a request that it be forwarded, if possible.

Greta remembered, crouching beside the trunk in the attic, how many times she had tried to write to Crain about the "miracle in Marby." The marks had appeared on her hands in late January; early in the month she'd received a letter he'd sent from Mexico before Christmas. A French aerogram, thin blue paper, one folded sheet, on which he'd superimposed Mexican stamps. Something about his having done this had disturbed Greta, although she had no idea what it was. She had read the letter hurriedly, skipping over news of school friends and Crain's reiterating how lonely he felt without her to the passage that seemed written in larger, more vivid letters than the others, given the way it pulsed and wouldn't remain inert.

"I am not *m'entending bien avec* my mother at the moment," Crain wrote. "She arranged my engagement party for December 30, the day after my father's birthday. On that day he and I always ride up into the mountains to Huayacheca (a silver-mining town) where we own a small hacienda, and we always spend the night because there isn't time to ride up and back on the same day. Now we won't be able to do that. Don't think this was any accident," Crain informed Greta. "My mother has always been jealous of this trip, because she suspects my father of being in love with the housekeeper in Huayacheca, and now she's found a way to keep us from going."

"Can't they go some other day?" Greta muttered—then glanced quickly across at her roommate to see if she'd heard. It's incredible, she continued silently, talking to Marie-Agnès, her roommate in France. *C'est incroyable!* she exclaimed, the lift into French making things seem more manageable. *Je n'arrive pas à comprendre pourquoi* . . . I fail to understand why . . . *Was* his father in love with the housekeeper? Was that fact so insignificant that Crain couldn't be bothered to say?

Greta had been reading and reading the letter in her dorm at St. Stephen's; it was the interval between the end of classes at four-thirty and dinner at six during which the girls were allowed to stay in their rooms, do laundry, take showers. Her roommate—a placid, sweetly pretty, slow-moving girl from North Carolina, named June, whose sympathy, Greta had learned, depended on her ability to find parallels in her own experience to whatever Greta spoke about in hers—was sitting on the other side of the room painting her toenails a dark apricot, swinging her bare legs off the edge of her bed to dry the polish. June observed Greta staring at her letter.

"Is somethin' wrong?" she asked, her feet poised in mid-air. "Bad news?"

"No, just the usual."

"Crain, you mean?" (June pronounced Crain like "crayon.") She let her feet down.

"I really think he's getting involved with some other girl," Greta said.

"That jerk," June said appreciatively. "Don't you just wish you could be a fly"—a "flah"—"on the wall, and see what he's really and truly up to? I know that's how I feel about Sinclair." A boy in the choir who, it was said, was going steady with a girl from town. "I would just like to *know.* But you know," she added wisely, "it could be sex."

"I don't think he would sleep with her," Greta said truthfully. "He wants to wait until he's married."

"And you believe him?"

"Why shouldn't I?"

"They lie"—"lah." "All men lie. At least when it comes to sex they do."

"He doesn't lie to me," Greta said.

Buoyed by June's righteous outrage, however, she denounced Crain's insensitivity in a letter.

> *Don't write to me anymore. How can you tell me about getting engaged and how you can't sleep for thinking about making love with me* on the same page?
>
> *As far as I'm concerned our relationship is over. I never want to see you again.*

Crain wrote back at once.

I don't understand why you're so angry about my letter. You knew I was engaged—this is just the formal announcement. How could everything not be on the same page? There's only one page in an air letter. I thought we were d'accord *that we would always be honest with each other. Would you prefer for me not to tell you how I feel?*

Greta felt paralyzed again by this logic that sucked the insides out of everything; how could this be the same person who'd been so upset when they said goodbye at the airport in Paris that he'd tried to change his ticket to Mexico City for one to Washington, D.C., and then all summer had called her nearly every day at the hotel where she and her father had been staying—which wasn't easy. He'd had to slip away from his family and go into town, wait in line at the public telephone exchange, wait while the operator put an international call through. . . . He was afraid if he told his parents about her they wouldn't let him return to school in France. If Crain had written that he no longer loved her, that seeing Julia again had made him realize she mattered the most after all . . . But all fall he had complained how nothing was the same without her; this would be his last year at the school—he wouldn't stay for Terminale, the final level, and if she was going to finish high school in the States he would try to convince his father to let him go to college there, although his father was insisting Crain go to Oxford as he had. "Crains from time immemorial have trod the paving stones of Christ Church," Crain quoted.

She tried next to believe that what Crain said was actually true: the engagement meant nothing; it was an obligation he had to fulfill, just as his marriage to Julia, making love to her, having children with her, living with her all their lives would also be an obligation . . .

"But what started all this up again?" Greta wrote. "It seems as if it's because I left that you're going through with it. Do you think I *wanted* to leave? You know my father made me."

"No more can I help it," Crain wrote back. "I promised. I gave my word."

"But I thought you were going to tell them you couldn't go through with it . . ."

Despite Crain's insistence that he didn't blame her for leaving, that that had nothing to do with it, she didn't believe him. This would never have happened if she'd stayed; if she'd been with him he would have had the strength not to do what his family wanted. This was really all her fault. She loved him but she had to admit he was weak. He was weak when she wasn't there to remind him who he was. Something—obviously his insane family and their insane dreams of titles and power—was making him afraid to stand up for what he wanted and she had to save him from them. But then she began to think of what he might be saying to Julia about the girl he'd "gone out with" at boarding school, and in this picture he ceased to be the Crain she knew—the playful, affectionate, thoughtful, devoted person—and became a stranger. You know it would never have happened if you'd been with me, Julia, darling, Greta imagined him saying, but I was far from home, and lonely—can you find it in your heart to forgive my weakness? She didn't mean anything to me . . .

Greta tortured herself with images of Crain and Julia together—she knew they both rode (it was at the stable near the Collège where Greta kept her horse that she'd first come to know Crain), and she imagined them on their Western saddles galloping through the cholla and maguey cactus fields behind their ranches where once or twice Crain had seen a rattlesnake. In a grassy hollow they would get off the horses, and Crain would be talking in his lowest voice to Julia, holding her hand, then bending to kiss her; he would insinuate his tongue into her mouth as he did into Greta's, he would trace the curve of her ears with his fingers, he would unbutton her shirt while pressing his forehead into her collarbone to see what he was doing—he might go no farther; he had said they had never even kissed and when he had said it Greta had believed him, but now they were engaged . . . He was *not hers, not Julia's*—how dare Julia think he was? Greta was the first person Crain had slept with; even if he hadn't said so his ineptness would have confirmed it. She had been inexperienced too, but compared to her Crain was in the Dark Ages. At least her mother had *talked* to her.

Greta had written Julia several letters, in which she told her about her relationship with Crain. "Dear Julia, You don't know me but last year I went to the same school in France that Crain does. I am his *girlfriend*. Do you have a clue as to what that means? Do you know all the things we did? Do you know what Crain writes to me about? Well, I'll tell you."

Greta would continue for pages, being as graphic as possible, embellishing nothing but omitting nothing, recording every intimate physical detail she could remember—and it relieved her to write this, to picture Julia's shocked reaction, her confronting Crain with the facts, denouncing him, she was breaking off their engagement immediately . . .

But Greta sent none of the letters. She knew before she finished writing that she wouldn't send them. The thought of what Crain might be driven to say in self-defense prevented her. She was a *putain*—a whore; he was a male, he had, pardon the expression, to get his rocks off somewhere, it didn't mean he *loved* the girl. . . .

The sores on her hands comforted her, in a strange way. She'd hardly remembered that she *had* a body since she had stopped sleeping with Crain and the itching and stinging reminded her that she was alive, at least; she was a person things happened to, things that had nothing to do with anyone else—not with her mother's dying, not with Crain's being engaged. This was her private relationship with the universe, that was what she felt—something told to her or *through* her; not a message, exactly, more like a reminder; something she already knew but was in danger of forgetting . . . She knew it didn't mean what everyone tried to make her believe, that she was singled out by God—if she was singled out, it wasn't by God. Anyone could get the marks if they weren't *inoculated.*

Worse than people thinking the marks were divine was their thinking she was pretending; she was dirty, a liar. In either case, they thought it was their business. *They* would decide what the marks meant; why didn't she just make it easy for everyone and admit she'd done it for the attention? Her mother had died, her boyfriend was going to marry another girl, her father was too devoted to his career to live in a place where she could live with him, her sister couldn't really feel sorry for her for losing her mother at sixteen when she'd lost hers at five—so no wonder Greta had imagined sores in her hands to get attention; her own mind had secretly done this to her. Even if she didn't consciously remember hearing about the stigmata, her mind could have retained the information, and what better way could anyone think of to get attention in a Catholic school than to have *them?*

As for the bishop, what did he want from her? At first he'd pretended to be on her side, listening sympathetically to her account of Sister Mary Catherine's interrogation—Sister Mary Catherine was a "zealot," he said, a fine woman in her way but apt to be rattled by anything for which her limited experience provided no ready explanation. The bishop had reminded Greta at first of her parents' friends—people who'd travelled and didn't think their own little world was the only one there was. But soon she'd begun to feel mistrustful; he cared too much what she said; he kept looking for clues, as if she had been sent to St. Stephen's to explain the workings of the universe to him. She knew he didn't believe she'd made the marks herself; she didn't think he even thought they were "hysterical." He seemed to think they really might be a miracle, but then was angry at himself for thinking that and tried again to trick her into confessing. But what did he think she had to confess?

In Thrush Hollow's attic, surrounded by Lucinda Dearborn's useless water-cure paraphernalia, Greta remembered trying to write about all this to Crain, trying to rescue herself from the mental fever brought on by too many simultaneous understandings; but just as with her letters to Julia, self-consciousness inhibited her before she could finish a single letter. What if *Crain* thought she had developed the stigmata as a way of getting attention, of trying to show him how upset she was by his getting engaged? What if he thought she really had gone off the deep end? She wouldn't be able to bear that, the one person still alive whom she trusted suspecting her the way everyone else did now—and then there was the sickening drop when she realized she didn't trust him anymore either; she wouldn't be uncertain of his reaction if she did.

She'd even tried to write about it *casually*. "Dear Crain, the strangest thing has happened . . ." "You'll never believe this . . ." "How much do you know about Christianity? We never exactly spent a lot of time discussing religion. . . ."

The joviality had been knives at her throat, threatening to annihilate her if she cried out; she was fighting for her existence but making a joke of it, lest someone accuse her of taking herself too seriously. How could *she,* Greta Sayre, a sixteen-year-old in the United States of America in the twentieth century, experience something that people were *sainted* for, burned at the *stake* for, the kind of thing that went down in history?

She gave up trying to write to Crain—about anything; fell back instead upon imagining him—tall, fit, poised—striding into McAndrew's cushy office and saying, What the hell do you think you're up to with my girlfriend? She's getting out of here right now!, McAndrew jabbering stupidly, I didn't mean . . . I didn't think . . . That's just the trouble, you didn't think! Come on, Greta, let's go . . .

Or if she could *shock* Crain, if she had some other news to go with that about her hands, then he couldn't think of her as mentally disturbed; he would be too surprised for that; if she could shock *anyone,* in fact, it might give her back the sense of herself she'd lost.

When a man has an erection, Greta envisioned herself saying to June, as if explaining a problem in geometry, the foreskin pulls back. The top of the penis is very sensitive. You have to use your tongue very gently—otherwise the feeling is too strong for them.

That would shut June up in a hurry, stop her saying, "It's a hard fate to be in love with someone who doesn't even know you exist."

Priests, as Greta had informed Ned, left the Church; sometimes it was because they had fallen in love. They had thought they could go through life without sex, devoting themselves to God, but that was because they had never known the former. Sometimes they left the Church for the woman they sinned with; sometimes they didn't. The illegitimate children of priests who wanted to force their fathers to admit paternity were practically a sub-specialty at Mistlefits, Chatterlane & Windeminion, and Greta continued to recast her past weeks in Priscilla Thwaite's language: "The bishop's interest in Miss Sayre could hardly be said to be purely professional." "Often, when she glanced up, she caught him gazing at her with a quizzical, ambiguous look." "He hung on Miss Sayre's every word." "The bishop could be seen to admire Miss Sayre beyond the bounds of propriety." "You stand in the face of the unknown and you don't flinch," was the kind of thing McAndrew said to her. "You have the rarest of qualities—the strength of character to live with the unexplained. All of society and history conspire to undermine it . . ."

In Priscilla Thwaite's *Agony at the Abbey* (set in Ireland; in England priests could marry), a young woman from the village, rosy-cheeked and ample of bosom, was cleaning the pastor's study. She chanced upon a love poem he had written; it was clearly not a hymn to spiritual love. She learned it by heart, then recited it to the good father one day, and was amused when he blushed. "You're a man like any other," she told him. "Contrary to what is commonly supposed," Priscilla Thwaite had written, "priests are more easily seduced than other men, and the higher they stand in the hierarchy the more easily they fall—perhaps because the element of surprise is so profound."

Even at the time, Greta had moved in and out of that language to describe to herself what happened. "Confused by the bishop's confessional, not *confessor's,* manner, the young girl thought that he wished her to 'give herself' to him . . ." "His manner was hardly that which one would expect of a headmaster with a student, let alone that of a bishop with a teenage girl. It was no wonder that she interpreted his suggestive remarks in sexual terms . . ."

Not only alliteration but the removal of responsibility for their actions from the hapless heroines made mystery novels popular, Greta was even then aware.

By the time she got back to the Collège after Easter recess, the scars on her hands had already begun to fade. Her father had met her in Paris as planned, but then had decided that they both could use a vacation, and they had spent nearly six weeks in Italy, where Greta had looked at scenes of the Crucifixion with a fresh eye, and felt superior to other tourists, who didn't have the personal experience of the Church's inner workings that she had.

She had been infected; that was plain. She'd had no immunity built up, either to the Church or to the country, and the virus had leapt at the chance to attach itself to a vulnerable host. From abroad, this seemed quite ordinary. She expected it was a common experience but people were embarrassed to talk about it, being made to feel as ashamed and singled out as she had been.

The State Department ought to issue a travellers' advisory, as it did for foreign countries in which U.S. nationals might be in danger. *Better not come home—you might catch something . . .* Of course, that would be bad for patriotism.

When her father left her off the Sunday afternoon at the end of Easter recess, the girls' dormitory was still mostly empty. The majority of students would arrive just at dinnertime in chartered buses from Paris, Montpellier, Lyon, and other places, so Greta decided to go for a walk. She wanted some time alone before facing everyone's questions. She remembered now that it had been about four o'clock, foggy and chilly, afternoon turning to dusk. It seemed to her that she had been shivering ever since she and her father had left Naples two days ago, but she hadn't brought herself to accept the fact that she was now back in a different climate and had not put on a warm coat. By habit she'd set off through the widely spaced pines behind the girls' dorm; it was the way she'd gone when she'd sneaked out at night to meet Crain—jumping down from a high window in the kitchen, the only downstairs window that wasn't locked. Crain had lifted her on his shoulders to climb back in.

Greta walked past the old stone farmhouse that had been converted to a dining hall and coffee shop; along the deserted, packed dirt path past the tennis courts; and then circled around behind the tall cement-block classroom building. *Bâtiment,* the French word for building, suited it, sounding as it did like "battlement." After thirty years, the smell of the halls—a mixture of chalk, sweat, and disinfectant—still came to Greta as vividly as if she'd just been inside. She could hear the abrupt thunderous noise following the hourly bell as students jumped up and hurried through the halls to their next classes, followed by the equally sudden decrease in sound to hums coming from behind closed doors as classes started up again.

After Easter recess, the windows were dark, the doors locked, and Greta felt like a ghost. It couldn't have been dusk—it had been only four or four-thirty—and yet her memory of the afternoon was of deepening darkness. She had her arms crossed in front of her and was rubbing them with her hands to keep warm as she continued past the classroom building and on through the pine woods along the narrow track that led to the back of the boys' dormitory: a long, low building, like an army barracks (unlike the girls' dorm, it was never locked at night). She had been there rarely—on the nights when she sneaked out, Crain had waited for her on the road to the village—and Greta stopped now at the edge of the woods and stood looking at the silhouettes in the few lighted windows as boys moved back and forth, unpacking. One came to his window and looked out, as if suspecting her presence, and instinctively she crouched down behind a tree, though it might have been too dark for someone in a lighted room to see outside. It bothered Greta not to be able to remember how dark it had been. Then she had realized that the boy was Crain.

At first she had leapt from behind the tree and waved, calling his name, but Crain had already turned and sat down at his desk. He was hunched over—it looked as if he were writing. A letter, Greta guessed, probably to his mother, to whom he dutifully wrote once a week. Or to Julia, telling her how much he already missed her. Or to her, Greta. She hadn't written to tell him that she was coming back.

She hurried down the slope, planning to rap on the window, but instead found herself standing on the other side of the glass, at the very edge of the window, watching Crain. The desk stood against a wall adjacent to the window, and Crain sat at an angle turned away from Greta. She could see now that he was in fact writing. If only she could see what, and to whom. Her heart was pounding; she was spying now. She should have knocked on the window, but instead she'd gone on standing there without making her presence known.

Then Crain turned, and Greta clapped a hand to her mouth, as if to prevent herself from crying out. She had acted without thinking, and at once took her hand away and called "Crain!" but she hadn't spoken loudly and he hadn't heard her; his eyes were blurred by tears, which he wiped angrily away with the back of his sleeve. The gesture was awkward, that of someone not in the habit of crying, and Greta, abashed, backed away. Her heart sank; she didn't know why. How could he not have seen her? Then Crain reached for the sheet of paper, crumpled it ferociously, and threw it into the wastebasket beside the desk. He stood and left the room, and Greta, terrified, as if he were headed outside to confront her, turned and ran. She hadn't stopped until she'd gone far enough back through the woods that she could have believably claimed—were Crain or someone else to come upon her—that she'd been walking in another direction and had stopped to rest on the way back. She sat with her back against a thick spruce, huddling forward with her arms around her knees, feeling like crying herself, trying to understand why she felt as if she'd lost something. She wasn't afraid of anything she could name. Right then, what she felt had little to do with the content of Crain's letter, whatever it might have been.

As she sat in the woods, huddled against the tree, shivering, she knew that she'd lost her chance. Why hadn't she rapped on the glass when she saw that he was crying and forced him to tell her what the matter was? What had she been afraid of? It had been her chance to confront him and find out what was really behind all his incomprehensible behavior but instead she had fallen back in fear—why? When it mattered the most, it turned out that she was a coward and now she would never learn what had upset him. This she already knew as an inexorable fact.

Greta felt physically ill, as if the disease she had contracted in Marby were now developing its secondary symptoms, and she shivered as she sat on the damp pine needles trying to calm herself, desperately trying to think of some way out while knowing there wasn't one.

How could she face Crain now? He would sense something—he was like a detective with her moods—but she couldn't tell him that she'd spied on him, she couldn't. She had enough courage to tell him, to explain that she'd been so startled to see him crying that she'd run away; that wasn't it. It wasn't telling him she was afraid of; it was knowing that if she did he would lie. She couldn't bear to have him lie to her. Not to her face.

Briefly, she considered trying to obtain the crumpled letter—she could go into his room when he went to dinner—but then she began to fear what the letter might reveal. What if Crain *had* been writing to her, to break off their correspondence? Julia had found out and wouldn't allow it—but in that case, Crain's crying would mean—what? That he couldn't stand to. But would she even want to know that he'd tried? Or maybe he'd been writing to tell her that he couldn't keep on with his engagement to Julia, it was a farce, given what he felt for Greta, but midway he'd realized that he couldn't, wouldn't send it, for whatever reason, whatever unimaginable reason tied him to Julia in the first place. If she'd knocked on the window, maybe he would have found the courage to take a different path, but she'd been a coward and now they were both trapped. Now *she* would be the one responsible for his hiding things from her—all his life. How could she blame him?

She didn't see him until that night after dinner, when a movie was shown in the boys' dining hall. Crain was standing outside with Dominic and other friends, smoking, all of them tall and stooped a little, as if they weren't used to their height yet, to being so far away from the ground.

"*Le voilà,*" whispered Marie-Agnès, and Greta had fought the impulse to run.

"*Il y a trop de monde,*" she whispered back. She didn't want to see him first in a crowd.

But Crain had already seen her. Breaking away from his companions, he exclaimed, "Greta! My God! You're here! What on earth are you doing here?"

His joy was unmistakable, and he grabbed her and swung her around. Greta flung her arms around his neck and pressed her face against his collar, breathing in his smell as if it were oxygen, trying to make up for all the months of being unable to breathe, and finally Marby and St. Stephen's did seem like a bad dream she was waking from at last, after many false wakings. Even the scene she'd witnessed before dinner seemed like a hallucination, and nothing Crain said or did, either that evening or during subsequent days, made it possible to believe that he was upset about anything. Everything was fine at home; everyone was well. The horrible engagement party was over with, the less said about that the better. Something would have to be done about "that whole situation," he remarked; he'd been a coward to go through with it, he knew, but for now, if she didn't mind (Why would she mind? She didn't mind anything!) he just wanted to forget about it. His younger brother, Fredrik—Federico; Rico, everyone called him—would be coming to the

Collège next year, when he was fifteen. Their mother didn't want him to leave, but their father insisted; his sons were to have European educations. If Greta was still there, then she could look out for him.

When the movie began, they held hands. Crain's fingers discovered the hard ridges of Greta's scars.

"Qu'est-ce que c'est?" he whispered.

"Oh, that," Greta said. "I burned them."

"Burned them? How?"

"On votive candles."

"Votive candles?"

"Taisez-vous!" someone behind them hissed.

"You know," Greta whispered, "the ones they light in churches to help the souls of the dead get into heaven."

"I know what they *are,* but how did you burn yourself on them?"

"Oh, it's embarrassing. They had this initiation ceremony at the school. The other girls. They kind of forced you to do it. They'd think you were a coward if you didn't. You had to hold your hands over the flame. The longer you did it, the more they respected you."

"But that's barbaric!" Crain exclaimed, in a loud whisper, and they were requested more vehemently to shut up. "Why did you care what they thought?"

"I didn't, but I thought that if they could stand it, I could. I have the record. No one had ever done it as long as I did."

"Is that really something to be proud of?"

"Is getting engaged to one person when you love another?"

"No," he murmured, after a moment.

They didn't speak again until the movie was over. Outside, in the shadow of the building as they kissed goodnight, Crain said, "It's obvious that neither of us behaves very admirably when we're not together."

McAndrew wondered if he had the energy—the flesh might be willing, but the spirit was weak. The first summer of his full retirement, and now this? A respite a lifetime awaited—to be snatched away just as it began? Seminary, army chaplainship, two decades' incarceration in the Church, then twenty-five years teaching what was hopefully called "Humanities," the last fifteen as headmaster of the prep school where by this time there was no one left who knew he'd once been a bishop.

He had served his time, he'd earned his parole, and now this letter from Ned Dene—he'd almost forgotten. Why would he wish to take up that dangling thread? Nothing could be easier than not to reply; he didn't expect that Ned would pursue the impulse to reconnect if he shouldn't respond.

Ned Dene and Margaret Sayre—Greta. He had never been able to bring himself to reduce the regal, time-honored "Margaret" to the little-girl sophistication of "Greta." They were a mere two hours' drive across the river. An old hotel—the image was suggestive, even without Ned's intentionally mysterious mention of "ghosts." McAndrew envisioned the turn-of-the-century towering structures that one by one, as if succumbing to a contagious disease, had burned or collapsed into lakes. The automobile had done them in—he and Ned and Greta could discourse upon the evils of the automobile; their set (surely they belonged to the same disaffected citizenry) waxed eloquent upon such topics. Ned Dene—a biographer and a university professor—what a disappointment, but what had he expected? Ned would have had to take refuge somewhere; what thinking person didn't?

Pruning the raspberries—that had been his task for the day. Pruning the raspberries and perhaps mowing the back lawn if it had dried out enough by mid-afternoon. Yet it *was* mid-afternoon and ever since he'd picked up the mail at the post office this morning he'd done nothing but sit in the maple-shaded sitting room with the letter—read twice on the walk home and once in the chair in which he had since remained immobilized—now propped on the mantel like Poe's purloined one, although with no hope of concealing its presence from himself.

I am content with my life, he complained; Sylvie was in college now, happy—he planned to offer her a trip abroad in two years when she graduated. (He hoped she might like him to go with her.) Her mother (he knew from Sylvie) had finally found a relationship again, almost twenty years after they'd lost Sarah, whose loss had cost them their marriage. Not having to think of Helen alone and grieving—that was a great load off his mind.

But now this. Where and how had Ned and *Greta* acquired the knack of appearing in his life at these moments when he was en route from one phase to another? What sort of harbingers, they?

Yet he would not be impressed by coincidence, he reminded himself. An order underlying events there might be, but since human minds were not constructed so as to grasp it, why seek to?

He had not forgotten, among other mistakes, his three-decade-old error in construing a young girl's disturbance as a message meant for him. She had been the principal, not he—but, oh, how long had he not been waiting for the world to offer a response to the tumult he awoke to each morning! At last! he had sung. At last! Fate stirred in the shadows. Its form was almost visible.

First the boy (as he'd thought then of Ned), next the self-important sister dragging the frightened but furious Margaret Sayre—found out!—into his plush study. After that had come the luxuriant metaphysical deflowering: he the one to seed her virgin mind with the seductive history of religious ecstasy and its ersatz forms. "Some are chosen, some wish they were."

"I don't see how this applies to me," she'd said, regarding him from somewhere beyond her sea-green eyes.

Insisting she was not marked; she drew no sustenance from her surroundings, how could they therefore design her?

He the one seduced in the end: perhaps her spirit *was* free; this shouldn't be inconceivable. Once in a while it must happen; he would like to see how she had turned out . . .

Mustn't think like this. What would it prove, either way? To find she was a creature of her era; to find she wasn't? *His* spirit was not free; no one's was; only by making a virtue of necessity could one approach the condition. Or so he had preached for a quarter of a century to fifteen- and sixteen-year-olds who had generally responded with fervor to whatever they had imagined him to be saying.

So she had married Ned. Margaret Sayre. "Mrs. Dene"—how wrong it sounded. How had it come about?

Introducing them, this had never been his purpose, indistinct though his purpose might have been. They had been two puzzle pieces he'd brought together to see if they interlocked, had seen they hadn't, but had left them adjacent while waiting for the missing intervening one—who or what would bridge their disunion.

They *could* have fit, and yet—he didn't know why—they didn't. They shouldn't. Ned with his overriding fear of venturing forth, credulity concealed behind his shield of skepticism—oh, Bishop McAndrew had wanted to make him *really* doubt. And Margaret—what had been so exceptional about her, after all? A deeper register of response than most, a sharper alertness to what she refused to accept as her birthright—but a *miracle?*

The unexplained was always a miracle. He had said this to her, and then had found that he meant it without irony. It was possible that it was still something he believed.

McAndrew stood and approached the letter, positioned between two empty pewter candlesticks like an object of worship—something he might have held aloft, invoking the Almighty's sanction, during his moment under the mitre.

There was no point in rereading it. He knew their son's name and age; the titles of Ned's books; he even knew most of what Ned wasn't telling him. Ned would not have written him had there not been a fault-line in the marriage; it led—or Ned believed it led—to the pain he'd experienced on learning from McAndrew that Miss Sayre was not the ascetic he'd imagined.

How and when, McAndrew wondered, had they discussed it? Had she made it seem as if the depraved bishop had been the perpetrator?

It was hard to know, even now, why he'd felt obliged (he still seemed incapable of being honest) to disillusion Ned. Ned had been his own younger self, of course, whose pretense at sophistication McAndrew had despised—every effort made not to let people know you didn't know what they were talking about. How he had warmed to the boy when he'd let his amazement gleam through: you don't eat bread and water and sleep on straw pallets! he'd all but exclaimed. McAndrew hadn't had the heart to tell Ned that his study reflected his predecessor's taste, not his own, which tended towards Puritan plainness.

What *had* the young Ned really made of Margaret, whose sensuality at that age had expressed itself as an extraordinarily intense *waiting,* so that finally (though would an adolescent boy react to it this way?) you wanted to see what she was waiting *for,* if it could possibly be *you.* You wanted to convert the watchfulness in her gaze to—oh, almost anything else: eagerness, welcome, satiety, knowledge. It was the watchfulness that was unbearable: could you measure up?

He was conscious of having felt that; he had been conscious then of feeling it, but what had happened was not inevitable, despite his being able honestly to say that he hadn't seen it coming. Even looking back, he found no clues that he had missed. True enough, as he'd said to the archbishop, he'd been improperly familiar, but he still believed that Margaret had reached a decision beforehand, and then had come to implement it. Implementing it, she had struck a sincerity that had taken over. He would admit to having colluded beforehand to the extent of never being satisfied with what transpired between them, and letting her know he wasn't; he had colluded *during* by responding with feeling—he supposed this made it irrelevant who had initiated.

The night in question, she had come up after dinner, as she had been doing every evening for ten days, for a "theological discussion." This meant that he mentally sniffed around the parameters of whatever she concealed, while she maintained that she wasn't concealing anything. She had been so exasperated by his need to know the meaning of what was happening to *her;* how could she have had any patience with his need to know what portion of it was intended for him? By that evening the impasse they'd reached had seemed unbreachable, and yet both of them had persisted in trying to find out what lay on the other side—he insisted on that, at least: he had not been alone in his curiosity.

Attempting if nothing else to gauge the dimension of what separated them, he'd remarked that he felt, in some way he couldn't put his finger on, that she was playing a game with all of them. "Oh, not, I hasten to add," McAndrew could recall himself pompously saying, that he suspected her of inflicting the wounds, nor did he mean to suggest that she manipulated for the meanness of it; it was something involuntary—something she was trying to make happen or that her body had caused to happen because she needed something so much . . .

"It's that inability to tolerate what's partial—that's the religion of our blood. That's our real emblem—up there, nailed to the Cross . . . Every now and then someone has to come along and offer up another sacrifice . . ."

Margaret had stared at him; suddenly she had begun to cry, covering her face with her mummified hands. It was the first (and only) time she had cried before him.

Ashamed (yet hadn't he also felt a measure of triumph?), he had knelt beside her chair and threaded his arm in around her shoulders.

"I'm sorry, Margaret. Forgive me." (He recalled saying "Forgive me.") He had done the secular male thing and pleaded with her to stop crying.

He had been holding her head against his shoulder by then and had been conscious of the sweet, grassy smell of her hair. He'd been recalling the last time he'd held a woman close enough to smell her: just after the war, when the mothers and fiancées of some of the boys he'd watched die as their chaplain had sought him out to hear an account of their son's or lover's final moments. Margaret's sobs had become intermittent and then she had mumbled something.

He had drawn back and asked her to repeat it.

"I'm not crying about what you think," she'd said.

"Not crying . . . I'm sorry, Margaret, I . . ."

"You don't take me seriously," she said, almost inaudibly.

"Seriously! I don't . . . What else is all this—these interminable catechisms—but taking you seriously?"

"I mean, as a woman."

"As a—!"

McAndrew had resisted the impulse to laugh, especially when she followed this remark with a second, "You're a man like any other," though she wasn't a good enough actress to keep looking at him while she recited it.

"Margaret, my dear," he said, "that sounds like a line. I would have thought you too young for that."

Embarrassed—or angry—she had risen and gone to the window. The heavy red velvet curtains had been drawn but she'd parted them and looked out. McAndrew followed and with her watched as two of the sisters, carrying freshly laundered sheets across their outstretched arms, methodically crossed the gas-lit cloister. What a confusing omen, he remembered thinking—the suggestiveness of sheets borne by beings who'd vowed never to delight in the activities that could take place between them. More gently he'd said, "I'm sorry, Margaret. I don't mean to make fun of you. But what you're saying is so . . . It bears no relation to your usual manner with me."

Silent, she continued to stand, watching the nuns until they went inside, and he tried to imagine what response she really wanted from him.

"My dear child, did I somehow give you to think . . ."

"I am not a child!" she exclaimed—this, though hardly original dialogue, delivered with more genuine feeling than her previous lines.

Before he had formulated an appropriate reply to this, she'd turned and thrown her arms around his neck. While he stood, completely wooden, his arms at his sides, she pressing her lips against his and trying to edge her tongue into his mouth, he had found himself thinking, of all things, that she wished he was taller than he was.

He broke away. "Margaret, this isn't . . . I don't . . ."

"Yes, you *do,*" she said. "Let me."

And then it seemed he did—in any case, he let her. That is, to a point. The point at which, both of them half undressed on the rug in front of the fire (recalling the play of firelight over her breasts, he could summon up no particle of shame, only regret), she had begun to undo the belt of his trousers, her bandaged hands loosening the buckle with some awkwardness. When he'd protested, she'd assured him that no, she wanted to, she liked "it," and this was what had sent him back to self-consciousness, this eagerness of hers to assure him that she liked what he didn't believe she possibly could have.

It embarrassed McAndrew now to think of himself—to think of her remembering him as—one of those men put off by a woman's eagerness to do the same thing they themselves were eager for.

"What's wrong?" she whispered when, all righteous indignation, he'd thrust her hand away and sat up. "You don't *want* me to?"

"It's not right," he said. "This just isn't right," wondering as he spoke where he'd learned to be such a prig.

"You mean, because of your vows?" she'd asked him.

"No! Not because of my vows! Or yes—I don't know."

His vows had scarcely entered his mind, he having made them in the spirit in which he'd done everything since the moment he entered the seminary: how far could he go and get away with it? How long before he was exposed as a fake?

There had been other opportunities to renege on his vows, but to date the potential complications—pragmatic and spiritual—had never seemed worth it.

"It's not right—between us—now—this way," he'd insisted.

"I don't believe you," she'd said.

Hadn't she encountered sexual repression before? he would have liked to ask her now. If I had it to do over again . . .

Though that was hardly the whole story either.

What did he imagine he would tell her? In the hope of—what? Of her absolving him of the sense of impotence he still carried with him from that time? And how did he envision this occurring? By the consummation that had not been achieved back then?

Though it wasn't sexual impotence, per se; not a question of performance. He could hardly say what it was. Was it that he knew, she'd made him know, that he'd missed his chance in life? He'd told himself that he didn't believe in missed chances; time turned chance into inevitability; and in any case could he really care how two people he hadn't seen in thirty years remembered him (or one person, since he wasn't sure he cared what Ned thought)?

It appeared that he did.

Though how could their thinking of him, one way or another, affect him now?

He might say that curiosity got the better of him: he wanted to hear the end of the story—though even this he thought he already knew. Compelled towards one another by the unresolved experience in their past, mysterious marks of which they could make no sense, Greta and Ned had remained together so that at least they could guard the memory, intact, within their intimacy, render its toxicity harmless by covering it over with new events, the way bees coated an invader, too heavy to remove from the hive, with a substance to contain its putrefaction. And he was culpable in this, wasn't he? He could have written to the boy. He might at least have apologized. Brother Dennis had let him know that Ned had come looking.

He had treated him badly, this McAndrew did not doubt; what he didn't understand was what in him still felt justified in having done so. Really, it was unconscionable. As a headmaster, he would have summarily dismissed any instructor who he learned had abused a student's trust as he had abused Ned's. So why was it, recalling the archbishop's inquest, his own consciousness of the real jury under the desk, did he still sympathize not only with his own adolescent pleasure in shocking a conservative superior but with his intention to twist the knife in the wound Ned had already suffered? Why had he sought Ned's confidence only in order to break faith with him? Taunted the boy with his mistrust while at the same time he strove to be sure he'd never trust anyone again . . . If he could answer that question . . . Had Ned any idea of the stakes involved?

McAndrew would have liked to think that it was the idea of showing Ned his hand (once he knew what he held) that enticed him as much as did the prospect of seeing how Margaret Sayre—Ned's Greta—had "turned out."

PART TWO

To reach Thrush Hollow, O. and his brother had to travel only from New Hampshire, where they were sojourning with friends in the White Mountains, but in 1865 it was a long trip: coach, train, and then, as Ned envisioned, horse and buggy out to the Hollow in the summer twilight. O. was so fatigued that he registered scarcely anything that first evening beyond the size of the house—so much grander and more elegantly furnished than his imagination had led him to expect—and the gracious manners of their host and Miss Dearborn, delicate and unstudied enough to suit even his already fastidious taste. The real thing, he said to himself, in his weariness not forcing himself to refine the epithet—or to note the similarity between his amorphous enthusiasm and that of his brother, S., of which he'd been scornful. "The man is . . . Captain Dearborn is . . . a man among men. You'll see." O. even found himself, as he drifted off to sleep, musing pleasantly upon the way Miss Dearborn had managed to be both present and unobtrusive at the same time, a quality he treasured but found rarely. Young women seemed in general to be trained to behave like butterflies: fluttering, showing their colors, flapping their wings . . .

He took himself to task in the morning. A maid brought hot water; he washed; he shaved, and stroking the renewed smoothness of his cheek stimulated thought. Already on the lookout for the sinister element in human intercourse, O. decided that exhaustion had rendered him vulnerable. The topics he had found himself thinking about, as he fell asleep . . . "A charming fellow," his brother had advertised Captain Dearborn to be, and charming fellows O. under any circumstances wished to avoid. *Charm* he defined as the capacity for reflecting back another person's deepest desires, spuriously owning the qualities the other had always sought, until, like Narcissus, the beholder leaned too far over the brink and drowned.

Perhaps the young lady was herself a "charming fellow"—like father, like daughter—and, as he descended the ample oak staircase on his way to breakfast, O. experienced a certain annoyance with Miss Dearborn, as if she had willfully deceived him, pretended to be something she wasn't. He meant to be cordial to her—naturally he would be cordial—but not forthcoming; he would not give her the access to his nature he felt he had somehow unwittingly permitted in his lassitude of the night before. He had accompanied his brother to visit a fellow veteran, that was all; in that role he could maintain himself for the duration of the visit, be agreeable but remain aloof, preoccupy himself with his reading, and observe.

At breakfast Miss Dearborn was nowhere to be seen. O. and his brother ate at a table with several other guests; Captain Dearborn stopped by briefly to greet them, bade them make themselves at home—he had to "see to things"—and then disappeared. O.'s brother seemed undisturbed. "He has a hotel to run," he said when O.'s raised eyebrows seemed to disparage Captain Dearborn's brevity. "He's a hard one to pin down," S. said cheerfully, as if Dearborn's slipperiness were a virtue. "And where is his daughter?" O. heard himself remark, in a disapproving tone.

"Miss Dearborn is indisposed," replied the young woman at that moment replenishing their supply of toast, and O. was now doubly mortified, both to be feeling such irritation over nothing and to have made his feeling public. Why not shout from the rooftop? The entire population of servants and guests would all soon no doubt be apprised of the fact that the elder Mr. O. had commented upon Miss Dearborn's absence at breakfast.

Another guest at the table—a weary-looking gentleman who repeatedly lifted a lorgnette to his eyes only to lay it down impatiently as if dissatisfied by what he had seen—offered rather querulously, "It is a most unusual circumstance. Miss Dearborn has never yet been unwell." O. politely expressed a wish that the indisposition should prove of short duration, but when he and S. were finally alone, O. vented his distress upon the maid. "Imagine answering something overheard like that! Clearly the Dearborns' civility doesn't extend to their servants!"

His brother, used to O.'s inexplicable moods—the family tolerated them by labelling them inexplicable—said, "Do come on. Let's go for a tramp." They set off through the shapely hills and valleys, an effort which ordinarily would have restored O. to good humor, but which now seemed instead to propel his mind along its same relentless track. Why was Miss Dearborn "indisposed"? She had seemed hale and hearty enough the night before. Had he unknowingly offended her in some way? Had his brother?

O. burned with the desire to ask S., now that S. had made the fabled Miss Dearborn's acquaintance, if she lived up to his expectations. Had S. been hoping that his friend the captain might consider *him* "good enough" for his daughter? (Reputedly, no one "up to snuff" had yet been found.)

But O. had of course never spoken to his brother about such things in his life (or to anyone else, except as a matter of speculative interest), and his tongue would have cloven to the roof of his mouth had he attempted to utter such words with it. What most humiliated him was his recognition of the reason he wanted to utter them. If his brother liked Miss Dearborn, then Miss Dearborn could not possibly be the sort of person in whom O. himself could feel any interest. His taste and his brother's had nothing in common; his brother was one of those young men for whom young women performed their butterfly dance. S. appreciated it. O. wished that he could lay the matter to rest. He had other things to occupy his mind, such as the plotting of the tale he had meant to weave about Miss Dearborn and her father. Why had a man so apparently well-educated and cultivated chosen to remove himself from his own kind— to live, as S. had put it (quoting Dearborn, O. supposed), as an exile in his own land? What did Dearborn apprehend about his fellows or what, conversely, did he fear they might apprehend about him? And how, in such isolation, had he, a widower, raised such a seemingly *finished* daughter? O. would like to fix her personality in his mind so that he could forge ahead with her development as a character.

But she was avoiding him! This seemed translucently self-evident. Then, in the next moment, his head ached at the absurdity of the notion. At its presumption. Who was he, to her, that she should avoid him?

She must have felt what he had, that was the only explanation. He couldn't doubt it. She had been as transported—and then as unsettled— by their meeting as he had been. She had seen in him what he had in her and was as afraid as he was to acknowledge it. It could so disrupt both of their lives.

But *what* had he seen in her? A brief exchange of pleasantries, a courteous goodnight—that had been all; whence arose these fantastic musings, this rush of the blood? Where was his thinking mind? Had he left it behind, in New Hampshire? Or farther back, in Boston? If only he could be *abroad,* as so many of his friends were lucky enough to be, then he would be able to see clearly, he would keep on an even keel. History would provide ballast. Yes, it was the fault of this blasted continent, reeking with promise. He had always suspected that it would deliver him to such a morass, infected as it was with hope and yearning like the darker continents with typhoid and malaria. You lived here and you *wanted* something. You breathed in youth. Contemplation went out the window. *There,* you absorbed the moderating wisdom of centuries of civilization from the very cobblestones, the atmosphere like a tonic to the nervous sensibility, reassuring one that one didn't have to do everything in one's own lifetime. It had all been done before and would be done again afterwards; one could lay down the burden of aspiration and know that others would carry it. One could simply live one's life.

But not so *here,* not in this infernally ambitious young nation, always *becoming,* everyone wanting everything and wanting it right now; everything that everyone over the whole dispiriting march of history had wanted and never had, every single one of them—of us, O. forced himself to amend—meant to have. No time like the present, that was the motto.

He didn't want to *want.* It was simple. That was what he would travel to get away from. Or he wanted to want those things he could *have:* agreeable surroundings, stimulating conversation, the time to write books. He preferred to observe. He didn't want this mania of the blood, this madness for more, this passion to realize dreams, which anyone with half a mind would know could never be satisfied by another *person,* and he wouldn't pretend, he refused! It was what other people did: married for love and settled into companionship. Revised their estimates of what was possible according to what they got. He wouldn't stoop to it.

O. looked at his brother, striding along beside him. He felt that he had been shouting aloud, but S. paced off the countryside as if the world were still the undisturbed place it had been less than twenty-four hours ago, when all such ideas as now clamored in O.'s mind had been abstractions. They were heading into woods; the track had narrowed and soon they were forced to walk single file. Neither knew where the path led. O. was usually particular about walks; he preferred to have a destination in mind, which, if possible, he could approach from one direction and return from by another. He didn't like to waste time looking at things twice until he had settled it that a site merited a return visit. Of course there were many things he would never tire of looking at, but there were also many things to be seen, and one should economize as much as possible in order to take the riches in. However, at this moment, O. did not concern himself with where they were going. He was wondering if Miss Dearborn often walked this way, and if there might not be a chance of their encountering her (her being "indisposed" did not necessarily imply that she was confined to bed), or, if not, if he might not become better acquainted with her by studying the surroundings in which she lived.

Rampant nonsense! Rubbish! Folderol! She was not a botanical specimen whose nature might be gleaned by investigation of the soil in which it flourished! Nor a woodland creature, to be stalked before capture. He didn't *know* her. He couldn't know her any better by observing the birch trees and pondering the fact that she strolled among them. Wildflowers grew in patches of sun: purple asters and blue chicory. She must, occasionally, pluck them. Did she weave them into her hair? Her burnished gold hair? Her nut-brown hair? The devil take it, what color was it?

Groaning aloud, O. sped up his pace. If he could not stop the frenzied activity of his mind, perhaps he could outrun it. Truly, his mind was as disordered as that of any of the hotel's patients who sought water cures for nervous ailments. He had encountered the species before now, having spent time himself in such establishments, seeking a reprieve from his eternal costiveness. Such water treatments as he had undergone had not proven noticeably successful, however, but perhaps Miss Dearborn might prescribe a different regimen. The cure might not lie in the prescription but in the prescriber. . . .

"I cannot concentrate!" he exclaimed. "I simply cannot keep my mind on the walk. I beg of you, let us turn back!"

S., startled, remonstrated mildly that a walk was not generally thought to require concentration, but he humored his brother. He shared the family view of O.: talented but in such an unspecific way that it seemed unlikely he would ever amount to anything. But this did not make him any less a beloved brother.

After half an hour's walk, they reapproached the hotel and climbed the steps to the veranda. Instead of entering through the side parlor whence they had exited, however, they circled around to the front so that, while they cooled themselves in wicker rocking chairs, they might admire the view. The gentle hills overlapping reminded O., as a century later they would another witness, of the downy scales inside a milkweed pod, which O. had stroked, wondering at their silkiness, at nature's reason for making them so soft, before he had pried them apart.

Lucinda Dearborn emerged onto the porch, carrying a tray on which stood a pitcher and several glasses, and asked if they cared to partake of lemonade. She had spied them returning, she said, and had anticipated their thirst.

Spied us from where? O. wondered. Had she been waiting, watching from her bedroom window? He could scarcely ask her where her bedroom was. But already his mind was relaxing out of its relentless self-analysis.

When it became clear that Miss Dearborn meant to share in their refreshment—she poured the lemonade and then drew a chair forward to form the third point of a wide-angled triangle with theirs—an infinite calm settled upon O. He wished to say, Don't ever leave my sight again, but since he could not say that, anything else was superfluous. However, it seemed that for now he might sit quietly, listening to his brother extoll Captain Dearborn's virtues as a commander and regret the fact that civilian life provided no opportunity for him to exercise them. "What a world it is," S. offered, "in which this should be the case."

What a lovely face the girl had, O. thought—her loveliness was unlooked for. All morning, he had been unable to recall the color of her hair or eyes, whether she was slender or robust. It hadn't mattered to him, but that she was sweet to gaze upon seemed an extra gift. But gift to whom? Did he mean to him?

For now, he could let such questions founder. He couldn't understand what had sent him into such a paroxysm of speculation on his walk. He'd contemplated instantaneous flight abroad. He'd blamed his native land for the fever of his blood. Now his blood flowed as coolly as a mountain brook. Lucinda Dearborn was an agreeable, kind, and intelligent young woman; O. felt as easy in her company as he did in his sister's. He had been imagining her vast, limitless, the world contained in her, but she was simply a nicely bred young woman wearing a modest, pretty dress, reclining in a wicker rocking chair sipping lemonade.

Then Captain Dearborn saluted S. from the lawn. "Corporal!" he called. "Croquet! Side lawn! Lickety-split!"

S. sprang to his feet, returned Dearborn's salute, and bolted down the front steps. Rufus Dearborn took his arm and, confabulating, they strode off. A cautionary sight, O. reflected: a person smitten. He would not wish to resemble such a person.

"You were unwell this morning," he said in a low voice to Lucinda, as if he had been waiting for the opportunity to speak. He was mortified to hear his confiding tone.

"I didn't sleep well," she said. "I lingered in bed awhile."

"I know what it is not to sleep," he said.

"I rarely do," Lucinda answered.

This response left O. more certain than ever that he had been the cause of her sleeplessness, and his briefly dissipated restlessness returned full force, and, with it, his irritation. Why could they not simply *discuss* whatever was befalling them—isolate it from themselves like someone quarantined with an infectious illness? If they could simply acknowledge that they had fallen victim to a spell, which had nothing to do with them as individuals—somehow a force of nature, or of history, had seized upon them and meant to work itself out through them. . . . Meant to make them do what? What force of nature? What did he mean? He needed Lucinda at his side to protect him from all the *space* that he had suddenly realized was all around him.

"Would you like, perhaps, to see how I pass my time?" she asked.

O. almost expected her to take him by the hand, he felt that hypno-tized. Did she mean to offer him one of her cures; did she perhaps think that it was in hope of one that he had come? What had his brother writ-ten to her father about him?

O. felt tongue-tied, a rare circumstance for him. You must think me very dull, he thought of saying. I am not usually like this. But what was he like? He had no idea, really. A young man who liked to read and think and converse about his reading and thinking with others who liked to do the same. Who longed to travel, to leave the glitter of the mind's life at home for its more constant gleam abroad. Who had no means of making himself a living. What had he to offer her?

Lucinda led him through the dining room and along a narrow hallway which skirted the kitchen and then turned twice before continuing on past three shut doorways on either side. She flung them open, one after another.

"No one's here now," she said. "The morning treatments are over. They take place between nine and eleven. The afternoon treatment is between three and five, but I prefer those to take place outside unless the weather is inclement. We have the pond, as you may have seen, and a brook."

"Then the afternoon treatments must of necessity employ cold water," O. said. "I should think that your patients might find you a rigorous physician."

Lucinda shrugged. "My patients would step off a cliff if I told them to. They have that much faith in my curative powers."

"You deem their faith misplaced?" O. asked.

"Oh, misplaced . . ."

O. couldn't be sure if she was impatient with him or with her credulous patients.

"What is it, precisely, that you do to them?" he asked.

"Precisely?"

They had entered one of the treatment rooms, furnished with a variety of tubs and hoses and pitchers with whose uses O. was familiar, and she turned to look at him. When she spoke, it was with a kind of indifference that told him she had no expectation of being believed.

"I return them to the source," she said. "To wherever the water comes from. I claim no understanding of the procedure, yet repeatedly I have observed a serenity and freedom from whatever troubles my patients replacing the anxiety and suffering so evident before treatment. The look I see in their eyes is of a person remembering something."

When O. said nothing and seemed to be merely sympathetically listening, she went on. "The baths were Father's idea—he said that we required something to distinguish Thrush Hollow from the many other resort hotels. Not only are we not by the seashore, the most popular location, we haven't even a lake to boast of. 'We have the brook!' I proclaimed, pleasanting—I was young—and he said, 'My dear, you've hit upon it! Cold water baths! We'll take their money so that they may sit beneath our country waterfall and be cured of their city ills. They'll flock to stand in line—believe me. I know human nature.' I laughed at him, but he refused to be dissuaded. He set off to make inquiries, and then he purchased bathing equipment from a gentleman in New York State and brought it home along with a pamphlet. *Hydrotherapy—Its Uses and Rationale.* This was before the war—all the equipment was installed—

but then Father went off to fight. The hotel was closed, so I could practice only upon myself and the servants. Eventually people in Stilling came to try my cures."

She paused.

"Pray continue," O. said.

"From the first I have been fascinated by the method, although the book's instruction is of the scantest. Recently a bookseller found for me a copy of Bell's treatise on baths, which I found of great interest, such as his assertion that although bathing can be considered the gratification of an instinct common to all living nature, modern civilization is far behind the ancient ones in its application. Most interestingly, he has observed that in the Anglo-Saxon branch of the great human family, a hydrophobic tendency is manifest in nearly all classes. Yet I have had to divine for myself when to apply the various techniques—though I will confess to you that I have not found it difficult. I sense, though I do not know by what mechanism, when a patient must recline, when sit, when stand; whether a running bath, a still bath, or a douche is to be employed; whether hot or cold or tepid; whether rest afterwards be called for or vigorous activity; when sponge baths or friction; when drinking and of hot or cold. Many are the variations and combinations, but rarely have I failed to prescribe the correct one. Father thinks it all nonsense—his opinion influenced, I expect, by the rather underhanded manner in which he put the spa into operation; he attributes all the cures to the fact that, as he says, I am pretty and my hands are gentle. I could apply milkweed juice and burdocks and the guests would pronounce my ministrations a miracle, he claims. Efficacy of any medicine resides in faith in the practitioner, according to him. But he's mistaken. Many of the patients are skeptics themselves before they undergo treatment. It is true I have never treated anyone with a severe illness except for Mrs. Draper's baby when she had the whooping cough and the doctor could not be found, and Mrs. Draper tells everyone I saved the little girl's life, but many of my patients have suffered greatly from chronic complaints, and I have not only been able to help most of them but to instruct them in remedies they can employ at home.

"Father may think what he likes, but it stands to reason that water comes from somewhere; it is not manufactured inside the pipes that transport it to us so magically through the walls. The brook comes from somewhere; our spring arises from a source unknown to us. Everyone must have a place to return to, or one can have no knowledge of home; thus it is also with the body. If we are not at home in it, we cannot be well. The vital essences come out of balance, too much blood flows in one place and not another. Running water over an afflicted part suggests to the blood how it should run when it has forgotten. This is no witchery; it is simple sense."

She finished speaking and looked at O., waiting for him to say something—something disparaging, she seemed to expect. He said only, "You evidently possess a talent." He had almost said, Water cures have never brought me any relief, but stopped himself for fear she would ask him to elaborate or, worse, construe his remark as an invitation to try her hand.

". . . a most effective cure for headache," she was saying. "To hold the hands in warm water. It draws the blood down from the head. Come," she said, "let me show you."

O. protested that he didn't suffer from headache at present, but Lucinda assured him that he would feel the effect nonetheless. He was polite, she said, but she could tell that he was not a believer.

"The fires will be out but the water should still be warm enough," she said, as she turned a faucet and held her wrist beneath the stream; then she stopped the drain and let the basin fill. She invited O. to sit on a stool before it and as soon as he was seated she positioned herself behind him and took hold of his hands, encircling his wrists and half of his palms; she lowered them into the water, forcing him to bend forward slightly.

He glanced at her, astonished. "What have you put into it?"

"Into the water? Why, nothing."

"Then what—?"

She released his hands and pressed her wet palms to the sides of his head, covering his temples. Now she was the one surprised, inhaling suddenly, as if afraid, though she didn't remove her hands. O. thought she'd whispered something, but he couldn't be sure. Still leaning forward, pressing his fingers against the bowl of the basin for support, he turned to look at her, forcing her to let go of his head.

"It's your hands, isn't it? There's something in your hands."

"I drew your blood to them," she said matter-of-factly, turning away. "I speed up the action of the water, that's all."

"No, I don't think that's all," O. said.

"Turn back," she said. "Keep your hands immersed in the basin," and he obeyed, feeling her hands this time before she touched him, a perturbation in the air about his head. Though their approach took no time at all, it was enough time for him to fear that they would not reach their destination.

Sighing, he closed his eyes; having heard his sigh, he self-consciously opened them, then closed them again.

Don't take away your hands, he wanted to beg her. Please don't ever take away your hands. But how could he say that?

Something passed between her palms, which she'd positioned again over his temples, or something in him moved to meet her. Had it been there all along?

I never want to open my eyes, he thought. I never want to open them again.

People must not know about this, he thought. If it were known about, why would they carry on as they do?

What did he mean by that?

"You fight me," Lucinda said softly. "You persevere in your resistance."

"Resistance!" O. exclaimed, opening his eyes. *This* you call resistance? What more could you expect to occur?"

Lucinda had withdrawn her hands. "You have seen," she said, nearly inaudibly.

Her technique, did she mean? What else?

He attempted to question her—how did she gauge resistance? how overcome it?—but she seemed reluctant to discuss her "method" now. She took a small white towel from a shelf and gave it to him. As O. dried his hands, he felt conscious of being alone with her in a way he had not since S. had left them. It seemed an intimate action, suddenly: to dry oneself, and he turned away, afraid that Lucinda would see his face flush.

Who was she—*what* was she? She was hardly simply a woman—a discrete being. It was as if she were not yet detached from whatever had brought her into being, like Venus in parturition from sea-foam. It seemed to O. that something vast resided in her, or that through her something vast could be reached.

"What is it?" she asked. "Did I frighten you?"

"Frighten me?" O. repeated.

Lucinda gave him a pained smile and turned away. O. despised himself at once for his disingenuousness, but Lucinda had already opened the door and, without giving him a chance to say another word, led the way back to the veranda. The bell had been rung for the midday meal and guests were climbing the front steps, some looking hot and dishevelled, evidently from their exertions during the croquet match. O.'s brother and Lucinda's father arrived and they all entered the dining room; O. and S. sat with Captain Dearborn and Lucinda at what was termed the "captain's table"—"captain" now taking on a nautical connotation which O. later on, in his letters, would expand to apply to all of Thrush Hollow. The time, he would write, had felt like that aboard ship: a company one delighted in while knowing that its assembly was inevitably temporary (he having no idea—or choosing not to censor himself if he had—how his attempt to make his time with Lucinda seem destined for conclusion would wound his correspondent).

But that was still to come. In O.'s mind it seemed, if not that all things were possible, at least that all things were not impossible. During the meal and throughout the afternoon and evening, he let himself sink into the sweetness that Lucinda's presence bestowed, particularly when the burden of rising to speech did not fall solely on him but was shared by his brother and Lucinda's father. Whenever she went away, it was as if a cold wind blew through the room, and he sat up, felt awake, and felt alone. He needed to tell her something, to apologize in some way for his moral cowardice of the morning in not having met her question head-on—I could think only of all that my answer might entail, he wished to say to her, if I said either yes or no. Yes would have been the truth, but to admit it . . . where might that have led us? However, to deny it, while, for one, being dishonest, has also landed us in a certainty of closer relation to come, if only so that I may exculpate myself. I thought that perhaps you wished me to lie. He wanted to tell her that he was not, at base, a coward, but that bravery required that one understand what was being asked of one.

That evening, alone again in his room, O. continued to take himself to task. With what was he faced? Was he being offered a great chance—or a temptation?

He loathed *striving*. It was so American—with all that he was coming disapprovingly to mean by that. He had thought of sex (when he had thought of it) as synonymous with the urge to transform oneself. To travel somewhere, using another human being as one's mode of transport. That many people colluded, even delightedly, in this employment of each other did not, in O.'s mind, make it any the less pernicious. Sometimes, however, he had imagined a sexuality not apart from the rest of life, but, rather, mixed into it, one not requiring one to step into a *role* in order to prosecute the satisfaction of one's desire. Satisfaction itself would not be an end but a beginning. He had imagined this, but it had been a fancy of dreams, in which one moved through all dimensions effortlessly; he hadn't believed it could exist.

Now, all in one day, it seemed to him that it lay before him; before him or all around him. He did not perceive Lucinda as distinct from the narrow green-clad valley in which she abode; she was a dryad, a creature not solely human although possessed of human form. He had observed the way that the other guests responded to her, the effect of her presence on them. They quieted, as if to hear a faint music, not the ethereal harp but Pan's pipe, sound blown through wood, not plucked from metal. He had heard them say to her, "Should I try the hot pack next?" and "Will you keep me on the running bath?" "My bowels have moved," one confided in a whisper, and Lucinda seemed to keep all the cases in order without difficulty, even though the details were not the point. They wanted to talk to her, O. could tell, to hear her voice, to feel her hand laid upon their hands. Their eyes followed her as she passed through a room with the adoration of a dog regarding its master. O. had noticed Lucinda's father, the captain (a bogus title, O. felt; why should what befell a man in war eclipse his previous identity?), as he sat in a wing chair in a corner, a newspaper open in his lap, unread; instead Dearborn watched his daughter with a kind of sardonic incredulity: wishing, so it seemed to O., to scoff at her ministrations but unable to deny the power she held over her patients. Dearborn had instituted the "water cures" cynically, as a way to pump up his business; according to S., he had been astonished to find that while he was away down South, fighting to keep the Union intact, his daughter had become a priestess of the waters.

O. has been standing just inside the doorway to his room. The door is shut behind him. He has been thinking, with his usual half-conscious distaste, of the sexual act: so animal, so removed from the life of the mind and spirit and appreciating senses which he leads. When he has permitted himself, after the marriage of one or another of his friends, to imagine what would occur on the nuptial night and—one presumed—on other nights thereafter, he balked at the moment of following them beneath the bedcovers, instead retreating back into less perilous thoughts quite as if he had actually entered a bedchamber unwittingly and were now backing out, apologizing for having mistaken the room.

But now he finds, to his amazement, that in thinking of Lucinda he does not back out. He goes into the room and sees her lying beneath the covers waiting for him. This should be enough, should startle or frighten him, but it does not. It seems the most natural thing in the world. He sees her smile and hold out her arms to him, hears her call his name out softly. He speaks an endearment in return.

O. is in his room; he doesn't realize that he has spoken aloud. It is night; he is preparing for bed; the curtains are drawn. He does not, however, see the bedroom at Thrush Hollow in which he actually stands, with the exception of those aspects of it that three-dimensionally furnish the two-dimensional images of his meditation.

My love, he says, and goes to the bed and sits down beside her. He strokes her bright hair as it lies, seraph-like, rippling across the pillow. She is the angel of his dreams, but she is not angelic.

Come to me, she says. She lifts her white arms from beneath the eiderdown: no nightdress. Of course not. Not for her the awkward fumbling and lifting. She is not afraid and neither is he, though they are both shy of the magnitude of their feeling, of this immeasurable new world upon whose shores they have disembarked. They can go anywhere in it. They may stake a claim, then espy a more tempting vista and go there. There is nothing whatsoever to be afraid of in all this vast space.

Lucinda unbuttons his waistcoat; he shrugs out of it. She commences the unfastening; he completes it. Soon his clothes are strewn untidily everywhere. He is so white; there is so much of him. Such a great distance of untouched flesh, from his chest to his ankles. Halfway, his genitals lie in his lap, like another person he hadn't known was present. He feels friendly towards them; it is a new feeling. He has always tried to avoid looking at them, but now cups his soft penis in his hand and thinks how soft it is, asking for nothing, and then it is her hand and it stiffens. How amazing this seems; how ingenious. It has a life of its own, but it is suddenly his life.

O. is now lying, nude, on the four-poster bed in Thrush Hollow's northeasternmost guestroom, pressing his lips into the pillow. It is warm in the room; it is an August evening, just barely night though it's late, and a delicate breeze rustles the flounced curtain at the open window. Though in his mind O. joins Lucinda beneath the covers, in the room he is hot and remains on top of them. He moves against her, against the bed, pushes himself into it, murmuring, his hands in her hair, her hands—where are her hands? He can't think. Their domain is infinite;

no wonder he can't see them. He remembers how, that morning, he felt his blood straining first in his wrists and then at his temples to mingle with her blood but then he was afraid; he resisted her; but now he doesn't, and he feels whatever it is flow out of him and into her and out of her and into him, a heat and aliveness that moves down from his head and neck and makes him conscious of a life that must have been in him all along but concealed from him until this moment. He feels it all through him, radiating across his chest and along his arms and down his back and legs and centering in his groin, and he knows that the thing to do is to give into it and he approaches the verge, he almost goes over it, but then perhaps a consciousness of where he is (he might soil the bed) or perhaps a wish to wait for her (it would be an infidelity to travel to this unknown destination without her) overcomes him and he lets out the breath he's been holding, leans over to blow out the bedside lamp, and lays himself back down, this time under the covers.

Lucinda would have preferred not to stay awake to greet their late-arriving guests, but her father had insisted. They were not just anyone, paying boarders whom the housekeeper could show to their rooms. She wasn't ill, was she? If not, why so reluctant to be up a little late?

Lucinda couldn't explain it. Her father would have laughed if she said she'd been overtaken by an unfamiliar sensation of ice distributed along her veins, impeding the flow of blood back to her heart, ever since, several days earlier, her father had told her that his former corporal would bring his elder brother along when he paid a visit.

"*Why* will he bring him?" Lucinda had exclaimed, surprising herself as well as her father with her vehemence.

"Why ever not?" Rufus Dearborn asked. "I should imagine because he believed it would bring pleasure to all concerned."

"It will bring no pleasure to me," Lucinda stated.

"Daughter, are you daft? What evil do you know of my soldier's brother?"

"I know nothing," Lucinda said. "We're very busy. We haven't the room."

"Nonsense," her father said. "It's a slow season. Half the ell stands vacant. Come, come, Lucinda, do you fear I'm wishing to marry you off? You know I've told you the decision is to be your own. Do you not believe me?"

"I don't know what I believe!" Lucinda exclaimed. "Please excuse me, Father, it's time for the morning treatments."

"Are you certain you're well enough?"

"Why would you make such an inquiry? I'm not ill!"

"No," her father said under his breath, as she flounced out of the room, "but as capricious as a mettlesome mare."

These "water cures" had brought it on, he didn't doubt, and he wished he'd never conceived the cursed notion—but how could he have anticipated that his impressionable daughter would betroth herself to the idea? He'd had no idea that she *was* impressionable! He had thought of taking the waters as another craze, an entertainment for the boarders along the lines of the bowling alley and the badminton court. Cures were all the rage, even if no one seemed to know quite what was to be cured. Now here was his Lucinda, ensconced among the gewgaws like a sibyl, like an interpretess at Delphi, translating the gurgling of the waters. He would think she'd gone mad—she *sounded* mad sometimes, the way she preached deliverance—were it not for the fact that she'd collected a congregation. Her own little flock of the faithful. They even came to *him* with their testimonials. Mr. Trevalyan, Mrs. Kingsbury—longtime paying guests, people whose perspicacity he held in respect. "I must tell you what a mighty alteration your daughter has made in my life . . ." "I don't recognize myself . . ." "How proud you must be to discover her possessed of such a gift . . ."

No, that proved nothing—that she had followers. They were daft, the lot of them. You didn't cure advanced dyspepsia and gout by dribbling water over the afflicted part! If such were the case, everyone in Christendom would be doing it. Yes, it was a time-honored method, he knew; Pliny discoursed upon the virtues of water; before him, the Greeks possessed their rhabdomancers—but what did that prove? The credulous strain in human nature had ever been in evidence. Alas, it was now his misfortune to witness his own daughter's immersion in it.

He blamed her being without a mother for her susceptibility. Always he had feared the effect on her of growing up without that necessary maternal influence. The nursemaids, nannies, governesses whom he had employed since poor dear Emily had been carried off by consumption when Lucinda was still but a babe in arms, however fond of the little girl they might have been, could never teach her what her own mother would have. Rufus Dearborn was convinced of this, though what it was that Lucinda's mother would have taught her he had no idea. That was the point; he couldn't do it. Lucinda's apparent complete lack of interest in any of the young men who seemed eager to be her suitors he also ascribed to her motherlessness. He had let her go too much her own way. He hadn't insisted that she acquire the social graces or learn to play the coquette—though somehow she had developed innate good manners; the grande dames from Boston were always complimenting him upon them and wondering how, in this out-of-the-way place, she had come by them. They beset him with invitations to send Lucinda to them for the winter; they would "bring her out," introduce her to society, but he had always refused. Perhaps he had been wrong, he thought now, been too careful of her. He'd told her, when she was of an age to question him, that he'd left his life as a "city gentleman" because he was tired of hearing people say things they didn't mean, of himself saying one thing and doing another. He hadn't belabored the idea, having made the remark offhandedly, for one thing, to stand in for a more penetrating analysis of his motives, a more specific explanation of his wish to withdraw from the course he sensed the nation embarked upon, but somehow his comment had taken root in Lucinda's own mind and flourished; she seemed to regard the world beyond Stilling as a great swamp of iniquity, and a descent into the social whirl of Boston or New York as a plunge into the murk of the underworld. The inhabitants of such places, to her mind, were forked-tongued, two-faced scoundrels, and the fact that the majority of the Hollow's guests came from these citadels of perversion— people whose company she enjoyed—did nothing to convince her to the contrary. They were the exceptions that proved the rule, the ones still possessed of enough moral vigor to escape to Stilling, where the hearts of the inhabitants, like the air, had remained pure.

He would have to persuade Lucinda to accept one of the winter invitations. He must convince her that he had exaggerated his dislike of cities and civilization—after all, he had fled under the cloud of her mother's death, thinking that if only they'd lived in the country instead of in town, as Emily had wished, she would not have contracted the deadly disease. What turned his stomach a little was his understanding of the society matrons' desire to show Lucinda off. They wished to produce her, like a genie, with a clap of the hands. They knew the effect she would have. She was not simply another pretty girl. It was the combination of her delicate, almost antiquated manners and her outspokenness that delighted people even as it startled them. The most outrageous remarks fell from her dainty lips. For, though she had somehow, almost supernaturally, learned ways of carrying and conducting herself that would not have been out of place in an old-world court, she had no sense whatsoever of what it was proper and not proper to talk about. The fact that she was instinctively kind might prevent her from saying things that she knew would hurt people—she never told a hideous old woman that she was ugly or taunted someone who spoke with a lisp—but did not prevent her from uttering what might mortify them with embarrassment. "My, how terribly ill you look this morning!" she might offer to a guest who everyone knew had been drinking far more brandy than was good for him the night before. "Does everyone in Boston converse as frivolously as yourself?" Captain Dearborn—and a collection of assembled guests—had overheard Lucinda say (with sincere curiosity) to a young gentleman from that venue who was currying her favor.

Rufus Dearborn would have thought his daughter's character formed by no influences other than those most evident—her half-orphaned state, her relative isolation from sophisticated society, her inheritance of his own distaste for cant—were it not for her seeming to know things and behaving in ways that could not be explained by any of these factors or their absence. Yet he preferred not to ponder the topic further—he was in danger of becoming as much of a gudgeon as she was.

Lucinda, meanwhile, had gone about her business. She did not, it was true, feel much like devoting herself to her patients at the moment; she was still too unsettled by the perturbation her father's news had set up in her, and she would have liked right then to strike out across the back meadow and through the birch glade to the spot in the brook where for many years she had practiced her own private water cures, not calling them that, kneeling in a tiny pool beneath the narrow waterfall that chased itself over the lichen-whitened ledge, so that the water fell over her neck and shoulders—did it notice that it struck flesh, not rock? she wondered—this mysterious aliveness, the only animate substance one could see through? It must, she thought; the way it hurried so to get wherever it was going, she only a further obstruction. Everything in the world was in its way; it was perpetual impatience, which must be why to contemplate its rushing past so soothed human beings. For once they could abandon their haste. *Destination,* urged the blood. *Why are you waiting?* But no one knew the destination.

When her father had come home, one day not long before he enlisted, with a wagonload of bathing apparatus and told her they were now to advertise themselves as a spa, she had thought it foolish, though no more so than advertising such things as "sweet-scented meadows, the music of songbirds, the soothing sight of mountains fading to blue in the distance," as Thrush Hollow's brochure promised. That people were so benighted as to live where they could not take these things for granted she supposed was a fact, so therefore they must also need to pay money to have water poured over them. The process whereby cures were effected by these various methods did not seem outlandish to her, however. She wouldn't have described water's working in the language of the pamphlet her father gave her; she thought its discoursing upon the permeability of the skin and the skin's communication with the internal organs a trifle showy, a fancy phrasing of the obvious; but if such language were needed to convince people, then let them abide by it. She didn't need to refer to the instructions to know what temperature the water had to be or what form its application should take for the various complaints people brought to her—still or running bath, douche, vapor bath, poultice. . . . To know that in ill health the blood's flow was impeded and needed to be drawn in one direction or another was no more mysterious to her than the fact that apple boughs underwent a pull towards water when she held them, a fact she'd discovered quite by accident, playing when young, learning only later that the practice had a name and a purpose. The only thing that really sometimes astonished Lucinda about her skill was the seeming incapacity of other people to practice it. To her mind they simply had not tried; it was as if they had sat all their lives in a chair and without having once stood on their legs complained that they could not walk.

She hadn't *known,* before she'd laid her hands on Mrs. Kingsbury's shoulders, that she would feel a near-scalding heat flow into her hands and up her arms, and the surprise of it almost caused her to cry out; as if she'd burned herself she instinctively pulled back her hands, but that didn't mean her newfound ability to diagnose the source of people's ailments struck her as anything outside of the ordinary course of events. She was sure there were other skills she possessed—that everyone possessed—if only they thought to practice them.

"What is it?" had exclaimed Mrs. Kingsbury. "Lucinda, have you hurt yourself?"

"I!" Lucinda exclaimed. "You have a raging fever! No wonder you complain of fatigue. I'm astonished that you manage to sit erect."

"I? A fever? Why, you're dreaming, child." Mrs. Kingsbury laid a hand on her forehead. "I'm as cool as ice cream."

Lucinda felt Mrs. Kingsbury's forehead as well; it was true.

"But just now . . ." Lucinda rested her hands on Mrs. Kingsbury's shoulders again. The same heat as before, but this time Lucinda forced herself to keep her hands there, and found that in fact, though the temperature was fiery, she was not burned. As before, the heat migrated up her hands, but now the two rivulets met at her neck and radiated across her chest; the heat wanted to travel down into her belly and then dissipate along her legs—she could feel whatever pathways carried the current all alert with expectation, but the flow did not come. There was some blockage. Instinctively, Lucinda laid a hand just below her rib cage; she felt a throbbing there, as if a wave were continually cresting and then receding. She knelt beside Mrs. Kingsbury and laid her other hand in the same place on Mrs. Kingsbury's abdomen.

"Is this where it troubles you?" she asked.

"Why, yes, it seems, now that you mention it, that's just where . . . But how did you know? Why, good heavens, your hand is on fire!"

"It's you who are," Lucinda said. "I'm drawing off your heat."

"How pleasant your hand feels there!" Mrs. Kingsbury exclaimed, laying her own plump, many-ringed fingers upon it. "It feels . . . I feel as if . . . The pain is moving away from you! It's trying to escape your hand!" Her startled eyes looked into Lucinda's. "Can you feel it?"

"Yes," Lucinda said, surprised too, until she recalled what it felt like to divine, how the tug increased or diminished depending on her proximity to water. Something similar was at work here. Whatever in her blood responded to the element of water responded as well to other people's blood. Maybe to the water in their blood. It didn't matter to know what. It mattered to know how to do it.

Now she felt confident. She laid her other hand beside the first and with both exerted a gentle pressure on the knot she felt inside. She moved her hands here and there, following the congestion as it tried to lodge in an untouched place. Then she felt it begin to break apart, like a hard lump of sugar in a pan of milk beginning to dissolve.

"Oh, my!" Mrs. Kingsbury exclaimed.

"Yes, it's dispersing," Lucinda said.

"It's going—it's travelling—I feel so peculiar!"

"There," Lucinda said, lifting her hands. Mrs. Kingsbury grabbed them.

"Please, no! It will come back! Oh, I'm free of it, free! For the first time in so long . . . I didn't realize." In gratitude and relief she began to sob.

"It won't come back," Lucinda said. "Not right away. I think I can teach you how to treat it yourself."

"But my hands don't . . ."

"With water," Lucinda said. "Applications of water. First heat, to draw the illness there; then cold compresses on your stomach and hot running water on your hands to draw it off—I will have to ponder it . . ."

This was the practice Lucinda had followed: placing her hands on her patients' shoulders or temples, locating the source of their blockage or discerning the temper of their blood, then prescribing appropriate water treatment. She had found that to have them immerse their hands in water while she conducted her exploration hastened her diagnosis, as if the disorder inside them could be healed only by reestablishing the broken connection between their circulation and that inside the earth. Sometimes she was able, as with Mrs. Kingsbury, to effect immediate relief; at other times more stringent measures were required. Illness was cunning; like a wounded animal, it shrank into a corner and would attack if threatened; its aim was to preserve itself, regardless of the harm to the body it fed upon. As from Mrs. Kingsbury's, sometimes it tried to escape into Lucinda's body; understanding this after that first unexpected attack, she knew, had made her less receptive to such assaults later on. It explained her greater or lesser success in dispelling an illness at first try. She had to maintain her impressionability, and this was something her own body naturally resisted. She had to pacify her own blood with the promise of cleansing later on; respite beneath the waterfall had never failed to purify her. The water washed her free of all impurities; it raced off with them, battered them against the brook's stones until they evaporated in a spume of bubbles.

This was why she wished, on hearing her father's news, to hasten to the brook to restore herself. She felt just as if she had laid her hands on a sick patient and absorbed his impurities, but she had of course touched no one, spoken to no one. Sometimes the valencies and accents in a guest's voice were symptoms that already worked in her towards a diagnosis before she ever laid hands on them, but she had never prognosticated in the absence of a physical being. She had never heard of this young man—"who we hope will amount to something, someday," as his brother had written, "though none of us is quite sure what"—why should she feel such alarm coursing through her? Yet that he was the source,

Lucinda was not in doubt. Hearing his name had broken the matrix of a new sensitivity: responding to hearsay as if it were substance. But whether he alone could provoke such receptivity or whether he was only the first, she didn't know. She knew only that she didn't like it; she could not see what use it would serve, and, that afternoon, after the midday meal (which she scarcely touched), when she lay in the stream and found that, this time, instead of carrying away her distress, the water seemed to part around her, to avoid what possessed her, she liked it even less. She wouldn't be rid of it, whatever *it* was, until she'd seen him—if she could be rid of it, of which she now did not feel sure.

She had told her father she did not wish to wait up to greet the new arrivals, but that had been only a half-truth. She was afraid; what if her symptoms were exacerbated?

In the event, this did and didn't happen. When she laid eyes on him— this rather austere-looking young man, though with a gleam in his eye and a way of inclining his head to the side when he listened that told of a lively mind within—she felt both becalmed and agitated. Becalmed because she could now have no doubt that he was the source of her unease; agitated because it was intensified by his proximity. She couldn't for the life of her sleep that night.

Finally she surrendered to her wakefulness, put on a dressing gown, and tiptoed downstairs through the great shadowy house; a lopsided half-moon shone in through the windows whose curtains had not been drawn and she hurried through the shafts of light as if someone in the heavens were searching the house for her. She let herself out through the kitchen and circled around to the outer side of the ell to see if the visitor's lamps were still burning. They weren't, and she felt both relieved and slighted. If he could sleep, it could only be because he had let her assume the burden of his restlessness. It was an ill omen. She felt such relentless urgency combined with complete impotence. And, then, worse: she recalled Mr. Limlaw's and Mr. Driscoll's abject witless looks when she had told them that she could not care for them as they did for her. She had found them so pitiful, so willfully thick-headed, but now it occurred to her that someone might consider her in the same light. The dark square of the visitor's unlit window brought that possibility home to her. But did she mean to say that this perturbation of her blood was *love?* It was simply a word. It could hardly contain the inebriated alertness she felt.

When she took hold of O.'s wrists the next morning, to hold them beneath the stream of warm water, her purpose was diagnostic: to learn more of what occupied him—and now her; but to her amazement she could feel nothing at all, so that when he asked, "What have you put into it?" and later, after she had moved her hands to his temples, hoping to feel something there, "It's your hands, isn't it? There's something in your hands," it was his feeling something which surprised and frightened her—his feeling something from her of which she herself was unaware.

She had answered calmly ("I drew your blood to them"), but she had not felt calm, not at all. Evidently she had exercised an effect on him yet she could not locate the source of his effect on her; something in him stood in the way; he could make use of her without her knowing how he did so. When, afterwards, he seemed uneasy, she asked him almost with eagerness if he were afraid of her; but he echoed her question without answering it, and she felt miserable. Why wouldn't he acknowledge her? What was he hiding?

She would not be able to touch him again. She could not invite him a second time to tour the bathing rooms. She could think of nothing else to do to gain access to the tributaries of his organism, which he kept blocked against her. Did he know that she could teach him things about himself which he might not know? But she could not tell him even that. In his presence, she stumbled for speech. He saw so much. His understanding was as extensive as hers, but so very different. He wanted to name everything. She understood in a vague way what he saw his task to be—to say what he saw, to save it by saying it—yet she wanted to tell him that it was no use; his self-sacrifice was misplaced. She could let him come into her world of water and rock; why could he not let her into his?

Sometimes she felt a slight give, a tiny opening made by a discrepancy between what he was experiencing and what he was willing to say, and it was at these times that she sensed a gentleness and kindliness within all his intellect and rigor, a sweet, enclosed space that was protected like a walled garden from all the necessity of *deciding*—but why he would cling to the form when he could sink into the formless, she didn't know.

All the while, over the next few days, while O. spoke of his longing to travel abroad, and Lucinda replied by enjoining him to send her descriptions of the sights he saw, this other argument went on beneath. To end it, he would have needed to say only, I want to go, but I want you to come with me, but he didn't say it.

On the morning of the day before he was to leave, Lucinda waited until they were alone. This had occurred not infrequently, since O. had no interest in the pastimes that entertained his brother and Lucinda's father: lawn games, target practice, and, chiefly, reminiscing about their exploits in the war—of which, Lucinda thought, O. was a trifle envious; she would have liked to tell him that the tales did not impress her.

It was a thickly hot day—"more suited to grimy Boston than your verdant hills," as O. said—and after they had mutually remarked upon this Lucinda told him that she liked to escape the heat of the afternoon by bathing beneath the waterfall. A sensible antidote, O. pronounced. This was all that either of them said on the subject.

But he would come, she knew. She had been there, waiting, it couldn't have been more than a quarter of an hour, when she sensed his approach. Even before she heard footfalls or pebbles loosening upon the steep path down to the brook, she felt a kind of wavering in the air, an unthreading of the weave of the atmosphere. She was sitting, already undressed, on a towel spread out along a shelf of rock beside the narrow leisurely waterfall. Her clothes were folded neatly out of the way, and beside her rested an oval basket holding soap, a hairbrush, and a hand mirror. O. stopped, out of sight, but from where, she knew, he could see her.

Their future, Lucinda understood, was contained, knotted and coiled, within the next few moments. She could say no more; she had said what she could say, and she could not convince him of anything. Nothing she did would make any difference, and yet the moment was still fraught with peril. He might or might not choose to reveal himself; she thought that he probably would not. She couldn't begin to understand what was happening to her anymore. What was she doing?

She stood to unpin her hair, removing the hairpins with one hand and collecting them in the other. The great mass of it suddenly fell, and she felt about for the pins adrift in it. She laid them in the basket and took up the soap, then waded into the shallow pool at the base of the waterfall— it came up only to her knees now at this, its shallowest time of year. She knelt and lowered her head and her hair fanned out around her in the slow-moving water like something spilled; soon the water soaked it and pulled it down. She rubbed the soap against her scalp until there was lather and then set the bar down on an outcrop of rock and reached under the water, seeking her loose hair, which, as if come to life again in its new, underwater world, swam about beneath the surface like swamp grass.

". . . with your tresses spread about the stream like a great water-lily . . ." O. later wrote. "I was transfixed . . . I thought: Never shall I forget this sight and yet, even had I been truly in danger of doing so I would continually be reminded, for I see you everywhere: I find you in Florence— Botticelli painted you . . . Raphael . . . All the great masters . . ."

When she had soaped her hair, Lucinda lay on her back and let the meandering current carry her hair downstream; she rested there like that, leaning back, supporting herself on her elbows, her head half immersed in the cold water. Her feet sank to the sandy bottom and she pushed off and then let them fall again. Miraculously, she forgot that O. observed her, that upon this moment's cornerstone weighed the entire structure of her future. She had bathed in the brook countless times, and in the pond below Thrush Hollow; she was wondering now what it would be like to bathe in the ocean, to feel the tide: coming in, going out. Again. Again. She couldn't imagine it.

Fresh water flowed in one direction only—downstream, towards the sea. Its flowing one way was a continual reminder that this was the only way it could flow. It reached the sea and became part of it, but then it was no longer itself. By what secret, circuitous route did it circulate back to its source in the mountains, divesting itself of its salt on the return trip? Moving from separateness to merging and back to separateness again, a continual change that continually remained the same.

She did not wonder how she knew that water made this circle; it didn't occur to her to wonder. Her belief was the natural conclusion to thinking that there was a finite amount of water in the world, which she believed without being conscious of believing it because she had always thought of rain as returning to earth what the earth had lost. It wasn't something new, introduced from without; it was coming home. The body was at ease, breathing deepened, when it began to rain; the blood knew that soon there would be more water to draw it to the ground. Without the water underground, the unmapped currents running through the earth, people would soon turn to weightless husks and drift aimlessly into the atmosphere like dead leaves.

When Lucinda stood, twisting her rinsed hair into a coil to wring more water out of it, she felt suddenly uneasy. It was the feeling of having forgotten something, of looking for something she knew had to be there but which she couldn't find, and even when she abruptly remembered O.'s presence and her hope that his witnessing this private moment might bind him to her in some way that he would be forced to acknowledge, it was as if the recollection didn't quite fit what she thought she had forgotten. He was the closest she could come to it, but the fit wasn't perfect. Somewhere in her daydream of water she had lost the sense of what it was she wanted. Inadvertently glancing up the slope, as if to see what was awry, she didn't see him, though she thought she caught a movement. She sighed and climbed out of the pool to towel herself dry. She felt so sad, suddenly; she ceased to worry about whether she'd revealed that she knew he watched.

How could it ever be right if it had to be so intricate? And it was terrible to guess, as she was beginning to, that it was the intricacy as much as anything else that might bind him.

She had envisioned the watching; she hadn't envisioned what would conclude it. She felt remiss, as if her lack of preparation were to blame for the impasse at which they now found themselves. She must have anticipated that at some point O. would take action. If she forced him to reveal himself, he might think she accused him of spying. Yet if not, all their future intercourse would be poisoned by a shared unspoken secret. She understood all too clearly why he did nothing, but why would he not do something?

Lucinda slipped. In tossing back her hair, she fell to her knees and, startled, cried out. O. came clambering down the path, calling to her.

"Are you hurt? Miss Dearborn, are you hurt?"

Lucinda stood, hastily wrapping the towel around herself.

"Thank you, no, I'm not hurt."

"You frightened me . . ." O. said, and then awareness of the situation (and perhaps of the fact that he was acknowledging what she'd asked him a week ago) overcame him.

"Forgive me," he murmured. "Please forgive me. I shouldn't have been here."

"No. I wanted you to be."

"We must tell no one," he said. "No one would understand our innocence."

"No," she said uncertainly.

"I will return to the house now. It would not do for us to be seen together."

Lucinda said nothing, and O. stood, indecisive, reluctant, as if awaiting her acquiescence. She refused to give it.

"The way you look at me . . ." he said. "I can't . . . I am not capable of . . ."

Later, when he was sure she would demand nothing of him, he was free to delight in the "primordial bliss of water and wood, leaves veiling, the dappling water dappling *you,* with your tresses spread about the stream, your face in their midst like the secret bloom within the flower. I was transfixed by all that was and all that might be. I could not move."

N ed told himself that he couldn't have cared less what the nature of O.'s sex life had been. What could he, Ned Dene, possibly gain by learning—*for a fact*—that O., as Ned was guessing, had "known" Lucinda, "known" her and then left her? (Of these "facts," which was the most important?)

That he was not alone in his speculations somehow made it worse. Revisionist biographies of O. appeared with the regularity of Loch Ness monster sightings, seeking to "prove" that O.'s fervid phrases in letters to the handsome Scandinavian sculptor or to his fellow expatriate, hostess of a nearby villa, had not been mere flourishes of the pen but commemorations of a corporeal rapture. Evidently people found it incredible that a mind of such penetration and sensibility could have known human beings without—as it were—*knowing* them. (More to the point, without wanting to.) And many who asserted that O. had not, ever . . . seemed to wish to pin his trenchant analysis of native character—its disjunctions and absences—upon a callowness in his own. It was not everyone's failure to meet and hold each other, it was his failure. He could not accept the inevitable discordancies of a mature relationship.

Ned could imagine what these Philistines would make of the passage from O.'s letters in which he spoke of the longing to submit "oh, but to submit" to one, all-embracing idea, to which all others would "henceforth be vassal." "They would pay their homage," O. went on, elaborating the metaphor, "be told their task, go about their business, content with their place in the greater scheme. Not for them—not for us!—this suspicion of authority, this pernicious 'thinking for ourselves.' One would emit a sigh of relief so never-ending that it would carry all before it, all our weary, uncertain days. Such a small step, and yet how splendid and immense it looms—how impossible!"

Had O. taken it? Yet even if he, Ned, had been present to witness O. and Lucinda's "episode" by the brook, and observed them engaged in "actual" lovemaking, what more would he have known than he knew now? O.'s betrayal of Lucinda—if that was finally what it was—would have seemed no greater than it did now.

Passion unrealized: that was O. and Lucinda's story. The revelation was the real person behind the recurring character: Lucinda's entombment in print. Ned began to wonder if it was *that* villainy with which he identified—the *fixing* of his nature—not, as he had first imagined, with O.'s reluctance or Lucinda's privation. The thought made him ill—it meant asking who had done the "fixing"—but he forced himself not to turn away from it. Nothing could be gained at this juncture by turning away, but, as had happened ever since Hudson Sleeper had unearthed the letters, facing something meant remembering something—this time the summer after he'd graduated from college when he'd remet Greta. That was when the obfuscation had really begun. Ned cringed to think of himself then, of his hesitancies and longings, his private view of himself as cut out for something better than the life he had lived so far . . . But was timidity a crime? And they had done it to him, hadn't they? She and her friend the bishop—with their not thinking him worthy of their confidence . . . Was it his fault that he hadn't insisted Greta reveal more to him than she found convenient? If he'd made a character of her, one which allowed her to cut off discussion when it suited her, wasn't it in retaliation for the one she'd made of him—the bumbler, afraid of the truth?

What if she hadn't walked into the shoe store that afternoon with her niece, where he was spending his days wedging shoes onto strangers' feet in order to earn money for graduate school in the fall? Would they have found each other again anyway? Marby was not large, and she was there for the whole summer, helping out her sister, who'd just had a second baby. Yet that she hadn't looked him up and had had no plans to had been clear.

Sometimes he thought that he would have found someone else, better suited to him, with whom he would not, in moments of difficulty, have felt such a prevailing sense of inadequacy. (That he and Greta experienced weeks and years of congenial living seemed irrelevant to these moments when the marriage was tested.) Yet mostly he believed that he would have still been there, morally speaking, in the shoe store, forced to listen to yet another lecture from unctuous Barry, the manager, on how to judge women's sexual readiness, or lack thereof, by their "footwear"—swearing to himself that this time he would walk out and never return, an intelligent human being could tolerate only so much . . .

"The black heels, with the tall spikes—well, I don't have to tell you what those dames want." Serving as Barry's captive audience had struck Ned as penance for sins specified and unspecified, a trial he was meant to endure before he would be released from this purgatory.

Ned smiled now, but then he was appalled, as Barry explained that a woman's choice of shoe indicated her degree of eagerness to be taken to bed, preferably by greasy jiggling Barry. All that could vary was the circumstance, the length of time required to persuade her, and the amount of distress she would manifest on being told afterwards that "this ain't no lifetime thing, baby."

"But, Barry," Ned would argue, "people don't go barefoot in our society. They have to buy shoes. So why does every shoe a woman buys reveal how eager she is for someone to get her into bed?"

"You college guys," Barry sighed. "You slay me. This what education does for you? What do *you* think makes the world go round?"

"Well, what about men?" Ned would counter. "I don't hear you talking about what men's choices mean."

"I don't need no extra equipment in the sack, Ned, if you catch my drift. Take my word for it, you look at a dame's shoe tree, you've got her basics all figured out. You experiment—you'll find that I'm right."

"How?" Ned asked, and immediately regretted it.

"Lost in the desert without a canteen?" Barry said sympathetically.

"Barry, I . . ."

"Now, now," Barry said, "don't you fret."

It was a funny word coming from brilliantine-haired Barry, and Ned almost liked him for a minute.

"Good-looking guy like you, they should be lining up around the block. You're just not picking the right *shoes,* I'm telling you. If I can give you a piece of advice. They want one thing and one thing only. They want to know you can't live without them but at the same time they like to suspect that you could take off without a backward glance. Take it from me, if you let them know you're wise to them . . . You'd be surprised, the number of dames that come in here I can tip over with a look. A firm hand on the ankle don't hurt neither. Feet are *private*. Someone takes hold of your shoe and you're sitting down and can't move—think about it. Ninety-nine percent of women, take it from me, you put your hand on them with authority and 'No' drops right out of their vocabulary. I know what you're thinking, What *kind* of dames? But *nice* ones, society types. I bet you it's the same with dentists."

"No doubt they sit around analyzing women according to their teeth," Ned groaned.

"Smart-ass," Barry said. "A little more education and I hate to think what you'll have left to send into the future."

At moments like this, Ned, sighing, asking himself in a mental stage-whisper what he had done to deserve this, had looked importunately around the shoe store, but he never found any solace in the displays of the shiny wing-tips and high heels, the provocative demands they made on would-be customers. He pitied these innocent victims until they came in, but then despised them for their capitulation in this contest they didn't even know they were engaged in. The worst was, Ned suspected that Barry was right, behind his bluster and exaggeration; he loathed the guy but couldn't deny that he felt a grudging respect, even as he heard him remarking, "Beautiful arches," and looked over to see him stroking the foot in question and then, if the foot wasn't withdrawn, moving up to the ankle or even the calf, as he murmured hypnotically, "Great ankles, strong calves, you need a good solid support," or, alternatively, "You have the kind of muscles that show up well in high heels. Lots of salesmen," Barry would explain, if the woman looked uncomfortable, "they measure your foot and that's it. Fitting a shoe right is a lot more complicated than that."

Incredulous, Ned would watch women nod, confide to Barry that they'd never been able to find a really comfortable shoe, and ask his opinion of their choices.

"Take it from me, Ned," Barry had told him, "most people don't know what they want, most of the time," and Ned could see there was truth to the presumption that if you simply barged in on people's psyches and told them what they needed, many would gratefully lay down the burden of their deciding selves and do what you asked. But then what—if you weren't impervious Barry—did you do when the other person capitulated?

That previous spring (Ned, half-shuddering, half-amused, recalled), he had informed two young women that he loved them, the same week. If he said it, had gone his vague reasoning, maybe he would feel it. He hadn't, naturally, been considering how *they* would feel. When speaking his lines hadn't engendered sincerity, it had seemed foolhardy to be scrupulous about how often he recited them, or to whom. Yet he'd soon felt sickened when his chosen subjects had appeared to believe him. Besides guilt for his dishonesty, he'd felt angry at the girls for their gullibility—at his expense, he felt.

His deception hadn't lasted long, that was its only redeeming factor. The college was small and, as he must have realized they would, Claire and Isabelle (even now Ned could mortify himself by recalling the tone in which he'd murmured their names to them) had discovered Ned's relation to the other and together had devised a plot: one invited him on a picnic; the other waited at the site and there they confronted him. What did he think he was doing? they demanded. Had he really thought he could have both of them? Did he think they were going to stand for it?

Ned had known he should feel remorseful or at least caught out, but by this time he had found all of them, himself included, almost ridiculous, as if they really were acting to a script—and the script of an amateurish, melodramatic play, at that. If only the director would shout "Cut!"

No, he said, he didn't think they were. No, he hadn't thought that. He didn't know what he was doing.

But which one of them *did* he love? Claire and Isabelle persisted, seeming to have agreed beforehand that she who was less favored would nobly relinquish the beloved, but Ned was silent. Love?

"I don't know," he found himself saying—to this and almost every subsequent question that was put to him. "I don't know why I said it. I said it to see what it would feel like. I don't think I love either of you. I don't think I'm capable of love."

Eventually, Claire and Isabelle had worn out their anger. They must have realized that he would never give them any satisfaction, in the duelling sense of the term. From habit, or because the food was there and it was a gentle spring day, they'd spread out the blanket Ned had brought as his contribution to the picnic and insisted they all sit down and eat together. Claire had made devilled eggs, which Ned had found especially bizarre—the fact that she would have laboriously prepared something while knowing beforehand that the picnic was only a ruse. The two girls had kept looking at each other, preparing, planning—he could not tell what. A ménage à trois, was that what they were concocting? Had they, in fact, loved him and found in each other a comrade in grief? And yet—having abandoned their interrogation—they more or less ignored him; they treated him like a wayward but doted-on younger brother.

The spot Claire and Isabelle had chosen was beside a river, on the lawn of a summer house, in mid-April not yet inhabited; the area had reminded Ned of Ravens' Point in Marby, though there the mansions were boarded up and bore signs warning "Danger—Entry Forbidden" or "Private Property—No Trespassing." He had never gone there with Greta, though he'd sometimes imagined, before everything had become so strange, that they would explore the place together, find ways into even the most securely sealed houses and discover what was being hidden from view. Here the estates were only temporarily closed, awaiting the return of their owners from their year-round lives—yet their simply standing there, as if inhabited, not knowing they were only "summer" houses, gave the whole area an uneasy and vulnerable air.

After lunch, one of the girls—Claire or Isabelle, Ned no longer remembered which—had suggested that they borrow the boat that lay upside down on the private dock, covered with a tarp, and go boating. That was what she said, "Let's go boating," a phrase that struck Ned as nearly fantastic.

"I'd really rather not," he said, but he had evidently lost the right to have his wishes taken into account, and was told that being a good sport was the least he could do.

Reluctantly he had gone down to the dock with them and helped them lower the boat into the water. He had no argument to make in his own defense, and yet he felt that their punishment was cruel and unusual: to have to drift in a boat on a lovely spring day with the two victims of his crime, as if it were a preliminary, not a final outing. He gave each of them a hand, because they seemed to expect one, and waited to get in until they'd settled themselves, one in the bow and one in the stern.

Suddenly, just as he was about to step in himself, to take his seat on the middle plank they'd left vacant for him, the most sincere emotion he had experienced in years overcame him—a great revulsion against every artificial exchange he had ever participated in—and instead of climbing down into the boat he had pushed Claire and Isabelle off with a great shove and called, "I'll wait here! You'll have more fun by yourselves!" and fled. He heard them shouting after him for only a short while before they floated, and he ran, beyond hearing distance.

When he judged the coast clear, he returned to the scene and gathered up the picnic things and loaded them into Claire's car, then found something to write a note with: "Dear Isabelle and Claire, I'm sorry, I don't blame you for thinking I'm unmitigated slime, but I feel too lousy to hang around. I'll see you back on campus. If you don't feel like speaking to me again, I'll understand." He had considered adding, "You certainly seem to have recovered from your shock pretty quickly," but had decided that there was no point in being nasty.

As he learned later, there had been no oars in the boat. He should have known it, even if he hadn't observed it—he had grown up by the water. People who left boats openly available kept the oars elsewhere to prevent just such unauthorized use of their property as he, Claire, and Isabelle had made. He must have known it—what other explanation could he have made to himself about their swift disappearance? Ned tried to recover a mental image of the boat, with its middle seat waiting, and it was true that he saw no oars in it, but perhaps this wasn't actually what he'd seen but an imposition of present knowledge on past experience. At the time, responding to a loathing as instinctual as a physical reflex, he had simply thrust them off and run.

The river, fortunately, was not a rough one but it was wide, and too cold and fast for swimming, and Claire and Isabelle had drifted, terrified, for a mile or more before they had been able to attract someone's attention as they sped under a bridge.

Ned had been summoned before the dean, who had said, holding up his thumb and forefinger a half inch apart and shaking them at Ned, "Do you realize that you were *this* far away from a charge of manslaughter? Another mile or two and they would have gone over the falls. Or did you plan the whole thing? I suppose it would have been one way to solve your romantic entanglements—which don't sound like much to be proud of. If you hadn't been such an exemplary student and weren't about to graduate in six weeks, I'd boot you out of here so fast you wouldn't know up from down . . ."

Ned still recoiled when he thought of the scene (though he also still heard how much the dean had enjoyed measuring the air with his fingers and telling him he'd been *"this* far from manslaughter" and trotting out such clichés as "knowing up from down"), and he had been, as he not infrequently did, recalling the events of the past spring and trying to wrest a meaning from them one morning in early July as Barry was giving him unsolicited advice about how to attract the "unfair sex," when a young woman came into the store with a little girl whom Ned assumed to be her daughter. Barry had flashed Ned a secret hand signal—*yours;* Barry hated waiting on customers with children. "The brats set up static on the vibes," was how he explained it.

The young woman had stared at Ned, seeming startled, but Ned had chalked it up to the generally adversarial behavior of people out shopping. Self-protectively, he greeted her from a distance, intending to let her look over the merchandise before he approached to offer help. This was his usual strategy, but in this case the customer didn't go about her business but, glowering, demanded, "Why didn't you answer my letter?"

The little girl looked as startled by the woman's angry tone as Ned was, and he scrutinized the child through a tumble of wild thoughts: had he impregnated a girl several years ago, whose letter accusing him of paternity he'd somehow never received? But if this was the case, couldn't she have written again? He could recall every girl he'd slept with, however—it didn't tax his memory—and this young woman wasn't among them. But by then he'd recognized her.

"Greta!" he exclaimed.

"Well?" she asked.

Ned stood speechless, and the little girl—three or four, Ned guessed—tugged at Greta's hand.

"Auntie Greta!"

Throwing Ned a disgusted look, Greta let her niece lead her away. Barry, who'd observed the exchange from behind the cash register, lurched over and inquired, with a meaningful glance at Ned, "Everything all right, Miss?"

Greta obliterated him with a stare, Ned was gratified to see, and then said icily, "I'd appreciate it if you'd bring me a pair of these for my niece." She held up a white patent leather slipper with a rosebud stitched to the toe.

When Barry, rolling his eyes at Ned, disappeared into the stock room, Ned went over. "Greta . . ." he began.

"I assume you got it," she said.

Ned had smiled then, though he knew he shouldn't; she sounded so exactly as he remembered. She looked much the same too, now that he'd recognized her: her wavy light brown hair still fell past her shoulders; she wasn't wearing a school uniform but her dress was conservative, the skirt to the knee, she evidently indifferent to the fashion changes of the past decade. She carried the same aura of intent stillness and watchfulness.

"It's really nice to see you, Greta," he said.

She'd seemed not to know what to say to this and busied herself settling her niece on a chair. Ned, conscious of Barry hovering nearby, spoke only of the shoes—a surreal exchange. ("No, the rosettes are stitched on quite firmly . . . Yes, there is a white polish, though we have found the finish remarkably durable . . .") After Greta had paid for the shoes, Ned followed her outside.

"I used to *know* her," he said disparagingly when Barry, on his return, pronounced, "Swift work. Nice specimen."

The next evening, drinking gin-and-tonics with Greta on a restaurant terrace above the harbor, Ned did what she had consented to give him an opportunity to do—that is, attempt to "explain." He'd come as far as apologizing for not answering her letter and begun to set forth his state of mind at the time as justification when Greta lost patience.

"How you could have thought for even one minute that the bishop might have been right about me! That is so insulting! He's twice my age!"

She had spoken as heatedly as if they were facing off in the deserted boatyard where they'd said their goodbyes seven years earlier, and even though Ned had been amazed at the readiness of her anger, he'd been feeling the upwelling of a joyous light-heartedness. Time had *not* stopped, then, as he'd thought it had. It had stalled, but now it could move forward.

"I didn't say I *did,* Greta. I only said I *wondered.* Is that so strange? There was so much I couldn't make sense of. It doesn't happen every day, you have to admit, a girl you know getting the stigmata . . ."

"Is that how you've thought of it?"

"Greta, it's *one* way. It's something that happens to saints and martyrs, not someone alive my own age. At least you could admit it's not a common occurrence."

"Maybe it's a phenomenon that goes underreported," Greta said.

Later, this retort marked for Ned the moment he had decided he was in love with Greta, the moment when he had chosen to define their relationship in the most conventional way possible—especially ludicrous given that the relief he'd felt at finding Greta again had arisen precisely because conventional was exactly what she wasn't. She'd never been willing to accept a single handed-down explanation about anything; if authenticity was to be found in this life, she was as close as anyone could come to it; she would never have let herself be rendered mute by the Barrys of this world, with their self-serving "theories"—but no. He could have taken her remark at face value, even if she hadn't expected him to, insisted that she speak seriously, faced the extraordinary *with* her—and who knows where they might have been today?

Instead he had smiled at her and reached for her hand—patronizing her, Ned saw now, even though she had clasped his hand in return and, later, twined her arms confidingly around his neck when he'd kissed her on the walk back to her sister's house. He regretted the gestures even while recalling their sweetness, all the uncertainty of the past so soothingly subsumed in those mutual caresses. They'd eradicated his younger insecurity—he wasn't mature enough or cultured enough for Greta, the world traveller, the girl who spoke four languages. Maybe for her it had put an end to the fear that he regarded her as a freak of some kind. Yet Greta was not the adorably feisty girl he had cast her as, sealing her into the character with that first physical claim. He knew it and she knew it, and yet it seemed she was grateful to be offered the part, so readily did she take it on—so hungry to be in the play that she'd accept any role, however unsuitable. He couldn't see, when he thought about it, any great difference between his own commandeering of the situation and Barry's presumptuous laying on of hands.

And once he and Greta had kissed, he could think of nothing else but how soon and where they would find the opportunity to consummate their relationship. He lived with his parents, and Greta was staying with her sister; he felt squeamish at the thought of suggesting they go to a motel. He briefly entertained a fantasy of their sneaking into St. Stephen's crypt and making love there, where he'd spent so many— could he exactly call them fond?—hours watching the votive candles burn out among the tombs. He'd taken the fantasy so far as to envision himself sliding a hand beneath Greta's head as she lay back on a sepulcher, cushioning her against the upraised profile of the effigy carved into the stone—a necrophiliac impulse, not the lovemaking on a tomb but its being to a memory, a girl he'd been in love with who had somehow been absorbed by this new, grown-up Greta.

His younger self might embarrass Ned, but he couldn't disown him any more than he could undo what had happened: lying one night on a floating dock in the middle of Piper Creek, to which he and Greta had swum, braving the jellyfish; Greta receptive, waiting—impatient too, not from desire, or not altogether, but as if, since they both knew that this was where everything tended, why not get there sooner rather than later? If they didn't hurry, they might end by confronting each other, and reveal—it was not clear what, but whatever it was might preclude their being in love.

Greta's impatience with him had seemed general, though she denied it—impatiently—when he asked her. A veiled half-moon hung over the trees at the shore; it was hot, out of the water, and their clothes, shorts and T-shirts, in which they had plunged into the creek, clung to them stickily. Ned had wished to say something to her first; he realized too late that this was not how he wanted things to happen. He had wanted this moment to be a culmination they had come to instead of something they did because they didn't know what else to do, but you did not lie on a raft in the sultry moonlight, with fireflies flickering and heat lightning exploding soundlessly against the suddenly visible horizon, with a girl you'd already kissed lying beside you on her back, her long legs thrown across yours, looking up at the starless sky and waiting, waiting for you to act, and not do what she expected.

Afterwards, Greta had been disappointed, Ned could tell, although she had politely pretended affection. The impatience he'd felt from her beforehand had never given way to satiety or gratitude. Something she'd hoped would happen hadn't happened—and never had. It was nothing as simple as physical satisfaction. They had no difficulty in "pleasing" each other, but this was something they did individually, at the same time, not a mutual occupation. He had never reached something in Greta, Ned knew; she had never let him or he had been afraid to go there because—he couldn't think why; this was where his thinking stalled— although by now they had pretended for so long that the distance they lived with was simply the inevitable separateness between any two people that they almost believed it.

Late in the afternoon Ned went to find Greta to ask if she wanted to walk after the mail. It was delivered around one to their box at the junction of the Thrush Hollow and Dalby roads, about a mile from the house; ordinarily one of them drove down after lunch, but today neither of them had bothered. With Henry at camp, their awareness of time was all awry—or so they said to each other.

Now the sun hung at the point above the horizon where at this time of year it always seemed to pause a long time before sinking, its light soaking more deeply into things than usual, gilding them with that lustre that was like regret. The air, on this early August day, smelled of leaf meal and dry, warm grass, and a particular ineffable odor that signalled the approach of fall, something like the smell of the past coming back.

How attached he was to this place, Ned thought, to its sights and sounds and smells, to his life with Greta and Henry in it. Throughout the year—with their hectic schedules, their never having time just to sit—the prospect of evenings on Thrush Hollow's back porch, the hours tending the garden, was what kept him going. Here was where he and Greta had always been happiest—in their summer place, their summer life. He'd taken for granted that it couldn't extend into the other nine months of the year—and this amazed him now.

Having walked most of the distance in silence, Ned broke it with a remark upon the pleasure of its being nearly six and still warm enough to wear short sleeves. It reminded him of his childhood, he went on, of staying out playing long after the usual time to be indoors. He mentioned his "old friend Anselm," with whom he had "navigated the neighborhood." If Greta noted his sly indirection, she didn't show it. She merely nodded, companionable, and wondered what it might have been like to grow up in a neighborhood. She saw how much it meant to Henry.

Henry, Ned thought, feeling somehow warned. As if she'd known (of course she'd known) what he wanted to talk about and meant to remind him of what they wouldn't have had if they hadn't learned to ignore whatever wasn't there between them. We hear *some* of what each other doesn't say, he wanted to point out to her; surely that counts for something.

Passing an abandoned orchard, they slowed; the road here paralleled the Hollow's brook, and they both gazed down at the clear stream, divagating over rocks—so instinctive, Ned thought, this need to watch water move, though it was a peculiar instinct; it was hard to see how it promoted survival, which instincts by definition seemed to do. Lucinda, perhaps, would have had an answer to that.

Abreast of a small intact cellar hole snug up against the road, Ned crossed the grassy median and laid his arm over Greta's shoulders. A butternut grew in the enclosure, marking its age; Henry, refusing to be swayed by the argument of anachronism, insisted there'd been an ice cream stand here; Ned and Greta guessed a mill; only recently had they learned from Nora Sleeper (how had it come up?) that the place had been a harness shop—"Someone in the Snow family had it. There are Snows across the way," she'd announced, tilting her head towards the graveyard, making them think for a moment that she meant right then, living people visiting graves.

"I'm sorry I've been so uncommunicative lately," Ned said.

Greta nodded.

He knew *she* knew he was hoping she'd say, "So have I." It was underhanded—to apologize for what he blamed her for.

"I've been so preoccupied with the correspondence," he tried again, and this time Greta complied.

"I'm sure there's a lot to think about."

"Yes," Ned said, sighing, as he returned to his side of the road. "I've read and read and read it. I continually feel I'm on the verge of figuring something out, but then it eludes me."

"Figuring out what?"

"I don't even know that. I hardly know what I'm reading for anymore."

"Maybe it's time to show it to someone else, then."

Ned didn't answer immediately. The logic of her suggestion was immensely irritating, as if she, not he, had brought up the correspondence and trapped him into discussing it.

"Maybe. On the other hand, it might make it worse. My learning what's at stake," he added, when Greta began to object. "I'm not talking about what I'll do in the long run. To think about that now would only cloud the real issue."

"Which is what?"

"What really happened between them," he said, exasperated. "O. and Lucinda. What else could you think I meant?"

"But you'll never know!" Greta exclaimed—as heated, suddenly, as he was. "How can you possibly know any more than you do now?"

"A month ago, I didn't know this much. Who knows what other discoveries the future holds in store?"

"Why not ask Hudson back with his dowsing rod? Maybe there's more buried in the cellar. Why not just dig up the whole cellar, for that matter?"

Ned sighed again. "Look, I keep thinking I'm on the verge of hearing it—whatever both of them aren't saying. The clues are all there, I'm convinced. If I don't get it, it's my fault, not theirs. My failure to receive, not theirs to transmit."

"But, Ned—transmit what? I don't understand what else you think you can know."

"How they lived!" he exclaimed. "How they lived with it. Or why. It's not just them—O. and Lucinda. They're not acting under their own volition. They couldn't do otherwise."

"I don't see that."

"I'm convinced of it. It was the climate—the day's climate. I don't mean it was known, but—O. wouldn't exempt himself from the common cause. Lucinda was his sacrifice. He saw what was happening and let it work itself out through him—through *them.*"

"Ned, I don't really see—"

"About her I'm not so sure," Ned interrupted. "Nominally she wanted to change things, but maybe—maybe not."

"Are you saying she *liked* never seeing the man she loved?" Greta asked. "How convenient—the secret desire not to have what you say you want. I thought you didn't want to psychoanalyze them."

"She doesn't *fight* enough, that's the thing. In all those pages, she hardly complains. She's in the 'right course' of her life, she insists. Only after O.'s few brief visits does she ever mention feeling deprived. 'I belong with him—our life is together,' she'll write, and you can feel her anguish in not living the life she believes she's meant to, but then before long she accepts its lapsing back into the hypothetical."

"Well, what choice did she have? What else could she do?"

"Kept railing against her fate, at a minimum. Stopped feeling ennobled by her privation."

"Maybe she just couldn't stand the sound of her own voice complaining."

"I suppose, yet there's still something I can't put my finger on—something in the tone, some secret satisfaction . . ."

"Maybe you can't believe that someone could live a whole life without having what she wanted."

"Can you?"

When Greta didn't answer, Ned added, "Maybe I can't, although it's fairly obvious to me that people do. This not admitting to things—well, if you don't have what you most long for, you don't risk losing it, do you? If other people don't know what you love, they can't take it away from you, can they? What, Greta? What *is* it?"

They were nearly to the mailbox by now and Greta had stopped, as if to study the life-sized deer, bear, and rabbit figures that surrounded the man-made pond beside the Thibeaults' shocking-pink house, as if the display were an object lesson in what Ned had been describing, this ostensibly decorative but obscurely hostile array.

"Greta, what's *wrong?*"

Ned's tone, his impatience abruptly dropped, reminded Greta of Henry's—the uncalculated distress. *What's wrong, Mom? What is it?* Could Ned really not know what he'd been saying? If he wanted her to think he knew what she was hiding, he couldn't have hinted it more plainly—this talk about secret lives. If he were laying a trap . . . But wasn't that what she'd wished? For him to have learned the truth without her having to be the one who told it?

"Greta, you look so disturbed," he said, taking her arm so that he could look her in the face. *"Can't* you tell me what's going on?"

This paranoia—Ned wouldn't try to trick her into a confession. He might not come right out and ask her what he wanted to know but he wasn't—he'd never been—devious.

She made an effort to smile, feeling as if she might choke. "We'd better get the mail. Mrs. Thibeault might accuse us of loitering."

Ned laughed, relieved. Their nearest neighbor had called the State Police the previous summer when she'd spied Olivia Tolliver and a friend skipping along the Dalby road (she said she thought they were drunk) and on another occasion when Henry had stepped onto her property in order to take a photograph of her browsing metal deer. (He'd written a Social Studies report titled "Death to Lawn Ornaments.")

Ned didn't speak until he'd drawn the flyers and envelopes out of the aluminum lunchbox-shaped box and they were out of sight of the Thibeaults' on their way back home. Then he said, "Just don't tell me it's nothing, Greta. It's your right not to talk, but don't tell me I'm imagining things."

"No," she said.

"I know I've been dragging my heels—I know people might disagree with me, about your right to remain silent. People think proximity entitles them to intimacy. I don't say this as a threat. We've never conducted our marriage like that."

"No."

"Maybe that's been a mistake, I don't know. Maybe we've respected each other's privacy too much."

"Is that what you think?"

"I don't know what I think. Sometimes I think it's what's kept us married for twenty years."

Greta didn't answer this, and Ned said, in a detached, musing tone that disturbed Greta more than anything he'd said, "On the other hand, maybe longevity's not the best gauge of success. I suppose the only gauge is one's own feeling about it."

Again he waited for her to speak—to make himself seem indifferent he looked through the letters.

"Anything from Henry?" she asked, to say something.

"Not today, lucky duck." Ned mimicked him. "But there's a card for you from Rachel and another letter for Henry from Olivia."

"He must not have answered the last one," Greta said, taking the postcard. "Otherwise she'd have his address."

"Love letters, wouldn't you guess?"

"Love letters! At her age?" Greta was looking at Rachel's card.

"She's thirteen," Ned said.

"That's what I mean."

"That's what *I* mean. What does Rachel have to say?"

"You mean about Livia?"

"No, Greta. I mean, what does she have to say?"

Greta turned over the postcard and scanned it. "Peter's mother's worse. They won't be back for another two weeks, and then maybe just Rachel and the kids."

"That's a shame."

"Yes," Greta agreed, thinking, however, that Rachel's having sent the information on a postcard instead of in a letter expressed her continued anger at Greta for having lied to her, at having been made complicit in Greta's deception of Ned (so Rachel had said), though (as Greta could have pointed out to her now; at the time she'd been too distraught) that was exactly what Rachel had been protected from by not knowing. The picture on the card, broken arches of a ruined abbey, Greta felt to be slyly emphasizing Rachel's unspoken message by suggesting that there was a whole world of sin and redemption (not to mention the visiting of its architectural relics) that Greta was barred from because, in Rachel's opinion, she had remained unrepentant about her deception. Because she had refused to place herself in the categories everyone else did.

"It doesn't mean I *liked* lying, Rachel," she had said, but Rachel was adamant. "Not liking it doesn't excuse it, Greta."

The postcard might even have been meant to remind Greta of her time at St. Stephen's, hinting that she'd left *it,* figuratively, in a ruin, its bishop resigned in disgrace, the sisters in an uproar, and Ned, there by happenstance, terribly wounded. If only Greta would learn to go to other people with her troubles when they first arose, instead of waiting until she couldn't hide them, then much destruction could have been avoided. "Dignity can become a fault," Rachel had said. Greta didn't think she was reading too much into the card's subject. Rachel considered landscape symbolically; she would be aware of what images suggested.

Greta had been longing for Rachel's return; Rachel was upset but they could talk about it; at least there would be someone she could talk *to*— but now, instead, she felt dread. If Rachel was this angry, if she still felt so implicated by what Greta had told her . . . In order to forgive her, Rachel would want to apply some pathological explanation to her behavior, to render her not responsible for her actions. What scarred and hampered soul would she have to agree to be for Rachel to take her back into the fold?

Greta glanced over at Ned, straining, without his glasses, to read the table of contents of a journal he subscribed to, and she registered for a moment the extent of her felt life with him, how familiar he was, and how comforting the familiarity.

Even so, she couldn't have it. She had forfeited all that. Crain was dead, and she couldn't go on living with Ned as if nothing had happened. Crain had lost his life, she had lost Crain, but it wasn't enough. She had to lose something else, of that she was convinced, although what it would be—what could be more than losing Crain . . . She didn't dare complete the thought.

Striding along beside Ned, with the lingering sun dappling the road's surface through the overarching branches, her mind washed blank as it always was when it reached this point, she was drawn out of herself into the sentient life of the place; recalled, as she and Ned rounded the last curve before beginning the long slope up to Thrush Hollow, to her first sight of the old hotel, long ago when they'd been staying with Rachel. It had been five years into her marriage to Ned, and until a little while before the visit to Stilling they had not been getting along: they were a mismatch, they'd more or less agreed; they respected one another but lacked some sympathy, some essential connection, and she hadn't gotten pregnant, as they'd both hoped she would—Ned in the belief that a child would supply what was missing, she in the wish to get even with Crain for having a family with Julia. Balance things out. Then maybe she'd agree to see him again, as he'd kept urging her to whenever he could get through to her by phone. In the end she had gone back to him anyway, hiding her unhappiness with Ned, though Crain knew—it was obvious from the gratitude with which her body responded to his. She didn't need to tell Crain how, at that moment when they should have been closest, Ned was always still on his own; she would have doubted her own knowledge of this, to condemn herself for wanting the impossible, if it hadn't been for Crain, who had never, not in that way, kept himself apart.

She had thought—telephoning Crain, arranging to see him—that she would be going home afterwards to tell Ned that their marriage was over; the meeting would give her the courage, reminding her as it would have of what she had been missing. All the way home on the plane (she had told Ned she was flying to Atlanta to look at a horse), she had rehearsed what she would say: I was lonely when I met you—the man I loved had just married someone else; I thought I could forget him, but I can't. The fact that you knew me at St. Stephen's when I was going through all I did there exercised some kind of pull on me . . .

When she opened the door of their minuscule apartment (Ned was in graduate school and she not yet with a clientele), set down her suitcase, and kissed him hello, she found instead that she was happy to see him. It was as if she actually *could* see him for the first time—his thoughtfulness, his fundamental uncertainty about his right to have what he wanted, his relentless questioning everything he thought he might believe—and she saw his real love for her, how he put up with whatever lack *he* felt so that he could be near her. To watch over her, even if she didn't want him to, because that was what made him feel alive.

All at once, she was not angry at him for not being Crain. (She still had Crain.) She had begun to love Ned then; far from divorcing him, she could actually be his wife (or, since it was Crain she felt married to, conduct a long, stable, clandestine affair with Ned).

It had been at the beginning of their new contentment that they'd gone up to stay with Rachel in Stilling. Greta had never been there, although Rachel had often invited her. On this particular afternoon, Peter and Rachel, pregnant then with Lenox, had gone into Dalby for Rachel's monthly check-up. Greta and Ned had set off on a hike, cutting across country, thinking they were headed for the abandoned Trout Hill copper mines when instead they had happened on Thrush Hollow. *Happened on* was precisely what it had felt like. Greta could still recall her first mistaking its bulk for a piece of gray sky, the illusion for a moment so convincing that she forgot that all around them that day the sky was a deep, opaque blue, interrupted only by a few luminescent fleecy well-defined clouds. When the gray patch looming at the crest of the birch grove through which they had been climbing took shape as the gable end of a building, she and Ned were both amazed: what could be that large—a piece of evidence overlooked, it felt—out here in the woods?

It was true that Rachel had mentioned an abandoned, half-burned hotel a mile or more up the back road, but the picture Greta had formed of another listing, weed-surrounded farmhouse dignified by the title had kept her at first from understanding what she was seeing. Even when she and Ned had circled the building and stood facing it from the front, and then could take in the charred wing whose craggy timbers stood out against the daylight sky like a building losing all but its outline at dusk, the original apparition had coalesced in Greta's mind not with any recollection of a defunct resort hotel but with a painting of Rachel's that had hung in Rachel's room when Greta first knew her in college: at a glance merely two parallel rows of black squares turning upward at a wide angle to the right, the squares etched with lighter crosses. As Greta had looked more closely, however, the squares had transformed themselves from spectral grave markers into windows and then she'd noticed faint lines suggesting clapboards, roof, doors, and a wide, airy veranda that had led her, when Rachel told her she'd painted the picture of a house near where she spent the summers, to place it at the seashore. It so convincingly bore the quality seaside houses have of letting in the weather that Greta had never thought to ask Rachel where her summer place was located, and even after she had learned that it was in Vermont, the only New England state without seacoast, she had never fully corrected her original impression.

Perhaps because of this, as she stood that bright, motionless summer afternoon in the tall grass that later she and Ned would cut back into a lawn, Greta had felt so distinctly that the sea was near that she had actually turned to look across the valley at the line of trees (which later she would identify as marking the road that led from West Stilling to Dalby), and though there was not even a pond in sight she could not rid herself of the impression. It was as if the tide were indefinitely held back, as if some cataclysmic event begun long ago—a sudden fissure in the ocean floor swallowing down the water from a vast area, a whole country—had yet to be resolved. As if one day the crack would close, letting out a centuries-held-in sigh, and then the water would flood back over the land. And even this summer, after so many at the Hollow, there were still times when the sea's absence was as palpable to Greta as that of a lover, an absence so enveloping as to have become a presence, as if the land longed for the sea with the same passionate disbelief in its disappearance that people felt at having to say goodbye to those they loved, as, that distant afternoon, gazing up at the great gray relic with Ned, whose hand she was fondly holding, she had suddenly felt for Crain, her longing only deepened by her abrupt, irrevocable understanding that, whatever the real reason, she could have him only if she lived without him.

She had thought of how, once, the sea had covered the land, how its hollows and slopes had felt the sea's penetration and caress; no emptiness had been left unfilled, so that, ever since the water had receded, the brooks and rivers travelling to the sea had molded the hills with their longing to return, and everywhere the character of the land had been shaped by this striving: to go back, sweet water joining to salt, back to where neither knew where one stopped and the other began.

If you lived inland, that was your character. You were formed by what you were not. No matter how deeply you immersed yourself, you were withheld; you withheld yourself. Like Lucinda, Greta thought, you lay in the brook meaning to abandon yourself to the stream but at the same time resisted it, braced yourself against the current. How could you not, unless you disintegrated and washed in elements down the rocks? And yet impatience would overtake you, a revulsion with what seemed to be your own refusal, a longing for union that could not be satisfied by anything in this interior country, until the only solution seemed to be to take yourself to the sea and throw yourself into it and then, like Lucinda, drown.

Every Sunday in summer, during the five years after the Civil War until Captain Dearborn died in 1870, the Thrush Hollow Resort Hotel and Spa for Ladies and Gentlemen served a free pancake breakfast. Captain Rufus Dearborn had offered it as a gesture of recognition and thanks to veterans and their families; any of them could eat a heaping plateful of hotcakes and bacon, a bowl of stewed apples, and drink as much hot coffee or iced lemonade as they could hold. Though any veteran from anywhere was welcome, usually only those who lived in West Stilling or up on Trout Hill, the village that had sprung up around the copper mines, took advantage of the offer. And though it was only a quick downhill walk from Trout Hill village to Thrush Hollow, it was a steep trudge home, and this dissuaded many from attending, though you couldn't beat the price and it was a pleasant setting, out on the lawn under the spreading maples if the weather was fine, and on the wide veranda if it wasn't. It was a chance to ogle if not to mingle with the city folk who could afford to come up to Stilling and do nothing except play croquet and fan themselves from week to week, to find some of them as uppity as one would have expected but the others nicer than one would have thought.

Among the veterans who hiked down from Trout Hill was a young man named Zebulun Snow. He had fought for two years and been wounded, and would limp all his life as a result. He was a handsome man, dark-haired, with eager, studying eyes and a large wavy moustache that he had decided to leave when he shaved off the beard he had grown during the war. The ladies found it dashing, but though Zebulun—Zeb, he was called—was pleased to accept the compliments, he wore it for another reason. He wanted ever after to be reminded, when he looked in the mirror, of the time when he had first grown it. He didn't want to forget what he had seen or what mankind was capable of. All his life, he promised himself, he would keep clear in his mind the discrepancy between what something could seem like before you did it and what it might be like when you were doing it. Born and raised in Stilling, brought up to farming, impressed into the mines for a brief interval when they opened in 1862, Zeb had had only a vague notion that the South even existed, and when he'd joined up to fight it had been as much out of a spirit of camaraderie with his friends and the desire to see something of the country as out of moral conviction. He couldn't much see what it mattered if some place so far away wanted to be a country on its own. After the Emancipation Proclamation caused him to think about it, he supposed he was against slavery; he knew he shouldn't like someone to own him and be able to tell him what to do, but he had never seen any Negroes and didn't know if there mightn't be something different about them that made it so that they needed to be controlled—if they mightn't be simple, like Isaiah Whipple's older brother Abraham, a grown man who could say only a few words but was happy all day long doing chores for his mother around the house.

Zeb learned differently after he'd met a few black people, fighting just like him for the Northern cause in their own regiments, and got used to looking at their dark, dark skin. What naked sowbellies we must look like to them, he thought. He was uncomfortable when a freed slave first addressed him as "sir." "No need to call me that," he said to the dark soldier. "No, sir," the soldier said, and Zeb thought he understood a carefully veiled antagonism in the phrase's repetition, and let it go. He had studied in school about kings and queens and lords and ladies, but in Stilling there were no social classes; everyone struggled alike, and the few who had more than others had either been lucky in trade or worked harder than anyone else. It had always seemed to Zeb that he could get whatever he worked for, and it was a revelation to him the first time he saw a great plantation manor and, a stone's throw away, the cramped cabins where the slaves lived. It wasn't fair, but the plantation house was beautiful, and it struck Zeb how easy it could be for people to get a wrong idea but think that they were right because they didn't want to give up what they had. Then it struck him that if he thought that about these Southern landowners, chances were they thought the same about him, and who was to decide between them? But, dammit, his side was *right*.

It must be right, he thought, it won the war; but what if the North had lost? He couldn't embrace the idea, but still it left him with the unsettled feeling that, but for the odd circumstance, anyone's life could have been someone else's. He could see why people were willing to die for what they believed: if they were willing to die for it, then it must be worth believing in, and if there were something worth giving your life for, then there was a reason for living. His head spun; he mostly was glad just to be back home, though he wanted to talk about what he had seen, what he had felt like being an instrument of death, killing boys even younger than himself because they'd happened to be brought up to believe in a different idea. Not even knowing they had been—till a bullet reminded them of it.

One day, Zeb's company had been fighting near a Mississippi swamp. A freak fog had risen towards late afternoon and it was impossible to see farther than a few feet. Zeb had received a superficial head wound, but didn't realize it or that blood had trickled down his face. The order had been given to retreat but everyone was milling around aimlessly and Zeb—like others, since hardly any two men could seem to agree— wandered off in what he thought to be the direction of the camp. It was so hot he could hardly breathe, and the singing of mosquitoes seemed louder than the shooting had. Before long he had become separated from the rest and figured he must be lost, but he was more tired than he could even comprehend and couldn't bring himself to care. His right shoulder, which he'd twisted somehow, ached and he needed to relieve himself. He wanted to lie down, but he didn't trust the spongy ground or what might come crawling along as he lay there. At home he wasn't afraid of snakes because there were no snakes to hurt you, but down here there were rattlesnakes and copperheads and water moccasins as eager as Confederate soldiers to encourage you out of their territory.

As he was thinking this and wondering how he'd gotten lost so fast, Zeb circled a big cypress and almost stumbled over a Confederate soldier sitting with his back up against the trunk. Before the soldier could scramble to his feet, Zeb had turned his bayonet on him. Instead of looking afraid, the soldier looked annoyed. He said, "It ain't no fair. I never seed you comin'."

He was so young—he could have been Zeb's fourteen-year-old

brother, Micah, who had begged and begged to be allowed to "go to the war"—and Zeb shook his head and put down his rifle. The boy looked incredulous as Zeb turned to walk away; when Zeb had gone only a few steps, a sound caused him to spin around and there was the boy whose life he had just spared aiming his gun at Zeb's chest.

"What the devil!" Zeb exclaimed.

"But you knew I was here," said the young soldier.

"Don't you have no honor?" Zeb asked.

"This here is war," the boy said. It sounded like "This heah zwah."

Zeb sighed. He should probably have raised his gun and attempted to shoot the boy first, but even the thought of raising his gun tired him too much.

"Oh, go ahead then," he said.

At least, when he was dead, he could get some sleep; when he woke up afterwards he would figure out what to do with this irritating youngster— really *just* like Micah, taking advantage of your good nature.

"That ain't no fair," the young soldier complained again. "I can't shoot if you ain't gonna resist."

"Then don't shoot me. Look, can't you just show me how to get back to my company—if you know where the fighting is, that is."

"Course I know," the boy said. He seemed miffed, as if Zeb had accused him of desertion. Maybe a deserter was what he was, Zeb thought, but Zeb decided he wouldn't annoy him further.

"I need to pass water," he said, wondering at his sudden formality.

"You go over thataway. Here, I'll show you."

The boy waited for Zeb to button his pants and turn to face him, then led him through the swamp until they came to more solid ground.

"How do I know you won't sneak back up and shoot me?" the boy asked.

"I might," Zeb said. "How long you planning to stay by that tree?"

"Till things quiet down some. I couldn't do no fightin' out there," the boy said, gesturing in the direction of the battle, which they could now faintly hear again. Up there, the fog must have begun to lift. "It was too much happenin' at once. I'd light out after some Yank but someone else would git to him first. I didn't know fightin' was like *that,*" he said. "So confusin'. Good thing we're wearin' uniforms. You could shoot your own men otherwise."

Zeb couldn't help laughing at the honesty of it, but stopped when he saw how insulted the boy looked. He felt sad suddenly, realizing how unlikely it was that this young soldier—a child in his mind and behavior—would survive the war.

"War is the worst sort of mess," Zeb agreed. "You go on now. I can find my way from here."

The boy nodded once and walked away as Zeb stumbled back up the rise in the direction the boy had pointed. Just as he neared the top, something made him turn around and there was the boy aiming his gun at him again. This time Zeb didn't think; he simply reacted. Raised his gun and shot. The boy seemed simultaneously to squeeze the trigger and to throw his gun into the air, as if in raucous celebration; then he fell backwards and lay still. He was already dead by the time Zeb, wincing at the pain in his leg, reached him.

When Zeb finally stumbled into camp a short time later, he was hauled into a tent with other wounded soldiers. He didn't feel his leg anymore and when he protested, in his exhaustion thinking they'd confused him with the boy he'd shot, someone swore at him and told him his face was all over blood and his trousers were soaked with it. Then the boy had managed to shoot him after all! Zeb thought joyfully, but burst into tears when he realized that the boy had never known it.

"He never said a thing!" Zeb moaned, and the men tending him thought he was delirious; they tied a rag around his forehead and forced him to lie down.

Never said a thing, Zeb meant, to give Zeb the opportunity not to shoot him; the boy had pushed and pushed until he'd pushed past Zeb's training to kill the enemy and provoked his instinct of self-defense—as if he'd wanted to see if Zeb had it in him. The boy had harbored no deep conviction about the justice of his cause. It was the inconclusiveness of the situation that had nagged at him like a mosquito, and he'd paid for wanting to be rid of what was really a petty irritation with his whole life.

Heavy as he'd felt the weight of the boy's death inside him, Zeb had never told anyone about him; he couldn't explain how killing this one particular soldier had been like shooting a dog or a baby—or explain the horror of understanding that a feeling that might arise from some source not connected to the present moment could nevertheless take someone over and completely change what happened. Even once he was home, Zeb could say nothing. He saw in other veterans' eyes the same hollow, haunted look he knew must show in his, but he could tell that all they wanted to do was to forget the misery and climb back into the idea of war they'd had before they went; their stories of heroic exploits and daring escapes were like ladders designed to help them scale the walls of forgetting. It was the easiest way to go on living, Zeb could see that, but every time he started to forget he thought of that boy, too foolish even to know what he was supposed to be there for, but getting killed for his confused idea of duty and his fatal hesitation.

          Zebulun Snow fell in love with Lucinda Dearborn in a matter of minutes. He laid eyes on her for the first time one Sunday morning when she stood beside him and asked if he'd care for more coffee. There were servants enough to do the waiting on table, but Captain Dearborn must have told his daughter it would be a courtesy to the veterans if a well-mannered young lady like her was personally to attend to their needs. Whatever it is that can make a person seem twice as visible as everyone else suddenly operated on Zeb when he turned to reply to Lucinda's question. He said only "Yes, please, ma'am" and "Thank you," but when he went home that day he knew that his life was changed. Though the steep hike down Trout Hill and back was hard on his bad leg, he made it without fail every remaining Sunday of that summer and most of the next. Each trip down he thought that this time he would surely think of something to say to Lucinda Dearborn besides asking her how she was that fine morning, and each trip up he wondered why he was struck dumb when she paused for a moment at his place as if to give him an opportunity to speak. He would never see her in any other circumstance, he knew; they belonged to different churches and bought what they needed in different villages. He thought of writing her a letter, but he didn't dare. Besides, what would he say? *I want to tell you about the time I shot a boy. Something makes me think you would understand . . .* He might have gone to his grave without sharing a conversation with her had Lucinda not finally brought it about.

"Mr. Snow," she said one Sunday, that second summer, "I wonder if you'd be so kind as to help me move the coffee urn out onto the porch."

"Most certainly I would," he said.

He stood and limped across the lawn beside her. When she noticed, she stopped.

"Why, I'm so very sorry," she said. "It's funny, but I've never seen you walk. I apologize."

"It's nothing," he said. "There's nothing I can't do."

"You were shot?"

"Yes. Yes, I was. Many of us were."

"My father wasn't," she told him. "I always wondered if he stood in the back and gave orders."

Zeb wasn't sure how to respond to what seemed to be a seditious statement. He said neutrally, "The commanders have to see what's going on."

"Do you think so?" she asked, giving him a curious look—half gratitude, half disbelief, and then she said, "Do you ever have the feeling you know what people are thinking, Mr. Snow?"

"No, Miss Dearborn," he said. "But I sometimes wish I knew what you were."

Lucinda blushed, and Zeb was afraid he'd been too forward. But then she said, "You wouldn't truly like to, Mr. Snow."

Zeb knew Miss Dearborn didn't feel as tenderly towards him as he did towards her—or, more precisely, he could tell that even if she came to, it would never mean to her what it did to him. He could tell that her eye was set on distant sights and that she would be merciless in brushing aside anything and anyone that obstructed her view, and something in that, though he couldn't say what, reminded him of that young soldier he'd shot and he wanted to do everything he could to keep her from the same fate. At the same time, it seemed to Zeb that he could see, as clearly as if both their lives were over and already written down in a book, how he would fall ever more deeply in love with her, only to watch her, each time she seemed ready to admit that she loved him back, raise up her gaze to the horizon on which she felt obliged to keep it fixed, and tell him that, however she felt, her destiny did not end with him. And he, after another year or more of trying to secure Lucinda's attention, would, out of desperation, marry someone else, hoping thereby to forget her—only to make his wife unhappy because he was always craning his neck to see around her as if she might be hiding Lucinda from his sight.

But this was all still to happen; it had to be lived through hour by hour, day by day, and so, when Lucinda asked Zeb how he came to be wounded, as if she knew there was more than the ordinary tale behind it, he told her the story. He watched her comprehend the unremitting, baffled pain the memory caused him, the incontrovertible experience he could not undo, as they sat side by side in two of the capacious wicker rockers that poked up every few feet from Thrush Hollow's continuous veranda, like a battlement, the others empty at the moment, keeping Zeb and Lucinda ghostly company.

However, this was not the end of their story; even though Zeb had foretold accurately, he had not foretold everything. To observers it appeared that Zebulun Snow was sweet on Lucinda Dearborn, but she thought she was too good for him; after a while he tired of waiting for her to come round and went off and tied up with a girl from North Hover, a Miss Amelia Blodgett, who'd come to Trout Hill as schoolmistress. As far as anyone knew, that was the end of it, and for several years it was. Zeb no longer hiked down to Thrush Hollow's Sunday breakfasts; he opened a harness shop and feed store in Trout Hill village; he was father to two small daughters. But all through that time he was waiting; for all he knew he might feel expectant the rest of his life, but when he heard, one bitter cold February day, that Captain Dearborn had suddenly been taken sick and died, he knew that his waiting period had been compressed to a few days: the time it would take for the neighbors to axe a temporary resting spot in Thrush Hollow's cellar, where Captain Dearborn would lie in his pine coffin until the ground thawed out in the cemetery and he could be buried the proper six feet down.

It was still bitter cold the day Zeb hitched his team to his sled and drove the long way round to the Hollow; the shortcut was impassable in winter, and Zeb sent a message home to Amelia from his store that he was heading to West Stilling to mend a harness and might be detained the night there. To make himself truthful, he stopped to deliver bags of feed to people he knew would be needing some soon and asked if they'd care to have him look over their harnesses while he was there; it was late afternoon by the time he arrived at Thrush Hollow.

Lucinda, as Zeb had expected she would be, was alone. In winter, she and her father made their home in only a few rooms of the immense place. Captain Dearborn had come to Stilling already a widower, and if he had any family nearby, they had never put in an appearance (though he'd had his wife dug up and brought to lie in West Stilling cemetery).

"Why, Zebulun Snow!" Lucinda exclaimed, pleased. "What brings you way over here, this time of year?"

"Came to tell you how sorry I am 'bout your father. Never been much at writing letters. I always was grateful for those breakfasts he gave. He was a generous man. Mind if I put my team in your barn?"

"I'll come with you," Lucinda said. In heavy coat and boots she helped

Zeb unhitch his horses, rub them down, water and feed them. Together they trudged back to the house.

"You'll have to stay the night," she said, looking at the darkening sky.

"I figured I might," he said.

That evening, under quilts piled a foot thick on Lucinda's four-poster bed, Lucinda Dearborn and Zebulun Snow came together with no pretenses and no promises. Nothing had been said at all, in fact, about what they meant to do, beyond Lucinda's "Will you come to bed?" and Zeb's "I will." Zeb thought, during one interval, of Lucinda's father, so recently dead, lying in his temporary grave two floors beneath them, and wondered if there was something sacrilegious as well as immoral about what they were doing, but the interval passed. He was surprised, and then he wasn't, at how unbashful Lucinda was; she was not like other women in other respects, why should she be in this? For the first time since the morning she'd asked him if he'd like more coffee, he felt as if he were living his life instead of waiting to live it and was so happy he didn't fret about whether or not Lucinda was thinking the same thing.

They fell asleep, and woke, in each other's arms, but not then or for a long time thereafter did they speak of what had happened between them, what would continue to happen, for the rest of Lucinda's life, whenever they could find an occasion. This was easier to arrange in warm weather, when they could meet in the woods between their houses; some winters they had to go without seeing each other once.

Except for the single entry, "Z.S. came late afternoon yesterday," which Ned Dene would puzzle over a century later, Zebulun Snow's name was never mentioned in Lucinda's diary. She left no written record even to permit speculation as to why this might be—unless the whole diary was such a record, protecting Zeb and herself from the forays of future investigators.

Lucinda loved Zebulun Snow—at least, so she murmured to him in moments of forgetfulness, for what other words can be found at such moments besides "I love you," however inaccurate or manifold in meaning they may be?

Yet Zeb knew very well that if he had asked Lucinda to fit her feeling into the forms others decreed for them she would have fought mightily to resist him. He understood this, and never held it up to her; he knew what could happen when someone who didn't fit the forms tried to make himself do so.

In the years to come, Zeb often pondered over how strangely things had arranged themselves. He had had to marry Amelia in order to become Lucinda's lover; she was the most blessed part of his life and yet no one knew about her. Since that February day, his marriage had grown peaceful; he no longer resented Amelia for not being Lucinda and saw her for the mild, obliging, loyal person that she was. It struck him as no end of peculiar that an arrangement that fostered the happiness of three people should have to be hidden both from public knowledge and from one of the three involved. The success of the arrangement *depended* upon its not being known, and it perplexed Zeb infinitely when he tried to understand how something could become something else according to who knew about it. He did not—he had asked himself this question many times—believe he was doing anything wrong even though he knew that the entirety of the town would condemn him if it found out, just as he believed he had done wrong to shoot that young Confederate soldier even though no one else would have thought so. Yet Zeb also knew that, if someone learned about him and Lucinda, and he, Zeb, heard of it, even if that person could be trusted never to tell a single soul, he himself would look differently on what he did.

"Zebulun Snow thinks deep thoughts," people said, teasing him about the deliberate stares he had come into the habit of fixing upon his fellows. "A penny for your thoughts, Zeb." "Zeb the seer," they teased him. "Zebulun the prophet."

If not thinking of his own circumstances, he was trying to fathom what other people could be keeping to themselves. It defied credence that, in all of Stilling, he and Lucinda were the only two who led secret lives. It went against plausibility. But why were there secret lives? What purpose did they serve? Could the world not be the world without them? And, if so, was the world at fault or were human beings? But how could the two be at odds when human beings had made the world and lived in it?

These were the questions that furrowed his brow and gave him the stern and trenchant look that his neighbors tried to jostle him out of.

B y seven in the morning, the front steps of Thrush Hollow caught a lone stripe of sun and Greta, up since five, having ridden for an hour, sat finishing a cup of coffee, as she flicked slivers of white paint off the door jamb with her fingernail. Even grieving collided with practical constraints, she thought coldly; there was not much time left before Henry came back to . . . If she didn't talk to Ned soon, there would be no time to . . . To decide what to . . .

Henry is not yours. His father is another man.

What are you talking about, Greta?

But he's dead.

Dead? Who's dead?

It was a fantastic scenario. She could not imagine speaking these lines.

"Sit down," people said, "I have some bad news." A cliché, though clichés, she'd learned, came back to life when someone you loved died.

"Mrs. Dene, I am very sorry to have to tell you . . ."

This seemed to be what she wanted to tell Ned—how then the words meant something they had never meant before, but meant nothing now, so that to tell him anything was pointless. She had slumped down on the tack trunk, and the telephone receiver, the news of Crain's death inside it, had pressed her hand against the trunk's metal strapping. Crain's secretary had sent away the news and so her telephone would not weigh as much. Greta had seen this with clarity—this and other details. The plane falling into trees; the pilot of the other plane, which Crain had not noticed until it was too late to do anything but swerve sharply, watching this. Crain's hands, his fine graceful hands, struggling with the controls, fighting to level out the plane. She would think, The branches will cushion the fall, he'll be able to get out—he won't die, they don't know. He laughed; she heard his laugh—all fluidity, as if he'd already been laughing before the sound became audible to others. He spoke; it was his voice, reassuring her. *Nothing's going to happen to me. Don't be afraid.* But this was her voice, reassuring him. Each time they separated he said, "I'm afraid I'll never see you again." "Of course you'll see me again. Don't be silly. Why would you not see me again?" "I don't know. Ever since I've known you I've been afraid of that."

The sound of an engine approaching distracted her. She wanted to say, *I can't hear;* she had to tell Crain that she understood why he'd been afraid now, that everything would be all right; but then she realized how rare it was to hear a car at this hour, seven a.m. on a Sunday, and she began to scan the road with the same fixity with which Nora Sleeper peered out the window beside her kitchen table whenever someone drove by. Greta saw metal glinting intermittently between the giant maples of the sugarbush and watched for the car to continue on up the hill towards Odder. She now wouldn't have been able to say of what she'd just been thinking, until she heard the car pause to make the hairpin turn into the drive, whereupon she leapt up, terrified—something had happened to Henry; she'd known all along that not everything had happened yet; only another event of the magnitude of Crain's death could dislodge her from where she was stuck, and only losing Henry could . . . But she shouldn't even think it. And she had insisted that he go to camp!

In a frenzy she began to run down the lawn towards the road, but at once stopped. The camp would have telephoned; only soldiers fallen in battle merited a personal visit—but could the telephone be out of order? They hadn't had a call in a couple of days. Maybe it was off the hook. Could she have left it lying on the tack trunk? But, no, that was three months ago. Crain had died over three months ago. She wanted to run inside to check the phone, but by then the car had come into view—a practically antique station wagon, wide, light green, with fake wood siding—and at the sight of it Greta knew that it couldn't be an emissary from the camp; it was the car of someone who didn't drive much and had kept it in a garage, washed and waxed it. An old person, she guessed (the elderly were not infrequently out and about at this hour in Stilling), who perhaps even remembered Thrush Hollow from the days of its operation—or who had picnicked on the abandoned property in youth.

Someone who no longer lived in the area and wouldn't know that the old hotel had been bought and reinhabited. How surprised the driver would be to see a woman sitting on the front steps! Greta exclaimed to herself. Suddenly she felt like an eager hostess, waiting while the car followed the backwards S-curve that looped along the edge of the lawn before circling around back of the house; with the sun striking the windshield head-on, the driver would be half-blinded and only vaguely see her, maybe in the glare imagine her to be one of the Hollow's former inhabitants, the ghost of Lucinda Dearborn herself, even, sunning off the chill of the grave!

The driver, turning back towards the house, slowed; Greta waved at him—a man, she could see—to go on up the slope, then set her coffee cup down on the steps before crossing the lawn. She still felt a strange expectancy, as if the visitor were actually calling on her, instead of coming as a tourist to see what had become of the old hotel.

At the top of the drive, instead of continuing around back to where she and Ned parked, the car came to a stop; the door opened, and a white-haired, not very tall man climbed somewhat stiffly out.

"Good morning!" Greta called, but the man said nothing. He stood with a hand resting atop his open car door, observing her, not smiling. Greta was taken aback and became conscious of wearing her jodhpurs and boots, as if it were her riding garb that explained his behavior.

"I'm Greta Dene," she said. "My husband and I bought Thrush Hollow fifteen years ago. It must be a surprise to—"

"You don't recognize me, do you?" the man said, and for a wild moment Greta thought that in fact he had mistaken her for Lucinda, which would make him . . .

"I had imagined . . . Alas, vanity—will there never be an end to it?"

He walked towards her, holding out his hand. "Jim McAndrew. You knew me as bishop at St. Stephen's."

Greta stared. She could feel her face flush—how could she not have recognized him? He was exactly the same, the same wry expression, the same eager scrutiny—and then she flushed more deeply when it occurred to her how he might interpret her embarrassment.

"From your expression I take it you had no idea that I might be paying you a visit."

"Paying me . . ."

"Ned didn't tell you that he wrote to me, I gather."

"Ned *wrote* to you?"

"Two weeks or more ago. The letter was forwarded twice. I have a summer home a couple of hours from here, across the river." McAndrew gestured east, towards New Hampshire. "Had it when I first knew you in Marby—it's a family home. It belongs to my sister Winifred and me now. Funny to think we've been within dining distance all these years, isn't it?"

Greta waited.

"I've stared at your husband's letter propped on the mantel of what it still pleases us to call our parlor for three days now, and this morning at five I was graced with a rare moment of moral courage and sprang to take advantage of it. That's my only justification for the indecency of showing up unannounced at this early hour—though I was possessed of the self-serving illusion, as I drove in, that you were waiting for me. Perched there on your front steps, keeping an eye on the road . . ."

"The sun's not out in back," Greta said.

At this rudeness McAndrew smiled and Greta, as if it had been what she meant to say, added, "I'm usually up this early."

"If I didn't know it to be unlikely, I'd say you hadn't changed . . . Greta?" McAndrew asked. "That's what you still prefer to be called?"

"Yes."

"Well, some consistency of character is a comfort. One wants there to be metamorphosis and yet something recognizable . . . Otherwise one feels that integrity has been sacrificed. I know I hope I've changed, but I daresay you and your husband will be the judge of that."

"Ned's still asleep. I'll go get him." She turned towards the house.

"Oh, don't wake him, please. I had said to myself that if there were no signs of life I'd camp out on your lawn until you woke up. I knew if I waited for a more civilized hour I'd never come. The risk . . . Picking up a dropped stitch like this . . ."

"There's no point in camping out on the lawn now," Greta said, when he didn't follow her. "You may as well come in."

"Thank you, then." In the front hall he stopped, gaping. "I *am* amazed. Ned wrote me that it was an old hotel, but I had no idea . . . Where are the mastiffs and the parlor maids? What on earth do you do with all this space?"

"Nothing, really. Just walk around in it." Greta pushed on to the kitchen. "Sit down."

He was studying her. "I'm sorry . . ." he said. "I didn't . . ."

He stood with a hand on the back of a chair and she looked at him, wondering why he hesitated, until she read in his face something that made her turn away.

Don't say anything, don't you dare say anything, she ordered him silently. How could it be *he* who noticed? How *dare* he? Or had Ned said something to him? Was that why Ned had written? To tell McAndrew—what?

What had been on her face? She'd been sitting on the front steps, thinking of Crain . . . Thinking of Crain . . . No, she mustn't. McAndrew would see. He'd already seen enough. Quickly she must move to some other thought. With Ned she had the habit of hiding but—so Ned *had* been keeping a secret, and this was what it was. It had not been only her own secrecy, reflected in him, that she'd sensed. He had summoned McAndrew to help him find out what was wrong with his wife. Well, if McAndrew thought he could walk in here, after thirty years, and chat as if they were old friends . . .

"There are times," McAndrew announced, "when I wish that I smoked."

Greta, caught by surprise, laughed and looked at him. He smiled back gratefully.

"I'm sorry I—"

"Are you hungry?"

"I could eat the proverbial horse."

"I only have a real one."

"Of course, you've been riding . . ."

"It's how I make a living."

"I'm impressed."

"You are? Why?"

"I'm inordinately impressed by anyone who can do anything physical at all well, but even more so when someone earns money at what for most people is an avocation."

"That's just the problem with it," Greta told him.

"What is?"

"Taking seriously something that most people you have to deal with don't."

"Oh, that problem." McAndrew laughed. "I thought that was living."

While McAndrew sat at the table, trying—she could tell—not to study her too closely, Greta brewed a fresh pot of coffee, fried bacon, scrambled eggs, toasted English muffins. How ordinary everything was, suddenly. *Everything was completely ordinary.* Was that what happened? You reached a point—you were stranded there—and then nothing could be strange again?

Ned must have been up late, for the smells not to wake him; she'd been asleep when he came to bed. McAndrew, whom Greta could not bring herself to address as "Jim," was telling her what he'd done since leaving St. Stephen's and the priesthood. A picture of a sprite-like young woman had been taken out of his wallet, his wallet taken out of his hip pocket. That gesture, more than any he'd yet made or anything he'd said, dropped him out of the Church for her. The girl was his daughter, Sylvie.

No other children? Greta, congenial hostess, had asked.

"No," McAndrew said, rather abruptly. Greta and Ned had but the one child themselves, didn't they? Ned had mentioned . . .

"Yes," Greta said. "Henry. At camp in Maine."

"That's Ned's name too, isn't it? Henry . . ."

"Edward Dene. Henry's middle name is Sayre. Would you like more coffee?"

"I've had two cups already. I'm supposed to be cutting down, though why, when I'm seventy-three, anyone should care . . ."

"Ulcers?"

"No—heart."

"I suppose coffee's not the healthiest thing."

McAndrew smiled. "Bless you, my child, for not having turned into a dietary expert."

"Oh, I'm hopeless. Ned is always after me to—"

"After you to do what?"

In the doorway, unshaven and with his hair uncombed, Ned stood looking at the two of them.

"Ned!" McAndrew exclaimed, pushing back his chair. "*You* recognize me, at least."

"Bishop McAndrew—how could I not?"

"Oh—Jim, please. Your wife didn't."

Ned glanced at Greta as they shook hands.

"I know you didn't expect me simply to show up like this. I've already explained to Greta that I was acting upon a momentary impulse of boldness."

"I'm glad you did," Ned said. "But how the devil did you find us?"

"Rand McNally got me to Stilling Center. From there I followed signs to West Stilling. I found a farmer in his milk house."

"Reuben Bliss," Ned said. He felt the coffeepot on the stove with the heel of his hand, then poured himself a cup and went to the refrigerator for milk.

That he was behaving as casually as if McAndrew were a neighbor in the habit of dropping by seemed to Greta quite in keeping with the whole phantasmagorical quality of the morning.

"Quite an estate you have here. You said 'hotel,' but I wasn't prepared for the size."

"Neither are we, when we get the tax bill. Imagine trying to heat this place in the winter."

"I have a drafty old elephant myself."

"His house is only two hours from here."

"You're kidding."

"Summer house," McAndrew said. "Your letter was forwarded twice. It reached me a couple of days ago."

"What's the town?"

McAndrew named it and Ned said, "You *are* kidding now. Come on, it's too early for practical jokes."

They both looked at him.

"Though you wouldn't have remembered, would you?" he said to Greta. "Unless you . . . This has to be a joke." He sat down. "That's the town where O. and his brother stayed before they first visited Thrush Hollow."

"That can't be."

"By 'O.' you mean our most famous expatriate novelist, I assume," McAndrew said. "The house he stayed in is just down the road from mine."

"I can't believe it," Ned said, shaking his head. "It's too much."

"That I summer in the same town?"

Ned glanced at Greta. "O. is one of the ghosts I mentioned in my letter. He corresponded with the daughter of the hotel's first owner. No one knew—I don't see how . . . He wrote fifty years' worth of letters to this young woman. Her name was Lucinda Dearborn. We found the letters earlier this summer, buried in our cellar, along with Lucinda's diaries."

"You found them?"

"We had a dowser up from the village when our spring went dry and he located them."

"I thought dowsers only found water."

"So did we. Evidently they also dig up the past."

"It was in a metal box," Greta said. "Some dowsers are sensitive to metal."

"Do you know his work at all?" Ned asked, a note almost of pleading in his voice.

"I've read the requisite titles."

"And his biography? How certain everyone's always been that he never had an intimate relationship?"

"I've heard rumors." McAndrew winked at Greta—Ned didn't yet know that among other subjects he'd taught literature for a quarter of a century.

"From the correspondence it seems fairly clear that Lucinda Dearborn was in love with him and he with her."

McAndrew laughed. " 'Seems fairly clear' seems fairly qualified."

"If you're familiar with his work, you'll know that that's about as close as one can come."

"And?"

" 'And?' Am I the only one present who finds the coincidence remarkable? First the letters, which propelled me to . . . And then you're living in the same town?"

"I do see how those two facts taken together would seem to demand some all-encompassing explanation. A discovery such as this, in your own cellar, with all that that implies . . . Whatever it implies. I can't say, of course, in your place, what I would make of the information. I *can* say that, in what's approaching a long life, I've come to suspect these circumstances that seem to suggest a direct intervention in our affairs."

There was a silence and then he looked frankly at both of them. "You have only to remember back three decades to know that I've had to learn this from my own mistakes."

Neither Greta nor Ned said anything, though they exchanged a quick look—just as they had in McAndrew's study, Greta was remembering. *Will you listen to him?* the look had conveyed then. Now it conveyed something like embarrassment. Here he'd gone on, grown up, and they—they were like children who understood too late what they'd been supposed to do when their parents left them in charge.

"Perhaps it's not the moment for us to dig all that up, but I can't sit here with the two of you, accepting your hospitality, without saying at a minimum that I'm truly, profoundly sorry for those things I've done that caused harm. I'm sure I don't even know all of them, but I know that these words are long delayed."

"It's—" Ned began, but McAndrew waved a hand.

"Please, not yet. I couldn't believe you, if you accepted my apology right now. You can't possibly know whether or not I've earned the right to offer it." He paused. "I seem not to have stopped pontificating, you'll be noting."

"I was going to mention," Ned said. They laughed—Ned sounding like Henry, Greta noticed—or Henry sounding nowadays the way Ned had back then . . .

"What I'd really like to do—if you have the patience—is to tell you both a story. Before the decades catch up with us and we notice that we're virtually strangers. Your astonishment at the coincidence of my living where your friend O. stayed is what made me think about it. It's nothing I've ever told anyone, not even my daughter, although it concerns her mother."

Ned stared. "I had no idea."

"No, I didn't suppose you would. I've filled Greta in on some of my post-diocesan history—I've been married and divorced, you need to know—but the rest can wait. It's a not too short story, I must warn you. To get to it, I have to go back to the Second World War, when I was a twenty-one-year-old chaplain . . ."

"That, I had no idea about either."

"Of course you didn't. To you I was and always had been a bishop, incontrovertible as the Church itself. It didn't occur to you that I, if not the Church, could change. In any case, my job, in the army, was to comfort the dying. You may imagine what a fraud I felt, being addressed as 'Father' by men scarcely younger than myself."

He looked from Greta to Ned and then at both of them, generally.

"The confessions I heard . . . The things that can still worry human beings on their deathbeds—it would amaze you to know. The world we have made is compelling, if it's nothing else. I tell you, though, I couldn't have lasted a month if I'd had to depend on my own belief in what I was doing. It was everyone else's in me that kept me going. Strange as it was to realize, I comforted people. Sometimes the tortured look in the eyes of dying men went away because of something I said, though I could never predict what it might be. It wasn't promising them that their heavenly Father was waiting to greet them. I couldn't. Not in those circumstances."

"No, how could you?" Ned murmured.

"It wasn't uncommon for them to give me keepsakes to be sent back home, afraid that things would be lost, or buried with them—or to dictate last letters to me, if they had time. After the war it was the letters that haunted me, with their promises of what life could have been. If only . . . I began to wonder how many women lived in the shadow of those letters—I didn't like to think about it. I was afraid I'd colluded in the creation of a whole population of would-be brides by scribing, 'I know how happy we would have been . . .' 'As I lie here, looking my last upon this world, I think of the children we would have had, the things we would all have done together . . .' 'Please spare a thought for me sometimes when I'm gone . . .' But I was twenty-one years old. How did I know that these were letters of *revenge?* 'You're going to keep living and I'm not,' that's what they meant. 'I'm dying for my country, so that you can live in it with some other man.'

"Maybe I comforted those dying soldiers when I said, 'You won't be forgotten,' though I didn't know in what way it would turn out to be true. After the war, thinking about it, I wished I'd snuck on a postscript: 'Remember, though you'll grieve for me, your life will most likely be just as happy as it would have been had I lived. Don't be seduced by the what-might-have-been.' Probably would have done no good—it's human nature to fix one's sight on that—but maybe I wouldn't have felt as complicit.

"However, the genesis of my cynicism is not the story here—though it was *your* misfortune to encounter me when it had reached its apogee. As I said, I wrote many such letters. Very occasionally, after the war, a wife or mother or fiancée—once in a great while, a father—would track me down and ask me how a husband or son or lover had died, how his spirits had been, what he'd talked about. I had my own shell shock to deal with, and these encounters helped me. Amazingly, I almost always could remember the men I was asked to. But soon even that experience was over and I had to readjust myself to the less than life-and-death concerns that mostly occupied my days."

He took a swallow of his coffee and made a face.

"No, no," he said, when Greta reached for the cup. "Now we're going to jump forward in time and land, some couple of decades later, in my post-ecclesiastical life. I was in retreat in New Hampshire, not having a glimmer as to what I was going to do with the rest of my life. I hadn't been in that situation since early adolescence, before I entered the seminary, after which all such decisions were seemingly taken care of for me.

"One day, at the home of neighbors, other summer people, I met a woman. The older sister of the wife of the couple. It was unusual enough to meet anyone new up there—no house in the neighborhood had changed hands in twenty-five years—let alone an attractive woman near my age. Thirty-seven, not divorced, not, as far as I could tell, involved with anyone, male or female. She was—is—an archaeologist, and had just returned after several years in the Middle East. My good fortune—she would be there for the whole summer. I was intensely curious as to how she'd wound up alone, but before I mustered the courage to ask her, she told me. One day on a walk. A spectacular June day.

"She was one of the young women I'd written a letter to. She'd taken the exhortation not to forget a little further than most."

"You don't mean she literally was," Ned said.

"One of the young women? Yes, I do. That's what broke down her reserve—or undermined her vow, as the case may be. She'd told me about the man she loved, though he'd been only a boy when he died. 'I didn't mean to stay single,' she said. 'I didn't set out to. There was just never anyone who measured up to Frank. I couldn't get myself to care.' She knew by then that I'd been a chaplain, and one day she showed me his picture and his last letter, which she kept in her wallet. It was written in my handwriting."

"I'm getting the shivers," Ned said.

"Yes," McAndrew said. "As did I. 'I wrote that,' I told her.

" 'What do you mean, you wrote it?' she asked.

"I told her that her fiancé—Frank—had dictated it to me, that I was his chaplain, that I did that for a lot of the boys, if there was something they wanted to say and were too weak to write. Besides, I recognized the photograph . . . I rattled on, giving her a chance to recover from her shock. Finally she began to cry. I took her in my arms."

McAndrew glanced at Ned. "Literally and figuratively. What else was I going to do? We fell in love—we got married. How else could we respond? It seemed intended. She felt reconnected to her fiancé, as if she were marrying his brother—if it couldn't be Frank, at least it was someone who had known and loved him. She imagined that I was such a person, that I loved in her the girl Frank had had to leave behind.

"The truth is, in a way I did. I was as much under the spell of the coincidence as she was. My heart went out to her for the loss she'd suffered, and I suppose I succumbed to the illusion that I could repay her for it. The pretenses under which we came together are no greater than those which bind most couples, I suppose—but then we lost a child. Nothing held, after that. Helen felt she was being punished."

He paused, not looking at Greta, staring, or at Ned, shaking his head.

"Sylvie was just a year old—she's twenty-one now," McAndrew said to Ned. "Helen was already forty-six when she was born—we'd given up expecting to have children, in fact, when she got pregnant. But the pregnancy was difficult and doctors advised against another. Still, Helen wanted to try. Then Sarah was born with a severe heart deformity. There was never any chance that she would live."

Greta drew a sharp breath. Her eyes filled and she blew out, once, twice.

"I'm sorry," she said. "I'm so terribly sorry."

Ned reached across the table and touched her hand.

"She would be twenty—a year younger than Sylvie," McAndrew said. "It took Helen apart. She blamed herself, to begin with—she'd let what she wanted override what the doctors had advised. The baby's heart problem was an anomaly—it had nothing to do with Helen's age, but she decided that she was being punished for marrying me, despite the fact that we'd had ten very happy years. She had to find a reason. She'd used to marvel at how strange the world was—if Frank hadn't died, she'd never have married me and had Sylvie. Everything seemed meant— meant for our benefit—but then Sarah died and her mind broke. If she hadn't married me, it seemed to her, Sarah would be alive. She couldn't bring her back, but she could leave me. She was being punished for the sin of having tried to be happy and if she didn't repent quickly, Sylvie would be next."

McAndrew stopped talking, and Greta and Ned sat in silence, Greta wiping her eyes.

"I had a reason for telling you this story," McAndrew said. "Which I have to admit that I've now forgotten."

"Coincidence," Ned said gently. "You wanted to warn me against being impressed by it. But it's not a story that needs a reason."

"No, I suppose not. Thank you, Ned." McAndrew shook his head, squinting. "All wounds time does not heal. Maybe by your time of life you know something about that."

McAndrew's arrival back in their lives didn't change anything—did Ned think it did? He was so cheerful after McAndrew left, as if whatever had been going on before had been dealt with and laid to rest. He couldn't really think that the whole trouble between them lay in their time at St. Stephen's, in their not having talked about it afterwards, could he?

Your son is another man's! Greta found herself exclaiming silently, as if she'd already *told* Ned and he was refusing to acknowledge the significance. Couldn't he see that her entire life with him had been a fraud?

It was everything the marks reminded her of, moreover, not the marks themselves, that she had no wish to remember. She'd never been averse to talking about the *marks themselves*—she never minded talking about what something *was*; it was all the talking about what something wasn't. McAndrew must assume she had told Ned about the evening in his study—how could he imagine that she hadn't? *The bishop tried to seduce me*—so McAndrew would guess that she'd described it. Ned would have believed that version; probably still would. McAndrew's trying to convince him otherwise would have the opposite effect. Well, maybe not. Not after the story he'd told. They respected him now, given the straightforward and modest way he spoke about himself. Yet she was having the same difficulty with McAndrew that she'd had with Crain—keeping his identity fixed when he wasn't present. He shifted back and forth between the bishop then and "Jim" now. For all she knew, McAndrew himself might remember the occasion as his seduction. His inexplicit but general apology had seemed meant to include that.

Well, you did *not* start it, she would tell him. Don't patronize me now by pretending I didn't know what I was doing. I hadn't expected to want to—that surprised me. Am I that good an actress? I wondered. But then it was just happening and I wanted it to happen. Whatever I had meant it to be, it became something else. I was never your prey—don't flatter yourself.

They would form a conspiracy of feeling sorry for her, the two of them. They might even feel sorry for *her* for having had to keep the secret she had kept all these years. That would be the kind of self-sacrifice that appealed to the two of them—all this time she'd lived a lie for the sake of her child . . . The supreme sacrifice of motherhood . . .

So what if she had used this excuse herself? She had known what she was doing, the lives she was risking. She had done it because she loved Crain, no other reason. She *loved* him, couldn't they understand? She *loved* him. They would take that away from her, make it less than it was. If she and Crain had really loved each other, they would say, they would have found a way to be together.

"I cannot tell Julia about Henry, Greta. I cannot. It would destroy her."

She had not wanted to hurt Ned, either, but Ned would have survived. Henry would have survived. People did. Men left their wives; the wives survived. How could Julia really be as vulnerable as Crain said?

So he'd said, Even if he left his family and he were free to be with Greta, how could either of them be happy, knowing the damage they had caused?

I could still be happy, she had thought. We were together first. You were going to be with me but something happened. You became afraid.

Or else he'd said, "We're so used to the secrecy, how do you know we would feel the same if everything were in the open?" "It wasn't secret when we were in school," she said. "Yes, it was," he insisted. "It was always secret from my family."

McAndrew had left about three. Afterwards Ned worked in the garden and Greta tried to read. Then it was dinnertime. Celebrating, it appeared, Ned had thawed out the venison Lyman Slack had brought them at the beginning of the summer ("saved for you," Lyman said, the implication being "since hunt season," though they knew Lyman had shot it off-season on their land).

Ned had fried the steaks in onions while Greta had made a salad and then he'd set the table in the dining room—"Everything's still in there from lunch," he explained, as if it would save them a great deal of effort not to have to carry the salt and pepper shakers and the placemats back into the kitchen, where they usually ate.

"How splendid to think Eden must have resembled it," Ned said, gesturing at the view as he sat down, requoting O., whom he'd quoted from the same chair to McAndrew at lunch.

"I haven't yet apologized to you for the surprise," he added. "I never dreamed that he might just show up like that."

"It doesn't make any difference."

"I thought he'd write back—if he did—and then I'd ask you . . ."

"Ask me what?"

Ned laughed. "I suppose I figured I'd know when the time came."

Greta nodded, as if this settled it. But then she looked up at Ned and asked, "Why *did* you write to him?"

"*Why?*"

"That strikes you as an odd question?"

"Not odd, no, just . . ."

"Just what?"

"Well, I . . . Unfinished business, I suppose."

"And did you finish it?"

He and McAndrew had taken a walk after lunch. Ned had as good as asked her not to come along.

"I'd put it this way—we acknowledged that it's unfinished. That's a start. But you heard him—you were there when he apologized."

"And you didn't discuss the past any more on your walk?"

"Not really. We talked about Henry and Sylvie. We talked about teaching. We talked some more about O. and Lucinda."

Greta sat silent.

"You appear not to believe me."

When she didn't answer this either, Ned shrugged.

"I didn't expect to like him so much. That's the great surprise. All that psychic manipulation he practiced—it's gone. There's much he hasn't had—he spoke more about his marriage, which overall seems not to have been very happy, despite what he said—yet he's not bitter. His good will seems genuine, not martyred altruism. I'd like to know how he got to that point. I'd certainly never have expected it, given the way he was when we knew him."

"The way he was?"

"Come on, Greta, you know perfectly well what I mean. His vicariousness. To tell you the truth, I think he was jealous of us."

"I'm sure you've already been over all this today."

"I've already told you . . ."

"You discussed me then—why wouldn't you now? It's what you asked him to come here for, isn't it?"

"Greta, I don't . . ."

Ned set down his fork and pushed his plate a few inches away from him and then pulled it back.

"Is that really what you think? Do you know, that never occurred to me? I wasn't thinking about you, to be frank. It struck me just how careless that had been when I walked in on the two of you this morning. Just like old times—having your tête-à-tête. How do you think that felt?"

"I didn't invite him back into our lives, Ned."

"No, I did. St. Stephen's—it wasn't finished. Not for me. Something about O. and Lucinda—to know whether O. knew what he was doing, understood his effect on Lucinda . . . It translated into whether McAndrew knew what *he* was doing. It provoked something in me—"

"But I was there!" Greta exclaimed. "Why didn't you ask me?"

"Ask you?" Ned asked curiously. "How could you know if he knew what he was doing?"

"Knew what he was doing about what?"

"To me," Ned said. "What did you think I meant? I suppose I still don't *know*—he didn't say anything beyond what he said this morning—but I didn't feel he was being evasive, only waiting till we got to know each other again before getting into specifics. My point is, Greta, it's a great relief. Can't you hear what I'm trying to say? I feel as if I'm letting out a breath I've been holding all these years, to have him corroborate my experience. It shouldn't matter—what happened happened; I should see it the way I see it—yet it does. I've never really been sure that I wasn't making too much of things."

"But what things?" Greta exclaimed. "I really don't know what you're talking about, Ned!"

"What he said about *you*, Greta. You must remember. I tried to discuss it when we met again in Marby but—"

"Oh, that."

" 'Oh, that,' she says. A bishop accuses a young girl of—I don't know what—making a play for him and it's nothing? Especially considering—"

"I wasn't that young, Ned. I was sixteen."

Ned gave her an annoyed look. "The point is, I'm crouching under his desk, wondering why he wanted me to hear this slander. Was it the only way he could get himself to talk like that in front of the archbishop? I came to understand that he needed me there as a way of magnifying his—I hardly know what to call it—misdeeds? What I never have been able to understand is that gratuitous bit about my being too young. What was the point, other than to hurt me, and why did he need to do that?"

"You had hidden under his desk but he knew you were there?"

Ned looked at her as if she were being intentionally obtuse.

"I didn't *hide.* He asked me to."

"While he met with the archbishop?"

"What did you think I meant? I told you about this. Don't you remember?"

"I don't remember anything about the archbishop or hiding under a desk. Ned, you've never—"

"Well, after all this time, it still rankles," he went on, paying no attention, "though that's scarcely the word. It embedded itself—that comment. Every inadequacy I've ever felt—it seems to be rooted there. That can't be, I know, and yet that's how it sometimes seems."

"Every inadequacy?" Greta hesitated. "Do you mean, every inadequacy you've felt with me?"

"Oh, among others. I'm sorry, Greta, it's absurd, but it still upsets me to talk about it. I can still hear the way he spoke about you—first the absurdity that you'd made 'advances' to him, and then his suggestion that introducing me to you might, well, draw off your interest, but you clearly found me too immature . . ."

"Well, I hardly . . ."

"Even though I *knew* he was lying, answering the archbishop's questions in such a way as to build a trap which he—McAndrew—could then walk into . . . He couldn't face the issue head-on, couldn't say, 'I want to leave the Church. I want a different life.' He couldn't take that risk. I understand that. I *understood* that. Things had to seem to happen against his volition, and in a way I still can't really express, I knew that he needed me to hear it. To disillusion me along with himself. But that other bit, my being too young—why did he need to *hurt* me?"

Ned looked at her, baffled, puncturing a piece of venison repetitively with his fork. He glanced down, laid the fork across the plate, and reached for his wine glass. For an instant Greta had the absurd thought that he was going to make a toast.

She picked up, then put down, her own glass. Speaking slowly, choosing her words, she said, "Ned, did you never think that what McAndrew said might have been true?"

"That what might have been? My being unworthy of your interest? Yes, on occasion."

"That's not what I meant."

"What he said about you? Of course not. I never for a moment considered it."

Greta was silent.

"What, Greta? You're suggesting I should have?"

She looked at him.

"But why? What good would it have done me to suspect you?"

"You give me too much credit, Ned."

"Greta, I don't—"

"Ned, I *did* what McAndrew said. I don't know if he 'scorned' me, but he stopped the proceedings halfway."

"He stopped . . . " Ned looked at her for a long moment. "Greta, you're joking."

"No."

"But I don't—I can't—"

"Maybe I was a little young, but I'm sure I'm not the only young woman who ever tried to make a priest forget his vows."

"Greta, you're angry at me for contacting him. Why else would you make up such an absurd story?"

"I was angry when I first saw him this morning, but at him, not at you. You would think I would be, but I wasn't. Then, like you, I realized that the Bishop McAndrew I've resented all these years no longer exists."

"Resented for what?" Ned asked, as if trying to catch her in a contradiction.

"For trying to find me out!" Greta exclaimed. "And then . . . And then . . ."

Ned nodded, relieved. "I think he was angry at me because I wanted something to believe in, and angry at you because you didn't."

"That about sums it up, I guess."

Ned looked at her. "What does that mean? Why that tone?"

"We're in this together, is that what you think? Ned Dene and Greta Sayre—What the Bishop Did to Them? And now it's all over? Bishop Buries Bygones?"

"Greta, I—"

"Ned." She pronounced each word distinctly. *"I did what he said.* He didn't invent anything. I went up to his study one evening with the idea of getting even—I'd sleep with him, then turn him in. I tried to talk him into starting it, but when that didn't work I did it myself. In the middle of it I found I wasn't having to pretend. We were half undressed, lying on the rug in front of the fire, before he got cold feet."

"Where was Bede?" Ned asked.

"Bede! He was . . . I don't know where he was! I suppose we made him move."

"It occurred to me to wonder. That was his spot."

Ned wouldn't look at her now.

"Do you believe me?"

Ned didn't answer.

"Is it worse or better—to know that he didn't make it up?"

"I don't know," Ned muttered. Then he did look at her. "How can you ask that? You're my wife!"

"It was a long time ago, Ned. Maybe it's time you . . . I wasn't quite the innocent victim you thought."

"You weren't the . . ." He stared, shocked. "You mean to say—the stigmata—you *did* cause them?"

"What? If I did one thing you can't imagine me capable of, then I must have done others?"

"Greta, I didn't say that, I just . . ."

"How could a girl who would bed a bishop on his hearthrug possibly be *pure* enough to receive the holy marks? That's what you're thinking, isn't it?"

"Greta, you know I'm not religious."

But Ned was watching her now—his expression somewhere between hurt and interest.

She said, "So something marked me—I'm not an idiot. But that doesn't mean I'm defined by the experience. I was singled out but I didn't bow down to my fate. That's what you can't believe. It's what McAndrew couldn't."

"I had been going to say something along the lines of 'It takes two to tango,' " Ned said. "So you had some schoolgirl plot—obviously McAndrew was receptive."

Greta made an impatient gesture.

"You're not in the world by *yourself,* Greta," Ned said irritably. "You can't take responsibility for everything. Besides, you'll have to forgive me if it takes more than an instant to refocus an image I've held for thirty years." He looked at her. "Why were you so outraged when I brought it up back in Marby? That I could even have considered believing it?"

"That was then."

"And?"

Greta shrugged. "You wouldn't have wanted to become involved with me if I'd told you."

"I see."

Ned said it with hostility, but it turned into something else while they sat there, gazing out the window at O.'s "Eden."

"I could have kept asking questions, you know. You deceived me, but I was your accomplice. And yet . . . Where do we go from here?"

"What do you mean, Ned? Where is there *to* go?"

"I don't know," he said.

She smiled at him then, liking him for that—and for not trying to persuade her to stay when shortly afterwards she pleaded things to be done: a letter of Henry's to be answered, Rachel's card . . .

"Go ahead," he said. "Leave the dishes. I don't feel overworked."

It was too much, too much too fast, McAndrew materializing, things rising to the surface after thirty years . . .

Ned must have known by then that there was more; he wasn't stupid. He had already drawn a connection between the letters and his own experience at St. Stephen's; it was only a matter of time before he drew other connections . . . And yet now he seemed willing to wait, as if he had something he wanted . . .

In a state of rising agitation, Greta took herself upstairs. In the bedroom across the hall from her and Ned's she sat at the trestle table she used as a writing desk and took Henry's most recent letter out of its envelope. The stationery was pale green, with a darker green wigwam set between two pines. Before lunch Greta had changed out of her riding clothes into a blue seersucker sundress and sandals and now she slipped off the sandals and folded one foot under her.

Dear Mom and Dad [she read],

Another bulletin from the loony bin. There's this guy in our bunkhouse named Matt who says whenever you ask him something like, "Do you want to go swimming, Matt?" "What's a swimmingmat, is that like a laundromat?" "Where's the soap, Matt?" "What's a soapmat? I never heard of a soapmat. Is that like a laundromat?" Everyone tries not to use his name but it's amazing how hard it is to remember. When you forget he gets this idiotic grin and you feel like killing yourself. Then there's this guy named Todd who answers almost everything with "Quoth the raven, nevermore." Remind me not to read that poem again for the rest of my life. I used to like *it.*

Greta didn't think about the content of the letter; she just heard Henry's voice, the entertained indignation and disbelief, and for a moment she missed him so intensely that she considered jumping in the car right then and driving the three and a half hours to the coast of Maine; she ached to see him. Nothing was normal without him around. He'd be surprised, but he'd be glad to see her. He had never—at least, not so far—experienced that adolescent embarrassment of his parents, though he did sometimes make fun of them, as when, long after he was too old, Greta still reached for his hand crossing the street. Mostly he seemed to sympathize with their predicament at having to impose rules and restrictions they both could remember very well resenting. Even as a small child, Henry had been strangely courteous and dignified, qualities he must have inherited from Crain, that innate aristocratic manner. How ironic when Ned told people that they took little credit for Henry's good manners . . .

How could she visit Henry? Like his father, he was too sensitive to her moods not to demand to know what the matter was, and without Ned as foil she might break down and blurt out the truth, and she couldn't; it wasn't fair—Rachel had been right about that, at least—it wasn't fair to tell Henry about Crain until she was sure it was the right thing to do—but how could she *not* tell him?

"Do you love me?" Crain had asked her, one of the last times they'd met.

"How can you ask that?" she had exclaimed. "Do you ask it just to upset me?"

They had been lying in bed, having just made love, and she had sat up to get a clearer look at him. He had asked the question before, it was a ritual, but the way he asked it this time was different; if he'd been another kind of man, she might have thought he was looking for an excuse to leave her.

"But Crain, how can you—"

"I was wondering, Greta, you see"—he was lying with his hands behind his head on the pillow—"if you go on loving me only because I'm your son's father. Perhaps you would long ago have told me goodbye if it were not for Henry."

"But Crain, what on earth . . . What's brought this up? How can I separate them?"

"Some women do," he said. "Some women have to."

But what did he mean? Why was he asking this now?

"Answer me this, then," he said, in the same conversational tone. "If Henry died, would you still love me?"

"Crain, please!" she'd exclaimed. "What is this all about? I love you! I loved you long before Henry was born and I've loved you after. I've lied for fifteen years to keep on seeing you!"

Do you know what it cost me? Do you?

"Yes, but Greta, do you know," Crain said, turning towards her and resting his cheek on his elbow, "I have lately been wondering about this. Whether if it were not for the hope of introducing me to Henry someday you would want to go on meeting me."

But didn't *he* want to see him? Didn't he want to see his son?

"My son . . ."

There'd been a look in his eyes she couldn't fathom—had she been inattentive? Was he really afraid that she might leave him? But why now? Had she made him feel too guilty about not being a father to Henry? Why did he look like that? She'd never seen him look like that—no, that wasn't true, she had: when she'd come upon him crying in his dorm room. But she didn't like to think about that moment.

Greta was still looking down at Henry's letter, but she pushed it aside and took out a sheet of her gray stationery.

"Dear Mrs. Crain," she wrote. (How absurd it sounded, like "Mrs. Santa Claus.")

"I hope you will excuse the liberty I take in writing to you," she went on, her language acquiring an uncharacteristic formality. It was Phoebe

Wilmot and Throckmorton's language—where else could she have learned it?—stored away until she needed it. What were they up to these days—old Throck and Phoebe? Surely Throck had long since tracked down Phoebe's malingering husband in the Arabian desert and shot him dead. Fair and square, above board, of course, in a duel, Throck having first told Wilmot what he thought of him—though without having had to "resort to imprecation"; from Throckmorton "such epithets as 'coward' and 'blackguard' " came "armed with a sting which lesser men could achieve only through profanity." A quote, Greta believed, from *Catatonic in the Cotswolds,* though the volume into which she imagined them reinserted had never been written.

> *Dear Mrs. Crain,*
>
> *I hope you will excuse the liberty I take in writing to you. I attended your husband's funeral, but I am sure that you could not possibly recall everyone who pressed their condolences upon you on that sad occasion. I was a business partner of your late husband's; he invested in horses with my advice. (I am a horse trainer by profession.) Ownership in the one horse we owned in common reverted to me upon his death, in accordance with the terms of our contract. However, to acquaint you with the nature of our business relationship is not my purpose in writing.*

Greta briefly set down her pen and smoothed her dress and hair, subduing the impulse to check her appearance in a mirror. She slid her feet back into her sandals and sat up straighter.

> *My husband and I spend our summers in a large old house (once a resort hotel, a water spa) in West Stilling, Vermont, and it occurred to me that you might find it a relief to spend a little while . . .*

Greta had almost written "fortnight," but put down "little while" instead.

> *. . . in a new place. You will forgive me if the suggestion seems impertinent. I knew your husband for quite a long time, and though I have never met you (excepting, so briefly, at his*

funeral), Crain often spoke of you and your children, and I feel
that he would have encouraged me to extend this invitation.

Of course neither of these things was true; Crain had spoken of Julia only rarely and reluctantly, when Greta had insisted; for them to encounter each other had been his worst nightmare.

You could be as alone here as much or as little as you
wanted. We have lots of space, lovely places to walk, a pond to
swim in. Please don't hesitate to accept my invitation if it
appeals to you.

N ed dawdled over the dishes, suspended in a kind of daze, then returned to his study, leaving the door open so he could hear Greta if she came back downstairs. Lately after dinner she'd said she had to write letters or "do some paperwork," but then a half hour later had wandered down explaining that it hadn't taken as long as she'd expected or she wasn't in the mood. He had pretended not to notice that, once evening came, she couldn't stand to be alone (she who had liked nothing better than to go for a walk by herself in the dark). They would sit, then, in the double-size living room or on the back porch if it was still light enough to read—or he would read and keep an eye on Greta staring at the pages of a riding magazine. Every night he swallowed the questions that he continually rephrased and which, he now was sure, she'd been waiting for him to ask.

He turned restlessly now in his chair to look at Greta's portrait— Rachel's painting—which he loved. It captured a characteristic gazing off into space of hers, an intent study of something not visible, and Ned thought, as he had before, that it was those qualities people were unaware of in themselves that made them most lovable. There was a childlike aspect to Greta sometimes, displayed in a gesture or an expression— a kind of bewilderment or impatience that always made Ned's heart go out to her. The protective character of his affection often irritated her, he knew, so he indulged it mostly in private, when she wasn't there to object. She'd been so adamantly self-reliant that he'd sometimes been forced to ask himself if it wasn't his own vulnerability which he attributed to her.

To look at the painting had reassured him that this wasn't true. Objective bystanders—first the camera, then Rachel's painter's eye—had seen what he had. There was Greta's pride, her stalwartness, her sternness even, but also that air of not seeing what she expected; that fleeting look of forlornness that never appeared if she knew someone was watching her.

"I love you, Greta," he said, then turned rapidly when he realized he'd spoken aloud. Then he shook his head and sighed heavily. What was he afraid of? That the woman he lived with would discover his feeling for the woman he'd always believed her to be?

But she already knew, didn't she? She had known all along. He would take this much of her and no more, and she had agreed to the bargain.

Why?

For twenty years Ned Dene cherished an image of his wife that was not in line with the truth . . .

Without her in the room, what Greta had told him had taken on an air of unreality. He'd been angry at her earlier, when there had still been a chance that he might get his own Greta back—when he'd still thought that that was what he wanted. He felt numb, and then he felt shame. If he hadn't been so terminally naive, she and McAndrew would never have been able to deceive him. He couldn't have asked more clearly, could he? Lie to me, lie to me. I can't stand the truth. Although they *had* told him the truth—first McAndrew and now Greta. He hadn't wanted to believe it.

Was that true?

What must McAndrew have thought he was up to—inviting his wife's former seducer into his home? Or *lover,* not seducer; Greta had insisted on that. Ned couldn't bring himself to think about it.

Ned Dene could not bring himself to picture his wife in the arms of another man . . .

Even though it had been thirty years ago; even though she hadn't been his wife then; even though the episode had not been consummated . . .

O. and Lucinda's word—"episode." But McAndrew was not O., and Greta was not Lucinda.

Or he couldn't think. The terms of comparison fractured and fell apart.

She and McAndrew had . . . Where was Bede? Ned kept thinking of the dog, his proprietorship of the hearthrug, his innocent witnessing, and their being conscious enough of what they wanted to do to make him move.

Of course he had forgotten to consider the evenings. It had not occurred to him that Greta might visit McAndrew at a time when he— Ned—wasn't there. While he was doing his homework, they had been deepening their intimacy.

She had wanted to seduce McAndrew and denounce him, she had said, but McAndrew wouldn't go along with it.

Ned found it difficult—nay, impossible—to believe that a man of the bishop's age, once the "proceedings" were under way, would have cut them short . . .

It still made more sense to think that Greta had been the one who got cold feet and McAndrew, angry, had retaliated by hurting Ned. Yet Greta urgently wanted him to believe otherwise. He had believed what she told him before; why should he refuse to believe her now? You couldn't live with someone if you weren't going to believe what she told you.

But how could a sixteen-year-old girl want to sleep with a man in his forties?

He himself was forty-five. Maybe she would want to sleep with him now.

Ned heard what he'd said.

Except that was hardly the whole story of their marriage. There were things he remembered, times in their windswept bed at the Hollow so sweet he carried the taste with him still. If that sweetness could exist only in the embrace of deception, then he preferred to be deceived. And he had had the arrogance and stupidity to invite McAndrew back into their lives, he had *taken it upon himself*—why? It was difficult to remember right now what his reasons had been.

Greta was upset. He did ask her what was wrong—it wasn't true that he'd never asked her—but he must have asked her in a way that made it clear he didn't really want to know, the way he'd made it clear back in Marby, sitting on the terrace above the harbor.

He would like to believe that he preferred the truth at all costs, but evidently he conveyed a desire to know first what costs would be incurred.

She had sent Henry away to camp. No, first she had come up early on her own. But she had seemed agitated for several days before that, since the weekend she had unexpectedly gone to Rachel's, leaving him only a note: "Rachel called suddenly and asked if I could come to New York. Henry's supposed to spend the night at Alex's house . . ."

"She and Peter are having problems," Greta said when she called. "I can't go into it now."

This had not surprised Ned; Rachel and Peter had "had problems" before and Greta was Rachel's chief confidante.

"It was exhausting," she said when she returned, "being in the midst of it"—accounting for what seemed practically nervous prostration. "What was it all about?" he asked, but she'd said she couldn't go into it. And then a week later she had driven up to Stilling. She needed a break from teaching. When he and Henry arrived six weeks after that, she had been calmer, but remote, unreachable, as if she'd been through some cataclysmic grief and were wrung out—but what?

Clearly, living with Rachel through her marital woes could not account for it. Things were better between Peter and Rachel, Greta had informed him when he'd asked recently. Peter's mother's illness had made their complaints with each other seem insignificant.

This had sounded too convenient to Ned, another sweeping under the rug, but then he wasn't in Rachel's confidence. And certainly not in Peter's—Peter with his Oxonian accent and stiff-upper-lip philosophy.

And what explained her sending Henry away to camp and leaving most of her horses at home? The money she made over the summer paid Henry's fall tuition and the taxes on the Stilling house. He could carry them for a while, but they didn't have that much leeway. This was someone else's wife, not Greta—this woman suddenly oblivious to financial concerns.

When he had been out of the room at lunch—in the kitchen making tea—he had overheard parts of her conversation with McAndrew, her telling him she'd decided not to show King's Ransom. She wouldn't "subject him to it," Ned had heard—King's Ransom, the most promising horse she'd ever had, as she'd bragged to everyone. But she had not seen fit to confide this to him; was he going to stoop to confronting her with what he'd learned through eavesdropping?

Oh, no. Far be it from him to confront her at all.

Ned stood, went to the door, came back, sat down again. He opened a volume of O.'s letters. He'd borrowed the complete set from the university library in order to compare the style, year by year, to that of the letters to Lucinda. He studied the frontispiece: the great man at midlife in a famous portrait, the powerful brow less imposing because shown in side view, the gaze ruminative—not regretful, precisely, though seeming to recognize what had not been and was not to be. Across the lower edge O. had written, "Yours unto death," and the caption beneath read: "The author in the 1890s, addressee of inscription unknown."

Who but Lucinda?—though the photo hadn't been sent. Why not? Too incriminating? Too heartfelt? Better to leave it like this: "Pine though I do for a glimpse of your adored face, *pining* as a method of living has not a little to recommend it—lending as it does a peculiar sharpness of detail to what the eye regards, clarity of outline needing, it seems, to be paid for in currency of loss . . ."

Pining as a method of living had not a little to recommend it.

Though to endure this for a lifetime? No, it was too sickening to contemplate.

"Eden must have resembled it," O. had written about Thrush Hollow, "in its being perfectly proportioned between the wild and the frequented, the splendid and the sweet . . . Yet Eden bore no man's mark, as your Hollow valley has done . . ."

What could he have meant, whether he recognized the connotations of his language or not? That she was ruined—Lucinda bore a "man's mark"? Eden, by definition, could not be returned to. "Pining, as a method of living, has not a little to recommend it . . ."

Yet the ideal, as in so many of O.'s stories, tired of being supplanted by the real, took on substance, its creator fell in love with it, and then it took its revenge.

Better not to give it a chance. To pine, yes, but in secret. Better to remain a caretaker, living in the dusk of the world you'd loved, leaving it in shadow, than to insist, like a fool, that it could go on when the bright light of history had shown that it couldn't. Glimpse it out of the corner of your eye—the world you thought you would inhabit if O. had risked it with Lucinda. Then you could feel that to sit on a veranda in the summer twilight, with one person whom you loved, apprehending the country's incomparable beauty, was to exercise one's patriotic fervor. To love would have been enough.

Giving McAndrew the tour of the old hotel after breakfast, Ned had said, explaining the unfurnished shabbiness, "We're just interlopers, you know. We've never taken up residence." Companionably, McAndrew had agreed, "Who can afford two houses?" He'd gestured at the long living room—the threadbare overstuffed couches and slip-covered armchairs overhung by reading lamps, the occasional tables strewn with books and magazines, the worn Persian carpets, the framed prints of well-known masterpieces interspersed with paintings and photographs by friends— and said, "The decor's as recognizable as Art Deco or Louis Quatorze— though what would you call it? Impoverished Gentry? Intelligentsia in Retreat?"

Ned had laughed—nice of McAndrew to come back in time to tell him who he was. "A votary of a different order—do you remember when you called me that?" he asked. "I always wondered what you meant."

"And do you know now?"

"I'm not sure. Some devotion to not having—something along those lines . . ."

"To not having—to not believing. You never know what belief might make you do. I don't know why I wanted you to admit it."

Ned shrugged. "It gets you in the end anyway. Too much skepticism leaves you as gullible as the most credulous idiot in the end—"

"There's no question," McAndrew said.

Yet what other defense was there against feeling not in the know, not privy to some comprehensive understanding he'd always believed other people took for granted? That he'd encountered scarcely anyone who seemed to *possess* such an understanding, some source of certainty to go home to, hadn't dissuaded him. As it happened, the only person he'd ever known who'd seemed to possess anything like it had been Greta. She had . . . *Had* seemed. Because now she didn't.

And suddenly he was full of dread.

Where was she while he was speculating? These days she never stayed this long at one task. Yet he hadn't heard her come downstairs. Usually he heard her by the time she reached the landing. Could she have gone to sleep?

Ned went upstairs but found the rooms dark; at a loss, he returned to the kitchen, where this time he noticed the note on the table, weighted by the sugar bowl.

Gone to put some letters in the box.
Didn't want to disturb you.

She had taken care not to let him hear her.

It was after nine, fairly dark; Ned trusted she had taken a flashlight. He'd argued with her about carrying one: "Yes, I know there's enough ambient light, but what if you hear something? What if you smell a skunk? Don't you want to know where it is?"

He'd better walk to meet her; she'd see the light but he would call to her as he drew near—"Greta, it's me!"—so as not to frighten her. He imagined her happy to see him, taking his hand as they walked back, surprised, as she sometimes seemed to be, by the strength of her own affection for him.

He meant to do this. He started down the lawn towards the road, then realized that he'd forgotten the flashlight and went back into the house to look for one. No matter how many flashlights they owned, you could never lay your hands on one when you needed to.

"Blast it all," he said.

"Say 'Blast it,' Dad," he heard Henry say—showing Ned off to his friends as if his father were an unusual animal. "What other father do you know who says 'Blast it' or 'Gee whillikers'?" Henry would ask with pride.

"Blast it all," Ned said again, for Henry's benefit, liking himself better, thinking of Henry's liking him. There, at least, was one aspect of his life in which he hadn't failed.

Ned returned to the front door and stood inside the screen, looking out. The evening breeze came and went like a cat that could not make up its mind and fireflies were signalling from random points in the darkness—green, translucent, hallucinatory. It reminded Ned of how the animals took over the place once the human inhabitants were gone: they came back in spring to find the cellar steps gnawed by a porcupine, spaghetti stashed under a pillow by a squirrel, raccoon hand-prints all over the pantry, inked by the stove blacking it had found its way into.

He stepped out onto the lawn and stood, listening. He heard crickets, then an owl. Hooting first from one direction, then another. Had it flown through the dark in the interim, or were there two owls? He heard a wood thrush, the Hollow's namesake, with its lush call that seemed to come from another century; it had sounded the same when O. sat with Lucinda on the hotel's veranda; it would sound the same after he and Greta were gone. In a strange communion with his own absence, Ned felt calm—how foolish his seemingly pressing concerns, how stupidly insistent his worrying about what everything meant. What difference did any of it make?

In the deep dusk he could make out the great bouquets of the sugar maples along the road, but nothing beyond. The dark intervals between their trunks seemed suddenly full of possibility.

In 1891, Zebulun Snow opened a small harness shop on the Thrush Hollow Road. The Trout Hill mines had been shut down for a while and his business had been falling off; Amelia saw the new venture as a necessary one and hadn't objected when Zeb allowed as how, to keep up business in the winter, the direct road being impassable, it would make sense for him to rent a room in West Stilling. The Thrush Hollow Hotel, he'd heard, had rooms to let cheap in the off-season. Miss Dearborn, the proprietress, didn't mind a little company with her summer boarders gone.

Thrush Hollow, even then, was isolated from other houses. Amelia Snow had been to West Stilling only two or three times in her life and never to the Hollow. It didn't occur to her to ask if there were other boarders (she sometimes, as Zeb had had occasion to observe over the years, evinced a notable lack of curiosity), and it didn't seem to occur to the inhabitants of West Stilling either that there was anything untoward in a married man's sharing a lonely mansion with an unmarried lady. That was how Zeb would have referred to Lucinda, though he knew other people considered her an old maid, a spinster—terms that suggested something youthful which had withered, a blossom left dry on the branch. Lucinda was in her mid-forties, and to Zeb as beautiful as ever— maybe more so, with her life now showing in her face—but he knew people didn't see it. They had never seen his Lucy as he did, lying unclothed on a bed, unashamed, her body little changed since he'd first seen it years ago, if softer now and fuller. They hadn't seen her with her hair in a tangle on the pillow, her face and lips flushed, her eyes shining like moonlight. They hadn't felt the deftness of her hands or known her yearning or heard her triumphant sighs.

Otherwise, they would never have made those worn-out jokes about "long evenings round the winter stove" or asked, with a wink, "What side o' the bed do her ladyship prefer?" If they'd really imagined that he knew, they would have spoken to everyone else about it, but not to him. The gallant in Zeb was offended that they considered the woman he adored such an unappealing creature, but to show offense would have been risky. For his part, Zeb had long ceased to care whether anyone found out; he *wished* to be found out, really, and sometimes it seemed to him that Stilling's obliviousness, Amelia's obliviousness, conspired to drive him mad, but Lucinda had never ceased to make it plain that she wished their love to remain a secret. "It would shrivel and die if anyone knew about it," she told him. Zeb didn't believe this—he was prepared to leave Stilling in a whisper and head out West to make a new life with her—but he believed that she believed it and in her stubbornness would bring it about.

Her stubbornness had to do, Zeb had figured out by now, with this writer chap who sent her letters from across the ocean. Zeb could always tell when Lucinda had received one. She was standoffish, haughty, as if she didn't think he was good enough for her; she made it clear he was unwelcome in her bed, but after a few days she was penitent, her affection redoubled. It happened at the outside every six months, usually oftener than that. It didn't bother Zeb—her repentance was worth the wait—except for its being what stood in the way of their living their life above board, even if he could hardly have said by this point why he still wanted this. Someone else might have said he had it about as good as it could get: a wife who loved him in a motherly, patient way; another woman who still warmed to his touch after twenty years. Since he and Amelia no longer shared that aspect of things, he scarcely even felt that he was betraying her. And he knew Lucinda didn't care about being acknowledged. So why did he spend long hours imagining people saying to each other in low voices, "Do you know what I heard? Zebulun Snow is two-timing Amelia with Lucinda Dearborn—can you believe it? Been going on for years, appears like. Who would have thought?" This fantasy brought Zeb infinite pleasure, regardless of the fact that its realization would almost certainly have brought him only grief.

In the beginning he had thought that Lucinda might have a child, and that this occurrence would force their secret into the open, but either she knew ways to prevent it or she was barren. They had never talked about it. She had never given him the impression that she regretted not being a mother.

As for this fellow she wrote to—her ghost suitor—what manner of man was he? Lucinda owned his books, but Zeb wasn't much of a one for reading. The *Illustrated Weekly,* now and again; that fairly satisfied him. He had sneaked a look at the man's letters, one time when Lucinda's remoteness urged and chance afforded, but he couldn't make much headway.

> *Great beauty there is in America yet it's fallow; mankind hasn't yet set his mark on it. As you know, making exception as always for your dulcet valley (but one cannot, alas, live entirely there!), I prefer a landscape graced by civilization, given a grammar, as it were, by the villas and olive groves of my beloved Tuscany, or by the more stolid and yet mayhap more mysterious country houses of my adopted homeland.*
>
> *Over here, one might opine, the dwellings have called the gardens into existence, or perhaps the obverse, whereas, in our native land, there is as yet only uneasy commerce between them. . . .*
>
> *She hasn't yet learned to conceal herself, our America; she's an eager child calling out for its mother to "Watch, only watch, Mama!" forgetting, alas, that she has no mama to watch, applaud, or caution. . . .*

And more such. What the fellow was on about, Zeb hadn't an inkling. Unpatriotic, Zeb called it. The fellow hadn't fought; he'd let his younger brother do that. Lucy's father had been the brother's commander; that was how come a fancy boots such as he was had come to an insignificant spot like Stilling. Though to hear the fellow rave on about its "bucolic virtues" was enough to make you ill. If he was so all-tarnation sorrowful about what his lost homeland was becoming, why didn't he come on home and say so like a man? You might have thought the fellow was behind bars, instead of free to come and go as he pleased. Zeb couldn't parse it, but he knew as clearly as he knew anything that whatever held the wordy fellow back held Lucinda back; as if with the smallpox, she'd been infected by his idea that to reach for what you wanted would be like trying to touch your reflection in water; your touch would dissolve it; there would be only water.

"You can't be on the bank and in the water at the same time," Lucinda liked to say—quoting the sage overseas, Zeb had no doubt.

"I'll take your leavin's," Zeb said softly, sliding the letters back into their envelopes. "You think you know what you're missin', but you don't. You don't know the first part of it. Lucy, she's plain and simply too polite to wise you up to that fact."

Zeb liked especially to recall the summer of 1870, the summer after he and Lucinda had first become lovers. The man was coming to visit—he'd been a year abroad—and Lucinda hadn't seen him for five years. Five years of passionate correspondence on both sides, so far as Zeb could gather, although trying to piece together an actual happenstance from Lucinda's dropped hints was about like trying to find someone to shoot at in the fog. Lucinda wanted, Zeb got the impression, for him to think she and the man had shared a bed, but couldn't quite bring herself to say so. This wasn't from reticence, but because it wasn't true, and Zeb would know it wasn't. There were ways of telling when you were the first.

This didn't keep him from being wild with jealousy, however. The man had lost his "dear cousin," Lucinda had told Zeb, and required consolation. The form in which Lucinda hoped to furnish this consolation, Zeb's imagination could all too easily conjure up, especially since he had the impression that the "dear cousin" might have been an impediment in the way of the man's giving himself heart and soul to Lucinda, the cousin's departure heavenwards leaving the way not only clear but her survivor hastening upon it. Zeb only hoped that when the fellow asked for Lucinda's hand, she would feel at least a twinge of regret at losing Zebulun Snow when she accepted. He couldn't hope to measure up to a world traveller, a man who wrote books, but he hoped Lucinda would miss him with at least a portion of the missing he would know for her.

Since Captain Dearborn's death, the Hollow no longer offered its pancake breakfasts and Lucinda had said it was too risky for them to meet in the woods when she had so many guests; either she would be missed and searched for or one of the young and hearty ones who tramped about in the bracken would stumble upon them. Therefore that spring they had agreed that at noon on the fifteenth day of September, rain or shine, they would meet halfway up the steep road to Trout Hill. If others were about, he and Lucinda would nod and pass on by, but, if not, they would steal away into a secluded spot and renew their acquaintance. But this plan had been made in April, before Lucinda had heard her correspondent's sad news and learned of his impending visit. That was in May, and Zeb had not asked if she still meant to keep their September meeting date; to remind her might have been to provoke a refusal. But he had waited with increasing despondency after the time of the bereaved cousin's visit, due in the summer, certain that either Lucinda would not come at all or would come only to tell him the news that she would be leaving Stilling to marry the man she truly loved.

At dawn on the fifteenth, it was raining, a steady, unhurried rain that meant to continue all day, and Zeb felt even heavier of heart as he went about his morning chores, ate his breakfast, and left for his shop. He asked Amelia to pack him a lunch; he'd work on through the noon hour today, he said, instead of trudging home in the muck. At a little past eleven-thirty, Zeb locked up his shop, propped a note in the window— "Back in the afternoon"—and started off down Trout Hill towards Thrush Hollow.

Lucinda, having stepped off the road under protection of the trees, saw him before he saw her.

"Zebulun Snow!" heard Zeb through the rain. "Over this way!"

"Miss Dearborn!" Zeb exclaimed, for the benefit of spectators.

No one at all was to be seen; nevertheless they waited until they were well away from the road to speak further. Both knew these woods; there was no dwelling for half a mile at least.

"I'm glad it's raining," Lucinda said, as she threw her arms around his neck. "That way we can do whatever we want."

"You don't mean . . ." Zeb asked.

"It's scarce wet at all underneath here," Lucinda said, crawling beneath a low-spreading spruce. "Come keep me company, Zebulun Snow."

It suited his Lucy, Zeb could not help thinking, to belong to him out of doors; she laughed when in a moment of haste his arm knocked a branch and drops of water sprayed across her face.

They'd joked to each other that even if someone came upon them they wouldn't be recognized, dripping wet and wearing no clothes.

Dressed, saying goodbye until the next time—two weeks hence in the evening; Zeb would say he had to repair a harness—Zeb, made brazen by Lucinda's ardor, couldn't resist saying, "And here I thought you would have something to tell me."

"To tell you?" Lucinda repeated.

"About your summer. Your special visitor."

She looked at him for a long moment.

"The hotel was exceeding busy this season."

This was all Lucinda said, and Zeb knew that good luck didn't like to be questioned. Still, he was curious. Had the fellow *not* proposed, despite Lucinda's expectations, and so her happiness at seeing Zeb came from relief that at least *someone* cared for her? Or was it that he *had* asked and, when it came to it, Lucinda found that she could not bring herself to accept? And if this were so, could the reason lie in her wish not to be separated from the man she really loved, one Zebulun Snow?

This latter alternative, scruple though he might not to flatter himself into believing, Zeb came to think the likeliest explanation for Lucinda's behavior. She loved him too wholly to be receiving his attentions as mere compensation. Whatever Lucinda might wish to *say* about the two of them, or about herself and that other fellow, her body didn't lie to him; no man could have asked for more assurance than she gave. He came to accept, understand it though he could not, that some people could feel something only if others didn't know about it; they seemed to feel the soil would not nourish them out in the sunlight. He would not have chosen to live this way, yet it was the way he did live, and he wasn't going to tax his mental powers overmuch in wishing it were otherwise.

After the one time, some years after this visit, when Zeb came across a few of the man's letters and read them, he never did so again. Nor did he ever read Lucinda's diary—he had not known she kept one—though clearly it had been left out for him, along with her correspondent's letters, with the assumption that he would do so, in the spring of 1915 when she took her trip to the seashore.

"Do what you want with these," she wrote in a letter left for Zeb. He'd gone home for the weekend and found it when he returned to the Hollow on Monday evening.

> *I cannot bring myself to destroy them. So much of my life is contained therein, even though it be a pretended life, that never really did exist.*
>
> *I have wronged you, Zeb—I don't ask your forgiveness. That would insult you further. Don't pity me when you read these pages. A mistake as lifelong as mine deserves no pity. I lived for nothing; my life has been one long emptiness. I believed that what a man said meant as much as what he did. I never even said to the world that I loved you.*

Zeb, choking, gasping for air, read on: the news that there had been a baby who died, one winter long ago when Lucinda had lived alone. It had been born months early, but she had been able to see that it was a little girl. She had made a coffin herself, which she'd buried in the cellar, in the same spot where her father had been buried, that winter he died. She'd be grateful if Zeb would see to it that the little girl had a proper burial. She did beg his forgiveness for not telling him. Some time after their daughter's death, Lucinda wrote, she'd visited a doctor in Boston who had told her she would never have any more children.

Lucinda wrote other things, which Zeb could scarcely read through his tears. She didn't tell him what she meant to do, but he knew. The clipping from the *Dalby Gazette* about the writer's death and the last line in her diary told him all that he needed to know. It was the only line he read. He had no wish to read any more.

It was April. In the cellar the frost went down only a few inches. Zeb chiseled away with a shovel. He was afraid to use a pick axe; he might shatter the box—he didn't know how deep Lucinda had buried it.

Two feet down, that was all. Lucky it had been winter when the baby died, Zeb thought; something might have smelled it and dug it up, otherwise. There were gaps in the foundation wall big enough for most anything to squeeze through.

The wood was still nearly intact; she must have used cedar. She would have known what to use. He kept himself working so that he wouldn't dwell on the picture that wouldn't leave his mind: Lucinda giving birth alone to a stillborn daughter, fashioning a coffin, burying it . . . His daughter. Their daughter. Lucinda hadn't given her a name, or if she had, she hadn't told Zeb.

Zeb wiped the small coffin as clear of earth as he could with his hands and then carried it upstairs—it weighed less than a good log for the fire—and set it on the kitchen table. In the hotel office he emptied the strongbox in which Lucinda kept the hotel's records and stacked her diaries and the letters from abroad in it. He fastened it shut with a padlock, pocketed the key, and then carried the strongbox down cellar and buried it in the same spot where his daughter's coffin had lain. He spent a good while smoothing out the ground, wetting it down with water, until no trace of disturbance remained.

Upstairs, Zeb went out back to the building that served as carpenter's shop and toolshed. He brought a hammer, nails, and chisel back to the kitchen.

He would have to look. There couldn't be much left—it must have been thirty-five or forty years ago, he guessed. How long ago that seemed, and yet how recent. He tried to recall when that spring had been when Lucinda's standoffish behavior had impelled him to look at O.'s letters, but he couldn't remember. That could have been the time, but it might have been any other too.

He pried open the lid, trying not to split the wood. Lucinda had nailed it every few inches all around. Finally it came up. First there was a folded cloth, which he removed. Then his dead daughter, a miniature, recognizably human skeleton, in a tiny, yellowed dress. He found it impossible to think that Lucinda could have sewn it before she had buried the dead child. She must have taken it off a doll.

Zeb didn't dare pick up the little skeleton but he laid his hands on it, one on the skull, smaller than a large apple, and the other across the chest, which his palm completely covered. After a while, he lit two candles and set them at either end of the coffin. He sat down beside the table, and remained there in silence throughout the night.

"Why didn't you tell me?" he said aloud, towards morning. "Why didn't you tell me?"

J ulia Crain sits on Henry's old swing, swaying back and forth, in and out of sight, behind the trunk of the dying butternut. Above her, the bare horizontal branch groans rhythmically. She doesn't pump but rocks herself gently, pushing off with the toes of her dainty white sandals. She wears a pale blue striped dress of sophisticated design dotted with tiny violets, and her black, gray-flecked hair is twisted behind her head as it was at her husband's funeral. This morning, for Greta, for the rest of her life, will always take place in the present.

In the beginning, Greta observed Julia from an upstairs window, taking care not to be seen although she knew that the way the sun hit the front of the house and blackened the windows made it unlikely that anyone would see her. Ever since Julia's arrival, three days ago, Greta had taken every opportunity to watch her when she thought Julia wasn't looking. Sometimes she had the impression that Julia was doing the same; feeling someone's eye on her, Greta would turn sharply, but Julia was always gazing placidly into the distance or examining her hands in her lap. Anticipating the intent stare of the Julia in her nightmare, whom she'd been expecting to confront—whom she'd been expecting to confront *her*—Greta found instead a diffident, grieving *widow,* a state as replete now with unassailable privilege as *wife.*

Now Greta waited for the branch from which the swing was suspended to rip apart from the trunk and crash to the ground. She wondered what she would do. Would habit send her rushing to Julia's aid or would she continue to observe, waiting to see how badly Julia was hurt? Ned had been threatening to cut the limb for several years now, since its extremities were dead, but each year Henry pleaded with him to spare it, and this year he had made Ned promise at least to wait until he came back from camp. One last swing, he said, for posterity's sake. It was an expression Henry used often, as he did others that took his fancy, heedless of their conventional application. "Come on, Mom, have another piece of pie—for posterity's sake." "Oh, for posterity's sake, would you get off the phone, Dad?"

Better Julia than Henry, Greta thought, as if she were required to choose which of them would be sitting on the swing when it collapsed. Better anyone than Henry. Instantly she strove to eradicate the thought. This terror that something was going to happen to him, that he was going to pay for her sins—even to consider it alerted those forces in the universe that would come dowsing for a substantiation. Worst fears could not be realized if you did not first entertain them. She had been fighting off the cold apprehension that had gripped her ever since the moment she'd watched from the back living-room windows as Felipe, Crain and Julia's son, had circled the car to open the passenger door for his mother, but her fear had only intensified, until it pressed on her almost unbearably, bending her towards its source. By now she almost wanted whatever was to happen, to happen, in order to be rid of the fear. Yet even to wish that wished doom on her child. Fear and wishing, inextricable. She tempted fate by not warning Julia that the swing was unsafe (though she had mentioned it to Felipe and to McAndrew's daughter Sylvie, who'd been taking turns pushing one another as high as they could), but fate responded unpredictably to tempting.

Greta had forgotten her original reason for coming upstairs, if she had had one. She watched Julia not from her and Ned's bedroom, but on the other side of the wide central hallway from the bedroom she'd assigned Julia. Greta had already looked through the closet and the bureau drawers and found nothing of particular interest except for two photographs of Crain—Lars, Julia called him. ("Lar-se," she pronounced it—a Spanish softening; though this was for strangers; "Renzo," she'd called him in person, short for Lorenzo, the Spanish for Lars.) One, recent, Crain in blue jeans and a short-sleeved plaid shirt, stood in a frame on the bureau; the other, an unframed snapshot of Crain and Julia in Mexico when they were young—it must have been taken not long before their wedding— Greta had found in the drawer of the bed table and now held in her hand. She glanced at it whenever she wasn't looking at Julia through the window, as if to be sure that the woman in the photograph and the woman on the swing were one and the same. In the photograph, Crain and Julia stood in a half embrace, turned towards the camera—a posed shot. The background—a crumbling stone wall and a field of towering saguaro cactus—seemed to accuse Greta: this was *their* world; she could never enter into it. She could never share with Crain the intimate knowledge of his country that Julia did. Greta wondered who had taken the photograph; probably Fredrik—Federico—Crain's younger brother (who had never, in the end, come to school in France); she couldn't imagine Crain showing his affection for Julia so openly in front of anyone else. He had mimicked his mother's urging him to kiss his fiancée—"Go on, you're engaged! You don't have to be shy now, *hijo . . .*" But perhaps he had done so easily, around anyone. He had been physically demonstrative in public with *her,* after all, before he had had to curb himself to guard their secret.

Greta wondered what Julia would do if she were to open the drawer that night and find the photograph torn in half—top to bottom, herself and "Lar-se" separated. Would she scream? Clap a hand against her mouth in silent horror? Pound on Greta's door and hold out the two halves to demand an explanation? Greta pictured each possible reaction in detail, as if she were writing a film script and wanted to choose the action that would most plausibly express the emotion she wished to convey. She did not think of the fact that she was occupied in searching a houseguest's bedroom, something of which, even a few days ago, she would never have imagined herself capable.

McAndrew had first appeared on a Sunday morning. That evening Greta had written to Crain's wife and taken the letter to the mailbox so that it would be picked up the next day. In one of the flukes of efficiency that sometimes overtook the postal system, Julia had received the letter on Tuesday afternoon. She had telephoned that evening.

She was so grateful for Mrs. Dene's kindness, she said, speaking in the soft, almost breathy voice and mild accent Greta remembered from Crain's funeral—in fact, yes, if it would truly be no trouble, it would please her very much to accept the invitation. She was—how did one say?—at loose ends. On Friday, she thought, her son might be able to drive her up—she was ashamed to say that she didn't drive—but of course he wouldn't stay . . . He would certainly be welcome as well, Greta had said.

Julia's son, Philip—or Felipe, as Julia called him and as Greta had always thought of him—who had driven her up to Stilling from New York, appeared to have fallen in love at first sight with Sylvie McAndrew, who had accompanied her father to dinner on Sunday, a week after his first visit. Felipe's room was across the corridor from his mother's; McAndrew and Sylvie, who at everyone's urging had returned two days later to spend a week at the Hollow, had rooms in the ell. Right now the two of them, with Ned and Felipe, were hiking up Trout Hill to explore the mines. They'd packed a lunch, and would be gone for several hours.

Julia was not a hiker, she regretted to say. Occasionally she strolled a short way up and down the road, or meandered around the lawn, looking at the flower beds; otherwise she sat in a lawn chair, on the porch in a wicker rocker, or in one of the soft shabby armchairs in the airy living room, crocheting a fringe onto a dresser scarf with fine thread. Her posture was alert, as if she were waiting for a receptionist to call her name and usher her into an inner office. Sometimes she paged through a magazine, but otherwise she didn't read. Invited to help herself to Greta's shelves of mysteries or the books in Ned's study, she apologized for never having learned to read comfortably in English. She added that "lately" she had been unable to keep her mind on anything—as if, so it seemed to Greta, Julia refrained from speaking her husband's name in Greta's presence. In the evening Julia played a card game with Felipe and once she played badminton with him after he badgered her to let him teach her; she proved adept, but he'd been unable to persuade her to play since. She continually offered to help with cooking or dishwashing, but the moment she was not required to be social her face assumed an expression of great distance and privacy, and she wandered off to sit somewhere by herself. Her remoteness infuriated Greta, and yet, against her will, Greta found herself behaving gently and solicitously towards Crain's widow. The word had attached itself to Julia like a tiara, crowning her with eternal possession of Crain and by Crain, now that he was dead.

Clear though it was that Julia was living in a state of deep grief, it would have been impossible for Greta to know how much of her behavior resulted from the shock of her husband's death and how much manifested a restrained, old-fashioned upbringing had it not been for Felipe's informative, confessional conversation. He had unburdened himself almost immediately, made half-frantic by his mother's near somnambulism; it was such a relief, he said fervently, to talk to a woman his mother's age who had known his father. "She has always been full of energy! You would not believe . . . None of us could keep up with her! We had a cook and someone cleaned the apartment but she was always busy directing, directing . . . My father used to say she would organize the houseflies if she could get them to pay attention to her."

Greta violently resented Felipe's assumption that she cared about his mother's state of mind, but she forced herself to ask, "They were happy, your parents?" as if to show concern, to gauge the extent of her guest's distress.

"Oh, entirely," Felipe said, with assurance. "They always got along. My father travelled a lot and she always missed him—maybe why she found so many ways to keep busy. She relaxed more when he was home. They knew each other all their lives—"

"Your father mentioned," Greta said.

"It would not destroy you if you were not to see me, but it would destroy her. You are the stronger—you do not need me in the same way."

"How do *you* know what it would do to me? You're not with me when I'm not with you! Do you think you vanish from my mind as I seem to from yours?"

"You know that's not true, Greta. You're on my mind all the time."

"All right, it's not true—but why do you make me say what I don't mean?"

Or had he meant it? Had all those trumped-up disagreements, as she thought, been sincere?

"How dare you? How *dare* you?" Greta said to Julia's dead husband, in Julia's room. Though what did she mean?

She saw Felipe again, circling the car while his mother waited for him to help her out, to lead her up to the front door as if she were a patient being shepherded to Lucinda Dearborn's water cure—because she was allowed. Julia was *allowed.* Crain had given her that right. Greta's anger swelled further, like a wave that continually accrued height and power but could not break. She had expected *something,* some false note in Julia's gratitude to indicate that somewhere, however unspecifically, Julia had known of her existence. But nothing. Nothing! She didn't need Crain to tell her that there was no volition involved in Julia's behavior. Julia was artless and unsuspicious, dignified and gracious, incapable of guile. Who wouldn't have wanted to be married to a person like that? Crain had been circumspect about Julia only because he hadn't wanted Greta to feel inadequate.

But with equal force, like the retreat of a wave, would come a memory of her and Crain's deep familiarity, their unquestionably belonging to each other; she remembered the desperation with which he had fought her suggestions that they ought not to meet anymore, if they could find no way out of their impasse. "I beg you to reconsider," he said, reverting to his youthful formality. Only in her presence was he convinced that he existed on this earth; only with her did he believe that it made a difference to have been here . . .

If she told Julia this, would Julia believe her? Or would she say, Oh, a man like my husband, he has other women—it's only you Americans, with your naive ideas of love and duty, who would find anything to remark on in this . . .

But he had loved her; Crain had *loved* her.

She couldn't comprehend it. How could Julia grieve so purely when her husband had loved someone besides her? Greta couldn't grasp it. She was travelling out of the present in two directions at once, riding a current going one way while across an expanse of water she witnessed herself simultaneously going another. Her mind would break apart. Only when she looked at Julia from a distance as she was doing now, when Julia was absorbed and unaware, could she imagine that Julia guarded some knowledge of her husband's infidelity: she was so insistently innocent; she'd never admitted that he needed things she couldn't give him, that he had a life in him she couldn't share . . . But in her presence Greta could not maintain this view. Listening to Julia's melodious voice, her faintly accented English, Greta, to her disgust, felt protective of her, wished to comfort her, to bring some liveliness back into her glance, as her son was so frantic to do. To blame Julia for any lack would be like blaming an animal or a flower, a being that existed in the purity of unselfconsciousness. There would be great peace in being the recipient of Julia's affection. Crain had been at rest with her; he had been home, something he had never been with her.

"But you are my home—that you *know* me is where I live. Why can't you believe me? Why would I tell you these things if they weren't true?"

Greta gave up trying to remember whatever it was she had come upstairs to do—if for a reason other than to postpone whatever would happen now that she and Julia were alone—and left the room. About to start down the stairs, she noticed that she had taken the photograph with her and she hurried back across the hall to replace it. As she shut the drawer of the bedside table, she glanced out the window and froze: Julia was no longer sitting on the swing. Greta listened, her heart beating faster. Was Julia on her way up the stairs, even in the hallway by now?

Greta heard nothing and decided she would look less culpable if she simply walked out the door and told Julia she had been looking for—what? A book? A vase? Yes, she was making sure that the flowers were still fresh—the daisies and chicory and Queen Anne's lace she had set in a mason jar on the mantel of the blocked-up fireplace. They were in fact wilted, and Greta grabbed the jar, relieved to have been made truthful by happenstance until it occurred to her that *Julia* would never have permitted the flowers in a guest's room to go unchanged for so long. Greta would have to apologize—"I'm not usually so distracted . . ." But that she couldn't say; Julia might ask what distracted her.

Wasn't that what she wanted Julia to ask?

On the landing, Greta paused to listen again. Nothing. No, sound. What could Julia be doing? Was she snooping as Greta had been?

A hand on the newel post, gazing at the wallpaper—narrow pale gray stripes overlaid with pansies, as if the design were an accident of printing, two discrete patterns mistakenly superimposed—Greta noticed the similarity of the pattern to that of Julia's dress and she could feel her mind lurching to establish a significance in this, some overriding explanation of resemblance. She shook her head, like Ransom when he balked, but she could feel the effort it took to resist. How much easier to give in, seek the message: it was meant for her; she had but to admit that and all would come clear.

Unwillingly, she descended the central section of the staircase into the downstairs hallway. Telling Julia about Henry might change nothing, but it was her only hope. It was why she'd invited Julia to Thrush Hollow, Greta forced herself to remember: something else had to happen to free her—she had to take back what Julia had stolen at Crain's funeral. What this was, Greta could no longer think. Though if in regaining it she broke Julia's world beyond repair . . . Had she any right to do that? Should she speak to Felipe first?

But only Julia had the power to free her.

Julia was sitting on the back porch now, gazing in the direction of the mines; the thought of her son in proximity to open mine shafts had terrified her until Ned assured her that one could not simply stumble into them; one had to enter the caves intentionally and even then the descents were gradual. "We will promise not to set foot beyond the entrance," McAndrew said, "if that would reassure you," and then Julia relaxed and said no, that wasn't necessary, she trusted their judgment. Though why they felt an interest in these bygone excavations, she did not succeed to understand.

"My mother has no sense of the past," Felipe teased her. "She's never had any interest in historical monuments or figures."

"A sense of the past, what is that?" Julia said. "I don't see that things are worth any more because they are old."

"Would you like some iced tea?" Greta asked Julia. "It's hot today."

"Yes, I find it so also. Thank you very much."

Together they returned to the kitchen; Greta flexed ice cubes out of a tray and poured from the pitcher of already cooled tea and asked Julia if she would like lemon. It had been a while since breakfast and so Greta also shook gingersnaps out of a box onto a plate and they carried everything back out onto the porch. There the two of them sat in the wicker rocking chairs, Julia in her simple but stylish dress and delicate sandals and Greta barefoot in the jeans and white V-necked T-shirt she had worn to lunge Ransom that morning. She hadn't been able to ride since Julia arrived. Ransom was impatient to work, but she couldn't free her mind sufficiently to concentrate.

Greta would have liked, now, to sit silently until the silence gained such intensity that one of them had to say something, was forced into revelation, but instead, even before she'd sat down, she began to chatter, to recount the history of the mines: their fortunes rose when the country was at war with itself and fell during peacetime—she couldn't maintain her reserve, let alone her integrity. Like a puppy, she leapt and whimpered, agitating for a response meant specifically for her. Julia inclined her head and nodded, attentive—she couldn't possibly be interested.

"It's hard to imagine what it used to be like here," Greta went on—the kind of imprecise, nostalgic-sounding remark she scorned when other people offered it. "So many more people—what that would have been like—instead of the outpost it is now. The world has changed so . . ."

"Mrs. Dene," Julia said when Greta left off, wondering what next, what further inanity she would seize upon to hold back the silence, hold back her fear . . .

"Greta," Greta said automatically.

"Greta," Julia corrected herself. "I am sorry—I've lived here so long, but I still am unused to American informality. Lars used to tease me. He said I lived in a—what is it you call it?—a time . . ."

"Time capsule."

"Yes."

Julia was rocking herself back and forth in the wicker chair, which creaked repetitively, and Greta had to prevent herself from asking Julia to stop the noise.

"My life has been my family," Julia continued. "I never wanted anything else. I've lived for them. I've never made close friends in the United States, though we've lived here since before Felipe was born and people have been friendly. There's no one to whom I can speak of certain things."

Greta, nodding, gripped the arms of her rocker, trying to quiet the noise of Julia's.

"You have been so kind—such a gift to me. I had thought that perhaps I might ask your advice."

"My advice?" Greta repeated.

It is here that time freezes, though within the frozen moment Julia continues to rock, and the trees at the far edge of the lawn swell forward and back, as if they are trying to approach but are arrested by a spell in their progress towards the house.

"It concerns my children," Julia goes on. "All their lives I have kept something from them. I am ashamed of it, but it was what their father— what Lars wished. Now I do not know if I should keep silent. I do not know what I should do. I do not know how well you knew my husband, but you did know him."

Greta realizes now that whatever Julia is going to say is not about her, not directly—she is not going to be accused—so then why does her heart pound so and her voice tremble as she replies?

"I will be glad to help if I can."

The strange thing is that she means this; and she will think, later, that she let Julia destroy her so that Julia could save herself, let Julia take away once and for all any right she—Greta—had to her own grief, and she won't understand why.

"No one alive knows what I am about to tell you," Julia says, and Greta imagines the dead who do know gathering in witness. "Perhaps no one should, perhaps I should not speak, but I am not strong enough to keep a secret like this alone—you will forgive me for burdening you. Here is what I must tell someone. Felipe and Teresa are not Renzo's children."

"They are not . . . I don't understand," Greta says. She notices that Julia has slipped into her familiar name for Crain.

"They are his brother's. Federico's. Federico is not alive either."

"Not alive . . ."

"He died several years ago."

"Yes, I know. I remember," Greta says inadvertently. Crain had been deeply distraught, though he hadn't seen his brother for many years.

"Rico married afterwards and had children of his own. They and their mother still live on the hacienda. I wouldn't want them to feel threatened. I'm not after money."

"Money?" Greta echoes. What hasn't she understood? What will happen when she does understand? She knows that she shouldn't listen to more; she should make an excuse—anything, no matter how foolish or transparent—so that Julia doesn't tell her the central fact around which they are circling, but she can't move. She even supplies Julia with the prompting she seems to be waiting for.

"You were involved with Crain's brother before Crain?" she asks. "But I thought . . . Crain said you were childhood sweethearts." Was *this* after all not true, the meetings in the moonlit cactus desert, which had caused Greta so much jealous pain? Had Crain stolen his brother's sweetheart?

"We were," Julia says. "We loved each other since the moment we met. We were both fifteen. I never thought of anyone else from that moment on."

"No," Greta says. I was fifteen too, she thinks.

"We were so careful. To prevent conception, I mean." Julia smiles. "In our clumsy, ignorant way. It was our first time. Renzo said we should wait, but we were engaged . . . Later, of course, I learned that if we had been able to have children our measures would not have been a success."

"Your measures?" Greta repeats. "If you had been able to have children?"

"I could. It was Lars who couldn't."

"Lars . . ."

Greta feels a strange rushing noise in her head, as if a plane, flying too low overhead, has rendered the conversation inaudible.

"But that's impossible," she says. "He has . . . Crain has children. How can he not have them?"

Julia looks at Greta a little strangely.

"I don't understand," Greta says. She tries to breathe, but can't tell if she should be breathing out or breathing in.

"He raised them as his, but they are not his. He could not have loved them more if they were, but he would never be convinced of that. It was his idea to ask his brother. Our children had to be his own flesh and blood, as close as we could come, he wouldn't adopt—but afterwards he hated Federico. He refused to see him after that, though when Rico died Renzo could not forgive himself. He always expected that one day he would find the courage to see him again."

At some point, Greta has no idea when, Julia has stopped rocking—whatever her rocking was meant to accomplish, accomplished—and now sits still, turned in her chair to face Greta. At each sentence she has spoken, as if someone were clicking a slide projector, Greta has seen a picture of Crain: requesting his brother to father his children; explaining to Julia—gesturing extravagantly, as he did when excited—why they couldn't risk "alien" blood; then persuading her to keep it all a secret . . .

"I respected his wishes—not to tell the children. I never liked it, but, especially when Rico was alive, I could understand it. Would Felipe and Teresa want to see him? It might have been very awkward. But that is no longer a possibility. Do children not have the right to know who their parents are? And their siblings? Yet I am so afraid they will feel betrayed, when Renzo is not here to explain his decision to them."

Now what Greta sees is Crain's expression as he studied Henry's photographs: wistfulness and longing, which always broke her heart, yet never the fatherly pride so apparent in Ned's face when he gazed at his son. Without even knowing she did so, she had looked in vain for a hint of possessiveness from Crain, while attributing his remoteness to self-protection, his knowing he couldn't risk closing the gap between himself and Henry lest he bring the whole fragile structure of his life crashing down around him. *But that is not what it was.* Not what she thought. What she thought was not what had been the case.

Out of the inadequacy of these phrases she sees Crain again, the day she told him she didn't see how she could be pregnant with Ned's child, the timing was all off; they'd been trying to have a baby for over a year with no success—"Are you sure?" Crain exclaimed. "You're absolutely positive? And you *are* pregnant? You've been to the doctor? Oh, Greta! Greta! I never hoped . . . I never dreamed . . ."

His wild delight she'd interpreted as his finally achieving the wherewithal he needed to be able to leave his wife and be with her; she could feel a hidden uncertainty gone; and she too became wild with happiness: she still remembered that vivid, wide-awake night. Later she had no choice but to accept his explanation: he was simply overjoyed that *they* should have a child. She was the woman in his heart. That didn't mean he could abandon his family.

But this was wrong. Neither was true. What was true was only this: Crain had been allowing himself to believe that, against all possibility, medical science had made a mistake. Maybe he *had* planned, once the baby was born, to leave Julia, but then he had concluded it could not be, and nothing had changed. Sitting on the back porch at Thrush Hollow, Greta tries and fails to comprehend that Crain would have left Julia and lived with her if only Henry had really been his son.

And now Greta remembers a hundred other things: Crain's closely examining Henry's successive pictures for resemblances to himself, his wanting to see pictures of Ned, refusing to accede to Greta's insistence that Henry had Crain's eyes and mouth. "No," Crain said. "No, he doesn't look like me.

"I sometimes wonder, Greta," he said, "if you would love me if I were not the father of your child."

Did she speak? Why is Julia still talking?

"I was brought up believing it is wrong to lie to anyone, for any reason, and yet I agreed to do what Renzo wished. But now he is dead. Must I still protect him? What sense does that make? Whom would I be protecting?"

"Protecting?" Greta echoes.

"He was a good father," Julia says. "I don't want Teresa and Felipe to feel that he wasn't."

"But he wasn't a good father!" Greta exclaims. "How can you think he was? A good father doesn't lie to his children—a *person* doesn't lie to someone who trusts him! Oh, my God!" she cries. "What right have I to say such a thing! My God!"

"Please," Julia says. "Mrs. Dene. Greta. I have upset you—I am so sorry. I didn't know . . ."

"Didn't know what? What do you know?"

"My question has upset you. Forgive me."

"How could he lie? How can you love someone and lie to her?"

"I do not know," Julia says gently, her expression disturbed and sympathetic. "There is something in your own life—"

"No!" Greta cries. "No!"

"I cannot defend my husband," Julia says, "but I cannot condemn him either. It never mattered to *me* that he was not Felipe and Teresa's father, but he never believed it. I had made love with his brother, and he could never forgive Federico. I don't think he ever forgave me, although it was his own idea. He didn't want doctors involved, or artificial insemination—then there would be a record. He said no records. The fewer people who knew the truth, the better. I should maybe have insisted on the modern way, the unknown donor, or not at all . . ."

There is still something she has not understood, it seems to Greta, something that Julia's words conceal, but she is too deafened by what Julia has said even to guess what this might be.

"Always his brother's shadow came between us," Julia continues, and, as if she's invoked him, the shadow in her talk seems to spread. "Federico and I—we had nothing in mind but to make Renzo happy. As for my children—you know, you are a mother. Your child is your child."

"You love the father of your child," Greta says.

"It depends," Julia answers.

On Thrush Hollow's back porch, it is very quiet. The deep silence of the summer afternoon, made more profound rather than interrupted by the hum of insects, has settled down around them. Soundlessly, unaware of herself, Greta is crying. She realizes this only when Julia leans forward and lays a hand on hers.

"I am very sorry—I have been thoughtless. I should not have gone on. I saw that you were upset. It was such a relief, such a great relief, to speak after all these years, that is my only excuse. I did not think of my question upsetting someone else. If it would ease your mind to speak to me in return . . ."

Greta turns to look at Julia. She gazes through tears at Crain's widow, and knows without reflecting that she won't tell her about Crain now. It isn't generosity that moves her, though she'll be generous without meaning to be. She won't say anything because she too is dead now, dead to the world, sealed in the tomb of her secret. The secret was never necessary, but the secret is all she has left, all that holds her back from the oblivion yawning all around her. She lied all these years to protect Henry, to protect Ned—to protect herself. So she said. She lied in order to lead two lives that could not be lived together, neither of which she could relinquish. But she lied for no reason at all.

Yet if she were to tell Julia about Crain—about his loving her, the things he said, his pretending to be Henry's father—no matter how vividly she could make Julia know Crain's passion for her, she fears, she is nearly certain, that Julia would feel only pity, a vast sadness and pity, but for Greta, not for herself. The poor woman, she would think, to let herself be so fooled.

Anger Greta could withstand—hatred, resentment. But not pity. Anger would call her back, resurrect her, now that she is no longer alive. But pity can never do this and she will not pretend to be alive to satisfy those who can't accept that she has died.

Greta was in the kitchen when Ned came in and she knew he could tell that something had happened; she was only washing her hands at the sink but maybe she went on too long or behaved oddly in some way because he laid a hand on her shoulder and said, "Is everything all right?"

"Yes—fine," she said, though her hands were bothering her so much that she could hardly think about anything else. They itched and throbbed and soon it would happen again; the pressure within was too great and her palms would erupt and then, as before, everyone would want to *understand* what had happened to her. They were *her* hands; *she* felt the furious itching that no amount of scratching could stop; *her* blood welled up against the skin, forcing its way out, but that would not matter to them. What happened to her happened to them, they seemed to think, and how could she withstand them now? Until a few hours ago Henry had been Crain's son and even though Crain was dead she was protected by the knowledge. She had thought she couldn't stand under the weight of the secret but it had been infinitely light compared to what it weighed now. Her life had been an impersonation, but not of her making, not the one that had kept her safe from immersion—in her marriage, in Ned's idea of her—she hardly knew anymore what.

Now she would drown; Ned was her husband and Henry their son, designations pressing down on them, pressing them underwater too, oblivious to their danger as they might be. Ned was Henry's father, but the Henry she had loved was Crain's son.

She had to get away from the Hollow, everyone watching her, waiting for revelation—Ned wondering what had happened while he was gone,

Julia wondering what she had said to upset her . . . Though she would never let Julia know *now,* let Julia think that Crain had kept on seeing her because she believed he was a father—*But that doesn't explain why you loved me in the first place or begged me to come back to you after your marriage. They will try to make me think you didn't love me—how could you have deceived me if you loved me? They will ask, and I don't know, I don't know . . .*

If I stay here I might try to find out from them—the way Ned thought he could understand O. by talking to McAndrew or McAndrew by reading O., mixing the dead with the living, the living with the dead, as if you could understand anyone in comparison to anyone else, as if anyone could take the place of anyone else.

I know how they'd think of you: liar, coward, pretender after titles . . . "A person can entertain an idea, can't he?" you said. I remember when you said it. It was just after I came back from Marby, a few weeks, no more, and we had gone to the village for coffee after riding. You had café crème and I had it black, with sugar. We both had those dense chocolate cakes—what were they called? You mentioned something about your "heritage" and I jumped on it. "Are you still thinking about all that? I thought you got over it," I said. "A person can entertain an idea, can't he?" you said, but easily, *Crain, and I knew it was all right. You wouldn't go through with marrying Julia—I knew it.*

And you didn't. You're no more married to her than I am to Ned and I know that but who in the world would believe me?

I will stay with you despite yourself, Greta said to him. It was more difficult but perhaps also easier, now that he was dead.

She went upstairs to change into her riding clothes, then down to the barn to saddle Ransom. It was mid-afternoon but it stayed light so late that she had four or five hours before real dark, easily enough time to get up to the mines and back—if she walked someone might offer to accompany her but if she rode no one could. Ned, catching sight of her from the living room, ran out and when she told him where she meant to go tried to dissuade her—"You didn't want to come with us this morning, why do you want to go now? Besides, it spooks Ransom, you told me so last summer."

Yes, it spooked him but that was why she wanted to go. She'd always known that something was up there; often when she'd look out at Trout Hill she'd think of what lay up above, a real ruin behind their picturesque summer one; Ransom's instinct told her even more surely than her own that something lurked there, exercising its malignant attraction. Already today, it had drawn everyone away from the Hollow so that Julia could deliver her fatal blow, and Ned must have sensed the danger. Yet she was less afraid now than impatient. What you did—what being brave had always meant—was to meet what you feared directly and, on Ransom's back, she wouldn't be able to pretend the danger didn't exist. This would be their real test, not international competition. Every impediment to unhampered movement had always terrified him, and no one had been able to train him because they thought his fear arose from first negative experiences of training, riders who had pushed him beyond his capability; cruelty, harshness. But they had been wrong about that; he'd always been capable of everything; it was his not understanding why strictures were imposed that stood in his way, bewildered him. Why do this now, and not that, why three paces instead of four? So her "cure" had been simple—she never ordered him to do anything. From a spectator's point of view, it looked as though she did, but that was not what happened.

She had known as soon as she laid a hand on his neck and he shivered, a great ripple spreading along his skin, how finely tuned he was; there would be no limit to what he could do so long as he decided to do it. On his back, she let him feel only the possibility tensed inside her, coiled inside her like time that would unwind when ready, and in response to what he sensed he *had* to move—he couldn't stand it, he had to play it out. He didn't *obey*. Six months after she first sat on his back, people who'd seen him perform before—or not perform, since he would do nothing—stood slack-jawed while he flawlessly executed *piaffes* and *passages* and the one-time changes, arguably the most difficult move in dressage. "What did you *do?*" they demanded, and she told them she hadn't done anything. She didn't say that she knew what it was like to have what you did, what it was in your nature to do, be defined and judgment brought to bear on it, *evaluated,* according to criteria that had nothing to do with you.

She had thought she would always be able to make it clear to Ransom that they were just pretending to do what other people thought they were doing; it might *seem* as if they were executing the movements prescribed by the test levels, but they did it only because they *could* do it, as a lark, to see what it felt like to do them. No judgment could touch them. Then

Crain died, and she thought, almost as soon as his secretary had hung up the phone: I'll never show Ransom again.

Overjoyed though he had been to see her approaching the paddock in jodhpurs and boots, Ransom still sniffed her warily as he rubbed his forehead against her shoulder. She hadn't ridden him for almost two weeks and he could tell that she had something unusual in mind. He tossed his head when she led him out of the paddock and down to the road. She would head up towards Odder about a mile, past where the road to West Stilling cut off to the left, and then curve back around to reach the mines; the track from the Hollow directly up Trout Hill was too steep to ride.

When she climbed into the saddle she could feel Ransom imperceptibly trembling, but he calmed down as they started up the road; maybe they were headed to the Tollivers'; she hadn't ridden him that way yet this summer. But when they passed the West Stilling road, he turned jittery again, and at the Trout Hill turn-off didn't want to take it; he hadn't forgotten where the road led although she'd ridden him there only once before and that the previous summer. She didn't click to him as she sometimes did, for encouragement, but instead sat quietly, letting him make up his mind, hoping he would understand that this was where they needed to go, this place Thrush Hollow fronted for, in its genteel decline: the old hotel a neglected grave marker in an unmown cemetery, not an abandoned hole in the earth—an unoccupied grave.

She slackened the reins and Ransom stood motionless, took a few steps forward, backed up. He did this several times. Then it was practically as if he said peevishly, Oh, all right. Better to see what it is than to wonder about it. He tossed his head and snorted but took the right-hand turn into the woods. Then they walked, at a good clip, for perhaps a half mile; the old road, after a gradual climb around the back of Trout Hill, leveled out.

"Home free," Greta said, and Ransom, hearing the unexpected lightness in her voice, danced within the paces of his walk. A foot held up higher than necessary, a slight sideways jog. An onlooker might not even have noticed it, but to Greta it was as flagrant as a shout.

"You want to run, old guy? Is that it?"

She gave the brief, *tsk*ing sound that reminded Ransom that cantering could be accomplished, though he was into a spring simultaneously with her asking him.

She leaned down and forward in the saddle like a jockey and patted his broad neck, realizing as she did so that the itching had subsided substantially since she'd left the house. She *tsk*ed again as Ransom joyously lengthened his stride into a gallop. The wind blew her hair back and she remembered how splendid it felt to race along a wooded road through the speckled afternoon light, the lively consciousness of this completely other creature radiating into her body through her hands, knees, and spine.

They continued to run, headlong, Ransom going as fast as he ever had, until the road intersected another. Here he slowed to a trot—which way?—and Greta leaned into the hairpin turn; the other, more gradual, led down to Center Stilling. She posted for a moment; then they slowed to a walk when the incline sharpened.

"That'll do for a bit, no? We got something out of our system."

She wanted, as she had when as a girl she rode bareback, to lie down along his broad back, but the saddle prevented her and instead she leaned forward again and ran her hand up and down his withers.

"We're almost there," she said.

Ransom, ill at ease, jerked his head forward in vigorous discomfort.

"Easy, boy. Easy does it."

He snorted and pulled at the reins.

In another moment they came out into the clearing and were upon the deathly place: the unsavory-looking hillside of bare, reddish, rock-strewn earth on which a few stunted trees but no grass or underbrush grew, the topsoil ruined by the copper tailings. Here and there, jutting out from the hillside, were half-rotted wooden platforms, like the landing platforms loggers had used before big machinery had made them obsolete. Hand trolleys full of ore had been rolled out on tracks from inside the mines. The miners' village, which had begun here and continued along the road, had long since gone—fallen in, rotted, burned. The hastily built shacks had not been set on foundations so it was difficult to tell even where they had stood.

Ransom was edgy, lifting first one forefoot and then the other, and Greta dismounted and stood by him, lightly holding the reins. She rested her other hand on his neck.

"Don't worry, old boy. It's all right."

Ritual phrases, but they soothed her too, and feeling her giving in to them the horse quieted and stood still, waiting. Greta waited too, for what she didn't know.

The air was warm, a lingering warmth; the top half of the hill already lay in shadow. With a sense of no time to waste and yet the feeling that all hurry was pointless, Greta led Ransom up the slope, picking her way through the orange slag heaps, until they came to the entrance to one of the mine shafts. It was the opening into a cave, where snow often lingered well into June. A column of frigid, dank air lay in the narrow gully before the yawning entrance and Ransom drew back in fear.

"Easy, easy—we're not going in."

This was the largest and best-known cave, and it had been fenced in with barbed wire and signs affixed to the posts warned people to keep out, but the wire had been stretched where people had crawled through. Greta and Ned and Henry had never ventured far beyond the entrance, and Greta didn't know if the adits descended gradually all the way or if, farther in, there were shafts into which men had had to be lowered with their tools. She wondered how they'd known where to dig. Reddish earth had told them copper ore lay beneath, but how did they know where to begin? Had dowsers, like Hudson Sleeper and Lucinda, directed them to the spot?

Greta felt sorry for the earth, its being used and discarded like this—*See what happens?* See what happens, she knew she meant, when you leave me? As if Crain's abandonment of her had somehow caused this devastation and she wanted to cry in frustration at the inability of her mind to distinguish one thing from another, at the foolishness of imagining that the world had been ruined because Crain hadn't had the courage he needed. Why couldn't she just face the fact that he was gone? Instead of telling herself that it was some sickness of the world he'd tried to keep himself apart from by keeping himself apart from her. As if, had they been together, in the open, he would have had nowhere to hide.

"It's too late," she said. "He can't come back, no one can come back," and Ransom took this as a cue to back away from the mine entrance, though Greta knew that in some way she would try to stay there, gazing into the empty darkness, wishing she could tell Crain that it was all right; she wouldn't demand that he leave Julia anymore, she would accept whatever he could give her. She had sacrificed herself before, but rebelliously; now she would give herself unflinching.

If I'd told you about my hands—what happened to my hands—would you have stayed with me? Would you have told me then what you *really suffered?*

But that was more foolishness—to think that if he'd known, really known, he would have been able to do something about it.

She let Ransom retrace the path back down the hill. No point in investigating any other entrances; they opened from the foot of deep ravines she could not lead Ransom into, but there was nothing more to find even if she could. She could come no closer to what she had lost; it was gone, it was missing; she knew now, for certain, that it would never come back. If she could remember that, then maybe she would be all right. The pure loss—what she didn't have—if she could keep it in sight . . . But she didn't have Lucinda's or Hudson's skill of knowing what was there that couldn't be seen, and without that gift how could she remember?

She had to go back down the hill, this time taking the steep, direct track to Thrush Hollow, leading Ransom, since it was late; Ned would send out a search party if she wasn't back soon. What was gone had taken refuge inside her, but it was too large for her and she knew, once she went back, that she wouldn't be able to contain it, that it would force its way to the surface.

So she went down the hill, not knowing (how could she know?) that not far off, just below the ridge, lay the tiny Trout Hill graveyard, where for one reason or another a few inhabitants of Trout Hill lay buried. Not many had elected to lie there; they had guessed, maybe, that the mines would cease operation and had not wanted the only sign of their having lived—their names, etched in stone—to be lost up in the hills too.

Among these forgotten dead lay Zebulun and Amelia Snow. Amelia had been buried much later. Her sister had said, "Amelia, are you sure?" when Amelia told her she meant to lie beside her husband. "He could do that and you'd still spend eternity beside him?" "We are husband and wife," Amelia said. "That's what the stones will tell. A hundred years from now, who will know?"

"Won't you go to the funeral?" Amelia had asked Zeb. "You boarded with her all this long time."

"She didn't invite me," Zeb said—Amelia's first inkling that anything was wrong. And Zeb was off his head; he kept talking about the war and a boy he'd shot. It was the war that did it, he said. It's the war, it's the war. Everything was all right up till then.

"No, it wasn't," Amelia said. "How could it have been?" Though she'd never been sure what she meant.

She never said a word to Zeb about what she heard—and she heard enough. For the next couple of years, till he was found in his shop hanging by one of his harnesses from a beam, no one at all said a word to him about what he'd done. And whether this was a kindness or a cruelty, Amelia could never decide.

In the days following the Trout Hill pilgrimages, as McAndrew thought of them, Julia Crain had come out of her depression—she the only one not to have taken that sinister trip. Every family had its ritual tours to which it subjected visitors, but a slag heap and ominous tunnels disappearing underground? McAndrew quailed before the manifold and theatrical symbolism.

Julia's newfound energy sought an outlet in cooking and cleaning, from which Greta, abandoning her hostess's role, no longer tried to dissuade her. Julia prepared elaborate Mexican dishes—mole, enchiladas, chalupas; other things McAndrew had never heard of—yet even locating the exotic ingredients required for these extravaganzas and assembling them was insufficient to absorb all her renewed energy and she embarked upon—it seemed nothing short of this—a complete reorganization of the household.

First she set about to wash the windows (something Greta and Ned claimed not to remember doing), insisting that her son climb a wobbly extension ladder to do the second-story windows outside. While he wiped them, she stood within, tapping on the glass to indicate spots he had missed until in exasperation he told her she must be imagining things. When this project came to an abrupt end after Philip rebelled and drove off with his inamorata Sylvie to visit the granite quarry a forty-five-minute drive from Stilling (their romance nurtured, it appeared, instead of by moonlit trysts or walks along beaches, by visits to excavations—for reasons McAndrew had not the energy to contemplate), Julia took on the rugs, dragging them outside and draping them over the porch railing, where she beat them relentlessly.

She was scrubbing the wide pine floorboards in the kitchen, singing in Spanish, *Ay-i-i-i, canta no llores . . . ,* when McAndrew, who'd taken refuge from this mania in his bedroom, saw Greta leave the house. He debated not at all before slipping out of his room, tiptoeing down the central stairs (the back ones, faster, would deliver him into the clutches of Señora Crain), and sidling out the front door. He circled the house but waited in the shadow of the large lilac bush at the northeast corner until Greta had left the field and entered the woods. Then he set off.

He had wondered if he'd have the stamina to keep up with her—an athlete nearly thirty years his junior—on the steep uphill climb to Trout Hill (where else would she be going? If he hadn't known better, he'd have thought from her surreption and haste that she snuck off to meet a lover), but he'd forgotten that the track forked before it began its ascent; some impulse told him to take the narrower left-hand path, down to Thrush Hollow's brook. Ned had pointed it out on their trek home the other day.

The descent to the brook was narrow and steep, and McAndrew dislodged several stones as he sought a solid footing. Approaching the bank, he had to duck beneath the low spreading branch of a hemlock. Sighting Greta, he started, then stepped behind the thick trunk of a spruce. She had paused on a strip of sand to take off her sandals, then, barefoot, waded into the stream and crossed to a ledge of rock. In the middle of the brook a narrow waterfall meandered down a broad, lichen-covered slope of granite, aiming at a shallow basin hollowed out in the rock by the water's continuous striking. Overflowing, it fanned out into a wider pool.

Greta now knelt at the edge of this basin, stretching out her hands beneath the tumbling water—palms up as if to fill them in order to drink, except that they weren't cupped but held out flat. Her back was turned towards the steep embankment and McAndrew, no longer making much of an effort to conceal himself, realized that she probably hadn't heard him over the noise of the brook.

As he stood studying her, her behavior confirmed a suspicion he'd held since that morning, when he'd observed her wince as she lifted a bucket of hot water out of the sink to take to Julia. "It must be scalding," Julia had commanded, "scalding! That is the true secret." Dutifully Greta had run the water until it steamed. Having Philip make off with his Sylvie before his very eyes was bad enough, McAndrew thought, but what kind of possession had Philip's mother taken of his Margaret?

While he stood debating his next move, McAndrew indulged himself, briefly, in pondering the strangeness of *his* being present at these episodes in Greta's life (according to Ned, there had, to date, been no recurrence—which was not to say that Ned yet knew what was going on; McAndrew rather guessed that he didn't), though he could hardly flatter himself that on either occasion he'd provoked them. On the first, he hadn't laid eyes on Greta until after the marks had appeared. He'd never had anything to do with admitting the girl boarders and that winter he hadn't been teaching. This time, he might conceivably have been a catalyst—though that role more plausibly belonged to Julia Crain. (McAndrew found it difficult to believe, as Ned claimed, that there was no prior relationship.) Ned, McAndrew could see, was becoming distraught, and yet Greta, for all that Ned insisted she was verging on a nervous breakdown, did not seem particularly upset. She seemed, instead, hopelessly remote, as if the deep solitude one had always sensed in her but could never really locate had been revealed, a rock rolled away from the entrance to the cavern, though even so one could not go through to discover whether or not she was still inside.

Although McAndrew had already stood without announcing his presence longer than he felt comfortable doing, he was afraid of startling Greta and afraid, too, of disrupting the water cure she seemed in the process of invoking. The phrase came naturally, given Ned's tales of Thrush Hollow's dead proprietress's reputed skill, though time seemed to have effected a reversal. The proprietress was now the one afflicted. The guests, however, were failing in their roles as healers.

"Greta!" McAndrew called, as he started down to the brook. "Greta!" he called more loudly.

When she turned to him, the helpless disbelief in her face shocked him and he was mortified—was he to do it all again?

This is not a passion play, Jim, he reproached himself. This is not an allegory staged for your benefit. You *happen* to be here—remember the lesson you propounded?

You should never have come back. The one visit was enough. You have no place in their present lives—what is it you're looking for from them?

He had lingered on at Thrush Hollow, knowing his presence could not be helping Greta, lingered in order—not to avoid cutting short Sylvie and Philip's idyll, the reason he gave to Ned (despite his fatherly grumblings, he rather liked Philip)—but to feel his equanimity slipping away from him, the retirement-age wisdom he had never really trusted being replaced by an excitement that sped up his circulation and left him avowing inwardly that nothing had really happened to him for thirty years. Not since his last days at St. Stephen's—these occurring, in his mind's eye, not in the rather plush encrimsoned office he'd inherited but in the black-and-white crypt, where he'd spent much more time than Ned had any idea, as if his job had been all about burial. It was here that he envisioned his conversations with both Ned and Greta as having taken place, although he'd been there only briefly in Ned's company and never in Greta's.

"Greta!" McAndrew shouted, about to take off his own shoes and go after her.

But at that moment she stood and waded back to the bank; though it had seemed to him when she'd first turned to him, stricken, that she'd scarcely recognized him, as soon as she reached the shelf of rock where he waited she said, "So you want to see?" and held out her hands. McAndrew looked down, then breathed in sharply in surprise. He glanced back into Greta's eyes, but her gaze was unfocused again—maybe she was seeing him as she had thirty years ago, when what was happening to her had happened for the first time. Except that it wasn't the first time; it was the *only* time. Given the gingerly way she had held her silverware at breakfast, the cautious lifting of the bucket, and certain subterfuges designed not to expose her palms to the eyes of the curious, McAndrew had been prepared to look once again upon the "holy marks" he had first been shown when Sister Mary Catherine had dragged Greta into his study and triumphantly thrust out the miscreant's hands at him. But now Greta's palms were perfectly smooth, only slightly red from their immersion in ice-cold water.

"Why don't you help me?" she cried. "You were a priest—do something!"

Relieved to hear her speak despite what it was she said, McAndrew answered, "Greta, you don't believe the things that might secure benefit from a priest, you know that. But let me talk to you. Can I at least talk to you?"

"I don't want to hear your theories. I heard enough last time."

"I have none. Believe me, I've learned humility. Please, let's sit down." He took her arm but she pulled away.

"Why did you come back? This would never have happened if you hadn't come back!"

"I don't know," McAndrew said. "Maybe not. But I'm not the prime mover. I wasn't last time, and this time is no different."

"No, you're a vulture, that's what you are. Ned was right about that."

McAndrew winced. "What's done is done, Greta. If I seem so again, it's not by inclination."

When she continued to stare angrily, he went on. "I've regretted for thirty years what I did that . . . for making it worse back then. Truly. I've said so to Ned, but I've had no chance to say so to you.

"Please, Greta, can't we sit somewhere? These old bones . . ."

Greta shrugged and turned to retrieve her sandals. She put them on and then led the way back up the path; at the intersection with the Trout Hill track, she continued straight on through a stand of birch and poplar until they came to a small field half overgrown by blackberry bushes, some berries among the green ones now bright red. She trampled a path through the briers to a circle of maples on the far side of the field and sat down on the grass just within reach of their shade.

She seemed calmer, almost passive now, and McAndrew asked, trying to sound casual, "Do your hands hurt?"

"Not much," she said, matching his tone. "They itched terribly and ached, but now that they've opened, they mainly sting."

"How long does it take them to close up?"

She shrugged again. "Last time it was a couple of weeks, but the swelling went on for much longer before the skin broke. Maybe the healing will be faster too this time."

"Did they require medication? I forget."

"Just something to guard against infection. The dressing had to be changed frequently." Greta laughed. "That made Sister Mary Catherine so furious—did I ever tell you? She used to take me to the infirmary, as if she thought I'd try to get out of it. She'd say to the nurse, 'The *real* ones wouldn't get infected.' "

"Poor Sister Mary Catherine." Then McAndrew asked, "Have you told Ned?" But this was the wrong question.

"No!" Greta exclaimed. "He mustn't know! It sickens him—he would leave me! He may leave me anyway but I'm not ready—I haven't the strength."

"What on earth makes you think Ned wants to leave you? I've never seen anyone more devoted than Ned is to you."

When Greta said nothing, he said, "Do you think the marks would go away if you were to leave Thrush Hollow? Go off somewhere?"

"Go off? Leave Thrush Hollow? Where would I go?"

"If *I* left, then? Since you tell me I'm an instigating force . . ."

"You can do what you like."

"Greta, I . . . Could you tell me who Julia is? Why you invited her here?"

"She's Felipe's mother," Greta said.

McAndrew sighed. "Let me speak in a more practical vein, then. If you want to be rid of her but can't, for whatever reason, send her home, I'd be happy to invite her over to my place for a while. You could make it clear that I have no designs on her," he said, when Greta looked suspicious. "It's fairly clear that the romance is happening in the next generation, wouldn't you say? I'm not in the least interested in the mother, except as a phenomenon, though I don't suppose you could tell her that without insulting her. God preserve me from innocence. That's really all I ask in my old age."

"Of course she's innocent," Greta said.

"I meant it pejoratively, Greta. But this is beside the point. I realize you may not have been imputing any such impulses to me, but—well, I don't have anything to give anyone anymore, not in any sustained way. The compassionate moment—hour or two—is the most I can muster. Thank God I know that. But, Greta, I *can* muster it."

"There's nothing you can do to help me."

"Are you living Julia's nightmare for her?" McAndrew ventured. "Is that what's happening?"

"I don't need to live anyone else's nightmare, your Excellency," Greta said. She held out her hands again, and McAndrew gazed at her unblemished palms, feeling witless, his cogitation plying such well-travelled avenues as wondering at the mind's power to believe in its own creations. He didn't for an instant doubt Greta's integrity. He remembered her explanation, at St. Stephen's, of how she could have come to undergo a transcendent Christian experience without having heard of it or being a Christian herself. "Ideas get loose," she said. "That's pretty obvious, isn't it? They wreak havoc in people who've never even heard of them."

McAndrew thought of asking what roving idea had taken up residence in her this time, but that would have been to patronize her, which, under the circumstances, maybe could not be avoided. Either he did not take seriously her condition, for lack of something more precise to name it, or else he believed that anything he could ask would be to take her too lightly. Nevertheless there were a hundred things he *wanted* to ask. How did she think things would have turned out if he hadn't let his better self (if that's what it was) get the upper hand all those years ago, if he hadn't so vaingloriously shoved her away from him? Why had she never told Ned about their encounter—until, that is, after his visit of a couple of weeks ago?

Ned had asked him to confirm her account of it, which he had done, as cautiously as possible. He would have liked to know, as well, if Greta had ever told anyone else about him, or about the stigmata, and, if so, what that person's reaction had been. Was this curiosity rooted only in his selfish longing to know if *he* had figured at all in her thoughts over the intervening years, or was there not, as well, an actual humility before this event which he could neither understand nor dismiss?

Something *happened* to you, he wanted to reassure her. You don't need to pretend.

Had she continued to insist on what had occurred as a discrete incident? (Though this was rhetorical; according to Ned, she never mentioned it.) Or had she ever, even as an indulgence, let herself believe that for a moment she had resided in the thick of the world's psyche, the wellspring where life's most basic questions were still potent and unsettled—maybe even let herself be flush with having been chosen, having been untainted enough, or genuine enough, to be one of the few to reach that place?

He believed this about her, but it made him uncomfortable. He didn't know if it was because he wanted his faith corroborated or because to believe it would mean that he too was somehow special: not the recipient of revelation but at least its witness.

As he had not infrequently throughout his life, McAndrew wondered what it was about some people—some rare few people—that aroused one's curiosity, when most were crude ciphers; what frequencies did certain sensibilities operate on that inspired one to articulate question after question when, before, one's mind had been a tedious repetitive roar? What was it about Greta, in particular—for him, in particular—that made him feel she could provide answers to questions he was able only, in her presence, to ask? And why (he couldn't help asking it)—why didn't she feel the same?

He decided to stop being cautious. What, for either of them, was there to lose?

"What's happened, Greta? Before I came, I mean. What's happened recently that's similar to what happened in Marby? What can explain the recurrence of the marks?"

"Thrush Hollow has nothing in common with St. Stephen's," Greta said. "It's an old hotel—a summer place now. Not a cathedral, not the home of a religious order."

"Similar in your experience, I meant. Not in the place, although—"

"Someone lied to me," Greta said, "if you really want to know. That's what's similar."

"Who did? What about?"

"My boyfriend. He couldn't go through with it, he said. Then at Christmastime they got engaged."

"Who did?"

"He loved me," Greta said, looking at McAndrew (he couldn't read her look), "but he married her."

She held up her hands again and stared at them, then blew on the palms as if to cool them. It reminded McAndrew, absurdly, of the way women blew on their fingernails to dry polish. "The fact is," she said, sounding in her sudden matter-of-factness like her younger self (unimpressed by miracles, McAndrew had used to say to himself admiringly), "no one contradicts what you think. No one really bothers to argue with you, even if they think you're wrong. So there's hardly any point to telling anyone anything, is there?"

"Is that really what you want? For someone to argue with you? That's hardly been my impression. You never seemed to want to discuss yourself at all."

He didn't know why he suddenly felt wary in the midst of his regret and concern. Maybe it was Greta's seeming to speak as if unaware of what she said or to whom she spoke while simultaneously, on another level, seeming to calculate every word. In a moment of stark astonishment, it occurred to him that, given a slight shift in their circumstances, he might not even like her. What right had she to be scornful of him for not knowing what she refused to tell him?

"If you hide someone's failing from him," McAndrew began, thinking of Ned, "if you try to compensate by paying for it yourself—"

"You didn't know him," Greta interrupted. "How could you say anything that would make a difference?"

"I didn't . . ." McAndrew began, but then shut up and waited. He watched Greta as closely as he dared, wondering if he had been too

intrusive and whether she would now withdraw. Her face was expression-
less and yet something seemed abruptly to illuminate it.

"All right," she said. "If you want to know . . . I've been talking about
Crain—Lars Crain, Julia's husband. We were in school together in
France. He was my first boyfriend. That Christmas when I was in Marby
he became engaged to Julia. It had been arranged, supposedly, but he'd
told me he couldn't go through with it. That's why I tried to get you to
sleep with me—to get even with him."

McAndrew, stunned, simply watched her.

"He didn't leave me—I don't mean that. My mistake was ever leaving
him. He couldn't believe in the two of us when we weren't together—he
couldn't believe in Julia when he was with me. When I was in college and
he'd graduated and gone home, they got married. So I married Ned.
They had their first child, then another. During this time, I refused to see
him, even though he called me every few weeks and pleaded with me to
change my mind.

"You understand, Jim," she said, "I loved him. I love Ned but not as I
loved Crain. It was simply a fact. Nothing could change it."

She paused and McAndrew forced himself to nod.

"Finally I gave in and saw him again. Ned and I weren't getting along
at all—both of us thought the marriage was about to end—and I couldn't
see what there was to lose. Then I got pregnant."

She stopped and looked at McAndrew.

"Oh, no, Greta, you don't mean . . ."

"Yes, with Crain's child. Crain is Henry's father."

The news hovered a moment before McAndrew said, "Dear God . . ."

"Ned doesn't know."

"No, I didn't suppose that he did."

McAndrew felt the weight of it lodged in his throat. "My God, Greta,"
he said, "I can hardly begin . . . How can you have lived with such a
thing?"

She made a gesture—a kind of desperate insouciance he hardly knew
whether to deplore or admire.

"I had Crain."

"And now?"

She said nothing.

Now you have me, it came to him. Someone had to know, if she were
to go on deceiving Ned.

As if she'd heard his thought, she said, "I always planned to tell Henry when he was older. Ned too. Crain wouldn't leave Julia and I didn't want to deprive Henry of the only father he knew. But now what's the point? What good could it possibly do?"

McAndrew exclaimed, appalled, "The truth can't be measured like that! It has no measure. It's its own measure!"

"I believed that once," she said, with a small, pained smile.

"Greta, I'm grieved for you—although that hardly begins to express what I feel. I'm so shocked I can scarcely think, but to know what you've lived with . . . the secrecy. Never being known." He shook his head helplessly. "I feel terribly sorry for you and yet—I never thought I'd find myself saying *this*—it's Ned I feel sorriest for. Ned and your son, but most of all Ned."

"I think you misjudge Ned," Greta said quietly. "Another man would have known. He would have been able to tell. Ned didn't want to."

"But Ned loves you!" McAndrew exclaimed.

"And I love him. Maybe you can't believe that, but it's true. Mostly we've been happy. But if I hadn't kept seeing Crain, we wouldn't have been."

"And now?"

"Now . . ."

"What about your son? Is he never to know who his father is?"

Pain crossed Greta's face. She said, "Ned *is* his father."

"Well, in a sense, but . . ." McAndrew shook his head. He leaned forward and lifted one of Greta's hands, held it palm up in his, then let it go.

"You know very well that I'll never tell Ned. Whatever dismay I feel, however I might judge you, my loyalty is to you. You knew that before you spoke, didn't you?"

She looked at him, with those fathomless eyes of hers.

"It's ironic, Greta—I have to say, what wish granted isn't? I always wanted to be something to you that no one else could be. I knew I couldn't be your lover—even if we had gone ahead, that one time, it couldn't have gone on—which is not to say I haven't wished to have had the memory. I couldn't be your lover; I couldn't be your husband; I couldn't, it seemed, even be your friend. I would remain an unpleasant memory. That was that, I thought, until a few weeks ago when Ned's letter arrived. I don't mean I've brooded upon that time all these years. But it nagged at me, and Ned's letter gave me the opportunity of putting it to rest. Hope—that's what I felt. Even wild and unbounded. I knew it was foolish—what did I hope *for?* Just something—something new in my life again, I suppose. One more contact with mystery. This time, I told myself, I wouldn't demand its solution. I'd be content with having been admitted back into it. Now I have been—oh, I have been! And there's no way out. I'm the prisoner who will take your place!"

"No . . ." Greta murmured. "Don't think of it like that."

"How else could I think of it? You've unburdened yourself. You've put me just where you were thirty years ago." He thought. "Does anyone else know?"

"A friend. Rachel."

"And Julia?"

Greta seemed to consider. McAndrew wondered how she could possibly need to think about this.

"I invited her here thinking I would tell her, but when it came down to it, I couldn't. She wouldn't want to know that about Crain."

"Of course she wouldn't. No more would Ned about you. But it's all wrong, Greta—your friend and I knowing what you won't tell your husband and son . . . what you won't tell your son's father's wife . . ."

Greta shrugged.

"What may seem to be a kindness can turn out to be something else in the end. Kindness can't be founded on a lie. Some things are absolutes."

"Maybe. Maybe not. I don't know anymore."

"How could you know? You've shut yourself out from them!"

Greta stared, then exclaimed, "Why? I still don't understand. Why you? Why you both times?"

"Well, Greta, I—"

"And Ned! As if you're the consequence. Why couldn't he see it? Why could he never see it?"

"See what? What do you mean?"

"What he leaves me to!"

"Leaves you to?"

"Strangers. Total strangers. I might as well be in a foreign country, for all that I will ever feel at home."

McAndrew thought about this. He had no idea if he sympathized with her or not. He said, however, "Don't try. Don't try to feel at home if you're not. Nothing good can come of that."

He wasn't sure what he meant, or how, really, it even applied to Greta, but she seemed at least surprised by what he said, and this gratified him.

"We'll talk," he said. "You'll tell me more, if you want. Maybe it will help. Right now I feel so tired. I can't think. I need to think."

He heaved himself to his feet and held out a hand to her. She didn't take it, he noted. If she was pretending, she was doing a damn good job of remembering her hands were sore.

"Come on, let's go back now. It must be lunchtime. Ned will wonder what's become of us. He's worried enough as it is."

Walking slightly behind her, along a former logging road that emerged on the east edge of the lawn back of Greta's horse barn—her beautiful horse whinnied and trotted to the paddock fence when he saw her—McAndrew tried to observe whether Greta held her hands any differently than she had earlier, but, if so, he couldn't tell. Climbing the rise to the house, they saw that Ned was out in the garden, weeding; he straightened up and waved; Greta waved back but said she'd go in and start lunch.

"Wouldn't you guess that Julia's already made it?"

"Probably. Why don't you tell Ned to come in in ten minutes?"

Did Greta hope he *would* tell Ned? Could that possibly have been her purpose after all? Well, he wouldn't oblige; he would not.

He noted and was revolted by the feeling of privilege. He was Greta's . . . Yes, that's what it was. Her confessor. All these years out of the priesthood and he was still sitting in the dark, facing the wooden wall, listening to the murmurs of sinners. And what did you do with all those whispered admissions? The sinners left cleansed, forgiven; you sat in the dark with all the misery you'd absorbed. All the secrets of humankind in its hopeless isolation, which maybe you could have alleviated if you'd been allowed to tell them about each other, but you were sworn not to, you *could* not, or they would not have spoken.

He told Ned only what had happened—what Greta thought was happening to her. He wasn't surprised that Ned seemed almost relieved. At least here was *something,* some indication of what was occurring inside. He agreed with McAndrew that it would be best to let Greta dictate the terms of revelation. Nothing needed to be said to anyone else, since there was nothing to see, and Greta's treatment of her hands was not really noticeable unless you were looking for it. Ned would have to hope that by next week, when he and Greta went to pick up Henry, the "situation" would have been resolved.

They agreed, in the garden, that they should be prepared for anything, but this promise seemed flippant when they entered the kitchen to find Julia bandaging Greta's hands. Greta was reclining in the stuffed rocking chair beside the wood stove and Julia was kneeling at her feet, winding a roll of gauze around her palms.

"She has hurt her hands," Julia said to Ned and McAndrew, as if Greta did not speak their language and required translation.

Greta looked at no one and Ned and McAndrew were speechless, although Ned, after a moment's stupor, moved to Greta's side and tentatively stroked her hair. She responded by leaning her head against the back of the chair and closing her eyes.

"The dressing should be changed frequently," Julia said. "These sorts of sores fester quickly."

Ned and McAndrew obediently nodded—what else could they do? It seemed too incredible that the wounds could have become materially manifest in the short time since Greta and McAndrew had separated, and subsequent experience (when Julia changed the dressings) confirmed this. Other explanations, however, also defied belief. Greta had told Julia that she bore the stigmata and Julia, less innocent (if that was even the word) than McAndrew judged, was humoring her? Or she now shared Greta's hallucination?

The latter explanation, incredibly, seemed to Ned and McAndrew best to fit both Greta's and Julia's subsequent behavior. Over the next few days, Greta took on the role of an invalid, dependent on Julia's comfort and ministrations, but at the same time that of someone privileged by a circumstance lesser mortals could not understand. And Julia treated Greta with a combination of reverence and solicitude, the way a devoutly religious person would behave towards someone she believed to be martyred for her faith.

Times had changed, Julia Velásquez y Pérez Crain confided to her new friend Greta Dene, from the age when a man like her husband could find his proper place in the world. It was such a pleasure to be able to tell Mrs. Dene what was on her mind; not since she had been a young girl in Mexico ("May-hee-co," she pronounced it) had she had anyone to talk to. She would eternally be grateful for Mrs. Dene's having let her share her secret. Somehow it did not seem to matter so much what she decided to do now that someone else knew the truth.

To help out in the house was the least she could do. Cooking, of course, that was a delight and a duty, but she wished to do more, and she had already cleaned everything that could be cleaned (polished the place within an inch of its life, Ned said), and soon she had hit on the perfect project: she would sew curtains for all the windows of the old hotel. She paid no attention to Ned's objection that he and Greta had not hung curtains by choice—what possible need for them was there, way out here in the middle of nowhere? Moreover they liked to look directly outside, unimpeded by frills and furbelows . . .

"But your wife is in favor of the idea," Julia pointed out—she had already borrowed her friend Rachel's sewing machine, and Mr. Dene would not want to prevent his wife from doing what gave her pleasure, certainly?

"No, of course not," Ned said, "But . . ."

"They don't like change, these men, have you noticed?" Julia asked as they measured the windows, Greta employing the tape measure because she was taller, while Julia wrote the lengths and widths down on a clipboard.

"They remind me of the tax assessors," Ned said to McAndrew, so that Julia and Greta could hear.

"Pay no attention to them," Julia replied. "They are only afraid that soon we will try to fix *them* up."

They drove all the way to Visby, where they bought several hundred yards of material, several dozen spools of thread, and placed an order for eight dozen curtain rods of various kinds and sizes. Julia insisted on paying for everything—it would be her small gift to repay the hospitality Greta had shown her. They converted an unused bedroom in the ell into a sewing room: two pairs of sawhorses laid with planks served as cutting tables. It hurt Greta's hands too much to hold the scissors, so she measured and marked the lengths and held the cloth steady while Julia cut. And all the while they cut material and sewed and ironed and hung curtains, Julia talked.

It was not a time for men like her husband to be alive, she had always believed, their strength and bravery twisted inside them like a tree trying to grow in a too small space. Could Greta believe it?—Felipe, her own son, had asked her on the trip to this northernmost territory (the first time she had come here although she had asked her husband to bring her, she had seen so many nice pictures in magazines) did she think she would ever marry again? How he could imagine that any man could take the place of his father—though Felipe, it was unfortunate to have to say it, was not like his father—at least not Renzo.

Julia had never told Renzo (though he must have realized) that Federico had been in love with her even longer than Renzo, and several times when Renzo was away at school Rico had tried to persuade her to go with him instead. She always refused, but she had to say that in certain ways Rico might have made her happier—he did not have such ambitions ("What ambitions?" Greta asked. For someone as effective and as influential as Crain, he had always seemed to her to have no particular aim— who was Julia talking about?), but it was her destiny to be with Renzo, she had always felt this, even when she was a young girl.

She had to say, and Mrs. Dene—Greta, she was sorry—Greta she was sure would understand, that although she had loved Renzo more than anything on earth, that did not mean she thought he was perfect. For example, she did not think he had always thought in the right way about what he should do. She did not blame him, it was the fault of the times he was born into, they gave him no way to be proud of what he was, but nevertheless she had her opinion. For example, his dream of winning back his family's lost lands and houses—it was foolish, didn't Greta think so?—although she had never let Renzo know she thought so. Did Greta think this was dishonest, not to say everything one thought? Didn't Greta agree that a marriage required a certain amount of privacy? People were foolish who thought otherwise. (Greta, who had thought both of these things, began to disagree vehemently. You don't know a thing about him! she exclaimed to herself.)

Maybe Greta knew, she and Renzo were second cousins through her mother, and Renzo's father had encouraged him to think already when he was very young that if he married her he would have a stronger claim to properties back in England, to a big palace of a house in Gloucestershire, Julia thought it was, though she could not be sure if that was where on their honeymoon Renzo had driven down a wooded lane and stopped outside iron gates, chained shut. "Look," he said, "when the wind blows the trees aside you can see the towers," but—if she could tell someone the truth finally—she had been able to see only more trees.

She didn't understand either why later he had wanted to come to the United States, a country she had always thought of like a bossy older sister, always getting her way, shoving everyone else around. (She hoped she did not offend Mrs. Dene—of course there were many nice Americans, it was their government she objected to. "It's hardly 'my' government," Greta said. "I grew up abroad.") She understood that he wanted to be far away from Federico, who he thought was gloating over him for being able to father a child when he, Renzo, couldn't. In fact, Greta would understand, being a woman, that Rico had suffered terribly, giving up a daughter in that way, although he had loved her, Julia, so much that he did it a second time, and also because he loved his brother, and would have done anything for him. "I don't know if you feel, here, the ties of blood as we do," Julia said.

They had gone, that second time, to stay in a hotel near the Pacific far away from everyone they knew, under a pretend name, telling no one, not even Renzo, Rico had promised, but she knew perfectly well that this was not true. Rico had never been able to keep a single secret from his brother (which was a reason, even if there had been no others, why she would not have tried to be Rico's girlfriend behind Renzo's back), and she knew that Renzo never would have allowed the two of them to go away by themselves. During the night, the bougainvillea vines rustled outside the window and there was no breeze. She did not make any effort to suppress the sounds she was making in the bed—she hoped she did not shock Mrs. Dene by speaking so directly, but she felt so comfortable it was astonishing, as if they had known each other for many years instead of having just met . . . She did not have to pretend anything with Rico; he was already Teresa's father—how could she not love him in some way? And she was so very happy because she knew that besides giving her a child, making love to Rico when Renzo was listening would make it impossible for him ever to leave her. (Greta was calculating; she knew when Felipe was born; some nine months earlier Crain had spent two weeks with her in Vancouver. Someone may have been listening to you, she thought, but it wasn't your husband.) She knew Renzo; he would be haunted by the idea that she might have preferred to be with his brother instead of him.

Renzo always had wanted whatever he could not have, whatever he could not be. His father was maybe to blame for this, telling him it was his duty to get back the lost titles, but Renzo didn't have to believe it, did he? (He didn't really, Greta didn't say. In the beginning, but not later on.)

Of course it was a terrible blow, to learn as Renzo had when he was only seventeen that he would not be able to father children. Even if he somehow found his way back into those towers beyond the trees which she could never see, there would be no one to carry on his bloodline. She knew that when he first told her the news he expected her to say, "Of course I cannot marry you then," since she had pretended that she cared as much about the imaginary inheritance as he did. She didn't mind admitting to Mrs. Dene that she thought he half hoped she would; sometimes she had wondered if he had met another girl at his school and wanted to break off their engagement but was afraid of disappointing his father. Renzo always gave in too much to his father, if Greta wanted her opinion. You wouldn't think it—he seemed so strong and independent—but it was true. He was so ashamed to find out he was sterile, as if a bad case of mumps when he was a child was his fault.

She had to confess—it weighed on her conscience, but perhaps Greta would understand why she had—she had let Renzo think she was taking him in spite of his infirmity; she had acted as if she were trying to hide her disappointment when the truth was she had really had to hide being overjoyed since a special sense had told her that now he would not be able to leave her. Instead of releasing him from their engagement, she had told him that she never broke her promises. If his fate was to be the last of his line, then she would die with him. That was what love meant to her, she told him. And this was true insofar as living without Renzo was not conceivable, and therefore anything she needed to do was permitted. Mrs. Dene would be thinking she was maybe not such a nice person to behave so, but every animal had an instinct to survive and she had hers.

Then, later, she suggested they adopt. Even though they were married she did not feel secure. She suspected that he had been involved with other girls—he was young, abroad for many years without her—what could be more natural? In her culture women often turned a blind eye, knowing the man would come back to wife and children when he tired of the novelty of another bed, but that was the trouble; there were no children to come back to. And children would make Renzo happy, even if he did not think so, she knew this about him.

So she had talked of adopting and he was the one who had wanted to ask Rico instead. She knew it was another foolish idea, but she must have already seen how it would tie him to her because she didn't say no. After Teresa and Felipe were born, it was not she, his wife, but they, her and his brother's children, whom Renzo greeted with relief and joy at the end of a workday or on returning home from one of his many trips. Perhaps Greta would find this hard to believe, since she had known Renzo only in a business capacity, but he could be very light-hearted and playful—not with her, but with his children. (And with me, Greta didn't say.) He loved them far more than he would admit, and always underneath was the fear that someday he might be exposed: not their father, not the papa they adored, but their uncle, a pretender.

It was ironic—was it not?—that in his work, too, nobody knew who he was. The better Renzo became, the less people could know what he was up to. No one knew how much power he really had. He couldn't tell even his wife much of what he did. (He had told Greta that he was in a position to "shuffle national economies like a pack of cards.") He would never have been given all the accounts he had if the people who trusted him with their money had known about all of his connections. After his death, Julia had had to go into Renzo's private bank vault and mail the letters he had already written to his secret clients (not even then directly to them, but to their representatives) to notify them of the steps they should take if they wished to close their accounts or, instead, to continue with another investor.

To Renzo, though, this work was all in preparation for the moment when he would take back his own important titles and properties, and maybe he was imagining how he would deal then with powerful men who were his clients not as a kind of servant of their money but as their equal. Renzo could have bought estates and titles with all the money he made, but what he wanted was to be welcomed home, the long-lost heir. He wanted the chained gates to be unlocked and swung open for him, for servants to be standing all along the drive, the housekeeper to be waiting on the front steps to say, "Welcome back, my lord."

It was silly too because once somebody had to start the title; somebody had to be first. Nothing was more real just because it had existed longer than something else; why did people think it was? It must be living in such a young country—people were so worried about what was real. Maybe that was why Renzo had wanted to live in the States. (He was here because I was here, Greta didn't say.)

This was a strange country; if Greta had not grown up here, then she would perhaps not take offense at her saying so. Julia had lived here for over twenty years but she had never got used to it. The truth was—she hoped Greta was not offended—but almost she had told Felipe to turn back; she didn't want to go any farther. As they drove north, the houses kept moving farther and farther apart, as if people could not stand each other's company anymore, and she truly did not see how anyone could live here—so adorable to look at in pictures, so clean with all the green grass and white houses, but neat and clean like an American cemetery, a place to go when you were dead.

Even now that she had stayed here, she didn't comprehend it. "Can I ask you—do you mind—why you are here? You and your husband and your son—all by yourselves in a house big enough for twenty? Forgive me for saying—I do not mean to criticize you—but you do not even take care of it. You do not paint it, you do not fill the rooms. You remind me of old people I have known back at home who have lost everything but refuse to leave their haciendas, except that you are not old and poor and you own another house besides . . ."

Greta had laughed, protested that they weren't going to let the place fall *in,* but Julia was having none of it. Why would you want to live in a place and watch it crumble about your ears? Surely they could find a use for it—a camp, a school of some kind, a riding camp . . .

"Oh, please," Greta said. "This is where I come to get away from all that."

"I could show you a place where you would really be away," Julia said proudly.

She told Greta of a place she knew, a hotel on Mexico's Pacific coast—yes, it was where she and Rico had gone—that was always full but where for unknown reasons few Americans came, where the two of them could sit on the terrace overlooking the ocean and drink *limonada*. From the windy terrace you descended steep steps and walked along the white beach, taking off your sandals, carrying them by their straps, and sometimes the waves thudded so loudly and the water hissed so long when it was sucked back that you couldn't hear to talk. Then in the evening you could sit on the terrace again, watching the sun sink over the Pacific, and drink margaritas. With real tequila—not what they used here.

She was so grateful to Mrs. Dene—to *Greta;* she promised not to forget anymore—for inviting her here (she hoped she had not offended by her remarks about their house). Really she could never adequately express her gratitude and she would like to return the favor, to invite Greta to her country—she of course would pay for everything, so money could be no objection.

Truly, perhaps she sounded foolish, but it had been so long since she had had a friend—even when she was young and had talked to her girlfriends about Renzo, they did not understand. What did she see in him? they always asked. To them he was a conceited foreigner who thought himself too good for the rest of them. It was true he was not always very nice to her in those early years, not until after she had the children did he really have the right respect for her, but she could not permit anyone to point that out to her or to advise her to find a different *novio.*

People here also did not understand the devotion she felt for Renzo. They saw him sometimes being condescending or impatient with her and they didn't know why she didn't stand up to him—"I wouldn't let *my* husband walk all over me like that," the wife of one of Renzo's business acquaintances had told her, but they didn't know what it meant to love someone; it didn't have to do with ideas like fairness or—how did they put it?—give-and-take.

Truly, she thought the women who criticized Renzo's treatment of her were just jealous—they wished they could feel so devoted to someone. But it didn't matter to her what anyone thought, Renzo was her whole life and there had never been anything she wouldn't have done in order to be with him. He was all in her life that she'd ever, truly, wanted, and no matter how much she missed him—she would miss him until the day she died and always regret that he had decided to meet Francisco, Federico's son, in Washington—"What?" Greta asked. Oh, had she not told Greta that that was where Renzo had been going when his plane crashed? He was afraid that Francisco knew his secret and was going to tell Felipe and Teresa, and Renzo might have been distracted, that may have been why he hadn't seen the other plane in time. And then, at his funeral, Francisco had come and said he had been hoping to reconcile with his uncle—he had never understood why his Uncle Renzo had never come to see them—so Renzo's worry had been all for nothing; though she wondered if maybe he hadn't been relieved after all, for the secret finally to be out, maybe he had been ready to face it. And she didn't mind admitting to Greta—Greta would understand how all kinds of things could go through your mind when someone died—that she wondered if he might have been planning to leave her. Teresa and Felipe were grown, not at home, the tie he felt to their mother might have been weakening, and sometimes when she couldn't sleep she thought about this—but what was she saying? She had been meaning to say that no matter what, no matter what anyone had ever said or would say about Renzo, she would always know that she had been his wife.

Rachel Tolliver walked in on Julia changing Greta's bandages. They were sitting at the kitchen table, Greta with her hands stretched out, Julia wrapping them in white gauze. A ceramic bowl of water infused with herbs had been pushed aside. An extra roll of gauze, adhesive tape, and a pair of scissors sat ready on the white enamel table-top.

"What's happened?" Rachel demanded, before she had said hello or explained her unannounced presence.

"Mrs. Dene has not been well, but now she is better," Julia said.

Rachel, looking at Greta, said, "Greta's not capable of speaking for herself?"

"This is Julia Crain. Julia, my old friend Rachel—we borrowed her sewing machine. We borrowed your sewing machine, Rachel. We didn't expect you before the end of the month. Your card—"

"Peter's mother died. The funeral was last week. Peter's stayed to settle the estate."

"I'm sorry—I didn't know."

"There was no time to write you. It's for the best, as they say. Peter's a wreck, but—well, you're supposed to be a wreck." Rachel glanced at Julia. "What did you do to your hands, Greta?"

"Oh, my hands . . ." Greta turned to see Olivia and Lenox standing uncertainly just inside the screen door.

"I didn't know you were here! Welcome home! Henry will be back tomorrow. Ned and I are driving over tonight so we can be at the camp first thing in the morning. There's a lunch for all the parents. Then we'll be back."

They smiled and nodded—polite children, Greta reminded herself to point out to Julia, who complained about American children's manners—but said nothing. Like their mother, they seemed astonished to find her being cared for by someone they'd never met. Greta supposed it was astonishing—if she could remember what it felt like to be astonished. Julia had finished bandaging now but remained beside Greta, a hand on her shoulder. Rachel stood on the other side of the table, staring at them. Finally Lenox asked, "Is the badminton net set up?"

Before Greta could answer, Julia said, "How nice that you enjoy lawn games. Felipe and Sylvie will be delighted to have more players. I believe they're out back in the hammock."

"Who are *they?*" Greta heard Olivia mutter, as she and Lenox dutifully headed outside.

"Sylvie?" Rachel inquired.

"Sylvie McAndrew. The daughter of an old friend of Ned's and mine."

"What old friend? I thought I knew all your old friends."

"Jim McAndrew . . ."

"Very nice gentleman," Julia put in.

"He was the bishop at St. Stephen's when Ned and I went there."

"*The* bishop?" Rachel looked down at Greta's wrapped-up hands. "You mean . . . you're not . . ."

Greta glanced up at Julia.

"*Cara,*" Julia said, stroking Greta's hair, "you sit and have a visit with your friend. I will get back to work. We are making curtains," she explained to Rachel. "It is quite a job, you can imagine. Ninety-four windows! It is so fortunate that we could borrow your nice sewing machine."

Rachel, speechless, watched Julia disappear down the hallway towards the dining room. Even after she'd gone, Rachel stood gazing in disbelief at the doorway. Finally she pulled out a chair and sat down across the table from Greta.

"Does she *know?*" Rachel stage-whispered.

"Know?" repeated Greta.

" 'Know . . .' she says. What on earth is going on, Greta? How long has she been here?" Then Rachel looked at the door to the back hall. "Where's Ned?" she whispered.

"He went for a walk with McAndrew."

"I meant, does she know about Henry, of course."

"Julia?" Greta looked thoughtful. "I . . . I'm not sure."

"You're not *sure?*"

"I think she may have suspected. Not my identity, but someone."

"But how does she come to be here?"

"I invited her."

"You invited her!"

"I thought I was going to tell her about Henry, but then—then I couldn't."

"I can't absorb all this, Greta. Crain's widow here, your *nurse,* and your hands again too—the same thing that happened when you were in school? That is what's going on, isn't it? And why the bishop's here?"

"Ned invited him."

"Well, I presumed that one of you did."

"Earlier, I mean. We found some letters in the cellar. Ned didn't want anyone to know about them."

"Letters? What letters?"

"From O. to Lucinda Dearborn. Sorry." Greta named the writer. "Ned has me trained."

"Here?"

"They knew each other. His younger brother was in Captain Dearborn's company in the Civil War. He visited Thrush Hollow with him."

"The letters were here?" Rachel repeated.

"Hudson Sleeper found them when he was dowsing for a new well."

"Give me a break. Dowsing in the *cellar?*"

"He was following a vein. Our spring ran dry, didn't I tell you? It's been a terribly dry summer, and apparently there was little snow last winter. Nora Sleeper says—"

"Greta, for God's sake! How can you go on in this matter-of-fact way? You didn't write a word about any of this!"

"Ned didn't want anyone to know about the letters."

"Ned didn't . . . Does *he* know?"

"No, he doesn't."

Rachel looked at her friend. "You sound as if you're not going to tell him."

"I don't know."

"Greta, how you can even . . ."

"I thought that was what you advised. When I came to New York in April . . . It would be unfair to tell the truth, you said, just to relieve my conscience. Quote unquote."

"Yes, then, when you couldn't even think straight. But now, especially if Julia suspects, you can't just . . ."

"Just what?"

"To be blunt, now Crain's dead, it might be easier for Ned to accept. He might want to formally adopt . . . Who did you tell him she *was?*"

Greta shrugged. "The widow of a client. Someone who needed a place to get away. Look, could we talk about this some other time? You just got back. I've spent the last four months thinking of nothing but this. I can't just sum it all up in a few sentences."

"Who's asking you to sum it all up? I wanted to know what's been going on. You expect me to come in here, find Crain's widow bandaging your hands because you're suffering a recurrence of—whatever it is—and not have some reaction?"

Greta didn't answer this.

"I've spent four months thinking about it too, Greta. I've kept your confidence for fifteen years but, frankly, I've often wished you'd never told me. I've . . . all I saw this summer was death—five people died in Peter's mother's nursing home the first two weeks we were there—and it casts a harsh light on everything, in case you haven't noticed. Sorry—that was unkind. I just don't see how you can forgive Crain for leaving you to clean up the mess, and I don't see . . . You let Ned live with something he couldn't forgive if he knew."

Greta watched her, and then said, "It's more complicated than you think, Rachel."

"Greta, what on earth do you take me for? The patronizing way you talk . . . Did I say it wasn't complicated? So you tell Ned, do you tell Henry? What purpose could it serve now? It's no pious point about the truth at all costs I'm making. But you speak so flippantly, I—"

"If you'd been through what I have, you might speak flippantly too. It might be the only way you could speak."

She'd be damned if she'd tell Rachel the truth after *this,* Greta was thinking. Ever since Julia had confided her suspicion that Crain might have been about to leave her, Greta had been drifting in a sweet haze, floating on Julia's warmth and affection. All the years of separation from Crain seemed, not meaningless, but muted somehow, subsumed by the confirmation that he'd meant everything he said, even if he hadn't said everything. What could be in greater contrast to Rachel's impatient directness than Julia's unquestioning devotion? Rachel, a staunch friend, but moralistic, unable to appreciate the nuances of things . . . The harsh New England glare, compared to the subtler understandings of older civilizations. Rachel either condemned her or felt sorry for her, neither of which Greta could allow. If she were to tell Rachel about Crain's deceit now, Rachel would forgive her for concealing her relationship with him all these years—hurt for hurt—but instead direct her anger against Crain, and Greta could not have that either. She couldn't let people who hadn't even known him criticize him when he was dead.

"What if we went for a walk?" Rachel suggested. "If you're allowed out on your own, that is."

"Don't be ridiculous."

"You can't blame me," Rachel said as they left the house and descended the front lawn. "To come home and find you in thrall to this . . . to Crain's wife! It's pretty macabre, Greta."

"Is it? It doesn't feel strange, really—it feels very natural. As if we've known each other a long time—I suppose in a way we have."

"Is she what you expected?"

"In some ways. In others not at all."

"You wouldn't care to be less cryptic, would you?"

Greta looked at Rachel and smiled, her resentment suddenly dissipated. "It's been hard having you gone," she said.

"Oh, Greta . . ." Rachel said. She stopped walking and threw her arms around her. "I'm so sorry—I'm so sorry for everything. For being such a prig, for . . . for *you*. I was so totally inadequate when you came in April. I've known it, but I couldn't say it. I couldn't write it. I was so angry that you'd kept seeing Crain secret from me all these years—your best friend. And now to see you so intimate with this . . . Well, never mind. No doubt it's all highly selfish of me, but there I am, highly selfish. I still love you."

"I love you too."

"I'm sure this is not the main item on your agenda, but I need to clear the air. I've had a lot of time, moldering in Cornwall, to consider my reaction when you told me about Crain. How I could have been so unable to comfort you."

They'd started walking uphill towards Odder but now Rachel stopped again. "When you said you weren't seeing Crain anymore, after Henry was born, I thought we were in the same boat. All this time it's what I've been thinking. You probably don't remember, but it was right around that time that Peter had his affair—oh, I still think he has the occasional fling," she added, "but that was his Great Love. He was all set to dump me and his two infant children for her—Courtney, Melody—I've blocked her name."

"You have not," Greta said, laughing.

"As you may recall, he made the great sacrifice and stayed with us—we came to an understanding that even if we weren't passionately in love that that wasn't necessarily the basis for a sound marriage. We were both devoted to the children. Do you remember our discussions about all that—yours and mine?"

"Of course I remember."

"At the same time there you were, giving up the man you loved so much for the sake of making a family with Henry and Ned. Not only that, but having to live with the secret you kept for their sakes. It was the mature and noble thing to do, I thought. We were all launched on the rocky seas of grown-up life together. And then this spring I learn that all this time you've kept the back door open—I felt so betrayed. The whole structure of belief I'd built up around my own marriage seemed to collapse too. Why learning that your life had been different from the way I'd thought it should have affected how I thought about *my* life, I don't know. Nothing in mine was any different than it had ever been, so why did it suddenly feel so empty and pointless? It makes no sense, but that was how I felt. I couldn't even see your loss. I'm sorry."

"You don't have to apologize."

"I hope you know I *have* thought about how you must feel. Knowing Henry will never now meet his real father—I can't even imagine what that must feel like . . . And now your poor hands—did it happen when the bishop came back?"

"Not right away. He showed up a couple of weeks before Julia. It . . ." Greta held up her mummified hands. "This only happened after Julia came."

"I can't imagine why."

Greta made a vague gesture. "They're actually fine now. Julia's being overly cautious."

"She likes to take care of you."

"I've told her I'm going to take the bandages off tonight before we leave to pick up Henry. That's the last thing a fourteen-year-old needs, don't you think?" Greta asked. "A mother with the stigmata. Parents are embarrassing enough as it is."

Rachel laughed, but said, "How you can joke about it . . ."

"What else should I do? I suppose if I had any sense, I'd set up a shrine. People could pay to come and gaze at me."

"I think you'd have to perform a miracle or two, don't you?"

"How do you know I haven't?"

"What, conjuring up Julia?"

Greta smiled.

"What does she think of your 'holy marks'?"

"Oh, she's thrilled," Greta said gently. "I'm her own private martyr. It's her new purpose in life—to care for me."

"What a world," Rachel said. "What a summer. I thought summers were supposed to be restful."

When they went back, it turned out that McAndrew (with Ned's encouragement) had invited Julia and Felipe to pay a visit to his place.

"We will see each other again soon, Greta, I am sure," Julia said tearfully. "But Jim is right, you and Ned should have your privacy. Your son will not want to come home from camp to find his house full of strangers. I regret not to have finished the work here, though. Perhaps soon . . ." Julia explained to Rachel, "Greta doesn't really know how to sew."

"Don't worry," Rachel said, "I do. I'll help her finish the curtains."

"Thank you," Julia said uncertainly. "I would not feel I abandoned everything so much then."

By eight o'clock, a last supper having been eaten and good-byes exchanged, the place was empty. Embracing Julia, who'd cried—then, half laughing, tenderly brushed tears from Greta's own eyes and thanked her meaningfully for "everything"—Greta had been overcome by panic; who else would ever talk to her about Crain? Where was he now? When would she see Julia again? And yet, as soon as the McAndrews' and then Julia and Felipe's cars were out of sight, Greta felt the almost giddy buoyancy that had affected her at private moments ever since Julia had told her, not knowing what she'd told her, that Crain could not admit even to himself how much he loved his children. Greta forgave him for that. And if he had let Julia bind him to her through his weakness, if he hadn't fought, wasn't it at least as much her, Greta's, fault for not realizing how unsure he was? She would bear that cross. She would always have herself to blame.

And then the lightness would become a cresting wave, pushing her high above the surface where she'd been lulled with Julia—it didn't change anything, not really change anything—how could it? Yet somehow it must, something must have, for how else could she feel this incredible lightness as she and Ned folded a change of clothing into a suitcase, climbed in the car, and drove off? They were barely out of the driveway when Ned pounded the steering wheel and let out a whoop of joy.

"Hooray! The vampire lady's leaving! Have fun, Jim!"

Greta, despite herself, laughed. "Ned . . ."

"I don't know what Faustian bargain you were paying off by having her here, but I certainly hope you've paid it."

"You really disliked her that much?"

"Oh, dislike . . . Do you *dislike* a sorceress? Recoil from, fear—but dislike?"

"You're not serious. You didn't really think that about her."

"I thought that about her effect on you!"

"Oh, on me . . ." Greta shrugged. "She's just going through a difficult time, that's all."

"And what were you?"

Greta pretended he'd asked the question rhetorically and merely smiled, then looked out the window.

"The last light is so beautiful, isn't it?" she said.

Everything seemed so without consequence. Crain was not Henry's father; Henry was not Crain's son; she was no longer the person she had been, so what did it matter what she did?

Turning after the Thibeaults' blazing pink house onto the main road, Ned reached over and took one of her unbandaged hands.

"Getting our boy, finally. It's been a long time away."

"All I want in the world is for him to be home," Greta said.

Ned glanced at her but—she could tell—refrained from asking why she'd virtually forced him to leave, then. He just kept holding her hand. He offered her this: to go on as before, to be mother, wife; not to have to explain. They would continue to see McAndrew—for one thing, Ned had entrusted him with the copies of O.'s letters and Lucinda's diaries, and anticipated discussing with him an appropriate means of announcing their existence to the world—Julia maybe not. At Sylvie and Felipe's wedding, it could be. Within six months, Greta felt sure, Julia would be back living in Mexico—what was there to keep her in this country now? She'd never liked it, she disapproved of it. For Greta and Ned this summer would become the "summer Hudson Sleeper found O.'s letters" or even "the summer that Henry went to camp."

Their lives could go on as they had before, if she accepted Ned's offer. What would he want in return?

"I'm relieved we won't have to explain our guests to Henry," Ned said.

"Explain, how?"

"Who they are and what they're doing here, what do you think I meant? What sort of a man was Julia's husband?" he went on, returning his hand to the steering wheel.

"Crain?"

"I thought his name was Lars."

"Oh. Well, that's what Julia called him to other people. She actually called him Renzo, short for Lorenzo—that's Spanish for Lars."

"But you just called him Crain."

"Everyone else called him by his last name. He didn't like Lars."

"You were pretty friendly with him?"

"I knew him since high school."

"In France?"

"That's where we met."

"You never told me that."

"No."

"It would have been easier to understand why you felt an obligation to his widow," Ned said, glancing at her.

"I told you I'd known him for a long time. He was part owner of Ransom."

"Yes, I know, but I . . ."

Ned sighed.

They drove for a while, past fields, some short with new grass after haying, some high with dark green streamers of corn; past houses, lights on inside, barns—lights on there too, summer milking hours; past the occasional gleaming church, steeple ascending into darkness, all backdrop, it felt like to Greta, a setting there only to provide a context for her role.

Halfway to where they would get on the interstate, Ned pulled off the road and parked beside an unused, weathered barn.

"What's the matter?" she asked. "Do you want me to drive?"

"No, no. I just have to ask you something."

Ned switched off the engine and the headlights and then sat for a moment, his hands on the wheel, looking straight ahead. Greta's heart began to pound—had he just been humoring her, letting her think it was all right with him to go on from there when really he was waiting for a moment when her defenses were down . . .

"I'm sorry," he said, "but I can't live with the suspense, Greta. I'd thought I could let you do things in your own time, but I can't stand it. Driving along with you like this, going to pick up Henry, as if everything were just fine . . ."

"What do you mean, Ned?" Greta whispered.

Could McAndrew have said something to him after all? She'd been unfair to McAndrew—a residual resentment, maybe, or simply because he'd happened to be there, as he'd been last time. She supposed that someday she'd have to tell him the truth, as she would Rachel—but not yet, not until she'd figured out how to keep Crain safe from them. Unless he'd told Ned to get even, in which case . . .

"I want to know," Ned said. His voice was taut and when he looked at her she could see the fear in his face. At that, she began to be afraid herself in a way she hadn't yet been—there was a way in which what she had done would never be real so long as Ned didn't know, though also a way in which it would cease to be real if he did.

"Greta, I can't face Henry, not knowing . . ."

"Ned, I don't . . ."

Please don't let's talk about this now, she was going to plead with him—*I* can't face Henry if you do know—but he didn't give her a chance.

"Are you planning to leave? Because if you are, Greta . . . I'm terrified of losing you, you must know that, but not knowing is worse. I can't live with it anymore. I'm sorry, but I just . . ."

"But, Ned, I . . ."

"I can't not think in terms of you—I can't. Even after you told me about McAndrew, back at St. Stephen's . . . I feel so inadequate, Greta. If I thought I could be whatever it is that you want, I'd offer to try, but . . . Oh, Greta, I'm just adrift. I've lost my bearings."

"But, Ned . . ."

His face was tensed, waiting. She shook her head.

"No, Ned. I'm not going to leave. If you can—if you can forgive me."

"What is there to forgive?"

"It's not *you,* Ned," she said.

The false generosity of this sickened her, but what was the alternative? To tell him about Crain, when he had all but told her he couldn't take it?

"No. I know there are things. Listen to us, competing to be the most culpable."

"I've never not loved you, Ned, that's not it. I just . . ."

"I know that," he said. "Otherwise I—"

"You're Henry's father," she said, and began to cry.

Ned leaned over and pulled her into an embrace—did it matter that he comforted her for the wrong reason?

Then he drew back. "Would you stay just for that?"

"Because you're my son's father?"

"Because I don't want . . . I couldn't, however much I wanted—"

"I want to have another child, Ned. I'm not going to be doing any shows for a while—I'd already decided not to show Ransom anymore, but then I've thought I'll take a break from the whole thing—not lessons, just the showing, and—"

"What?"

"Well, that's always been . . ."

Ned stared at Greta incredulously.

"Yes, I know that that was the reason you gave—too hard on your body—but, frankly, I never believed you."

"No," Greta said.

"But now you're ready?"

They looked at each other, trying to make out the other's expression in the growing dusk.

"I don't know," Ned said. "I can't . . . I've been a weathervane to your emotions all summer, Greta. Is the weather going to settle down again?"

He waited, then said, "I wouldn't like it said of me that I'm a man who can't live with a mystery, but . . . I don't know, Greta. I believe in spacing children too, but fourteen years—?"

She laughed at this, and then he laughed. "Come on," he said. "This is becoming surreal. We've got two hours still before we hit the coast."

"You sure you don't want me to drive?"

"I'm all right."

"Maybe we can switch at Concord."

"Let's see how we feel then."

Both of them blushed when, in the car on the way back the next day, it being the first time the three of them had been alone together, Henry said, "Well, Mom, so are you pregnant?"

Ned and Greta glanced at each other, then back at the road.

"What makes you ask such a thing, Sherlock?" Ned asked.

"We discussed it—it seemed like the best explanation."

"We?" Greta and Ned repeated.

"At camp, my friends and I."

"You discuss your parents' sex life at *camp?*"

"Not sex life, Dad, give me a break. We were talking about why we were there. You think there's just one reason why people go to camp, but there isn't. I always *wanted* to go, but it would have been easier to crack the access code to the Pentagon computer than to get you guys to let me. Then all of a sudden this summer Mom's practically pushing me out of the house. Not that I mind. Don't get me wrong. I had a great time, despite all the rampant insanity I had to deal with. These places attract maniacs—or they attract parents who have given birth to maniacs. The point is, this one guy, Regis, who I was pretty friendly with, he told me that last year he came back from camp and found that his mother was going to have another kid. He's an only child too. When he said that, it all clicked. Obviously you'd want me out of the way if you were going on your second honeymoon."

"Obviously," Ned said, glancing at Greta.

"Just do me a favor. Don't tell me I'm going to be the 'proud older brother of a bundle of joy.' That's what Regis's parents said, I kid you not. Those exact words. If you ever told me the news in such a nauseating way I don't think I could even look at it. Don't get me wrong. I'm too old for sibling rivalry. It would be kind of entertaining having a little squawker around. Just don't be all goo-goo about it. If you can possibly help it, that is."

"Understood," Ned said.

"So are you or aren't you?" Henry leaned forward. "You're awfully quiet, Mom. Did I steal your thunder? Really, I'd be happy however you told me. I'll even baby-sit."

Ned said, "Henry, I suppose such a thing isn't impossible—we're not quite over the hill yet—but so far as I know no such event is imminent."

"Oh, geez," Henry said, sitting back, mortified. "I'm sorry, Mom. I was just kidding around. I didn't mean to upset you. I'm sorry, really. Are you mad? Do you want me to go back to camp?"

"No!" Greta exclaimed, turning sharply to look at him. "Don't even say such a thing! I could hardly stand it from the minute we left you there."

"Then why—?"

"Don't expect consistency from adults, Hank," Ned said. "You're bound to be disappointed."

"No kidding," Henry said, ill at ease.

"I thought I should learn to stand it," Greta said. "It's not all that long before you'll be off on your own. I was afraid I—I don't know—needed you too much."

"Mom, that is *so* dumb," Henry said at once, his voice full of relief. "It's the dumbest thing I've heard in a long time, and believe me, I've heard a *lot* of dumb things in two months at Twin Pines for the Criminally Insane. Why would you want to *practice* feeling lousy? That's demented."

"Aren't you the boy who stuck sharpened pencils in his arm in first grade when he knew he was going to have a shot so he'd get used to the pain?" Ned asked.

"So I'm related to her, big deal. That should come as no surprise to you. It's still dumb. Everyone inherits a few dumb genes."

"All from my side, I take it," Greta said.

"I *wish,*" Henry said. "I said 'Gee whillikers' at camp. Not once, mind you, but *twice. In public.*"

"Sorry, friend," Ned said.

"Oh, everyone is flawed," Henry said magnanimously. "It could be worse. I could have gone around muttering 'Nevermore.' So, can we stop for lunch?"

"I thought that was lunch," Ned said.

"Cream-cheese-and-olive sandwiches and carrot sticks? Dad, do you have sunstroke?"

"What did they feed you normally?" Greta asked.

"*Normally?*" Henry asked. "*Normally* I can't tell you. *Normally,* whatever they ladled out of this cauldron the size of a washing machine was not analyzable into separate components. I'm not even sure if it was animal, vegetable, or mineral. The *sandwiches* were meant to impress the parents. They wanted you to think that over the summer we actually ate some foodstuffs known to man."

Greta and Ned were laughing and Henry, warming to his task, went on embellishing until he sighted, on a billboard, the symbol for his fast food of choice.

A few days later, one morning around eleven, Greta and Rachel were drinking iced tea and sitting in lawn chairs in Rachel's front yard, talking.

"You can't have a child to improve your marriage," Rachel was saying, "I agree with you absolutely, but that doesn't mean you can't have one."

"It took long enough the last time," said Greta. "And we were a lot younger then."

"So do what other people do. Take your temperature. Stop drinking coffee. You know, Greta, people have children for all kinds of reasons. Then the reasons are beside the point. They just have the children."

Greta nodded. "You know, I'd like to have that letter to Henry back. Is it still in your bank vault?"

"Oh, my God!" Rachel exclaimed. "It's in the attic! I took some papers out of our safe deposit box, meaning to sort them out this summer—all of my parents' correspondence was in there—and then we left so suddenly. I forgot about the letter. I should have told you. I'm really sorry."

"There's no harm done. I'd just like to have it—not to have it floating around."

"Of course. Let's do it right now."

Upstairs, in her bedroom, Rachel's daughter, Olivia, was lying on her bed crying, getting up periodically to study her face in the mirror above her dresser to see how she looked, trying to guess how Henry might react if she cried in front of him—whether it would make him take her more seriously, make him laugh at her, or disgust him. His letter had just arrived that morning, remailed by her father from England, and she had been rereading it every few minutes, unable to believe it really meant what it said.

He didn't want to hurt her feelings, Henry wrote, "since we've known each other since the dawn of time," but he really just liked her as a friend, and he thought that she must be thinking he was something he wasn't. Olivia tried to find hope in this last statement. If she could convince Henry that he was what she thought, would he love her back?

She had horrible visions of his showing her letters to Lenox and the two of them making fun of her, and if that happened she would have to kill herself; at least then Henry might realize what he'd lost, and she tried to think of a method that would be both painless and not leave her looking disfigured. She thought of sleeping pills, but she didn't like the idea of lying there knowing she was dying. A gun would be quick, but she didn't know how to get hold of one, and, besides, if she shot herself in the head her brains would explode and if she shot herself through her heart it would probably leave her with a horrible expression. Drowning was probably the best, except that if she wasn't found quickly something in the water might have nibbled her.

From time to time, Olivia went to her window and stood behind the curtain, trying to hear what her mother and Mrs. Dene were talking about. Her mother didn't know she was in the house—she thought she was out in the woods with Lenox, repairing their tree house. Hers and Lenox's and Henry's—it was on their land but Henry had built it with them.

She'd heard Henry's name once or twice and then the words "letter" and "bank vault," from which she gathered that some secret involving Henry or his parents' relationship was being discussed but she couldn't make out what. Instinct told her that valuable information was to be had if she could but get hold of it—valuable, that is, to her in her campaign to convince Henry to take her feelings seriously—but she didn't dare try to eavesdrop from downstairs. She and Lenox had told Henry about all the people who'd been staying at Thrush Hollow until the night right before he came back, and he'd joked about his parents getting rid of him so they could rent out his room, but Olivia could tell he was upset to be hearing about the guests first from them. Now here might be the explanation.

But then her mother and Mrs. Dene came inside; she heard them starting upstairs and she panicked—she'd been seen and they were coming to accost her, *together,* but then they went on up to the attic and she heard the scrape and thump of boxes being moved. She opened her door a crack and stood just inside it. Before long they came back down and she heard her mother saying, "I wouldn't keep it around if I were you. There's no need for it now," and Mrs. Dene gave a big sigh and said, "No. No, I know there isn't," as they continued down to the first floor. The evidence, whatever it was, was now gone.

Greta had been inside, reading over the letter she'd written to Henry almost fifteen years ago (he was an infant of two months, she'd told him, just beginning to smile—she asked his forgiveness for deceiving him; she hoped he might understand someday why she had), trying to muster the resolve to burn it in the wood stove, when Henry himself came into the room. Before he'd said a word she could tell that he was furious.

"I want to know what's going on!" he exclaimed. "First you banish me for the summer, then you dig up letters in the cellar, then you have all these people I never heard of staying here, but you make sure they're out of the way before I get back—*what,* exactly, is going on?"

The last question, angrily spoken, was one Henry often posed in jest, and Greta half smiled.

"Is it a big joke to you, keeping all these secrets from me? What did you just go up to get in the Tollivers' attic? Livie heard you. You and Mrs. Tolliver were talking about me. She heard you."

"Livie heard us? How?"

"She was in her room. She heard you talking. What's that?" Henry demanded, pointing at the letter on Greta's lap. "Is that what you got from the attic?"

"It's a letter," Greta said, slipping it back into its envelope, which she folded several times and put in her jeans pocket. "It's nothing that concerns you."

"How do I know if you don't let me see it?"

"Henry, it isn't any of your business."

Ned came down the hall from his study. "What's all the commotion? Or is it a private matter?"

"He thinks we're hiding things from him," Greta said, looking at Ned.

"Is this about the guests again?" Ned asked Henry.

"That's part of it. I know they're part of it. You're just not telling me something. Livie heard Mom and Mrs. Tolliver talking about me."

Ned looked at Greta.

"We often discuss our children," Greta said.

"So tell me what you said, then."

"I thought Olivia told you."

"She couldn't really hear."

"Well, Henry . . . Of course I won't tell you what I said. I have the right to have private conversations with my friends, just as you do with yours. I never grumble about you behind your back, if that's what you're worried about. You know I always tell you if something's bothering me."

"Dad . . ." Henry complained.

"I'm afraid I agree with your mother on this one. She has a right to talk to Rachel about whatever she wants without being eavesdropped on. And we've already been all over this 'secret visitors' business. We've told you who the people were and that they left out of consideration so that we could have time alone as a family. Jim McAndrew and Sylvie will probably even make it back for dinner before we leave. It's your friend Olivia who's made it into a drama. We weren't keeping anything from you. We talked about other things on the way home and the next morning Lenox and Livie were over here at the crack of dawn to give you this supposedly clandestine information."

"I still don't believe that's all there is," Henry said, and Greta and Ned looked at each other, then back at Henry, scrutinizing them.

It was one o'clock. After Greta had left, a little after eleven, Olivia had run to the tree house and demanded to speak to Henry privately; Henry had arrived home a half hour after Greta. Ned now said, "Could we do something so mundane as to eat lunch? I don't know about the two of you, but I'm famished."

"Of course we can eat," Greta said.

"Don't think I don't know you're trying to change the subject," Henry said.

"We won't," Ned said.

Halfway through their sandwiches, they heard a car gunning around the house and a squeal as it lurched to a stop. In another second, Rachel slammed through the back door.

"I think Livie's gone off somewhere to kill herself!" she screamed. "She left a note. It was all about Henry—she took my sleeping pills. I routinely hide them, but I haven't unpacked . . ."

Greta and Ned were standing now, Greta beside Rachel.

"Where is she?" Rachel asked Henry. "Where would she go? Lenox already checked the tree house."

"I don't know. Why would I know?"

"Think, Henry," Ned said.

Reluctantly, Henry suggested, "Maybe the waterfall."

"Which waterfall?" Rachel shouted. *"Where?"*

"He means ours, don't you?" Greta asked. "Just up the brook?"

Henry nodded, his eyes filling with tears, and at his nod Rachel was out the door, running. Ned took off after her.

"You'd better come too," Greta said.

Henry, looking stunned, stood and followed his mother out into the back yard.

"No one's blaming you, Henry. But I don't want you staying here by yourself right now. Come on." Without thinking, Greta took his hand and (she noted this) he didn't take it away until they'd left the lawn for the tall grass.

"What happened between the two of you?"

"Do you mean now?"

"Just what happened, Henry. She wrote you letters all summer. I guessed you weren't writing her back since she didn't have your address."

"I did write her, but she just got the letter."

"And it upset her so much she's tried to kill herself?"

"Mom, no! Not just the letter. The fact that I won't . . . I mean I don't want . . . Jesus, Mom."

"No one's blaming you, Henry," Greta said again.

He sighed deeply. "Okay. Here's the whole soap opera. Last summer I kissed her. *Once.* We were at the waterfall by ourselves. Lenox was somewhere. It was no big deal—I just did it. But she seemed to think it meant I'd vowed eternal love. I thought she'd get over it during the year, but this summer it was worse than ever. She wrote me all these love letters. I tried to be nice, but I had to tell her the truth, didn't I?"

"Yes, of course you did. Thank you for telling me. It's not your fault, Henry."

"It's not? Whose fault is it, then?"

"It isn't anyone's."

"It must be someone's."

"It's the way of the world, I'm afraid." Greta looked at him. "Some people learn how they feel about things by doing them and others look for events to fit what they feel. Eventually it evens out."

"Oh, great," Henry said. "Wisdom." Then he said, "She kept trying to make me think there was some big secret—I mean this morning. She kept hinting that she could tell me more than she was and I got mad. Then she got really upset. I think that somehow she thought it would make me love her if I thought you and Dad were up to something, I don't know why. She said I'd be sorry someday that I'd lost her. I didn't think that this was what she meant."

"No," Greta said, afraid. "No, why would you? Come on, Henry, let's run."

Out of breath, they had scrambled two-thirds of the way down the path to the brook when they saw Rachel and Ned climbing back up, Olivia between them. She was sobbing hysterically.

"It's *okay*," Ned mouthed to Greta, who heaved a long breath of relief.

"Let's head back," Greta said to Henry. "Livie will feel mortified if she has to face you right now."

"If I leave she'll think I hate her," he objected.

"Yes, of course she will, you're right."

Olivia wouldn't look at Henry or Greta as she approached.

"I'm sorry, Livie," Henry said.

Ned said to Rachel, "Maybe they'd like to have a moment alone. Would that be all right, Livie?"

She nodded without looking up.

"No," Rachel said.

"Rach—" Greta began.

"No!" she exclaimed. "No more secrets. I've been worrying about this all summer. I want to hear whatever it is. If it can't be said in front of us," Rachel said to Henry, "then don't say it."

"No one's worth it, that's all I was going to say," Henry said uncomfortably. "No matter what you feel about them."

"That's true," Rachel said. "Thank you for that, Henry."

"Are you all right?" Henry asked, ignoring Rachel, and Olivia seemed to cheer up at this remark. She continued up the path and Henry followed her. Rachel hung back with Ned and Greta.

"I suppose you're right to let them talk," Rachel said.

"If they don't now, they'll feel too embarrassed later," Ned said.

Rachel said to Greta, "She had the pills in her hand. If we'd been five minutes later . . . I dumped the whole bottle in the brook. I hope it won't put the fish to sleep. Look at this." She held out her hands. " 'Her hands shook . . .' I always thought that was a figure of speech."

Greta held her. "It's all right. It'll be all right, Rachel. At least you can talk to her now. I'll tell you what Henry told me."

Rachel nodded, wiping her eyes. "But right now let's go. I can't bear to let her out of my sight."

"O. and Lucinda," Ned remarked to Greta, as Rachel started after Henry and Olivia.

"Yes, I know," she said.

"Whatever that means."

"If it means anything."

On the day before they were to leave to drive south, Greta rode over to West Stilling, as she did each year, to say goodbye to Nora Sleeper. The keeper of the city, Ned called her, for her having somehow acquired the role of welcoming committee and spare-key-retainer for all the summer people.

It was a ceremonial ride, along the back road from the Hollow to West Stilling, past the Tollivers' old farmhouse and fallen-in barn (she'd stop to visit on her way home), until, half a mile farther on, she came to the village. Once a thriving settlement, now an artist's sketch of one—a few dispersed clapboard houses, a faded church with its steeple removed, the one barn that still stabled cows—as if to suggest what the place would look like if actually populated.

A lush breeze blew as Greta set out, and the air seemed full of unfallen rain. From beneath the canopy of trees the leaves were silver and the lowered sky was a strange translucent underwater green, heavy with all it held back. It was warm, balmy; there was practically sea-spray in the air, as if waves were breaking somewhere just over the horizon. Ransom, sensing Greta's anticipation, whinnied, seeking confirmation of his urge to run.

Having wished the Sleepers a good year and apologized for Ned's last-minute occupations—bolting the shutters, draining the pipes—that had prevented his coming with her, Greta told Ransom, after tying him to a fence post in the field beside the Sleepers' barn, that she'd be just another minute. Then she crossed the road and went into the graveyard. Nora, who had accompanied her out onto the front porch and had been waiting to watch her ride away, looked momentarily puzzled but then waved and politely returned indoors, as if Greta were someone recently bereaved.

Greta hadn't ventured into the cemetery since the first years they'd been in Stilling, and she didn't recall ever looking closely at the Dearborns' graves. Ever since Hudson's discovery she'd been telling herself that she would visit Lucinda's, though she wasn't sure with what aim. In Crain's will, Julia had written to her (she had not been able to bring herself to tell Greta in person—it was a painful subject, even though she understood that it had been Crain's feelings about Federico and then Mexico that had led him to make the request)—in his will Crain had asked to be cremated and his ashes scattered at the school he'd attended in France, and Greta had written back a sympathetic note. She was sure that Renzo (Crain was an altogether different person) had not meant to hurt Julia; Julia should disregard the instructions, she advised, if she would feel better scattering his ashes in Mexico—although Greta knew the exact spot where Crain had wanted to rest. She would think of him waiting there for her now, free and happy as he'd been that first year they were together, before he'd clung to the belief that he was damaged—there beneath the pine tree where they'd used to meet and kiss.

It wouldn't be long now—just a lifetime. She forgave him his betrayal; he could forgive hers in staying with Ned. He could have fathered the whole world, if he'd wanted. If he'd told her. It seemed he was admitting that to her, in the end.

The Dearborn monument, in the northeast corner of the graveyard, was a tall granite spire, rising from a block etched with the family name. The monument was that of a prominent, prosperous family—meant to commemorate many bearers of the name, yet there were only three small stones, flat in the earth, to mark individual graves. From a few feet away, Greta read the inscriptions. "Rufus Augustus Dearborn, 1818–1870." "Emily Eustace Dearborn, 1820–1847." "Lucinda Emily Dearborn, 1846–1915."

Reaching into the pocket of her summer dress—Crain had never seen her in this particular one, but he'd liked it on the rare occasions when she wore a dress—Greta took out the envelope in which she carried the letter to Henry, already torn into tiny pieces. Holding the envelope upside down, she shook it, and the pieces floated down, looking like apple blossom petals where they came to rest on the grass.

She noticed, at the same time, another stone. It lay close to Lucinda's, half covered by earth. She hadn't seen it at first. In contrast to the others', its engraving looked roughly, amateurishly done, though the name and inscription were perfectly legible. Greta knelt down and held the grass aside to read it.

"Lucinda Dearborn Snow," it said. "Died before she was born." There was no date.

A NOTE ON THE TYPE

The text of this book was set in Simoncini Garamond, a
modern version by Francesco Simoncini of the type attributed to the famous Parisian type cutter Claude Garamond
(ca. 1480–1561). Garamond was a pupil of Geoffroy Tory
and is believed to have based his letters on the Venetian
models, although he introduced a number of important differences, and it is to him we owe the letter that we know as
old style. He gave to his letters a certain elegance and a feeling of movement that won for their creator an immediate
reputation and the patronage of Francis I of France.

Composed by ComCom,
an R. R. Donnelley & Sons Company,
Allentown, Pennsylvania
Printed and bound by Berryville Graphics,
Berryville, Virginia
Designed by Anthea Lingeman